MW00617389

The
Ultimate
Evil

To Doris—
Gee, now you're my
instructor!
I wish you well always.

[signature]
2/2/10

Titles by Larry Wonderling:

Nonfiction

SEDUCTIVE ILLUSIONS, How the Resist the Lure
Of Society's Smoke and Mirrors
SAN FRANCISCO TENDERLOIN, Heroes, Demons
Angels and Other True Stories

Coming Soon

DR. LARRY'S MINDING YOUR MATTER

The Ultimate Evil

A Mystery Novel
By Larry Wonderling

Cape Foundation Publications
San Francisco

© 2005 Larry Wonderling. Printed and bound in the United States of America. All Rights reserved. No part of this book may be reproduced or transmitted in any form or by any means without permission in writing from the publisher, except by a reviewer who may quote brief passages in a review.

This story is fiction and any resemblance to real incidents or events is purely coincidental. As for the characters, some are real friends of the author, while their characterizations are "mostly" fictional.

Cape Foundation Publications
San Francisco, California

Library of Congress Catalog Number: 2003115771

ISBN: 0-9659415-5-8

Cover Design by: Norman Cyr and Ben Levy

This book is dedicated to my friends. Although their actual names are fictitious characters in my novel, their friendship and loyalty are nonfiction.

PROLOGUE

In astrology, early *April* represents Aries, the first sign of the Zodiac. This sign is obsessed with mastery and winning at all costs. In numerology, the number *eight* signifies power, achievement and strength, skills necessary to win at all costs. In witchcraft, *Wednesday* is Woden's day of the planet Mercury—a planet with a devilish sense of superiority, the catalyst behind winning at any cost. Then there's the *full moon*, which activates and intensifies these New Age energies. When combined, these phenomena can ignite the worst of evils.

The death of eight people on a Wednesday in San Francisco is really no cause for alarm. As far as San Francisco residents are concerned, eight people just happened to die on the same day. Their deaths occurred around the city in random areas of wealth and poverty. The victims were unrelated, old and young, rich and poor. Times of death were equally scattered throughout that particular Wednesday. How they died seemed as different as where or when they died. Causes of death included everything from drowning and poisoning, to crushing. Even why they died seemed random—an assortment of murders, suicides or accidents.

When Inspector O'Shea of the San Francisco Police Department was assigned those eight cases, he and his partner, Sergeant Ellis, knew that in a city of over 800,000, eight random deaths on one day weren't really unusual and certainly not foreboding. How could they have known that these cases would gradually emerge as the most baffling and sinister they had ever encountered?

After several weeks of standard investigative procedures, getting them nowhere, both detectives had an eerie hunch that they were missing something. It was a hunch that plunged them deep into an unholy abyss where they would discover, to their horror, the sheer terror of that *Wednesday, which also happened to be a full-mooned April 8ᵗʰ*.

Acknowledgements

No matter how hard I searched, I could never find all those misspelled works hidden in my manuscript. Besides, spelling isn't my strong suit, neither is grammar. I also desperately needed to know from someone other than myself if my story was clearly written and fascinating. So I am sincerely and humbly grateful to Marja McGraw, Shirley Kennedy, Jim and Grace Ginella, Mary Lou Ramage, Richard Bender, Dona Richards and Bob Hanna for your line editing skills, review of this book and indispensable feedback. Also, thanks to my editor, Carol Eversole, for going through all the many rewrites and completion of this book.

CHAPTER 1

Helen Hansen was one of nature's rare gifts. At thirty-five her natural beauty was as ageless as the songs of birds to the early morning sun.

She seemed to have it all, while all she ever wanted was to care for others. Safely cloistered in wealth and security, Helen chose community service in poverty and danger. Her volunteer work was in Hunter's Point, lower Mission and the Tenderloin—all poor areas of San Francisco, swarming with angry minorities resenting those, like Helen, with plenty of everything.

Married to a handsome, successful and very rich attorney, they lived in a magnificent two-story house in San Francisco's exclusive Sea Cliff district—an elitist community imbued with fame, fortune and high security. Her typical day was steeped in hard work and verbal abuse by many she tried to help, yet she chose to avoid the press or any other recognition. During Thanksgiving and Christmas, when the rich offered their toothy smiles to the cameras as they served the poor, Helen stayed home.

Her love of home was totally unrelated to wealth. Home provided Helen with privacy, a place to relax, to cook, read mysteries, wear jeans and an old sweatshirt and enjoy her favorite music—New Age and Flamenco.

Helen was an early riser. She treasured her morning strolls before spending the day with the disadvantaged. She was usually out of bed by 6:00 a.m. This provided her with time for a leisurely shower, a fresh cup of coffee and her cherished walk. Upon returning, Helen

2 • Larry Wonderling

would prepare breakfast for Derrick, her husband, whom she awakened at 8:00 a.m.

What a wonderful day, Helen thought that Wednesday as she bundled up for the trek to her favorite morning spot. It was a five-minute walk to a panoramic view unsurpassed anywhere in the world. High above Baker's Beach and the rugged, rocky shoreline, the sun had just cleared the Berkeley hills. It sprinkled the San Francisco Bay with a sparkling shower of golden embers, dancing westward along the choppy water until the entire Bay was ablaze.

She had seen this unveiling often, yet each time, it was a new, breathtaking thrill. Like a curtain rising in the east, the stage glowed, spotlighting the grandeur of the Golden Gate Bridge, Point Bonita across the Bay and nearby Mile Rock. Standing there on the edge of her special cliff, Helen felt serene, enthralled with the awesome beauty of it all.

Then, suddenly pressure on her back, loss of balance and her sense of peace was shattered into convulsive tremors of terror. Within seconds, Helen was again at peace, lying on the rocks two hundred fifty feet below.

📖 📖 📖

It was 10:00 a.m. Wednesday, an hour before Bill's weekly session with Dr. Jerry Wunden, his psychotherapist. Bill Winston had been released from San Quentin Prison about a month earlier. There he had served fifteen months for forgery. Larceny was the least of Bill's problems. He was a psychological and physical mess, with no interest in improving his mind, and a relentless drive to dismantle his body.

From the start, Bill was congenitally malformed. He was born with a left leg three inches shorter than his right, a partially developed right hand resembling a claw and a large dome forehead towering over a receding chin that could have been part of his neck. By age twenty, he was oblivious to women and obsessed with young, aggressive men. During his youth, he had another more dangerous obsession with masochistic implications. He was determined to change his unattractive physical appearance. While still a teenager, he ripped off most of his right ear with a saber saw. He was trying to reshape his floppy earlobes. It didn't work. He also tried stapling his eyelids to eliminate their squinty, droopy-eyed look. That didn't work either.

Bill was HIV-positive, and since he didn't attract men by his orphaned personality and alien appearance, he favored sadists. Even in San Quentin, he constantly provoked other cons into hurting him, and a few months before his release, he was placed in one of the Spanish-type isolation cells as a serious management problem. During his stay in isolation, he sliced open his scrotum and cut out one of his testicles with his contraband razor blade. Before guards heard his screams, Bill managed to swallow the testicle. He just hated being alone and unnoticed.

Bill couldn't stand psychotherapy. He certainly didn't need it, he'd argue to himself. Neither did he need any more prison time, which was a convincing reason to comply with the Adult Authority Board's order. He must undergo psychotherapy as a condition of his parole—or else.

After downing his fourth cup of coffee, Bill reluctantly dragged himself off his couch, grabbed a coat and left his small studio apartment for the ten-block walk to Dr. Wunden's office. As he walked up Leavenworth toward Post Street, he tried to prepare himself for the session. *Wunden isn't such a bad guy*, he thought. *Besides, it's only about forty-five minutes of my time, and then I'll be free for two more weeks.*

When Bill reached Post Street, the explosive jackhammer blasts were deafening. "They're always working on these lousy streets," he grumbled. Then the noise quickly began to fade into more pleasant thoughts of a wild, erotically painful night with his lover, Jason.

Crossing the street at Post and Leavenworth, he suddenly felt a slap on his left ear. "Ouch!" he said. That was his last word as he crumpled to the pavement—dead.

📖 📖 📖

In his late fifties, Emil Anderson had worked hard all of his adult life to support his devoted wife, Rachael and their rebellious son, Ralph. Despite the expanding shadow of giant supermarkets obscuring "mom and pop" stores, he had successfully maintained a small neighborhood grocery store in the Richmond District for over twenty-five years. Tragically, his wife died of cancer the year before, and now it was his lonely responsibility to maintain the business and supervise his troubled son.

Ralph had been in juvenile hall several times for thefts and assaults on younger kids. Approaching thirty, Ralph was a big, flaccid, sloppy looking high school dropout. He typically slept till noon, refused to help his father in any way, ate everything in the house and stayed out most of the night. Ralph was a classic product of an over-indulgent mother and an overly permissive father. He grew from spoiled kid into a self-absorbed, demanding adult, who easily manipulated his father. Tuesday evening, however, nudged Emil over the brink of tolerance into the depths of frustration.

Emil closed his grocery store at 9:00 p.m., and by 10:30, he was alone in his living room, sipping a can of beer while watching *NYPD Blue*. The sound of his doorbell had that continuous shriek of urgency—the kind that sent low voltage current through your stomach in uneasy anticipation. Turning on the porch light, Emil could see Mrs. Leon, holding her eleven-year-old daughter's hand. Lorene Leon was a single parent neighbor, with a fixed income and tight budget. She had been shopping at Emil's store for over a year, mainly because he let her charge groceries toward the end of the month when she was usually broke.

"What's the matter Lorene?" he asked, as he ushered them into the living room.

Lorene looked down at her daughter, Cindy, then almost furtively into Emil's eyes. "Your son tried to molest Cindy today." She had learned from her daughter that on the way home from school, Ralph had beckoned her with a wave. When Cindy approached, he pulled her into the bushes, tore down her pants and began to fondle her. Just as he was unzipping his fly, Ralph was startled away by two adults walking nearby. Cindy stayed with the adults until Lorene returned later that evening.

"Cindy's OK now, and you've been so nice to us, I didn't want to upset you. But Ralph is dangerous and I just don't know what to do."

His head throbbing with a mixture of shock, disgust and anger, Emil dropped his eyes toward the floor and sat silent for a moment. Then he slowly looked up at both of them. "Don't worry, Mrs. Leon, I'll make certain Ralph doesn't bother Cindy any more. I'll call you tomorrow. OK?"

Mrs. Leon gave a faint, smiling nod.

Emil barely slept that night. His head still pounded in frustration over his only options. He realized he had no control over Ralph, and talking to him would be useless. Ralph still wasn't home, and God only knew what he was up to now. Emil knew Lorene wouldn't go to the police without his sanction. He also knew Ralph was dangerous, and he had to do something. Then he remembered his old high school friend, Richard Bender.

Bender was his hero—the best boxer on their team while Emil was the worst. Nevertheless, they became good pals, with Bender always defending his friend and Emil always praising Bender. After graduation from high school, Emil quickly got a job and Bender easily got an athletic scholarship. Emil remained Bender's most loyal fan, with letters and telegrams of congratulations for Bender's many athletic and scholastic achievements. Ranked number one in his class at law school, Bender had been working as a San Francisco deputy district attorney for about ten years. Emil knew he could count on his prudent advice.

Next morning, Emil left a message for Bender at his office, "Your old friend and fan, Emil, needs your help. It's about my son, Ralph. I'll come by this morning and hope to see you at ten."

At a cafe near his grocery store, Emil decided to have breakfast before visiting Bender. He'd been there many times, and the owner reliably left a small table by the front window available for Emil every morning. Seated at his usual table, Emil ordered a light breakfast of coffee, orange juice and cereal. The cafe was mobbed with noisy customers, and maneuvering to the rear restroom was unusually difficult for him. Finally, returning to his seat, he sat oblivious to the bodies bumping against or leaning on his table. He was preoccupied with his wife's loving warmth, his failure as a father and his meeting with Richard Bender.

Emil arrived at the DA's office at about 9:45. Seated in the waiting room, he absently picked up a *Time* magazine, without reading a word. He thumbed through the pages, wondering where his son was and what Bender would advise. He wasn't feeling too well, a little strange, but figured he was just nervous.

When the receptionist announced Emil's arrival to Bender, he was delighted. He hadn't seen Emil in years, which didn't dim memories of a fine high school friendship. After reading a few memos, looking over his court calendar for the day and pouring a cup of coffee, Bender walked out to the waiting room to greet his old friend. Slumped on the chair with the *Time* magazine lying across his knees, Emil was dead.

📖 📖 📖

"For Christ's sake, Jim, now what's your fuckin' problem? What's the stink eye for this time? You look like I just ripped off your wallet."

Jim stood silently, posturing like an old warrior, with clenched fists, wide stance, piercing stare and twitching jaw. "You don't like what ya see? Let's go outside, Harry. I'll take you on outside. You're the problem, asshole. Let's get it on."

Harry stared back, nodding slowly with a deep sigh that formed a faint smile. "Jesus Christ. Let it go, Jim. Grow up."

Harry and Jim were once good friends. They had known each other for virtually ever and no one's clear, including Harry or Jim, what triggered their decade old feud. There's some consensus that rivalry had something to do with it.

For his age, Harry Sutherland had an enviable appearance. At eighty-two, he was still over six feet tall with a muscular frame, hard, well-contoured chest tapering into a narrow waist, a strong, craggy face and a neck that was still at right angles to his firm chin. Tucked beneath his visible muscles, however, Harry's skeletal structure was a wreck. Fossilized bones, ending at dry jagged joints, were barely held in place by brittle, cracking ligaments and tendons that had lost their springy resilience long ago.

Severe arthritis had been pulverizing his bones for years and his valiant struggle against his condition was a standoff. "Use it or lose it," was his motto, so every morning, instead of medications and rest, Harry dragged himself off the bed onto the floor where he slowly and painfully stretched and exercised his limbs until able to walk again. Swimming was another daily remedial activity that kept Harry's body from seizing into a knot.

Following a healthful breakfast of dried fruits, oatmeal and Metamucil, Harry drove to Aquatic Park. There, with old cronies, he reminisced about the good old days and slowly swam exhausting laps within the protective Aquatic Park buoys. He had been a member of the Aquatic Park Porpoise Club for over ten years.

Jim Robinson was Harry's reverse image. Other than his fifteen-year Porpoise Club membership, whatever he and Harry once had in common was a well-kept secret. Despite a sagging chin and an enormous belly announcing the arrival of his 5'10" frame, Jim was as strong as a gorilla, healthy as a young elephant and mean-tempered as a trapped panther. A great college athlete, Jim hadn't exercised in years, yet he was as agile as a deer. He thrived on greasy meat and well-salted potatoes that he washed down with plenty of booze, And at eighty-five, Jim had no aches or pains. Also different from Harry, Jim didn't swim for exercise; he simply enjoyed effortlessly swimming and floating around Aquatic Park. He never seemed to tire.

Walking by the Porpoise Club locker room during the rancor, Don Dutil flashed a placating smile at Jim and Harry. "Don't you guys ever stop? Why don't you declare a truce?"

Jim grunted something, grabbed his blue swim cap and walked away while Harry, looking at Don, threw up his hands with wide-eyed agreement.

By 11:00 a.m. that Wednesday, Harry slid his red cap down over his ears, splashed some cold water over his lightly greased body and plunged into Aquatic Park water, where he began his slow swim to the buoys. At 11:30 a.m., Don Dutil clamped on his nose clip, slipped on his white cap and started treading water to the Aquatic Park buoys. He gave a quick wave to Jim Robinson, who was on his way back to the beach. *Why is he coming in so soon?* he wondered. Don was a twenty-year veteran of the icy Bay waters. He was in great shape for a ninety-year- old and proud of his endurance. Regardless of Bay conditions, he could always stay out longer than the youngsters like Jim and Harry. Yet, after today, he'd feel much older and tired.

Reaching the middle buoy, Don Dutil rolled over to begin a few backstroke laps. After three easy, graceful strokes, the back of his right hand hit something awash. Startled, Don flipped onto his stomach as both of his hands fell over submerged shoulders and top of a red swim cap. Pulling on the shoulders, a head surfaced within inches of Don's face. It was Harry with wild, bulging eyes staring vacantly in terror. He was dead and Don was very sick.

📖 📖 📖

In San Francisco, homelessness has been a tragic human issue, a sensitive social issue and an embarrassingly insoluble political one. It becomes even more of an issue when a homeless person dies on the streets and the death has racial implications. Then the *liberal left* and the *righteous right* unite, and the Mayor's thick oak door rattles with protests of indignation.

When a poor, old, black drunk was torched into grizzly pieces of charcoal within the rubble of the demolished Embarcadero freeway, the blaming was thunderous. Every committee, even remotely related to homelessness, race or crime prevention demanded action. The solution to this fury was Officer Bob Nelson of the San Francisco Police Department. He was the token taskforce of one, assigned to catch the perpetrators who could have been anyone, including other homeless. No one really cared about the nameless victim or, for that matter, the "perps."

Big cities are all about issues, organizations, constituencies and image—especially the Mayor's office. So with a well-choreographed display of compassion, the Mayor promised to arrest the bad guys.

Officer Nelson was a black, twenty-five-year-old college graduate with a Bachelor's Degree in Criminology. Being ambitious, he jumped at the opportunity to exchange his uniform for the ragged, soiled clothing of a bum. He had been on the police force for less than a year, which meant receiving all of the off-hour assignments his seniors hated. He roamed the Hunters Point streets as a beat cop, directed early morning traffic and occasionally got to drive a cruiser. Nelson had anticipated at least five years of uncritical uniform duty before being considered for professional detective work. This undercover job was a real career break for him even though he wasn't a detective and no one but another rookie would have considered the job. For Officer Nelson, he was thrilled with his undercover assignment. It didn't matter to him that his hours were still graveyard, his plain clothes filthy or that his salary was the same.

To other cops, Officer Nelson's assignment was viewed as anything but courageous or romantic. Armed with a flack jacket, Nomex flame-proof sweater and head liner, walkie-talkie, .38 snub-nosed revolver and an oversized dirty old coat, his job was to wander the demolished Embarcadero freeway area, check in with a nearby cruiser hourly and bundle near some rubble, feigning drunken sleep. His police back up, waiting in a cruiser, was thirty seconds away, and since the police figured the assailants took several clumsy minutes to torch the unconsciously drunk victim, the precautions were almost excessive. Besides, even the chief thought the operation was a waste of time. The fiery murder was an isolated incident and unlikely to happen again.

It was unusually cold and foggy when Officer Nelson bundled up in some old tattered blankets to await the remote possibility of his heroic arrest of the predators. This was his fourth night of vigilance, cold and boredom. At 2:00 a.m. Wednesday, he made his third call on the walkie-talkie. "Mike, it's Bob. All's cool."

Fighting a big yawn, Mike replied, "OK, Bob. Out."

Officer Nelson failed to make his fourth call, and when several cruisers arrived after 3:00 a.m., there was no fire. Nelson was still bundled up, yet with a huge block of concrete freeway embedded on the ground, where there was once his head.

📖 📖 📖

In the shadow of venerable old Kezar Stadium, Polytechnic High School was in good company. Never heralded with as much as a footnote for its academics, Poly had become an athletic giant—especially in football. Nine of the last ten football championships were owned by Polytechnic, and each year the All-City Football Roster contained 80% Poly players. There was also wide national recognition with many Poly players achieving high school All-American honors. There were eleven other San Francisco high schools, all panting enviously at Poly's supreme sports dominance. Some of the schools boasted a sort of moral victory when they lost a game to Poly by only one touchdown.

Early in Poly's history, it was traditionally a school of discontented, angry, poor youth jammed together in an educational system irrelevant to their uninspired lives. Most of these kids didn't fit a high school regimen with its preparation for a middle-class lifestyle they never had. Their goals were much more basic and appropriate to their present young lives. Get a job, get a scam, hustle or just get out of school so you could make some money. These kids had hung on through junior high with no practical payoffs. They were just burned out and restless.

Then Bob Lualhati came along. Young, energetic, charismatic and an ex-pro athlete, he was hired as the football coach. Bob immediately felt the unbridled power generated by the sheer tension, frustration and physical potential of his wayward charges. In only two seasons, he managed to harness this diffuse energy into a well-organized, highly motivated athletic team. Now, twelve years later, his football teams were some of the best in the nation and any kid with sports fantasies was eager to enroll at Polytechnic High School.

When Al Rubio, the talented assistant coach, left for a head coaching job in Southern California, Bob had a half dozen applications for the prestigious position within a week. As the list of candidates grew, Bob already knew that his choice was reduced to two teachers at Poly. Dick Boyd, a history teacher, had been volunteering for several years to help coach the backfield. A fine college athlete, Dick was a well-liked teacher. He loved sports and knew the game of football exceptionally well. He had also earned the respect of the team, who barely knew André Likert, the other candidate.

Likert was the drama and language arts teacher in a school where "jocks" still felt such elective courses might contaminate their masculinity. Nevertheless, it was never really a contest.

Decidedly, in Likert's favor was his friendship with Lualhati. They and their wives had been close friends for years. Bob's wife Alice, a plain, somewhat dumpy looking homemaker, had dreamed of an acting career. Instead, she had settled for Likert's offer of a voluntary position as prompter for his student actors' biannual school play.

Bob and Alice reciprocated by attending André's weekly auto-crosses. These were amateur parking lot speed trials through a series of pylons. André had become the Don Quixote of the autocross circuit. On weekends, he was Sterling Moss, Jimmy Clark, Fangio and Andretti, all compressed into a racing suit not really necessary for the parking lot. His windmills were the other weekend competitors and their cars.

Everybody at Poly knew and joked about André's fantasy racecar career. Most of the school also seemed to know, before Boyd, that André had been appointed assistant coach.

"I don't believe it, Bob. How could you appoint that candy-ass version of Barney Oldfield to a job he doesn't know shit about? Stick the twerp up your own ass and tell him I'll take him on anytime, anywhere." That was happy-go-lucky, likable Boyd in his enraged mode.

That same evening, a very contented André jacked up his TR-4A "race car," removed the front wheels and slid under the frame, where he would tinker for the next two hours with its suspension and disc brakes. This was a Wednesday pre-race ritual, and with garage door open and Rimsky Korsakov's "Scheherazade" blaring in the background, it was a ritual experienced by the whole Parnassus Street neighborhood.

Humming along with the music, André noticed a pair of loafers approaching. After peeking out for a quick look, he slid back to work. "So, what are you up to?" he asked. "Hey don't do that…."

André was found a few hours later, crushed to death under the car.

📖 📖 📖

Carlos Villa was a genuinely religious, mild mannered, dependable father of six, loving grandfather of fourteen and a potential great-grandfather of at least several dozen more. He was one of those few select Mexicans to become a U.S. citizen after legally immigrating to the United States with a work visa forty years ago. He was never a heavy drinker, drug user or wife beater. He had no vices or bad habits, and despite his meager janitorial earnings, he'd managed to help three of his kids through college. That's probably why he was still driving a twenty-year-old, 350 Chevy, three-quarter-ton pick-up that he used to collect bottles and aluminum cans for resale. Carlos acted like a saint while looking like a swarthy, overweight, double-chinned, bushy-haired, disheveled old Mexican junkie.

Leona, on the other hand, succeeded in looking more like his daughter than his fifty-year-old wife. She had great genes, great make-up, a great physical fitness trainer and nothing but leisure time. The only thing she'd never had was a job. There wasn't a trace of the old lizard look that welcomes the onset of the fifties. Her skin was like a flexible new inner tube that never revealed a crease. She wore low cut blouses presenting full, firm breasts and high cut white leather boots introducing well-contoured thighs. Completing the alluring appearance were her skirts of bandanna length. When Carlos and Leona walked down the street together, there were muffled sounds invariably coming from gawking neighbors—*hmmmm*.

Carlos left his old truck parked on the street in front of their home, situated on Twenty-Fourth Street and Dolores. Leona parked "their" Camaro in the garage. Carlos didn't mind. The body of his truck was beyond street damage and he took good care of the operational parts of the truck. The engine had recently been overhauled, the automatic transmission shifted smoothly, all four tires were brand new, and living on a hill, his brakes were carefully serviced every few months.

Wednesday was especially hectic for Carlos and his family. Their youngest daughter, Stephanie, was marrying into the Italian Ginella family at the Mission Dolores church on Saturday the eleventh. Tonight was the big rehearsal at the church with Carlos' bridesmaid daughters, little granddaughter as flower girl, bride-to-be and a whole flock of Ginellas. Leona and Carlos were jointly giving away their daughter.

He knew that after work he needed to order more flowers, to endure a final fitting for his rented tux and to drop by Carl's Bakery to make certain the monstrous cake would be ready and delivered to the reception hall. Leona's schedule was equally as busy. She had to endure a half-day at the beauty parlor following an exhaustive aerobics workout, she explained to Carlos.

Carlos got up earlier than usual. He wanted to complete his janitorial duties by 2:00 p.m., providing more time for his personal obligations. As he left his house he had a fleeting glance of somebody walking away between his truck and another parked car. Otherwise, the streets were empty.

The old three-quarter-ton Chevy broke the morning silence as it burst into throaty grunts with a touch of the ignition. In a minute, the uneven explosive grunts became a smooth powerful purr. Carlos backed away from the curb and, as he had done thousands of times, he was on his way to work. Usually, he would drive a block to Twenty-Fifth, turn left at the stop sign, left again onto Guerrero, which took him to the downtown area. Today was different.

In the middle of the steep Dolores hill, Carlos applied his brakes. There weren't any. Several more frantic pumps slammed the useless pedal to the floor. Carlos looked up to see a terror stricken, wide-eyed woman holding a child. She was in the intersection desperately trying to avoid the on-coming truck. The impact knocked mother and child over the windshield, onto the actual top of the cab. Frozen in shock and trying to stop the truck with his hands, he nearly bent the steering wheel in half while his feet kicked and pounded the brake pedal. The truck finally slammed into several parked cars, throwing mother and child back over the hood onto the street. Mother was dead and her four-year-old child critically injured.

📖 📖 📖

Gently stroking her tiny, bony hands, Terry Digness looked up toward the ceiling, pleading through deep convulsive sobs, "Please die, my dear sweet lady, please die." He was floundering in a cruel gray sea of sadness, and there could be no rescue—no happy ending. His wife of fifty-two years lay motionless beneath clean, white, unwrinkled covers in an ICU room at St. Mary's Hospital. Terry hadn't left Grace's room since she slipped restlessly into a peaceful coma two days before, on Monday, the 6th.

Physically exhausted, emotionally ravaged and nearly delirious, Terry numbly followed the countless tubes and wires from hanging bottles, digital boxes and strange machines. They all led to a mask-like face of thin, off-white porcelain, barely concealing the deep hollows of a skull. Many of the tubes seemed to have twisted and slithered their way into Grace's nose and mouth, distorting her once beautiful features. His eyes burned and his vision blurred with the days of constant weeping. "That isn't my Grace." He winced, backing away from her bed. "That's not human, it's a robot, a humanoid. Oh God, what can I do." Collapsing across her bed, Terry's dreams were more merciful.

Waking from his brief dream, Terry felt a cold, jabbing chill. Looking at his wife's cadaverous body, he was reminded of his mounting despair during the past five years when radiation, chemotherapy and surgery failed to stop the spread of Grace's cancer. As Grace continued to deteriorate, she lost bowel and bladder control and could no longer care for herself. That was a year ago, when Terry embraced her emaciated little body with a promise he would euthanize her when she was ready. Last week, before the coma, Grace had mumbled her readiness and Terry succumbed to agonizing conflict.

Kneeling at the edge of Grace's bed, Terry again prayed for an answer, yet there was nothing but his sobs and muffled shrieks of torment as he buried his tear streaked dripping face into his hands. Then he struggled to his feet and ran, almost hysterically, from the room. He had to get away for just awhile.

Fifteen minutes later, Mrs. Hanna, the head nurse, was returning to her ICU nurse's station when she noticed that the monitor to Room 136 was not working. It was 4:15 p.m. When she checked Grace's room, to her horror all of the wires and tubes had been ripped out of her body and the plugs yanked from their wall outlets. Grace was finally dead.

📖 📖 📖

Viewed from a distance, eight unrelated deaths in San Francisco on the same day approach obscurity in significance. They may have rated the afternoon *Examiner's* D Section, probably as fillers, while offering well-distorted one or two liners. "Wealthy Seacliff woman found dead on rocks, body mangled in fall and partially dismembered by seals...." "Mexican kills mother and critically injures child with truck, bodies crushed on impact...." "Intensive care patient dies when life supports yanked. Crazed husband prime suspect. Doctors report wife's condition was treatable and prognosis fair...." "Grotesque demise of principal witness in DA's waiting room. Death suspicious...."

Other than a few close ties, who really cared about the initial accuracy of these stories? Certainly not the public or journalists. Like trash collectors, reporters waded through the daily collection of newsy garbage gleaned from coroner's and police reports, where they would salvage a few tempting morsels for a couple of lines in Section D. A few reporters may even hit the big time rating a byline in Section A.

Ask the average reader of those two-liner tragedies about the eight Wednesday deaths, and they'd selectively remember that some guy was mangled to death under his racecar and some gal was eaten alive by seals. To most San Franciscans the victims' names weren't relevant any more. What was important was the perverse fascination imbedded in the horror of their agony. How they died, not who they were, was the lure of the story.

Of course, if the victims' deaths on the April 8th Wednesday were all somehow mysteriously related, that would be another story.

CHAPTER 2

Lieutenant O'Shea must have been the only person in San Francisco who cared about all of Wednesday's eight victims. Not because he really cared. How could he; he didn't know any of them. He was ordered to care about them by his captain who dumped the victims' files in his IN box. Now they were an official part of his caseload, at least some of them. As usual, his first assignment would be to identify any of the eight as homicide victims.

After six years as a homicide inspector, when O'Shea arrived at his Bryant Street office, which was a cubicle, his morning routine was well established. Read some of the morning paper while enjoying his morning constitutional that he called a "Jimmy Brit," grab a cup of coffee, black, no sugar, check for urgent memos and calls, and finally check the IN box. This morning was only slightly different. O'Shea's eyes narrowed as he stared at the towering stack of eight cases. "Holy Jesus! What the hell's going on?" he muttered. Lifting the pile of files, O'Shea scanned each cover to make sure they were all their referrals. *Yeah,* he thought, *they're all ours. Oh well.*

Dropping the last of the eight on his desk he absently followed a female cop's posterior as she swished by his desk. In the next cubicle a detective was telling a joke to his partner. O'Shea had heard it before and didn't think it was funny. Refocusing on the pile of cases he shifted to his more attentive, professional reading mode. He considered this part of his morning routine while unaware that these cases would be anything but routine.

📖 📖 📖

Inspector John O'Shea was a genuine *purist*. He was *pure* Irish, as any good size leprechaun, *pure* cop since grammar school and a *pure* binge drinker since college. At seventy paces his red hair still easily announced his heritage, yet he wasn't that arrogant, insecure kid with the cherub face any more. Thick as a cashmere rug his carrot red hair had dulled a bit with his fifty-two years, along with temples now sprinkled with flecks of gray. The years had also altered his once smooth, freckled skin into a weathered, ruddy complexion and time had carved furrows above his bushy eyebrows. Even the few hairline veins on his nose and the clouding whites of his blue eyes were signs of age and booze. Curiously, his more chiseled, craggy, sagging features atop his robust 5'11" frame had actually transformed this baby-faced kid into a ruggedly handsome authority to be taken seriously.

O'Shea's career began as a school traffic monitor at age ten. In college he majored in football and criminology; and during the Korean War he was a Marine captain provost marshal in Japan. Then it took another twenty of his twenty-three years with the San Francisco Police Department to achieve the rank of lieutenant. He was well aware of the struggle for advancement in a department larger than some small towns and permeated with ugly politics. During his career struggle he had made as many police enemies as friends, mainly because of his impatience with incompetence and lackeys, in addition to his attitude, which saddled him with a rebel reputation.

His bi-monthly binges, or "runs" as he called them, further fueled the controversy when he'd disappear for eight or nine days. What preserved O'Shea's job and allies were his excellent investigative skills and sobriety on the job. No other cops ever saw him drunk and where he went on his runs was a secret he shared with only his civilian friends. Although O'Shea rarely socialized with other cops, he loved being a cop. That love affair sparked his recent ambition to be *the cop*—Chief of Police. Of course, O'Shea hadn't the political skill or a police endorsement. He did have, however, Judge Arnold Hall, a mayoral candidate, who virtually promised O'Shea the chief's job if he'd help him win the election. Having lost his once cherished family in divorce, O'Shea had too much leisure time on his hands that he ironically used to become Arnold's lackey.

📖 📖 📖

"Mornin' John."

O'Shea nodded an acknowledgment to Ellis, dropped one of the case files on his desk and leaned back, clasping both hands behind his neck. He respected Sergeant Paul Ellis, his new black partner. He was a bright, dedicated cop with a wife, three high school kids and a retarded sense of humor. O'Shea had worked with Ellis for several years in narcotics and when he recently transferred to homicide, O'Shea was delighted. Although Ellis had no homicide experience he was a quick study, a careful investigator and a remarkably penetrating, objective observer. Part of his competence was his eagerness to listen and learn; and O'Shea was a willing teacher.

At forty-seven, Ellis' smooth, light tan skin, short neatly trimmed black hair, and delicately handsome, yet unremarkable features provided a portrait of a younger man in a more sedate profession— perhaps music or medicine. Despite his 5'9", hundred and forty-five pound frame, in high school and college he was a fine miler in track, outfielder in baseball and a champion welter-weight boxer. Ellis was all business on the job with no interest in pursuing rumors about O'Shea. While working in narcotics they had developed a solid professional relationship that gradually grew into a friendship.

This bond occurred despite their obvious differences. On the surface Ellis was everything O'Shea wasn't. A devoted family man who rarely swore, he was also exceptionally meticulous and patient. A sense of humor, however, was something Ellis never quite figured out; whereas O'Shea was noted for his quick, stiletto-piercing humor. Yet, beneath the surface lurked their more compelling similarities. Both detectives realized a deep sense of loyalty to each other and an exquisite sensitivity to others.

Sitting on the edge of O'Shea's desk, Ellis glanced at the pile of new files. "Looks like we've got a few new ones today."

O'Shea leaned forward with a wry smile and grabbed his cup of coffee. "A few? What an understatement, unless eight new cases is a few. Some seem to be definitely homicides, a few could be accidental and there might even be a suicide. So that's our first job, to establish the reason they died. As usual, Paul, this first part of the procedure for us is routine—search for witnesses to the actual deaths, look for homicide or suicide motives and determine the actual cause of the deaths through the medical examiner."

As usual, Ellis laced his cup of coffee with three sugars and half milk. O'Shea watched the vigorous stirring. "You know, I could never figure out why you bother with the coffee part."

Ellis sat down at his desk with a squinty-eyed puzzled look. "I really like coffee."

Ellis' desk was adjacent to O'Shea's, within the same cubicle, which provided some semblance of privacy.

"Here are four of the cases. Look them over and tell me what you think." O'Shea randomly handed Ellis four files before opening the file on Helen Hansen. "For example, this one out in Seacliff could be a homicide, suicide or even an accident. The victim, a thirty-five-year-old woman, was discovered crushed to death below a two hundred fifty-foot cliff near her house. She could have just slipped, or thought *'Oh screw it'* and jumped, or she could have been pushed. Each possibility would have resulted in the same landing on the rocks, mangled and dead."

"Yeah," said Ellis, without changing expression.

O'Shea continued. "She might have been standing there when a pissed-off neighbor walked by and gave Helen the nudge of her life. Then again, maybe a big, happy dog put his big paws on her back and knocked her off the cliff." O'Shea looked at Ellis and smiled. Ellis nodded back without even a slight guffaw. Both resumed reading the files carefully.

During the next few days the two detectives spent their working hours visiting crime scenes, reviewing police reports, medical examiner findings and developing a list of friends and relatives of victims that might help illuminate the eight crimes. These basic procedures frequently result in more questions than answers—and this week's routine was no exception.

Their first stop had been to Seacliff at the spot from which Helen fell. Approaching this cordoned off area, O'Shea noticed a leashed Great Dane dragging his owner down the street. "See, it could have been a big dog after all." As O'Shea laughed, Ellis didn't even smile.

Helen's footprints had been identified by police forensics despite other footprints. The last of her two footprints were about a foot and a half from the edge. "Jesus," O'Shea exclaimed, "she obviously didn't have—what do you call it—acrophobia. A big wind could have blown her off the cliff. Check for paw prints."

Ellis ignored the last comment and examined Helen's footprints carefully. "Well, she either jumped or got a strong push. Her fall was no accident. Otherwise, wouldn't there have been some signs of feet shuffling or slipping before the fall? Some effort to regain her balance? The footprints are too clear."

"You're right," O'Shea said. "It's like one moment she was firmly standing there and the next moment she was flying."

📕 📕 📕

Pressing the doorbell to Derrick Hansen's home, O'Shea was greeted by a melodious *Clair de Lune* chime and a cheerful reply. "Come in honey, the door's unlocked."

Slowly opening the door, for a moment O'Shea thought he was entering the Museum of Fine Art, with pedestalled statues, huge oil paintings and tapestry filling the enormous, beautifully chandeliered foyer. *Wow, this is living*, O'Shea thought.

As Derrick approached from the closest of five doorways, his broad, rosy-cheeked smile quickly rearranged itself into a grayish, frowning stare. Derrick Hansen, Helen's bereaved husband, could have been a *Gentlemen's Quarterly* model.

O'Shea made a couple of obvious mental calculations. This guy's expecting someone else and what he's wearing must cost more than I make in a month.

Dressed in a finely tailored, brown, double-breasted, gabardine suit, cream-colored silk shirt, rust colored tie and matching pocket-handkerchief and reptilian shoes, Derrick asked dryly, "Can I help you?"

O'Shea quickly flashed his badge and a smile. "Hi, I'm Inspector O'Shea. Didn't your secretary tell you I'd be here about noon?"

"Your hand's covering your I.D. I can't tell who you are by a badge," Derrick replied.

"Oh, I'm sorry," said O'Shea, while thinking—*Oh shit, what a way to start an interview.*

Derrick was a tanned, handsome, six-foot, medium build, black haired fifty-year-old, with graying temples and rather hard, yet nicely sculptured features, without a trace of wrinkles or sags. While Derrick carefully inspected the I.D., O'Shea wondered how many face-lifts he had. With a sense of irritation, tinged with envy, O'Shea figured the black hair was dyed, leaving just enough gray to create a distinguished look. O'Shea also figured Derrick probably worked out daily to prevent any bulges in the tailored suits, except maybe one around his crotch.

After an insultingly long examination of O'Shea's I.D., Derrick returned it with a crisp, delayed comment to O'Shea's original question. "No, I wasn't aware you were coming, and I have another pressing business appointment with Ms. Evermore, my legal secretary. We have to go over some depositions this afternoon."

Just when O'Shea was wondering why the lengthy explanation from Derrick who was so terse about everything else, the *Clair de Lune* door chimes introduced one possible explanation. Carol Evermore was a stunning blond in her middle twenties, with erect breasts, probably as firm as Derrick's face. Her long gorgeous legs meandered upward into muscular thighs, disappearing under a tight black knit dress that traced the contours of her full feminine hips and tight curved buttocks. *What a knockout*, O'Shea exclaimed to himself.

Carol sashayed toward Derrick with wide, fluttering eyes and slightly parted, pursed, cupid lips, until Derrick managed to stop her forward motion. "Hi, Ms. Evermore, I'd like you to meet Inspector O'Shea."

Carol's eyes easily narrowed into slits as she turned toward O'Shea with a thin, tight-lipped, strained smile. "Hello," she whispered.

"Nice to meet you, Ms. Evermore," O'Shea offered with a nod. He then shifted his glance to Derrick. "Can we get together tomorrow?"

Derrick widened the door opening as a good-bye gesture. "Certainly, is tomorrow at 1:00 p.m. OK?"

"That'll be fine Mr. Hansen. It's been my pleasure, Ms. Evermore."

📖　📖　📖

The next day, while Sergeant Ellis was charging around Sea Cliff looking for witnesses, Clair de Lune's reply was almost cordial. Derrick greeted O'Shea with a hardy handshake and casual smile, as if yesterday didn't count. This was really their first meeting. Even his clothes were casual—cashmere sweater, over Levi's, over Docksiders.

"Inspector O'Shea, it's good to see you. Come in." Derrick led O'Shea through the "art gallery" into the living room that was about the size and grandeur of the Morocco Hilton lobby. O'Shea sat in a cream-colored overstuffed leather chair that practically buried him.

Then before O'Shea could express condolences, Derrick smoothly offered his own. "What a gruesome accident. I'm still in shock. Helen had such a deep appreciation for life and she never took anything for granted." Derrick slowly shook his head and dropped his eyes toward the rich Persian rug. "We were so much in love."

"Please accept my condolences," O'Shea interrupted before Derrick could prolong the eulogy. "Was there anything at all your wife might have been upset about?"

"What the hell are you suggesting?" Derrick abruptly asked.

"I'm sorry, Mr. Hansen, but the evidence at the scene of the fall suggested she either jumped or was pushed. We've interviewed every neighbor and anyone who might have been in the area last Wednesday morning. So far, no one has reported seeing anything."

Derrick dropped his eyes again, as if in deep thought. "That's impossible," he insisted. "I just got through telling you that Helen loved life and even the slightest possibility of enemies is preposterous."

O'Shea sat awkwardly silent for a moment. "Mr. Hansen, I'm sure you know there are a couple of routine questions I have to ask. Were there any problems between you and your wife?"

"Absolutely not!"

"Could you share with me your activities last Wednesday morning from the time you got up?"

Derrick shot a scowl directly into O'Shea's eyes. "The phone awakened me at about 7:30 a.m. It was my good friend, Arnold Hall."

Oh shit, O'Shea thought.

"Arnold was confirming our golf game. We talked for about five minutes, then I showered, shaved and heard the housekeeper let herself in at about 8:20. Helen usually wakes me at 8 o'clock, and her absence was beginning to worry me. At 9:30, I called the police, who informed me that a female body had been discovered on the rocks. It was Helen. Now get out!"

📖 📖 📖

Sergeant Ellis' day was even less productive. Every doorbell seemed like a prelude to some classical masterpiece, and even though he couldn't identify them all, Ellis began to enjoy the crystal pure notes resounding into pleasant melodies. What he didn't enjoy was the curt, snobbish answers to the chimes. "I'm sorry to bother you, I'm

Sergeant Ellis with the San Francisco Police Department. Did you notice anyone or anything unusual about 7:00 to 7:30 a.m. this past Wednesday?"

"I'm sorry sir, the owners are on vacation and I saw nothing" (Slam).

"No!" (Slam).

"The residents were asleep, they shouldn't be disturbed now" (Slam).

"Do you have a warrant or something?"

"We have no interest in what others do on the street" (Slam).

Hoping for a more receptive audience, Ellis shifted to people outside. Actually there wasn't much difference from the people inside, he noticed. Along with his request of them, most walked by without a glance, probably figuring he was trying to sell them something. After an hour the only ones willing to talk were a weird old man with a funny looking old dog and a teenage smart-alec.

When Ellis approached the old man walking his dog, he tried displaying his shield. It must have resembled an arrest, since the old man obediently dropped the leash and threw up his hands, with a ready confession.

"I knew you'd catch me. My maid isn't just my maid, and I knew she was an illegal from Mexico. What are you going to do to us?"

"Nothing," Ellis replied in surprise, as he pocketed his badge. "All I want to know is if you saw anything or anyone unusual between 7:00 and 7:30 a.m. last Wednesday."

"No, I was with Rosita."

"Have a nice day," Ellis said, rapidly moving on down the street.

Walking in the opposite direction was the teenager. He was fiercely bouncing a tennis ball high in the air, spinning around and catching it with his outstretched palms behind his back.

"Hey, chum," the kid shouted when Ellis caught the ball the kid had missed. "Don't fuck with the ball," ordered the kid, "I'm working on a routine."

Handing the ball back, Ellis tried a smile, "Oh I'm sorry." The kid was tall, slender, with Aryan blond hair, handsome, squared features, Levi's and a red and black jacket. "You go to Poly?" asked Ellis.

"So?" was the kid's reply.

"My daughter goes there, her name's Beth. Thought you might know her."

"No!" snapped the kid.

"Do you live around here?"

The kid levied a frowning sigh. "What are you, a cop?"

"As a matter of fact, I am," added Ellis, flashing his badge. Pointing to Helen's house, he said, "I'm looking for anyone who might have known the lady who lived across the street, saw her or noticed anything unusual last Wednesday between 7:00 and 7:30 a.m."

"No, I don't know her, I've never seen her, there's nothing unusual and, yes, I go to Poly. Anything else?" the kid blurted.

"Thanks." Ellis said without the smile. "Have a nice day." As the kid walked off, fiercely bouncing the ball, Ellis decided to try another home.

This next home shifted his barely tolerable day to a nearly disastrous one. After listening to the chimes resonating a relaxing spiritual message, Ellis stepped back as usual, to avoid frightening anyone who answered the door. This time it didn't work. As the giant white door, with its stained glass centerpiece opened, a young woman blasted Ellis with a shrill, explosive scream. The shock wave sent him reeling backward where he missed his footing on the top step. He desperately grabbed for the polished brass banister, another miss. Airborne, he practically pirouetted down the three beautifully tiled entrance stairs until landing face down on the sidewalk with his feet still on the second stair. By that time the door had slammed and all was quiet, except his throbbing knee.

The papers he had been carrying in a folder were scattered over, under and around him. *At least there's no wind*, he thought. Ellis slowly slid down the remaining stair, rolled over and spent the next few minutes picking up papers and examining his wounds. He had a tear in the right elbow of his new brown tweed sport coat, a rip at the knee of his gray polyester slacks, along with elbow and knee abrasions matching the tear and rip.

Just when Ellis was thinking, at least no broken bones or gawkers, he heard a car skidding to a stop behind him. "Now what!" he muttered, as he turned to see two very nervous looking security guards leap from their white car brandishing big Smith and Wesson .38's.

"Down on the ground, down on the ground, hands behind your head," they shouted like some discordant duet of Keystone Kops. Ellis quickly realized that even a friendly, non-compliant comment by him might result in "dead bones." Before they could assume he was resisting anything and shoot him, Ellis was back on the pavement with hands behind his back and a wider knee abrasion.

Now he could say it. "I'm a cop, Sergeant Paul Ellis with the San Francisco Police Department. When you search me, you'll find my shield, I.D. and gun."

As one security cop pointed his gun at Ellis' head, the other trembled his way into Ellis' coat pocket, while screaming, "Don't move!" All three of them were relieved when his identity was finally established. By then, however, there were three San Francisco Police cruisers on the scene, a small crowd and heads peering from every nearby window in the neighborhood. While everyone was arguing, apologizing or just chatting, Ellis quietly limped away before the screaming lady reappeared. *I'd better quit work early today*, he thought.

CHAPTER 3

Finishing his usual morning office routine, O'Shea wondered why his partner hadn't arrived yet. It was 8:30 a.m.

That's when Ellis came limping into their cubicle. As he carefully eased himself into his desk chair, he looked up at his partner with a frail smile. "Sorry I'm late, John, I was in the captain's office."

Captain MacInerny had been a tough street cop, who single handedly wrestled thugs to the ground and rescued victims in the once rough Fillmore and Excelsior districts of San Francisco. That was thirty years ago. Today, at sixty-three, he was a pot-bellied worrier, who had lost his guts years ago and couldn't rely on the intelligence he never really had. But, he was a legend, a hero as the most decorated officer in the history of the San Francisco Police Department.

Like an old honored flag you can't burn or get rid of, you just leave it symbolically displayed somewhere. For MacInerny, it was last year's promotion to captain, a kind of honorarium that was his symbol. Although he had no organizational or investigative potential, he had become a useful sycophant for his superiors. This had sadly reduced him to a messenger, either mistrusted or not taken seriously by those in his command. He was also O'Shea's supervisor.

📖 📖 📖

"What the hell happened to you?" O'Shea asked as Ellis limped to his desk.

"You know, I'm not sure. Yesterday was one of the worst days in my working life. Even the captain heard about it and wanted to know what to tell the chief. I suggested he tell the chief nothing. God, John, I'm surprised it's not on the bulletin board."

Ellis detailed the whole day to his partner, who quietly sat biting his lip to keep from laughing. "After I got home, Elizabeth and the kids laughed when I told them about the header down the stairs. What's so funny? Now *you're* laughing."

O'Shea tried biting his lip again; and when that didn't work, he burst into a laughing, head shaking apology. "I'm sorry, Paul, you take everything so damn seriously, it is funny."

Ellis got up and hobbled around the side of his partner's desk, then he looked around and leaned toward O'Shea as if in confidence. "You want to know what bothers me? What really bothers me is why the lady screamed. Is it a racial thing, a menacing black guy in a white neighborhood? Did I do something to scare her, or was she just crazy?"

O'Shea got up and put a hand on Ellis' shoulder. "Are you ready for this one? I heard from the uniformed cops, it had everything to do with your appearance, but not like you think. The lady was a light black maid, with an estranged boyfriend who threatened to kill her. You had the misfortune of looking just like him."

Ellis momentarily relaxed his usual sober expression into a wide-eyed, toothy grin. "Wow, so that's it. Poor lady."

O'Shea dropped his smile. "Now can we go to work?"

"Sure," Ellis replied soberly.

📖 📖 📖

O'Shea gathered up the eight cases scattered around his desk. Inserting a few more notes and documents into some of the folders, he stacked them in a neat pile. "There's about two feet worth and they're growing," he said, looking at the stack.

Ellis quickly scanned his own desk. "Have all my notes and stuff been filed?"

"All but the back flip off the stairs." O'Shea grinned. Ellis was back to his all serious mode.

"Anyway, I stayed last night until about 10:30, pouring over all the accumulated information on each case. I even tried to decipher some of your scribbles."

Ellis looked up as if a bit startled. "Why didn't you call me? We're partners you know."

O'Shea's four kids were grown and Mary, his wife, had divorced him two years ago. "You've still got a nice family. I got the TV, a book or a gin mill down the street. OK?"

This time Ellis got up and patted O'Shea on the shoulder, "OK, but I'm always ready to share the load."

O'Shea grabbed the top file off the stack. "Let's go over the Hansen case again and we'll work our way through the pile before it gets any higher. This will be our preliminary assessment of the evidence, the development of our hypotheses and strategy. In other words, what we got, what we need and where we go from here." O'Shea grinned again and Ellis' expression didn't budge.

"The medical examiner's report on Helen doesn't tell us much we didn't already know. She was crushed to death on impact with the rocks. It was a bone shattering splat that even drove the splintered bone in her left forearm beneath the sternum into her heart. There were no fingerprints, palm prints . . ."

"Don't say it," Ellis interrupted.

". . . or paw prints on what was left of her jacket. There were also no medications in her system. We still haven't come up with any witnesses, and there's not even a grain of evidence at the scene of the fall. Thanks to you, we can rule out accidental death, it's still suicide or a homicide."

Ellis was listening intently while he vigorously stirred his creamy sugared coffee. "After reading your interview with the husband, I think we can concentrate on homicide."

O'Shea agreed. Aside from disliking Derrick, he had already concluded that the tryst with Carol Evermore was a strong motive for murder. "Besides," O'Shea added, "no one, including her physician, noticed any behavioral changes suggesting a downward mood swing. Helen didn't know, or didn't want to know about the girlfriend. So where we go from here is back to the Hansen house, re-examine every move Derrick took that morning, re-interview the housekeeper and anyone else nearby, except the screaming lady. I'm laying all of this on you, because Judge Arnold Hall is both Derrick's pal and my advocate."

Ellis looked at O'Shea with a knowing nod. "No problem."

📖 📖 📖

"At least we know from the start that the Bill Winston case is a homicide."

"Yeah," acknowledged Ellis, "the .22 bullet through the side of his head, with no weapon around, is hardly an accident or suicide."

"Ballistics indicate the shot was fired from about thirty or forty yards," O'Shea said.

"The bullet's path through the head suggests that the shot was from about fifteen feet high. Maybe a doorway or first floor window," Ellis added.

"The perp must have been a pretty good shot," O'Shea reasoned.

Standing over O'Shea, Ellis read the ballistics report again. "Yeah, he was a heck of a shot, especially if the weapon was a handgun. The bullet was too smashed to determine the type of weapon. But, this is interesting; the perp might have been in the National Guard. The report says that a .22 shell casing, matching armory target ammo, was found down the street."

"Yeah, I noticed that," O'Shea said. "Let's see if Jason, his lover, was in the Guard. By the way, you know the victim was being seen by a good friend of mine, Dr. Jerry Wunden. He's a shrink, ex-jock and a regular guy. I'll try to see him this weekend at the Java House, our old hangout. I'll also check out the lover. He tends bar at the Full Load on Castro Street."

"Don't let 'em get you drunk down there," Ellis admonished, like some unthinking, well-meaning uncle.

O'Shea's Irish face flushed and sizzled with annoyance. "I'll try not to let them fuck me either."

"I'm sorry, that was stupid. I know you don't drink when you're working."

O'Shea's red faded, along with his grinding teeth. "Forget it. No big deal." Then changing the subject, "Why don't you check the Post Street area again for witnesses, even though it's probably a waste of time, with all that jack hammer construction noise and the heavy traffic. He could have been shot with a grenade launcher, and I doubt if anyone would have heard it."

📖　📖　📖

O'Shea slid the next two files off the top of the pack. "Christ, this is a mind-boggler, Paul. Two more of my best old pals are linked to these two cases. Dick Boyd, my buddy, was the guy aced out of the assistant coaching job at Poly by André Likert, the guy who had his chest caved in by his racecar. It had to be a homicide. The hydraulic jack handle was fully released in a counter-clockwise direction; the jack was negative for leaks and the drop light plug had been kicked loose, probably by the perp. No witnesses, of course, and Dick is the primary suspect. In fact, he's the only suspect for now.

"This'll really blow you out. The garage floor was clean, except for an oil puddle near the rear jack wheels. That's where, yesterday, forensics found a partial shoe print about the size of Sasquatch, you know—Bigfoot."

📖 📖 📖

O'Shea tucked all of the papers back into the folder and opened the other file with a broad grin. "I didn't really know Emil Anderson, the guy who got poisoned on his way to see Richard Bender, a deputy DA. Rich was one of the best middleweights in California, and one of the brightest guys around. I agree it's pretty obvious that Emil's son, Ralph, somehow poisoned him, but what the hell, even if his kid confesses, it'll be fun interviewing Bender."

"We have to find Ralph first," Ellis added. "The lab report indicates Emil OD'd on Phencyclidine."

"That makes sense," O'Shea noted. "Ralph is a loser and a user with easy access to PCP."

Ellis wasn't particularly concerned about investigating the Anderson case. It seemed pretty straightforward to him. A spoiled son did something heinous enough to finally fuel his father's anger and bolster his courage into contacting the DA's office. The kid squirms in desperation, but he can't bully his father any longer, so he follows him to the restaurant and poisons him with over a hundred fifty milligrams of PCP.

Ellis was, however, really concerned about the Likert case. He was worried about his partner bending procedural rules for a friend. "Let me interview Boyd, OK? I've never met any of your close buddies."

"No, I'm going to interview him because he is my buddy."

"Come on, John, he's a suspect. He's the main suspect. What if he really did kill Likert?"

"I've been a cop for over twenty years and Boyd's friend for over thirty years. That's over fifty years of instinct that tells me Dick didn't kill anybody."

"But what if he did?"

O'Shea looked at Ellis coldly. "If he did kill him, Likert was an asshole and deserved it. Get the picture?"

"I didn't hear any of this, Lieutenant."

📖 📖 📖

O'Shea's face softened a bit as he again changed the subject by handing Ellis the next two files. "You've done most of the leg work on these two; have you any ideas about what happened?"

Ellis thumbed the case on Sutherland, re-reading his scribbled notes. "These were all Porpoise Club old-timers. Their average age is about eighty. You've probably seen them swimming within the Aquatic Park buoys."

"Yeah, they always reminded me of little balloon heads with arms, and they still wear those rubber caps."

"Well, it keeps their head warm, and the head's supposed to be the body's radiator. I can't even wade in that water, it's too cold."

O'Shea gave a mocking frown to Ellis' last comment. "Sometimes you act older than the average age of those old timers. I bet you can't swim."

"That's right I can't, but I can beat your butt at handball."

Ignoring this reminder, O'Shea just cleared his throat. "Tell me more about Sutherland. I think I remember him from high school."

"Come on, you know everybody."

"I should, I was born here. I'm not an ex-patriot from Hayward like you."

Ellis picked up the ME's report, scanned it, then looked at O'Shea. "What do you think Sutherland died of?"

"What is this, a game? How about dehydration."

"That's pretty close," Ellis said nearing one of his almost smiles. "He drowned."

"No shit, Paul, those coroners really do a thorough job. Tell me something I didn't know."

"Harry Sutherland was a well-liked, retired chiropractor. He was also an ex-athlete. You probably knew that part."

O'Shea nodded.

Ellis continued. "He was still in fine physical condition, with no medical problems and an active social life, especially with women, probably because they tend to outlive men. Apparently most of his male friends were dead, except for Don Dutil. He's a retired banker who sponsored Sutherland's Porpoise membership. And there's Jim Robinson, an ex-old friend who hated Sutherland. Dutil apparently witnessed an argument between Sutherland and Robinson about a half hour before the body was discovered. Robinson called Sutherland out for a fight, and Sutherland reportedly just ignored him. Later, at Aquatic Park, Dutil noticed Robinson, with his blue cap, coming in shortly before Dutil bumped against Sutherland's awash body."

"Wow." O'Shea chuckled. "Dutil could make witness of the year. He seemed to witness everything but Sutherland's last breath. By the way, could it have been an accident?"

"There was nothing wrong with the guy. He was a good swimmer; and there was no medical evidence of heart failure, seizures or any other problems that might have killed him."

O'Shea rolled his eyes up toward his forehead. "I think I remember a guy named Jim Robinson. As I recall from my father, he was a real hothead in school."

"Come on, who the hell don't you know?"

"I don't know anyone else from Hayward. Anyway, Robinson sounds like a prime suspect to me."

"I agree," said Ellis. "Robinson was reportedly as strong as an ox, an endurance swimmer and besides, there are no other suspects or witnesses."

"Have you questioned Robinson yet?" asked O'Shea.

"No, I'm waiting for a forensics report on some material found under Sutherland's fingernails. Maybe we can hit him with some hard evidence, like skin or something. There were also some fresh bruise marks on Sutherland's legs."

"Sounds right to me, but if Robinson's got scratches, don't wait till they heal before you interview him."

"Good point." Ellis dropped the Sutherland case before picking up the other one on Carlos Villa. "This other case is real loose. The intended victim was in jail for manslaughter until this morning. He drove his old truck down Guerrero Street into a Dorothy Torres and her three-year-old daughter, Melody. Mother's dead and the kid's critical in a coma. I really feel sorry for the old guy, Carlos Villa. Jailers tell me he cried practically the whole time in jail. They finally had to sedate him. Everybody just assumed he was a reckless, irresponsible driver, probably because he got two speeding tickets last year. No one believed the guy's brakes failed, and the police impound garage mechanics didn't get around to even checking the truck brakes until yesterday. They were all cut."

O'Shea slowly shook his head, "So the perp is now the victim?"

"Well kinda, you know how cops try to snug up their cases. Before I had a chance to see him in jail, traffic had already gotten involved. Then some racist cop brought in narcotics. Any swarthy looking guy named Carlos Villa, has gotta at least be a user."

O'Shea leaned forward over his desk. "Who's the narcotics cop?"

"Your friend, Mahoney."

O'Shea grimaced and pounded his fist on the desk, "Ah, shit, go on."

"Well, narcotics wanted to prove Villa was driving under the influence, but they haven't been able to link him to a marijuana seed, let alone hard drugs. Then the brake-cutting discovery yesterday kicked Sergeant Mahoney right in the butt. So narcotics has changed their strategy. They're convinced Carlos is a dealer because of his pretty wife's expensive lifestyle. Carlos is squeaky clean, but you know Mahoney."

O'Shea knew Sergeant Lloyd Mahoney too well. Mahoney had resented him for a variety of reasons. During a high school street fight, he had broken Mahoney's jaw with one punch. O'Shea always scored higher on exams, and even though Mahoney had two years police seniority, O'Shea was always promoted before him. Eight years earlier their smoldering relationship festered into a pathological hate, especially by Mahoney. At that time, Sergeant O'Shea was Mahoney's superior in a narcotics unit. When large sums of money were seized during a bust, discretely sharing five to ten percent with all cops involved was quietly condoned. On one such bust, Mahoney got greedy and had to take $500 from a $1,500 bag of bills. O'Shea had caught him in the act, had him transferred out of the unit, yet told no one why. That didn't matter to Mahoney; he never stopped hating or blaming O'Shea for everything.

O'Shea fumed. "Mahoney's going to fuck Carlos over and roust his wife, just because it's one of my cases."

"I agree, I've checked around and there's no way Carlos or his wife are into dealing. But that won't matter to Mahoney, he'll come up with something."

O'Shea sat back in his chair and momentarily closed his eyes. "I should probably break that asshole's jaw again. You know Captain

Mac ain't willing to help, and most guys in narcotics avoid me since Mahoney started running the unit and his mouth. You know, maybe Ginella can lean on Mahoney."

"You mean the father of the groom who is supposed to marry the Villa kid?"

"That's right, Paul. I've known him for years. Jim's a great guy with a lot of influence."

Ellis slapped his forehead with his right palm, "I don't believe it. You did it again."

"Hey you forget, he's not from Hayward."

📖 📖 📖

"So, what about the last two cases?" asked Ellis.

O'Shea picked up the remaining files and dropped them on Ellis' desk. "We don't have to bust our hump on these," O'Shea grunted through a huge yawn. "Grace Digness seems like a classic mercy killing. Her husband, Terry, was seen running out of her hospital room, down the corridor, shortly before she was found dead. They had some sort of a suicide pact and he's not denying he pulled the life support stuff. He's in jail on a suicide watch."

Ellis flipped through the file. "Has he been arraigned yet?"

"Yeah, he's been charged with second degree murder. He'll probably plead to a manslaughter before the trial sometime next month."

"How about this one?" Ellis asked.

"That last one on Officer Nelson is another low priority for us," O'Shea said. "The whole goddamn police force is tripping all over themselves, looking for the perp. At least twenty uniforms thoroughly mauled and trampled the whole area. The only evidence left is the finger and shoe prints of twenty cops. But that didn't stop them," he added. "After trashing the belongings of all the homeless in the area and booting them all out to nowhere, the frantic twenty arrested two vagrants who had been looking at the guy with the concrete block for a head."

Ellis was following along with the police reports. "Their names are Scotty Harvey and Ron Tuttle, with priors for drunkenness, fighting and disorderly conduct."

"I knew one of them during the days I was a beat cop south of Market," O'Shea said. "Old Scotty Harvey was a career wino who wouldn't hurt a flea. If he was ever arrested for fighting, it's because somebody was beating the shit out of him."

"How come you don't know Tuttle, the other guy?" Ellis taunted.

"Because he probably *is* from Hayward," O'Shea replied slowly with one of his full-face grins.

CHAPTER 4

Carlos Villa sat on the edge of his bed, heaving deep sobs of torment. His blood red eyes were almost swollen shut by the constant flood of salty tears dripping from his nose to his chin, onto his upturned palms resting on his knees. He was paralyzed in grief and his only movements since his release from the county jail were volleys of convulsive shivering when he tried to catch his breath.

Falling asleep meant the terrifying plunge of his two-ton truck down the steep Guerrero hill. The horror of grotesque bloody faces smashed against his windshield. Bodies vanishing, then reappearing with dead eyes as the truck slammed to a stop.

Staying awake flooded his mind with searing grief and blame, exploding into obsessive thoughts of torturous *what ifs*. He shouldn't have left home so early that day. He should have pulled hard on the hand brake, jammed the automatic transmission into reverse, steered away from mother and child. He had frozen in panic.

There was no escape. No way to stop the thinking. Carlos shuttered with throbbing thoughts of doubt and guilt. *Police now say they thought the brakes failed because of my drug dealings. How can they know what I don't know? Did I sell drugs? Was my wife, Leona, involved? I don't remember, but the police say it was my fault the brakes failed. All my life I thought I was being good, and now I'm bad. I can't bear being bad. I can't bear dreams or thoughts anymore. I need sleep without dreams.*

Carlos dried his hands on his pant legs, reached across the bed and grabbed the old .38 his father had left him. He put the barrel in his mouth, pulled the trigger and heard a click. He pulled it again and found his dreamless sleep.

A week later, when O'Shea learned of the suicide, Mahoney had his second broken jaw. That was another sleepless night for O'Shea. He couldn't turn off those gnawing thoughts. *Why would anybody try to kill this good guy? Is there a possible drug connection? No, not him. Maybe somebody sabotaged the wrong truck. Ah shit!*

📖 📖 📖

O'Shea was an excellent homicide investigator, with a bright, hard-working, painstakingly thorough partner. Yet they didn't seem to be getting anywhere with most of their eight cases. *Plenty of motives and very little evidence*, O'Shea thought. *Now, a straight, conscientious little Mexican was brainwashed into suicide because of his rigid morality, respect for authority, a rotten cop and an unknown killer.*

O'Shea took a deep breath and slowly sighed, molding his angry frown into a pensive grin. He was looking at his bruised knuckles. He knew he had alienated a few more cops, but that didn't matter; it was worth it. It was a one-punch triumph and some sort of requiem for a good man, who died thinking he was bad.

📖 📖 📖

Sixteen-year-old Jerran was a straight A student at Polytechnic High School. Four years earlier his father had deserted the family for another woman. This compelled his pregnant mother to work as a full-time maid in some of San Francisco's big hotels. As the only male in his small family, Jerran was very protective of his mother and little sister. He often thought that once he completed his education and became a physician, he would always care for them financially.

Beep . . . Beep . . . Beep . . . Beep. Exhausted by the grieving and sleepless vigil, Jerran was kneeling against his sister's hospital bed, with head resting on his outstretched arms across her. He could only watch and listen to the sterile, metronome rhythm beeping its tentative promise; there's some life beneath the layers of blood stained gauze bandages and tape concealing four-year-old Melody's broken, lifeless body. Jerran's face and arms were smeared with traces of dried tears. He still cried in deep sobs, but there was no moisture left for tears. He half lay there with little hope and worst of all, unbearable guilt. A week earlier—when time had lost its meaning—Jerran's mother, Dorothy, was killed and his sister critically injured by a runaway truck. "What went wrong," he gasped. "Karma has made me an orphan." Beeeeeeeeeeeep . . . . .

Three days after his sister's death in the intensive care room at San Francisco General Hospital, Jerran was found dead, hanging by his belt from a pipe in the boys' gym at Polytechnic High School.

📖 📖 📖

Arnold Hall's insistence that his friend, Derrick, was innocent had come close to collapsing O'Shea's endorsement and political ambitions. He had resisted Arnold's friendly warnings to back off, until Ellis discovered the overlooked gardener who swore Derrick never left his home that morning. His girlfriend's three-day visit to L.A. was also solidly verified. Still disliking Derrick, O'Shea had apologized to Arnold and again fantasized about being the chief cop. *Yet, there's always a down side*, he thought, still grinning. *Someone pushed her over that cliff; maybe it was the big dog after all.*

"Nah."

CHAPTER 5

O'Shea was looking forward to the next day's Java House get-together with some of his oldest and most loyal buddies. Curiously, other than their athletic backgrounds, they had little of the obvious adhesive that tends to bond people together. They had different professions, nationalities, interests and physical appearances. Even their hang-ups, as well as their family involvements, were different. To an acquaintance of theirs, or casual observer, they really had nothing in common.

Most conventional observers believe people hang together principally because of their similarities; perhaps because the average person doesn't look beyond the superficial to the uniqueness of each individual. True, doctors typically socialize with other doctors, lawyers gather with lawyers, and housewives with their neighbor housewives. Ghetto blacks have their brothers, students their sororities and fraternities, snobs with their snobs and Chicanos their homies.

None of the stereotypes that qualified as group identities applied to O'Shea's pals. If anything, their unique values and individual identities generously seasoned the bonding. Wunden, the psychologist, was bored by colleagues. Deputy D.A. Bender thought most attorneys were crooks, educator Boyd nodded off at just about every teachers' gathering and Ginella, the most influential, knew everybody while barely tolerating anybody. O'Shea, of course, was no exception. He loved the life of a cop, but not a life *with* cops.

Despite their athletic backgrounds and interests, none of the five were common interest groupies. They weren't joiners who needed to hang out with other athletes, reminiscing about their good old days. None of the stereotypes that qualified as group identities had ever applied to O'Shea's pals. The main bonding ingredient was their unqualified trust in each other. Early in their youth, these five earned their loyalties, which each quietly honored with a deep sense of pride.

In the 50's, Second Lieutenant John O'Shea, U.S.M.C. had partied all night with Boyd and Ginella. He intended to drive to Quantico, Virginia for Military Police training, after dropping off his buddies and grabbing a few hours sleep. Roaring drunk, O'Shea momentarily lost control of his car and sideswiped three parked cars near Ginella's house. As he kept driving, all of their laughter was suddenly stifled by a big red light and shrieking siren. Boyd, in the rear seat and Ginella in front, knew O'Shea's career was over if caught. Almost simultaneously Boyd dragged O'Shea into the back seat as Ginella slid into the driver's seat. Then he stopped the car and surrendered to the police.

A few years later, a drunk Bender and Ginella broke up a Polk Street bar, while flattening the bartender and Pete Gillette, the owner, who had tried to throw them out. This time Ginella got away and Bender maintained "the other guy" was a stranger. Wunden, then a probation officer, knew Gillette as a low-life crook, with outstanding warrants and a low-life brother on probation. When Wunden learned of Bender's arrest, he leaned all over Gillette with vague, convincing threats, until the charges against Bender were dropped.

These exchanges of loyalty and unsolicited rescues had persisted into their middle age years. Ironically, they rarely saw each other; yet in a crisis, they were suddenly together, unflinchingly prepared to lie for each other. Fortunately, however, there were fewer crises for the five, since all but O'Shea no longer drank.

📖 📖 📖

On Sunday, O'Shea arrived at the Java House early enough to chat with Phil before his friends began wandering in. Complimenting this unlikely group of friends was Phil Papadopoulos, owner of the historic Java House—a remnant of those last San Francisco waterfront cafes. These old longshoremen cafes flourished in the forties and fifties when San Francisco was a bustling seaport. Sadly, the old Java House was gradually sinking beneath a sea of yuppie breweries and Starbuck coffee houses.

Papadopoulos wore Zorba on his face with a superb handlebar mustache that rivaled Salvador Dali's finest. "Where ya been?" boomed a voice through the monstrous mustache that hid most of a huge grin. He was a proud prototypical Greek—with an attitude. His ponytail was the first clue that beneath the Greek heritage was the unmistakable aroma of hippy, mixed with rascal. Papadopoulos loved to schmooze with his customers, embarrass them with his radical ideas and laugh them out the door if they squirmed too much. O'Shea and his pals were Papadopoulos' favorites, probably because they laughed with him and never squirmed.

O'Shea returned the grin. "What's it to ya, what do you think you are, a cop?"

Aproned Papadopoulos dried his hands and walked around the counter, separating tables from the kitchen. "No, but you are, unless you lie." Papadopoulos gave O'Shea a bear hug greeting. O'Shea gave one back, before sitting at a large table near a window.

"All my old friends are coming here this morning, Phil. You know them all—Ginella, Bender, Boyd and Wunden."

Papadopoulos returned to the little kitchen where he could work and talk. "All you guys haven't been together here in years. I see the doctor once in a while, Big Jim was here last month, but I haven't seen Boyd or Bender in a long time. What are you guys up to, anyway?"

Ignoring Papadopoulos' question, O'Shea glanced out the window at the huge South Beach Harbor. "It's sure changed since the freighters used to dock here. How about some grease and coffee before the others arrive?"

Sensing something was seriously up with O'Shea and friends, Papadopoulos dropped his original question. "The usual—sausage, cheese and pepperoni omelet with sourdough toast?"

O'Shea got up and poured his own coffee. "You remembered, Phil, extra sausage, you know how I love grease."

Just then, tall, lanky Richard Bender came in with hands buried in his khakis and a furtive area-scanning look.

"Who the hell you think you're lookin for?" challenged Papadopoulos.

As Bender tensed up and spun around, his frown collapsed into a relaxed smile. "My God, Phil, it's been awhile. I didn't recognize your voice."

After a second bear hug with Bender, Papadopoulos pointed to

O'Shea's table.

O'Shea leaped up, grabbed Bender's hand and they engaged in a mock hand wrestling match for old times. "Always great to see you, Rich."

"Likewise, John."

"You know I'm glad you got here early. Why don't you order and I'll bounce a few cases off you."

Breaking his vegetarian diet, Bender ordered about a half-pound of bacon, sausages, four hot cakes and plenty of butter and syrup. "This is what I've been waiting for, John, real food."

Like a couple of ravenous hyenas after a kill, O'Shea and Bender slurped their plates clean without saying a word. Wiping the grease from his mouth, O'Shea finally broke the eating frenzied silence. "That must have been a hell of a shock to find an old friend dead in your waiting room."

Thoughtfully nodding his head, Bender sponged up the remaining morsel of grease with his last piece of pancake. "At first I just couldn't believe it; one of those cognitive dissonance things. I knew he was asleep, even though he wasn't. Emil was a good friend and one of those rare, fine human beings."

Downing his second cup of coffee, O'Shea nodded sympathetically. "I didn't know Emil well, but everyone seemed to like him. As of this morning, we're still looking for Ralph, his son, the most likely suspect. Did you get my message about the kid's sexual molestation of a neighbor?"

Bender was nodding before O'Shea finished the question. "Yeah, sure did, but we already knew. Mrs. Leon, the kid's mother, reported it when she learned Emil was dead. Our office is also looking for the son now. He's the perfect suspect. He knew Mrs. Leon would tell his father, and, as a junkie, he had access to and knowledge of PCP, the stuff that killed Emil. Ralph's also a psychopathic low-life."

"All we gotta do is catch this one." O'Shea smiled. "Well, that's one out of eight."

"What do ya mean?" Bender asked.

"Last week I got saddled with eight new cases, and none of them feel quite right. That's one of the reasons I wanted to see you guys. A little business with pleasure. Did you know that André Likert got squashed under his car and it's probably a murder?"

Bender looked a bit surprised. "I read about it in the paper, but we haven't gotten that one yet."

"Then you probably didn't know that Boyd is a possible suspect," added O'Shea.

Bender really looked surprised. "Jesus, what's that one all about?"

O'Shea explained about how Boyd threatened Likert when he lost the assistant coaching job to him, all of which occurred a few days before Likert's death.

Bender heaved a deep sigh. "You know we've gotta help him either way."

"Yeah, Rich, I know."

"Hey, what's happenin', can we flop here?" The voice was unmistakably Ginella's foghorn blast. With him was Jerry Wunden, who was slightly hidden behind Ginella's gigantic girth. Spearheaded by Ginella, a few more bone crushing hugs followed. "I saw this guy in the parking lot, anyone know him?" Ginella laughed.

"I think that's Doctor Something-or-other." O'Shea smirked.

Wunden slithered in front of Ginella. "What am I, just a sour hunk of nothing?"

"That's not a bad self-assessment," quipped Bender, as he slapped Wunden on the back.

When the foursome finally settled down, Ginella—who had eaten breakfast an hour before—gave Papadopoulos his order of two hamburgers with French fries. "On second thought," Ginella bellowed, "hold the mayonnaise, I'm on a diet."

"Hold the mayo," Papadopoulos repeated, as he wrote the order with a frowning smile. "You eat too much."

Wunden ordered his usual cheese and mushroom omelet with wheat toast, just as Boyd walked in. This prompted another onslaught of hugging, back slapping and wise cracking before they again settled down.

Boyd, tall, lean and in good shape was the handsome, over-indulgent womanizer during his youth. Now, he was into sensible moderation. He ordered two eggs up, wheat toast and tea.

"How's Poly reacting to Likert's crushing finale under his car?"

Boyd, now seated by the window, dropped his fork full of eggs and stared directly at Bender.

"No, I didn't kill the asshole, if that's what you're asking, Mr. Deputy D. A."

Bender threw up his hands with wide eyes. "Lighten up, Pal, I haven't even got the case yet. O'Shea just started to talk about it when you guys came in. You know damn well we wouldn't roust you."

Picking up his fork, Boyd looked at all of his friends and grinned. "I know that. I'm sorry. It's just all the jokes, sly glances and innuendoes at school. Do you think murder's my style, Dr. Jerry?" Wunden quickly shook his head. "No, Dick. You'd have waited until he slid out from under his car, then you would have beaten the livin' shit out of him."

"Thanks, Jerry, I needed an accurate clinical profile."

Reaching over the table, O'Shea squeezed Boyd's arm. "I know you didn't do it. Your foot's half the size of a partial print we found. Got any ideas who offed the jerk?" asked O'Shea, still squeezing.

Sipping his tea, Boyd shook his head with a blank, searching stare at the table. "Half the teachers and jocks couldn't stand him. He had a talent for pissing people off; and that probably included half of his neighbors. I guess the real question is, who's capable of killing someone disliked or even hated."

Ginella was vigorously nodding as he downed a few more French fries. "That's a great point, Dick. Punching out somebody you can't stand is one thing; we've all done that. But deliberately killing somebody, that takes a certain type of person. Right, Jer?"

"Yeah, I agree, Jim. Most people will argue that they'd kill in defense of family or themselves. Yet, even under those extreme circumstances, most people couldn't consciously snuff somebody out. Even under orders in combat, killing face-to-face, up close and personal, was overwhelmingly tough for most and impossible for others. Then there were those who loved it. Probably the best predictor of murderous behavior is past behavior—like kind of a profile of kids who like to torture small animals just for fun. Otherwise, there's no psychological test that can identify one of these potential killers. Maybe it's in their genes."

"How about mercy killers?" asked Bender. "We've got one now. I think his name's Terry Digness. He's a mild-mannered, law-abiding guy in his seventies, with no prior arrests."

Wunden downed another swallow of coffee as he thought for a moment. "You know, Rich, I don't think mercy killers are killers. It's an oxymoron."

"An oxy-what?" demanded Ginella with a puckish grin. "Are you still eating those damn psychological dictionaries?"

Bender laughed his way into the conversation before Wunden could reply. "That's not a psychological word, Jim."

"Oh shit," Ginella muttered. "Here comes the lecture."

Wunden dropped his remaining piece of toast on his plate. "For Christ's sake, Jim, we're not going to jam a new word down your throat. You're not interested? No big deal."

Ginella gave Wunden a sheepish smile. "All right, all right, you win. A quickie definition."

Wunden stuffed the last piece of toast in his mouth and looked at his friends. "Is everybody ready for the lesson?" Wunden gave his buddies a polite finger, as they sarcastically sneered, grunted and applauded. "An oxymoron is two terms that tend to contradict each other, like 'religious wars' or 'friendly fire'. Most real mercy killers have all the feelings killers never experience, like compassion, empathy, selfless courage and humanity. They have no intention of killing anyone. They must help end somebody's life as a way of ending the unbearable suffering. For most of these gentle people, despite their deep grief and pleas from their loved one, ending a tortured life is an overwhelming decision. It takes monumental courage, especially in the face of society labeling them mercy killers, the oxymoron."

They all applauded.

O'Shea easily telegraphed his feelings. His face had changed to an enriched beat red from his usual ruddy beige. "Are you thinking what I'm thinking, Bender? Terry's no killer. He didn't kill his wife, even though she probably begged him to. When she was found by the nurse, the life support tubes and wires had been almost barbarically ripped from her face. It was really a grotesque sight."

Bender sighed. "I'm inclined to agree with John. You too, Jerry?"

"I'd stake whatever reputation I've got left on it. A killer murdered Terry's wife, not Terry."

"All in agreement raise your hands," proposed Bender.

All five raised their hands. Standing nearby was Papadopoulos. "Me too," he said.

"Goddammit," quipped O'Shea, with a pleased look on his again ruddy face. "Now there are four primaries that are no longer suspects. Terry couldn't have killed his wife, Carlos didn't cut his own brake lines, Boyd would rather fight than kill and Derrick's alibis are solid."

Sopping the burger grease with his last fries, Ginella added, "Maybe I didn't know an oxymoron from a real moron, but I did know Terry and his wife Grace, as well as Carlos. I knew them most of my life. You guys may be the morons. Digging into their backgrounds, you'll never find prime suspects, because anyone who knew them truly liked them. I think whoever is responsible for those deaths didn't know them. Maybe they were mistaken murders, or random mischief, just for kicks."

They all sat silently for a while as Papadopoulos poured more coffee and told a couple of corny jokes.

O'Shea wanted to bring up a few more of his eight cases, but realized that was enough for one day. The rest of their afternoon together was spent reminiscing about the good and lousy old days.

CHAPTER 6

O'Shea could barely sleep Sunday night. *Maybe it's too much coffee, or maybe I'm becoming an insomniac,* he thought. *Hell no, I'm no neurotic so it must be the coffee,* he argued. *Then again, maybe I think too much. No, it's the coffee.*

He kept thinking about the Java House, his friends, their comments and even his thorough investigations that seemed to be leading him backwards. There was also his gnawing cop intuition. He was overlooking something disturbingly obvious. Each crime seemed clearly unrelated to the others. They were all discreet, isolated incidents requiring separate investigations. Yet, he was as confident that a single negative energy, something out there, linked all eight crimes together. He knew there was a connection; he just didn't know what, or where to start looking.

Seven a.m. Monday, O'Shea was already at his desk. He had begun to carefully review each of his eight expanding files. He couldn't help but remember, with mixed feelings of professional pride and disappointment, that less than two weeks earlier each folder contained only a page or two of brief reports. Now there were pages of interviews, other types of investigative reports by Ellis and him, in addition to state or federal agency documents, medical examiner autopsies and supplemental police reports. Yet, they seemed to be getting nowhere.

Looking over the PCP poisoning death that occurred in Bender's waiting room, O'Shea sat back for a moment, rubbing his eyes. He thought aloud, "At least this should be one less case once Ralph, Emil's son, is picked up."

"Did they catch Ralph?" Ellis asked as he entered their office cubicle.

"Not yet. What are you doing here so early?"

"Probably the same thing you're doing. Trying to solve some of these cases. Were your buddies any help?"

O'Shea shook his head slowly. "Well, we can truly rule out Boyd—honest! I'm also convinced Terry Digness didn't kill his wife. Don't ask me to explain my reasoning."

Impassively, Ellis grabbed his half-full cup of last Friday's sweet, soured milk cold coffee. He took a long, satisfying swig, as if it were freshly brewed. "You're right, John. Terry's too gentle and loving to end his wife's suffering by ripping her face apart."

"Christ, Paul, you keep amazing me. Anyway, that's four out of eight without the viable suspects we thought we had. Any ideas?"

"Just to keep digging, take up the slack, don't let any lead get cold, keep reviewing all we have and what we need. You taught me all of that. I also get the feeling these crimes are related in some sinister way, which means maybe we should look beyond the obvious."

O'Shea looked up at Ellis with an all-knowing, nodding smile. "I needed those reminders. You're one hell of a fine partner. There's nothing wrong with our investigative skills; we've just got to keep at it. And that last point of yours, you must have read my mind!"

"I guess for cops, patience is the ultimate virtue. I can't help feeling that after busting our humps, turning over every rock for nearly two weeks, we're no further from finding the bad guys than the day we got these cases."

This time, O'Shea vigorously shook his head. "Come on. I just snapped out of my slump, don't put me back there. Police work's a lot like any scientific investigation. Every rock we turn over is one less rock. Proving somebody's innocent is as important as proving their guilt. So anything we do, tells us something." O'Shea grinned. "So far, we've come up with more good guys than bad guys. That's progress."

When Ellis gave a vigorous nod, O'Shea added, "I've notified every agency, bureau, neighborhood watch group, professional informant and street snitch to contact us if they have information about anything unusual that was reported in any of the eight crime areas two Wednesdays ago."

"That's really a good idea. After reading your list, I added a few of my own."

"How the hell did you know about my list? I just sent the inquiries last night. Christ, you are a mind reader."

Ellis remained expressionless. "I dropped by the office for awhile last night. Must have been right after you left."

O'Shea gave Inspector Johnny Drocco a quick nod as he walked by. "He owes me a pedro. He said I'd be suspended if I punched out Mahoney.

Ellis watched Drocco disappear down the hall with a big smile and thumb-to-index finger OK sign. "Inspector Drocco's sure in your corner, huh. He's obviously glad you weren't suspended. By the way, how much is a pedro?"

O'Shea slapped his forehead with his open palm. "You really did lead a sheltered life in Hayward. It's five dollars."

"Oh," remarked Ellis blankly.

"So, who's on your inquiry list?" O'Shea asked.

Ellis grabbed his list. "Every soup kitchen in San Francisco, including St. Anthony's and Glide, to spread the word to all homeless about the Embarcadero murder two weeks ago. Then I also sent requests to the Coast Guard and yacht clubs about anything unusual reported along Sea Cliff or Aquatic Park, and faxed the Strider Security Agency about any suspicious actions two weeks ago at St. Mary's Hospital, the Sea Cliff or the outer Richmond, where Likert was splattered. That security agency patrols all those places. I'm also hoping we can get a better profile on some of our victims, suspects and their acquaintances. So I've contacted Villa's janitorial union, his wife's physical fitness gym, PCP dealers, autocross associations, the Department of Corrections and the Castro S & M clubs."

O'Shea had been listening and absently watching the uniformed female police officer with the well contoured posterior. She was making coffee down the hall. "You're a piece of work, Paul. That covers just about everyone in the City. How about an inquiry through the newspapers to the entire population?"

Unperturbed by O'Shea's comments, Ellis thought for a moment. "Maybe an article on the eight crimes would be worthwhile."

O'Shea got up and headed for the coffee maker down the hall. Looking over his shoulder, he changed the subject. "When I get back, let's critique the four cases that still have some bad guys."

Ellis waved an acknowledgement.

Like a homing beacon, or werewolf tracking its prey, O'Shea followed the young, firm butt right up to the coffee machine. Furtively scanning her posterior, as well as the rest of her body, he wistfully thought to himself. *Wow, she even has a pretty face.* Holding his empty cup, O'Shea stood next to the female officer, while staring at the full coffee pot. "Coffee ready?" he asked.

"Oh, hi, Lieutenant. It's ready. Would you like me to pour you a cup?"

O'Shea grabbed the pot, filled his cup and slowly eased away from the pretty face, without looking at her. "No thanks." He was uncontrollably clumsy and shy around pretty women.

"You got a thing going with that lady cop?" Ellis asked when O'Shea returned.

"What lady cop?" O'Shea quickly changed the subject, again. "Where are we on the other four cases?"

Ellis was holding the Aquatic Park case open on his lap. "Well, I did initials on Dutil, our witness, and Robinson, our primary. I also interviewed the Porpoise manager and all the park rangers on duty that Wednesday, including the rangers who work the ship museum, the Balclutha and the ferry boat near Aquatic Park. I came up with a big fat zip!"

"Christ, I thought we just got through with agreeing that coming up with nothing is something."

Ellis dropped the file on his desk and glanced at O'Shea with one of his rare sighing hints of impatience. "I know that Loot; I haven't finished."

Staring momentarily at the bottom half of the female walking by, O'Shea threw up both hands with a broad, impish grin. "Sorry, I lost my head for a moment. Go on."

"You know what I think? You're horny and it's interfering with your concentration."

O'Shea sneered. "Go on, Aquatic Park?"

"Well, if you really want to know, Dutil will be a great witness to all the circumstantial stuff. He's clear, articulate and unwavering. He saw everything but the murder by Robinson."

"You're sure it's a murder?" O'Shea asked.

"Absolutely! According to the coroner, Sutherland was in good cardiac and respiratory health, with no seizures, strokes or any other internal causes for his drowning. As you know, bruises on his legs also indicate he was held under and the tissue found under his fingernails suggested he fought for his life." Ellis picked up the file again. "Then there's Robinson, a real uncooperative hot head. He's cooling his heels in jail."

"In jail?" O'Shea repeated.

"Yes, while interviewing him at Aquatic Park, he told me to, uh, go screw myself and pushed me away. Fortunately Big Red (a 6'4", two hundred and fifty pound uniformed cop) went with me. So Robinson didn't resist when I arrested him. I figured he might be a bit more cooperative in jail."

Carefully slurping his hot coffee, O'Shea grimaced as the steaming coffee nearly burned his puckered lips. "For zip, you sure got a lot done yesterday. Robinson's where he belongs."

Dropping the Aquatic Park file, Ellis picked up the one on the Post Street sniper.

"Is that the one on Winston?" O'Shea asked.

"Yeah, but you first, John. Didn't you interview his lover, Jason, last week?"

O'Shea blew on his coffee and tried another cautious swallow. "That fuckin' interview made my skin crawl. Goddamn coffee is still too hot." Slamming the cup on his desk, O'Shea continued as he wiped up the splashed coffee with a couple of Kleenex. "The bar is right on Castro, right in the heart of 'Fagville.' With a name like Full Load, I should have brought a woman cop with me."

"For protection?" Ellis asked.

"Well, yeah," O'Shea grunted. "I knew when I walked in, our worst drug bust would have been a cake walk compared to this. They should have called the place 'Grab-a-Joint.' When I opened the door and flashed my buzzer, the music was blaring hard rock and guys were dancing together all over the place. The ones who weren't kissing and hugging were stroking somebody's dick."

Ellis looked a little puzzled. "Why'd you flash your badge? Were you gonna bust the whole bar?"

O'Shea blanched, realizing the badge was unnecessary and better left unsaid. "I suppose it was my only protection, and don't ask me why I needed protection. Anyway, Jason was waiting for me. He's a wiry little shit with a ton of crap leaving his mouth every time he talks."

Ellis came close to grinning. "Maybe that's why he's such a little shit. Get it?"

O'Shea shook his head and sighed. "I just said that. Anyway, Jason was up front about his hot S & M sex with Bill Winston and practically everybody else in the bar. He gets off on bondage; torturing his partners without seriously injuring them. He says some like real pain, like broken bones or ice picks through the hands or feet, requiring emergency hospital treatment. Nothing modest about this guy, he let me know he's a real artist, kind of an S & M specialist, who could even fist fuck his partner without ripping his asshole apart. The arrogant little fart also had his own special 'up your ass' alibi. Some of his following verified their all-night orgy with Jason well into the Wednesday afternoon, the day that Winston got whacked."

"You think it's true?" asked Ellis.

O'Shea downed the rest of his cooler cup of coffee. "That's the worst part of it. Yeah, I do. Last night I also called my buddy, Jerry, the shrink. I forgot to ask him about his patient, Winston, while we were at the Java House. He said the two guys had a great symbiotic relationship. Jason got his rush and a few bucks hurting Winston, and Winston got his rocks off being hurt. There was really no reason to kill the guy. Jerry said it's also improbable that a sadist like Jason would hide out and shoot one of his fans, for whatever reason. As Jerry put it, if Jason was going to off someone, he'd more likely rip out the guy's throat with a screwdriver and let him bleed and scream to death. I hate like hell to say it, but I've gotta agree."

Ellis casually nodded. "Me too. There's no record for Jason owning a gun or being connected with any group that gets bullets from the National Guard."

Looking down at his empty cup, O'Shea lamented, "Well there goes one primary suspect I really wanted to bust—just because. Now we have an innocent bad guy and no leads. Dammit, we're back to the starting line."

Gritting his teeth a little, Ellis stared blankly at O'Shea for a moment before replying. "Not quite the starting line, Loot. Remember, we established a man's innocence. Now we don't have to use any more of our time on Jason. Besides, he serves a community need, for all those guys who want to be hurt."

"Up yours, Paul. Look over the next case that still has a primary. I'm gonna get some more coffee." Walking down the hall, O'Shea realized he was scanning the corridor, doorways and cubicles for a glimpse of the great posterior and the pretty face. Pouring another cup of coffee from the nearly empty pot, O'Shea looked around. There was no one in sight. *Oh well,* he thought, trudging back to his desk.

"I saw her leave about five minutes ago," volunteered Ellis.

"Who you talkin' about?"

"You know, Ida. The pretty cop with the neat butt."

Trying to sneer through his flushing face, O'Shea poised his cup over Ellis' head. "You wanna wear this? Just keep it up." As he put down his cup of coffee, O'Shea added with a feeble air of indifference, "So, Ida's her name?"

Ellis sat quietly, looking over the Nelson case.

"Well?" asked O'Shea.

"I thought you weren't interested."

"I'm not," O'Shea quickly lied. Realizing his defense was excessive, and ridiculously transparent, he added in a softer, more matter of fact, chatty tone, "I'm just curious. What's her name again?"

"Ida, she's twenty-five, been on the force for three years, works all over the department, filling in for 'no-shows,' she's straight, doesn't have a boyfriend and right now she's doing PR work at City Hall. Now, do you want to go over the Nelson case?"

A bit slack-jawed and nearly speechless, O'Shea rallied a faint smile. "Uh, sure. Thanks."

Ellis closed the Nelson file and slid it across his desk. "Dammit, John, this case is a rotten mess. Our uniformed cops, in all their anger and incompetence, really blew this one. Two winos are going to be arraigned next week on a murder one. They were staggering by the Nelson corpse when back-up cops arrived. Boy, our cops were thorough. They trampled the scene, beat the piss out of the winos and probably alerted the real killer to run for it."

O'Shea slammed his fist on his desk, again splashing coffee from his full cup. "Shit, shit. I should have known this would happen. Those Keystone cops felt humiliated. The cops were supposed to find the killer. They weren't supposed to be killed by one. That's our goddamn case and they've already closed it on those two poor winos. Those bastards, who's the asshole in charge?"

Ellis grabbed the file and found the arrest report. "Sergeant Sullivan. Another twenty-year redneck who knows nothing about investigations and cares less about following procedure."

"That's not all," added O'Shea. "He's tight with MacInerny, who won't side with us, even though it's our own case."

"That's no problem." Ellis beamed. "You knew those two winos, Scotty Harvey and his buddy, Ron Tuttle from your south of Market patrolman days. I checked them out carefully and you're right, they're a couple of harmless drunks who are always at the bottom of the wino pecking order. They were regularly mugged by the bully winos. Anyway, I talked to them in the City Jail. They were all bruised and I think Scotty had some broken ribs. Poor guys, they thought they were in for drunkenness.

"I also checked their medical records at General. They both have emphysema and cirrhosis, and I'll bet each one of their scrawny bodies weighs less than a hundred pounds. They're so weak they can barely pick up a half empty wine bottle, let alone a huge slab of concrete."

O'Shea shook his head pensively. "That won't stop Sullivan and his buddies from hanging those poor guys."

Ellis smiled. "Bender will. I told him the whole rotten story about the bungling uniform cops, the frail winos beaten and never Mirandized. I gave him the whole nine yards. I also told him we were partners and good pals. Bender said he'd make sure those winos never got to court. I found out this morning they're dropping the case and releasing them to General Hospital. I called Bender last night. Is that all right?"

It was O'Shea's time to beam. "You are a pal. Next time we get together, you gotta meet Bender and my other buddies. What the hell, one more case without a primary suspect."

They both laughed.

◫ ◫ ◫

Wiping up the fresh coffee stains on his desk, O'Shea stopped laughing. "Just how many primary suspects do we have left?"

Ellis had also stopped laughing. "I think it's two out of the eight. At least they're both solid. All we need from Robinson is a confession. Of course, it wouldn't hurt if we got some physical evidence like those tissue samples with his DNA."

O'Shea furtively scanned the empty hallway.

Ellis grinned. "I told you, she's at City Hall."

O'Shea shot Ellis an angry glance that quickly morphed into a grin. "You don't miss a thing do ya? Anyway, we've got enough circumstantial evidence for formal murder charges now. We've also got his ass in jail, where we can bust his balls. We'll alternate. I'll be the hardass and you the more sympathetic."

"Yeah, but I should be the bad cop," quipped Ellis. "I jailed him, remember?"

"I know," said O'Shea, "but I make a much better prick."

"You said it, Loot."

O'Shea acknowledged that last comment with a broad smile, a third finger and another changed subject. "Where the hell's Ralph been hiding out? You know Emil Anderson was a good friend of Bender's."

Ellis grabbed the Anderson file from the bottom of the stack. "There's been an APB on him since Emil died in Bender's waiting room. This guy's a real putz. He had no friends, treated his family like lackeys and had no job. He's one of those bad seeds. You know, born rotten and evil. A thief, a bully, a junkie and child molester; then to top it off, he murders his own father. I'm sure he's somewhere in San Francisco. We're bound to find him; we've got his picture posted everywhere. And when we find him, we'll both play bad cop."

O'Shea nodded, "I know just how you feel, Paul. But this one's gotta be exactly by the book. We can't blow this one and give this asshole any legal loopholes. Bender would flip out. At least, this is one we can close when we find him, as long as we keep cool. What the hell is a putz?"

📖 📖 📖

On the Tuesday before Anderson's murder, Ralph's attempted sex with nine-year old Cindy ended in a panic run when some passing adults began shouting at him. A half-hour later, Ralph was nervously wandering Market Street; afraid every cop already knew what he had done. In desperation he hid in one of the cheap Market Street theaters where he watched the same two movies twice. It was evening when Ralph finally left the theater. Shrouded by the night he felt safer, as if invisible. He was even beginning to believe he hadn't done anything wrong. Besides, he thought, no one would recognize him; and Cindy knew better than to say anything. Just to make sure, he decided to head home to find out from his dad if anyone had reported him. He knew he could handle Emil, maybe get some money and leave town until all was forgotten.

As Ralph approached his house, he was stunned by what he saw. Holding Cindy's hand, her mother, Lorene, was standing at the open front door talking to Emil. Ralph couldn't hear the exchange, but when Lorene and daughter entered the house, he knew he was busted.

Again, in panic, Ralph needed an escape, while knowing he had nowhere to go. He had no friends, no hideout and about $19. He couldn't even go home for his clothing or a few of his dad's valuables. It didn't take Ralph long to come up with his habitual solution to any problem. The great escape into drugs. By midnight he was walking the Tenderloin area looking for a heroin fix.

"Whatcha lookin' for, man?"

Ralph didn't know the two blacks, but he knew they were ready to sell him just about anything. "Got smack?"

The blacks moved in closer, looking over their shoulders. The tallest one, with a fixed frown and ring through the right side of his nose, lightly brushed Ralph's shoulder as if swatting a fly. "What kind of bread you got?"

Ralph was having the usual hot and cold flashes, aching bones and muscles, tremors and nausea that come with stress and a day and a half lag since his last fix. His discomfort was approaching the intolerable stage when caution and common sense no longer matter. He needed more than just a taste of smack. Ralph pulled his small wad of $19 out of his pocket just far enough to expose part of the top $10 bill, concealing the denomination of his remaining $5 and four $1 bills. "I've got five more of these," he casually whispered, trying to hide his increasing shakes. His brainless plan was to get $60 worth of heroin, look surprised when he pulled out $19, apologize for his mistake and promise to pay them the rest tomorrow. Ralph knew better. Yet, like most desperate junkies, he wasn't in the mood to think.

These two street hustlers were always thinking, scheming and suspicious, especially of a shaking low-life they didn't know. Glaring at Ralph, they had seen those body signs before. A guy trying to act cool, who painfully needed a heavy hit of smack with only enough bread for a light fix. One more quick glance over their shoulders and the two blacks went into action as if following a well-choreographed script. With lightening speed the tall guy pulled the cash from Ralph's pocket, while his short husky partner drew a six-inch switchblade from his jacket. As the knife opened with a snap, the blade silently tore through Ralph's clothing, piercing his flesh a few inches beneath his sternum. Effortlessly the blade slid into Ralph's body up to the handle, then a clockwise twist and the blade was withdrawn. The short guy adeptly sidestepped the trail of spurting, gurgling blood. This all happened in an instant. The rest was in slow motion.

Ralph was alone, sinking down the side of a lamppost until he sat on the pavement, gripping his saturated clothing and staring in disbelief at the bloody geyser slowly weakening to a trickle.

Discovered about an hour later by a passing patrol car, Ralph had quietly bled to death. He spent the next two weeks in the morgue as a John Doe.

φ   φ   φ

Born on a full-mooned April 8th in Hamburg, Germany, Elvin Streichner, Jr. had all the advantages of rich, brilliant parents along with all those stifling disadvantages of bigotry and arrogance.

Elvin Streichner, Sr., his father, was born on an April 15th. He was canonized as one of the great post-war German athletes in pole-vaulting. He was head of the prestigious Chemistry Department at the University of Leipzig, and a Nobel Laureate in Biochemistry. He was also a proud Aryan, who mourned the death of Hitler and the destruction of the Third Reich. He believed in the invincibility of the Aryan race and the parasitic inferiority of non-Aryans, including blacks, Jews and hybrids. Of course, he deeply resented Americans as mongrel low-life cowards who beat the Third Reich dishonorably.

Streichner's mother, born on an April 30th, equaled her husband in brilliance, social prominence and the intensity of beliefs. Her gifts, however, were cosmic, spiritual and penetratingly magical. She was well known as a *sensitive* with verifiably inexplicable telepathic and clairvoyant abilities. In contrast to her husband's social bigotry, Elizabeth was a soft-spoken, intense humanitarian, who used her astrological acumen and psychic powers to help others.

At age three, young Streichner was delighting both parents with his intellectual and physical excellence. He learned to read by following the words as either parent read to him. By age five, astrology, parapsychology, arithmetic and politics were his favorite subjects, and gymnastics his favorite leisure activity. To his father, Streichner, Jr. was achieving Aryan perfection. His mother, however, already recognized that he possessed the sensitivity, insights and concentration of a mystic.

CHAPTER 7

In the early afternoon, Ellis was the first to take the short walk to the City Jail where Robinson, one of their remaining two primary suspects, was confined. Most law enforcement officials, including the sheriff's deputies who work as jailers, could barely tolerate the City Jail. Ellis was no exception. He had first hand experience that it was a place where severe headaches and duodenal ulcers are made. Every time he approached the jail he thought of bad breath, foul body odors mixed with smells of disinfectants, beans and other unappetizing foods.

The City Jail is noisier than any construction site and more abrasive. Everything is concrete or metal, with no sound-absorbing materials. Steel doors are never closed, they're slammed with an ear splitting, vibrating, crashing sound that rattles every cell. *People don't talk in the City Jail,* he thought, *they all shout.* Once inside, it's a sneak preview of Dante's Inferno—a cacophony of shouting, belching, screaming, banging, slamming and gaseous bowel noises that persist twenty-four hours a day. "Oh well," he muttered to himself, "sure glad I don't live here."

Locating one's interviewee in the City Jail was another irritant. As usual, Robinson was lost and it took about fifteen minutes of sitting alone in one of the small stuffy interview rooms, before a fat, sour-faced deputy gave Ellis the good news. "We found Robinson. He'll be here in a few minutes."

Ellis offered a strained smile. "Thanks."

Over ten minutes later, a sullen-looking, messy-haired Robinson, clothed in beige coveralls, entered the waiting room. When Robinson stood silently, glaring at him without saying a word, Ellis felt a bit intimidated. He also doubted even a semblance of cooperation and decided to just assume a role of cool civility and professionalism. "Please sit down, Mr. Robinson. I need to ask you a few questions."

After looking around the small room, Robinson yanked the farther of two chairs from under the table, shoved it to the back wall, turned it sideways from the table and slouched on the chair with arms folded and feet outstretched. Still silent, Robinson stared at the wall with tight, quivering jaws as if daring Ellis to talk.

Ellis glared back, as he resorted to his rare use of a few swear words. "You think you're some kind of bad ass? In here, I'm the bad ass because I can keep you in this stinking jail for a long time. You assaulted a police officer, and you're the primary suspect in the killing of Harry Sutherland." Mellowing a bit, Ellis added, "We don't know the whole story, but we do have enough circumstantial evidence to book you on murder one. For all we know, maybe you two fought in the water and he drowned. So, for now, just give us your side of the story. Of course, we'll drop the assaulting an officer charge."

Robinson spun around in his chair, slammed both hands on the table and slowly got up. Leaning across the table, he glared back at Ellis. "You're right. You're the bad ass, not me. I haven't done anything. I gave you a little shove and you call it assault. Fuck you."

Before Ellis could reply, Robinson opened the interview room door and quickly walked out in the corridor to a nearby deputy. Ellis said softly, "End of interview." As he got up to leave, Ellis watched Robinson being led back to his cell by the deputy. *I'm not really a bad ass,* he thought.

📖   📖   📖

When Ellis returned to their cubicle in the Homicide Division of the San Francisco Police Department, O'Shea was beet red, standing by his desk gripping his phone. "My God, he's gonna explode," Ellis gasped, as he eased closer to his partner.

"...Oh shit! Has he been positively identified? You'll fax us a report right now? Thanks." O'Shea slammed down the phone, took a deep breath and looked up at Ellis. "Ralph didn't kill his dad. He's got a bulletproof alibi. He was dead."

Ellis shook his head. "Sit down, John, before you blow a fuse. Take a few real deep breaths and tell me what happened. Where in the world has he been hiding dead for the last few weeks?"

"In the goddamn morgue," growled O'Shea. "Here we have an APB out on this loser, with his face on bulletins all over the place, including the morgue. Some cops pick him up in the Tenderloin, dead from stab wounds the night before Emil Anderson died. He was a John Doe on a slab until it dawned on a coroner's assistant to check bulletins for missing persons. He was positively I.D.'d this morning by Emil's brother." O'Shea had calmed down sufficiently to take another deep breath and give his partner a grin of resignation. "Go on, say it. Say what you know I'm thinking."

Clasping his hands in front of his mouth, Ellis closed his eyes for a moment. "Well we had to go with the obvious first. We've done that, now we just have to move on."

"What about our last obvious, Robinson?" O'Shea asked with a hint of sarcasm.

"He ain't talkin' to me except to insist he's innocent."

O'Shea leaped to his feet as if to enter the ring. "It's my turn, Paul. I'll get that son of a bitch to confess one way or another."

As O'Shea hurriedly walked down the hall, Ellis knew better than to caution his boss. "Go get um, Loot."

📖   📖   📖

O'Shea was so preoccupied with confronting Robinson, he was, for once, oblivious to the disagreeable odors and harsh sounds associated with life in the City Jail. Although used to the long wait while deputies searched for inmates, today O'Shea was unusually impatient. After twenty minutes alone in the interview room, he tapped on the window to get the attention of a passing deputy, "I've been waiting a half hour for Jim Robinson. Has he escaped?"

Not at all amused, the weary, disheveled deputy concealed his own annoyance. "I'll see what's keeping him. Maybe he's on a detail."

Five minutes later, a still aggravated and wild-eyed Robinson was standing in the doorway, glaring down at O'Shea. This was the first time they had met during the investigation, and O'Shea simply stared back with a strange curiosity. "Did you by any chance go to Sacred Heart?"

Startled by O'Shea's initial question, Robinson unwittingly relaxed his jaw a bit and sat down near O'Shea. Trying to maintain his defensive posture, Robinson delayed his reply for a few seconds. "Yeah. So?"

O'Shea hadn't planned a disarming strategy. He was simply beginning to remember this older man, and his interest was genuine. "As I recall, you were a great All-City lineman at Sacred Heart back in the 20's. You were also one hell of a tough middle linebacker at Cal. Didn't you make the All-American team?"

Now Robinson was becoming curious. "Honorable mention. How do you know all of this? You weren't around then."

O'Shea grinned. "My dad was. He was second-string quarterback when you were a senior at Sacred Heart. His buddies always called him Jackie."

Robinson stared pensively at O'Shea for a few seconds. "Jesus, you look kinda like him. Yeah, Jackie was a good guy. He made All-City in his senior year. How's he doin'?"

O'Shea offered a soft, reflective smile. "He died of cirrhosis a few years back."

By now Robinson was nodding slowly and listening carefully. "Was he a heavy drinker?"

"He never went to college. He could have become a great athlete. He worked in the City most of his life as a bartender and part-time drunk." Neither smiled, and after a brief silence, O'Shea added, "When I went to Sacred Heart, I saw your picture in an old trophy case down in one of the old storerooms. You were honored as one of the school's best athletes. Did you know about the trophy case?"

"Yeah, I knew, but you're the first guy to ever tell me about it. Ain't that a bitch? In here of all places."

O'Shea laid down the notebook he'd been holding since he entered the interview room. "I also know you were line coach at Sacred Heart for two years. You probably don't remember me. I was a freshman during your last year. Practically the whole team thought you should be head coach. They said you knew football better than Coach Kumorik and you could teach the game. You used to get in there and mix it up with us. All the players knew you were a good athlete and you inspired us. Why'd ya leave, Coach?"

Robinson gave a wry smile. "Guess I was like your dad; a binge drinker. I never drank on the job and you know, I don't think any of the kids ever saw me drunk. I'd just fall off the wagon and go on a run for about a week."

Sounds like me, O'Shea thought.

Robinson continued, "The school put up with my disappearances about every other month, then I got a DUI. Somebody in court reported me to school officials. They put me on probation. A couple of months later, some parent apparently spotted me shitfaced, staggering out of a Mission Street bar." Robinson peered up at the ceiling shaking his head. "When I started drinking, I used to always hang out in the Mission. I never thought I'd be spotted there. Anyway, I was, and whoever saw me reported me to the school board. Guess I could have denied or fought the charges, but what the hell. I admitted it, and I was allowed to resign."

Nearly a half hour had elapsed since Robinson entered the interview room. O'Shea realized neither had even mentioned Harry Sutherland's death. It was more of a chat between two geezers than a formal police interrogation. *Robinson reminds me of one of my old loyal pals, especially Boyd*, he thought. O'Shea was beginning to like the guy. Yet he also knew the interrogation was inevitable. *After all*, conceded O'Shea to himself, *Robinson's the primary suspect and I'm the detective in charge of this investigation.* "What really happened the day Sutherland drowned?"

Robinson looked directly into O'Shea's eyes. "You're either a smooth operator or a genuine guy."

"I've never been known to be smooth or clever. I came in here to rip you up, and now I'm just hoping you'll keep talking to me and be honest."

Robinson maintained his sober expression and unflinching stare into O'Shea's eyes. "I'll tell you all I remember and it'll be the truth. Harry and I were best friends. I admired him. He was tall, muscular and tough when he played tackle at Poly. When we played them, we lost the game because of him. We had some good backs at Sacred Heart, and Harry stopped them at the line of scrimmage. He was all over the place, especially in our backfield. Later, when I was at Cal, we played St. Mary's College. In that game, Harry threw a block that picked me up and drove me backwards a good five feet. We beat St. Mary's that day, but Harry beat me and I told him so.

"At any rate, we became close friends, until I heard that he told somebody I drank too much. In retrospect, that wasn't much of a reason to end a friendship. Maybe I'd always wanted to see who was really the toughest in a fight. Harry never let me find out. He always backed down. I guess it became a routine with me. I liked to provoke him and watch him back off.

"The day he died was really no different. He backed down as usual. I felt I won, even though I knew he wasn't afraid of me. He just didn't want to fight me. Once he backed down that day, I ignored him and went for a short swim. I had an appointment with my urologist for a prostate check at 11:30 a.m."

O'Shea was concerned about his own prostate because of his constant need to urinate. "I'm due for an exam myself. I'm sorry." O'Shea added. "Go on."

Robinson grinned. "Well, there's not much more. I took a few quick laps, went back to the locker room and took a hot shower. I got to Dr. Reimer's office about 11:15. That's all, Detective. I really ignored Harry. In fact, I don't actually remember seeing him in the water. There was no confrontation, and I didn't sneak up and drown him. Yeah, I used to be a hot-head fighter, but I've never been a killer."

O'Shea reviewed a few notes he'd taken. "One thing's certain, you were in the water when Harry was swimming. Did you notice anything unusual, anything at all?"

Robinson thought for a moment. "No, well, I don't know, maybe one thing. I did notice two black wetsuits. I could see their snorkels, tanks and regulators. They were probably fifty feet from me. I don't think I'd ever noticed divers before inside the Aquatic Park anchorage and swimming area."

"Anything else?"

Robinson paused, shaking his head. "No, nothing—that's it."

O'Shea slowly stood up, extending his hand. "That's all for now. Thanks for talking with me."

Robinson got up and responded with a firm handshake.

As O'Shea opened the door, he again turned toward Robinson. "By the way, do you have any questions?"

"The black detective I pushed, is he going to press charges?"

O'Shea smiled. "I doubt it."

📖 📖 📖

Leaving the tumultuous City Jail, O'Shea pondered his bungled marriage, his selfish kids and his three main objectives in life. More than ever he wanted to be Chief of Police. This meant courting Arnold Hall, whom he didn't particularly like. He'd also feel more confident in his professional abilities if he started solving some of the eight cases. Then it would be nice if he could date Ida. O'Shea reconsidered. *At this point, I'd be happy with one out of three.*

When he returned to homicide, Ellis was on the phone and Ida was nowhere in sight. *Still at City Hall,* he thought. O'Shea sat down at his desk, quietly staring at the pile of files. For the first time in years he was professionally frustrated. He couldn't help feeling that the cases were mocking him, laughing at his puny investigative efforts. Yet, he was ironically pleased with today's interview.

Robinson reminded him of his friends, even himself; which he realized might tend to undermine his objectivity. O'Shea really wanted to close one of the eight, and Robinson was the best possibility. In fact, he was the only remaining primary suspect. Just above a whisper, O'Shea began thinking aloud. "Hell, he drowned Sutherland, probably by accident. How could he, when I believe his story, well most of it. Yet, how could he have ignored Sutherland after such a violent argument? And those divers, they seem like a fictitious alternative suspect. Ah, shit."

Ellis hung up the phone and walked to O'Shea's desk. "Were you talking to me or yourself?"

O'Shea looked up, "Maybe both."

As usual, Ellis was unaware of even the possibility of sarcasm. "Can you tell me again, I didn't hear what you were saying? But first, did you break Robinson?"

O'Shea rolled his eyes toward the ceiling, shook his head and sighed. "In the first place, I was talking to myself. It was a private conversation and don't ask me why I said both. As for Robinson, no I didn't break him; he damn near broke me. This will blow you out if anything can. Robinson calmly talked to me for about a half hour and I kinda believed his story."

"Wow, what do you mean by kinda?"

O'Shea smiled. "Well, at least, I got a wow out of you. The guy's a hothead like I was."

Ellis softly interrupted. "You still are, aren't you?"

"Not like I used to be," O'Shea replied. "Anyway, he seemed like a regular guy—a straight forward, hip-shooter. Nothing sneaky about him."

"In other words, you're telling me you liked the guy."

O'Shea caught himself about to frown, then he grinned. "Yeah, kinda like you, only with a sense of humor. Now can I continue?"

"Sure, Loot."

"I guess it's sort of a Dick Boyd kind of a thing. I really doubt this guy would sneak up and murder someone. He's more likely to kick shit out of somebody and accidentally kill him. According to him, Sutherland was his hero, until some trivial show of disloyalty. Apparently Robinson had considered Sutherland the toughest football player he ever knew. Sutherland was top gun and Robinson admitted he might have secretly needed to find out who was the toughest. But Sutherland always backed down; which may have made Robinson feel like the top gun. In any event, I'm not convinced he's innocent. I just think if he killed Sutherland, it was a fight, combat and an accident. I don't buy his claim that he ignored Harry in the water. He also mentioned seeing a couple of SCUBA divers. I don't go for that either."

Ellis had grabbed the Sutherland case and scribbled a few notes on the inside cover. "Sounds like we have a manslaughter."

"So you tend to agree?" asked O'Shea.

"Well, I can't disagree, as long as he's still a suspect."

O'Shea sensed that was as much as his partner was willing to concede. "Was the phone call anything worthwhile?"

Ellis shrugged his shoulders. "We may have a more viable suspect in the Villa case."

"You don't sound too enthusiastic."

"It was from Officer Logan. He said he got a hot tip on the perp who did the brake job on Villa's pickup. Through an informant, they learned that Leona was doing some local dealing and owed the suppliers a lot of bucks. The debt pissed them off and the alleged dealers hired a Juan Rodriguez to cut the lines. Logan said that since it's our case, we could do the bust. He gave us an address and said the guy's headed for Miami in a few days, but would be home tomorrow night after 6 p.m."

O'Shea shook his head. "Christ, it's too goddamn convenient, and who the hell are these 'theys' and 'thems'? Doesn't Logan work for Mahoney?"

Ellis nodded. "They're also pretty tight. They still hoist a few together at Tommy's Joynt and do the barbecue weekend thing with their wives."

O'Shea got up and paced around the cubicle. "I think it's all bullshit. A set-up engineered by that asshole Mahoney, and we've got to check it out tomorrow night."

Ellis looked surprised. "Why? I agree it's most likely a set-up."

"It's a no-brainer. If we don't go, we can't prove Rodriguez isn't the real perp. We have a professional obligation to check out every lead, especially from other cops. Besides, I can't break any more of Mahoney's bones unless I'm certain it's all a lie."

Ellis nodded. "I'm with ya all the way."

CHAPTER 8

A few days before Officer Logan called O'Shea's office, Sergeant Lloyd Mahoney hunched over his desk, fuming with a smoldering hatred about to burst into a deadly plan. Each time his bloodied tongue probed the sharp wires holding his broken jaw in place, he knew he had to somehow destroy O'Shea.

Mahoney personified just about everything most people fear or despise in others. He was a viciously greedy, vindictive bully with a thoroughly entrenched sadistic streak. He worshiped the unrestricted authority and power of a job that legitimized the worst in him. Early in his career his badge and gun effortlessly transformed him into a fearless giant, more dangerous than most hardened criminals. As a police officer he easily became a self-appointed predator knowing that his criminal prey was in no position to report him.

The narcotic unit was the perfect assignment for him. Plenty of junkie informants who would turn in their entire family for another fix, relaxed police procedural rules in dealing with the illegal drug world and an endless flow of confiscated drug money. Besides the cash he seized during drug busts, Mahoney enjoyed pistol-whipping drug pushers and dealers, while stashing some of the drug contraband, which he could later sell.

Mahoney's appearance matched his behavior. He was an ugly combination of slovenly over-indulgence with odiferous, hoggish qualities.

Actually, Mahoney was only 5'7" with an enormous belly spilling over his belt like a bag of sloppy swill that sloshed when he walked. Both belt and fly were well hidden beneath a gelatinous bulge of flesh that relentlessly strained his shirt buttons. He reeked with the stench of sweat, cigar smoke and old garbage odors that could have been eliminated with a little soap and water. His squinty eyes embedded in his fleshy face concealed the slightest hint of openness. His huge jowls dangled on his dirty collar, and his brown stained teeth announced his bad breath. Mahoney was disgusting to look at. He was a pig and even looked like one, with up-turned nose flaunting two big nostrils, greasy grayish-black hair and a day's growth of prickly beard that roamed the lumpy contours of his triple chin.

Mahoney had no neck, no conscience and no loyalties. He was a lousy cop and even a worse street fighter. He was just a slob with the authority and back up to bully and brutalize others with impunity. How and why he had remained on the force so long was a mystery to anyone who knew him. Some figured he must have been an Internal Affairs snitch. Still other police officers simply tolerated him as an obnoxious irritant that wasn't going to go away.

Of course, being sergeant of a narcotic detail was further assurance he wouldn't go away. Mahoney could easily intimidate the police officers who worked under him. They liked the added income as well as the other perks that came with their less regulated undercover work. As career cops, they also needed to protect their jobs by pleasing and protecting their sergeant. Even so, most of them quietly questioned many of Mahoney's tactics. Officer Logan didn't. He was young, strong as an ox, ambitious and not too bright. He had all the ingredients of a potential bully, who actually liked his boss, in addition to those perks working in a narcotic unit.

When Mahoney wound up with another broken jaw, Logan had quickly offered to "beat the shit out of O'Shea." Mahoney realized, however, that O'Shea was tough and Logan might end up being forced to kill him. *That won't do*, he thought. He didn't want to lose Logan. He was a good man who would always watch his back.

As Mahoney sat brooding, Officer Logan stopped by his desk with some information that unexpectedly triggered the planned revenge against O'Shea. "Hey, Sarg, on the street the word's out that our snake, Rodriguez got a bunch of automatic weapons. He's selling them to a couple of bad ass Chicano gang members."

"When?" Mahoney mumbled through his wired teeth.

"The deal's going down next Tuesday at 6 p.m., his place. Should I call the SWAT Team and Robbery? It ain't drugs this time, and whoever does the bust will need lots of back-up."

After a heavy breathing pause, Mahoney scanned the area for privacy. Then he looked up at Logan with one of his fiendish sneers. "I got a better idea. This is between us. It's time to fuck up O'Shea. Tell him Rodriguez cut the brake lines on Villa's truck. Give O'Shea his address and put him there at 6:15 p.m. He'll follow it up, I know the son of a bitch. Him and his nigger-ass partner'll go it alone. No back up. If the cholos are still there, they'll waste the pricks."

Massaging his aching jaw, Mahoney winced, then turned back to Officer Logan with a guttural snarl. "You get word to Rodriguez that two plain clothes cops'll pound on his door Tuesday at about 6:30. Tell him they're tryin' to set him up for a bogus fall, let him know the cops are snakes and he's got the right to defend himself. Got the idea? O'Shea and Ellis are dead either way. They'll either interrupt the cholos or Rodriguez'll be waiting for them after the deal."

Logan sneered back with a nod. "Sounds good to me boss. I'll take care of our pal, Rodriguez.

Juan Rodriguez was a junkie, amateur hit man for $50 a pop, snitch and cop hater. But he owed Logan, who, for more than a year had supplied Rodriguez with drugs for strong-arm work and street information. Rodriguez did a lot of the cops' dirty work; and despite his hatred for cops, Rodriguez' loyalty to Logan was real. When Logan was a beat cop, he had witnessed Rodriguez killing a dealer, and at Mahoney's request, Logan never reported the murder. That marked the onset of their unholy relationship. Mahoney took advantage of it, knowing he had more than a reliable informant. He had his own personal assassin.

After calling Sergeant Ellis with the false information, Logan checked with a few of his Mission Street snitches to make sure the 6:00 p.m. gun deal was still on. It was. He then contacted Rodriguez personally.

The set-up was in place and Mahoney was thrilled. He didn't even care if Rodriguez got killed. He just wanted O'Shea dead, or at least seriously injured. As much as he hated to admit it, Mahoney knew O'Shea was a fierce adversary and wary cop. He'd be hard to bring down. He also knew that the two Chicano gang members were added insurance in case Rodriguez failed. They were mean, psychopathic killers who wouldn't hesitate to kill a cop in their way. Besides, he thought, even if O'Shea lives through it, we'll deny the tip and he'll be remanded for a reckless bust without proper back up.

📖 📖 📖

At 4:00 p.m. Tuesday, Lieutenant O'Shea and Sergeant Ellis were on their way to Capp Street in the Mission District, in an unmarked car. Both were armed with 9 mm automatic handguns, back-up 12 gauge sawed off shotguns and an arrest/search warrant provided by O'Shea's political friend, Judge McMahon. O'Shea had also taken advantage of a few contacts from the old narcotics days. These were contingencies Mahoney overlooked, while seriously underestimating O'Shea's street savvy and cautious intuition. An hour before their departure, O'Shea learned from an old snitch about the 6:00 p.m. gun sale with Rodriguez and two gang members. Needing Rodriguez alive, O'Shea and Ellis decided to avoid SWAT team support or any other help that would inevitably result in another Keystone Cop, blazing guns. O'Shea had, however, alerted his friend, Johnny Drocco, who agreed to await a call.

Regardless of the outcome, O'Shea and Ellis knew this one had to be perfect. Every "t" crossed, every "i" dotted. If Rodriguez were the prime suspect in the Carlos Villa case, the legality of his arrest was vital. More likely, if it were a set-up against O'Shea, police procedure still had to be meticulously followed to legitimize re-breaking Mahoney's jaw.

Parking across the street from Rodriguez's Capp Street first floor flat, O'Shea and Ellis sat quietly. After rechecking their weapons, they soberly focused all of their attention on the house, the sidewalk, the street and all movements. Like two world-class athletes, they were experiencing the intensity of absolute concentration—a mental and sensory state that rejects even the slightest distraction, which might, just for a second, misdirect them from their objectives. It was 4:15 p.m.

In the San Francisco Police Department, O'Shea and Ellis' surveillance skills were unrivaled. Wunden had once told them it had something to do with their visual, spatial perception, memory, concentration and plenty of hard work. They agreed with the concentration and hard work part.

Arriving early gave them at least an hour and a half to clearly learn all the baseline activities, background constants and details on Capp Street. This would facilitate quickly knowing changes in the background that weren't expected or didn't fit the activities. They observed the rows of similar old Victorian type houses bordering each side of the Rodriguez address. Each had a wrought iron fence, with a closed gate in front of the house. Within the gated wrought iron fence, there were five steps leading to the front porches and doors for the lower and upper flats. There were also walkways on the left side of each house, leading to their back yards.

A man and woman in their thirties were chatting near the second house, east of the Rodriguez address. They were smiling and hugging each other. Four Hispanic teenage males were laughing and joking, as if oblivious to anything else on the street. They were sharing a smoke and the distinctive aroma was no doubt marijuana. These teenagers were standing next to the green house, which was the house west of Rodriguez's address. Three kids under the age of ten, two boys and one girl, were riding their bikes back and forth down the sidewalk off the east curb cut on the street and back on the sidewalk over the west curb cut. O'Shea and Ellis, on the south side of the street, had a direct, right angle view of Rodriguez's house. The unmarked car was parked across the street in the last parking space before the white passenger zone in front of a huge convalescent home.

Three wizened old ladies were seated on a bench beneath the long porch that led to the convalescent home main entrance. Nearby there was an assortment of decrepit men and women with canes, walkers and wheelchairs. They were trudging up and down the gradually sloping disabled ramp that joined the porch. A four-step stairway, about twenty feet east of the bench, also led directly to the entrance. This accommodated the more spry staff and visitors. *What a mess if there's a gun battle*, O'Shea thought.

Almost simultaneously, Ellis gave O'Shea a quick, glancing comment, while still carefully scanning the neighborhood. "You know, we've gotta pull this off without shooting up the neighborhood."

O'Shea was watching a young woman carrying a sleeping baby as she pulled a basket of laundry past the Rodriguez house. "Yeah, I know."

Squinting carefully at the upper windows, Ellis shrugged. "At least the upstairs flat seems vacant." It was 4:45 p.m.

📖 📖 📖

Rodriguez was a nervous wreck. He slept fitfully, aroused easily by the slightest noise. He was a small-time pusher, mainly to support his own drug habit. He would do anything illegal for money and he especially enjoyed assaults or killings. He wasn't at all worried about Logan's warning. He'd kill both cops before they opened their mouths. This gun sale, however, was big time, a professional deal. If all went well, he'd no longer be considered an amateur, and he'd have some big money, at least $500. If he blew this one, he'd no doubt lose his life.

The gun dealers were real pros who wouldn't tolerate mistakes. No second chances. The gang buyers were even meaner losers. They would torture Rodriguez before killing him. The ten AK47's with thirty round clips were in five reinforced Safeway shopping bags— $15,000 worth. The initial exchange had been made a week earlier in a nearby busy Safeway parking lot, where bags and shopping carts were not suspicious items. Since then, Rodriguez had hovered over the guns that were hidden underneath his bed. Afraid to leave his flat, he sat for hours watching the front door, armed with his .357 Magnum revolver.

That morning the ringing phone had practically startled him through the ceiling. He knew the voice, crisp and unwavering. Only two icy words, "Five o'clock."

Rodriguez's reply was equally brief, but far less self-assured. "OK." He trembled.

This pre-arranged call abruptly reminded him the deal was on an hour earlier than scheduled. In a way, Rodriguez was relieved. He had been uneasy about the original time. He had boastfully told a trusted buddy about the 6:00 p.m. deal. Shortly after, he realized he didn't have any trusted buddies.

Nervously pacing the front room, Rodriguez walked to the window where he carefully moved the curtain about an inch from the window frame, just enough to view Capp Street. *Nothing unusual*, he thought. Returning to the sofa, he grabbed his .357 Magnum, opened the cylinder and re-checked the bullets for the umpteenth time. As he sat facing the front door and window, he stroked the loaded gun resting on his lap. His eyes and ears strained for the slightest unusual shadow or sound. Rodriguez was ready.

📖 📖 📖

Despite their decades of police experience, the usual anxiety was reminding them that anything can go wrong, and sometimes does.

Beneath Ellis' silent, unflinching concentration were those annoying stomach butterflies, urge to urinate and that telltale dry mouth. Those were the familiar feelings he used to tolerate while awaiting the first round of each of his collegiate boxing matches.

Sweaty palms, waves of nausea and an almost unbearably itchy scalp belied the coolness and calm of O'Shea's steady eyed vigilance. These were the same symptoms O'Shea used to experience prior to each kick-off during his college football days.

Ellis was the first to notice the Ford van that had just parked five houses east of the Rodriguez address. The van had circled Capp Street twice—*a bit unusual,* he thought. The three guys emerging from the van were also a bit unusual. The shortest of the three wore a huge black coat down to his black boots and a black velvet hat that seemed to rest on the tall, turned-up collar. His hands were buried in the big coat pockets and, with his face obscured by hat and collar, he looked like a strange silhouette of some cartoon villain. In contrast, the other two were a foot taller with Frisco jeans, loafers, arrogant jutting jaws, earrings, furrowed angry brows and narrow, dark bluish sunglasses with gold rims. The one with the black pea coat wore a Dodger baseball cap, with visor backwards. The other had a "Sharks" jacket and red headband above his shoulder length ponytail.

Equally suspicious was the man seated behind the steering wheel. Another pea coat, collar up and a dark watch cap pulled over his ears. He was looking around with no sign of leaving the van. Ellis gently nudged O'Shea's shoulder without taking his eyes off the three men.

"Yeah, I know," acknowledged O'Shea in a whisper. "The black van, the driver and the three silent, shifty-eyed studs don't fit this part of Capp Street."

"Those buttoned up coats don't fit either. It's too warm out. I bet they're packing something," said Ellis.

O'Shea flicked a glance at his watch. "Dammit, if it's them, they're an hour early with double the guys."

Both detectives silently watched in disgust as the three cocky gang "cholos," with heads bobbing and twisting, strutted down Capp Street until they reached Rodriguez's front gate. The shortest guy, with the biggest coat, stopped a few feet before the gate, lit up a cigarette and leaned against the fence. He was obviously the lookout. The other two closed the gate behind them, walked up the five steps and stood at the front door for only a second, before the door slowly slid open about two inches. Seconds later the door opened just wide enough for the two men to enter.

As the front door quickly closed, O'Shea grimaced a deep sigh. "Shit, shit, shit, this could be another 'OK Corral'."

Ellis was intently watching the guy in the van nodding to the lookout. "Yeah," he replied. "I saw an old version of that movie last week."

After darting a quick glance at Ellis, O'Shea paused for a few moments before speaking. "No way can we shoot it out with these guys, and we sure as hell can't let them have a bunch of automatic weapons."

Mentally weighing the possibilities, O'Shea paused again. "OK, here's the plan. You stroll by the van, get its license number, walk around the block to the nearest phone and call Inspector Drocco on his cell phone. We don't want the whole force on this. Give him the address and all the details, then tell him to ready the SWAT team; and when these guys leave, tell Drocco to have them tailed until they're hopefully in a more remote place to make the bust. When you get back, I'll use our police phone to give Drocco the final go."

📖 📖 📖

The squeaking front gate sent Rodriguez a shock wave of apprehension. Then heavy footsteps up the front stairs. It was almost 5:00 p.m. and there was no turning back. *This is it*, he thought. Leaping up, he cracked open the door just slightly.

"Hey blood, five o'clock," snarled a heavy voice from the porch.

Shoving his gun behind the nearby TV, Rodriguez swung the door a little further, and before he could say a word, both men were in the front room.

"You alone, Bro?"

"Yeah."

"Show us the stuff, man."

Still intimidated by the two gang members, Rodriguez complied without asking about the money. He quickly pulled the five shopping bags from under the bed, while both cholo gang members stood over him.

When Rodriguez started to reach into one of the bags, the biggest cholo grabbed his arm. "Don't touch, man. We check the merchandise."

For the next twenty minutes the ten AK-47's were carefully examined, loaded, unloaded and playfully aimed at Rodriguez's head. They had known in minutes that Rodriguez was weak, which meant he could be bullied and used. With a knowing nod of agreement, the gang members told Rodriguez the original deal was off. They figured if he were weak, so were the gun suppliers. "You get seven five, half the fifteen G's. This stuff is 'mierda'."

Rodriguez knew he was a gonner. The suppliers would kill him if these guys didn't. In desperation, he made a move for his gun behind the TV. One clumsy lunge was as far as he got. As the knife blade slid through his back muscles into his right lung, Rodriguez felt dizzy. Then with a crack on his head with the butt of an AK-47, he was out cold.

While they hadn't planned on killing him, that sudden movement changed their minds. *What the hell*, they thought, *now we can keep all the money.*

📖 📖 📖

O'Shea was becoming a bit restless since the two gang members had entered Rodriguez's front door. "I wonder what the hell's going on in there? Maybe they're having dinner? It's taking too damn long. It's been about a half hour."

Fixated on the van driver, Ellis knew O'Shea was thinking out loud. He answered anyway. "There may be a lot of automatic weapons to examine and then they've got to negotiate the deal. Anyway, Loot, we've gotta wait till they leave."

"I know all that," snapped O'Shea.

Ellis was reminded O'Shea's worst quality was impatience. O'Shea was in the first, testy stage and Ellis knew better than to say more.

O'Shea gave Ellis an eye-rolling frown and they both silently resumed their vigil. Five minutes later, their wait was over.

O'Shea was so intensely scanning the front door; he noticed the front door knob slowly turn, seconds before the door actually opened. He gave Ellis a quick nudge. Pressing the police phone lever, O'Shea whispered in a loud rasp, "Drocco!"

The reply was almost instantaneous, as if Drocco had never taken his hands off the phone receiver. "We're ready, John."

O'Shea sighed, "Thanks, pal, stand by." He was relieved, knowing he had back up that he could trust with his life. Lieutenant Drocco was an absolute professional and one of his few genuine cop friends.

Ellis' unflinching attention was still glued to the van. He saw the driver nod and lean forward slightly as the engine shattered the calm with a roar. As both detectives watched every move, the intensity was so electric it could have powered generators.

They had it all—the automatic weapons, all the money and as important, powerful credentials for their résumé. This heist would bolster their reputation as the toughest gang in San Francisco. They out-slicked, outgunned and dethroned a fierce gun dealer. Now they were the best—top guns. Dragging the five shopping bags out the door, both cholos were bragging to themselves. There was no stopping them. They were now the self-proclaimed leaders of their gang.

Silhouette, the lookout, ran up the stairs to help with the bags. Dodger hat and ponytail didn't need or want any help. The guns were their trophies; and as they strutted by, Silhouette knew better than to touch their prizes. The gang driver, alerted by the lookout, had eased the van to the front of the Rodriguez house. After sliding open the side door, the driver stood by as the two cocky, self-anointed leaders stacked the bags under the rear seats. Ponytail pulled two fully loaded AK-47's out of the last bag. He openly handed one of the weapons to his Dodger hat partner, and with a yell of triumph, both waved the AK-47's over their heads. They were showing off, bullying the public. These cholos were now itching for a chance to try out their weapons. They were out of control and deadly dangerous.

Shouting and laughing like they had just won the World Series, the four gang members brazenly waved at timid onlookers and passing cars before entering the van. Silhouette sat next to the driver and the two gun toting leaders piling in behind, shouting and waving their weapons. Spinning the rear tires, the van fishtailed north on Capp Street.

"The deal's complete. All four are in the van moving north on Capp. OK?"

Drocco quickly answered O'Shea's call, "We see the van. License # B26484. It's on."

The way the gang shouted and waved worried O'Shea. "Be careful, Drocco, these guys are crazy."

Another quick reply, "Thanks, John. Don't worry."

O'Shea slowly shook his head as he watched the van disappear, skidding right onto 17th Street. "Good luck, Drocco," he whispered to himself.

Ellis lost sight of the van, swallowed and turned to O'Shea. "He's a pro. He'll handle those amateurs. You ready?"

O'Shea was still gazing down Capp Street. "Yeah, let's grab this asshole."

Both detectives unobtrusively unholstered their 9 mm automatics, checked the clips, released the safeties and slipped the weapons into their more accessible pockets. As they opened the car doors, neither took their eyes off the front door of Rodriguez's house. With one hand on the 9 mm in their pockets, O'Shea and Ellis slowly walked across the street, making sure there were no bystanders near the house. In the middle of the street, a '60 something Chevy sedan approached fast. Ellis instinctively spun around, dropping behind to cover O'Shea's back. The car sped by, missing Ellis by a couple of feet. Once on the sidewalk, they re-scanned the immediate area. The streets were clear and no words were necessary. Like a precision machine, they knew exactly what to do and when. It was 5:40.

Fortunately, the old rusty front gate to the Rodriguez yard was wide open. One less squeaking alarm to alert Rodriguez they figured. While Ellis stood at the foot of the five stairs leading to the front porch, O'Shea walked softly along the narrow cement path along the right side of the house. The left side was blocked by dense shrubbery. The yard at the rear of the house was strewn with empty bottles, beer cans and a wide variety of other garbage that led to an overturned garbage can. There were also piles of feces scattered on the ground like little land mines, with a warning to walk carefully. O'Shea complied, then he noticed a big bowl of water and a long winding chain. O'Shea froze as he followed the chain toward the three back stairs. There, an enormous black and brown mongrel, with obvious Rottweiler lineage, was sprawled on the ground. Its bowling ball sized head was resting on two huge front paws. The dark, piercing eyes were staring at O'Shea as black gums started twitching just enough to expose fang-like teeth.

Still motionless, O'Shea slowly moved his eyes across the yard until he found the end of the chain anchored around a tree stump. Following the chain's irregular course from tree stump to dog collar, gave O'Shea a rough estimate of the dog's range. He guessed about thirty feet. O'Shea was a few feet past the edge of the house, about twenty feet from the huge head when he heard low volume snarling growls. *Damn it,* he thought, *it's a no win. I'm in range and if Fang barks, Rodriguez will put me in range.* As if in a slow motion movie, O'Shea began moving backwards—frame by frame. After three delicate, nerve wracking backward steps, he was again out of sight around the side of the house. Holding his breath, O'Shea slowly eased his gun from his pocket. He was expecting the dog, still in range, to explode around the corner. It didn't, and O'Shea could breath again.

Ellis was on the front porch when O'Shea virtually tiptoed back to the front of the house. Following a pantomime of Fang chained out back, O'Shea pointed to the rear of the house as he widely mouthed, "Big dog!" His partner's quick nod said he got the message on the first try. O'Shea pocketed his weapon and stood below the stairs looking up at Ellis. He was wondering why his partner was already on the porch. That wasn't in their routine. O'Shea quickly complied, however, when Ellis motioned him up the five steps. He trusted his partner's judgment, besides this was neither the time nor place to question it.

In a low whisper, Ellis explained about the two kids playing catch with a baseball that hit Rodriguez's front door. Before one of the youngest could retrieve the ball from the porch, Ellis had eased up the steps, grabbed the ball and threw it to the kid. "I gave him a mean scowl, shook my fist and sent them running up the street."

Staring at the silent doorknob, O'Shea had to smile. "I knew you had a reason."

Like telepathy they were both thinking, *now what?* "Those cholos probably wasted Rodriguez," whispered O'Shea.

Without taking his eyes off the front door, Ellis gave a quick nod, "That ball hit hard, and after, not a sound."

O'Shea pointed toward a front window, the blind was open a couple of inches. Cautiously he peered inside. Startled, O'Shea grabbed for his gun and dropped to the porch floor. Rodriguez was sitting on the living room floor, leaning against the wall, as if staring at the window. Not a sound. After a few minutes, O'Shea risked another peek. This time he realized Rodriguez hadn't moved and his stare was unblinking, empty. There was also blood oozing from beneath him.

O'Shea looked at Ellis, "I think he's dead, Paul."

Ellis crept to the window. "You're right, dead or dying. Let's go in. He's still a possible suspect."

O'Shea nodded.

Ellis carefully tried the doorknob. The unlocked door slowly creaked open. Still grasping his automatic, O'Shea scanned the street just long enough to make sure no one was nearby. It was too long. As he turned back toward the door, he heard the harsh sound dreaded by all law enforcers. It was a thunderous bang, sending Ellis flying backwards off the porch.

O'Shea tore the weapon from his pocket, as he recklessly blasted his way into the living room. There was no one there except Rodriguez, who was still against the wall and looking dead. After thoroughly checking every room, O'Shea returned to Rodriguez. That's when he noticed the .357 Magnum resting in blood at his side. O'Shea quickly felt the body—still warm. There was no pulse and the barrel of the revolver was still hot. *God dammit*, he thought, *he wasn't dead, he was waiting. I blew it.* Slamming his fist against the wall, O'Shea cried out. "I'm a fucking asshole!" Now he had to help his friend, who was probably dead as well. When O'Shea spun around toward the front door, Ellis was leaning against the doorjamb.

Clutching the flak jacket over his chest, "We both are, John," he added softly.

O'Shea ran to him and gently pulled him to the floor. Cradling Ellis in his arms, O'Shea barely noticed his own blurring eyes. "Don't move, partner. You'll be fine, I'll take care of you."

Ellis looked up with a sheepish grin, "I'm not dying, but I think I busted a rib. This vest probably saved my life, huh?"

Still blurry eyed, O'Shea helped Ellis remove his coat and flak jacket. Carefully unbuttoning his shirt and lifting his tee shirt, O'Shea saw the huge red welt, slightly left of Ellis' sternum. "Jesus, that was a hell of an impact, but the skin's not even broken. That bullet was headed for your heart. How's your back?"

Leaning against the side of the door, Ellis felt around his upper body. "Guess I'm getting used to flying backwards down stairs. I'm really OK, John. Just my chest hurts. Let's get out of here and call in."

O'Shea helped Ellis to his feet and draped Ellis' coat over his shoulders. They both noticed the huge hole in Ellis' coat.

A small silent crowd had formed in front of Rodriguez's house, typical of too many neighborhoods, especially in drug-infested areas. No one knew O'Shea and Ellis were cops, no one knew who was shot and no one really cared. They were just curious. They weren't even concerned enough to call the police. O'Shea waved his badge anyway, just in case there was some good citizen out there.

Slowly weaving their way through the crowd, neither said a word until back in their unmarked car. As the curious peered at them through the windows, O'Shea called the City's emergency medical team, the coroner's office and the police.

Ellis examined the hole in his coat. "Think I can get this mended?"

O'Shea managed to head off an eye-rolling glare. "I'll buy you another coat, Paul. That one's useless unless you want to frame it." O'Shea widened the big rip in his own coat pocket. "Look at this, mine's worse than yours and I did it myself, trying to pull out my gun."

Ellis was massaging around the painful red welt. "Boy did we blow it. Like rookies, we made too many damn assumptions too hastily."

O'Shea looked out the window beyond the gawking crowd. "I wonder how Drocco's doing?"

CHAPTER 9

Parked on Capp Street two blocks north of the Rodriguez house, Lieutenant Drocco and Sergeant Bare waited for the final word from O'Shea. Detectives Ron Lunsted, known as Slim, and burly Frank Guiliani were in No. 65, a second unmarked car parked two blocks south on Capp Street. A back-up SWAT team with five officers in No. 102 van was parked two blocks west on Valencia. Drocco was in command of the operation.

Dark complexioned and craggy faced with thick gray hair; Drocco looked more Mafia than police. Yet, a twenty-five year veteran, he had earned every conceivable commendation. Bright, courageous, honest and witty, he was that rare cop virtually everyone liked and trusted.

His partner, Sergeant Bill Bare, was a tall, well-built, movie star handsome college graduate. Number one in his Police Academy class, remarkably he had advanced to detective in two years and sergeant after an unheard of four years. He was the envy of the department and considered the most likely to eventually succeed as Chief. Bare had requested Lieutenant Drocco as his mentor. He knew Drocco was one of the best, most experienced detectives in the department. Sergeant Bare was also aware of Drocco's intense loyalty to his partners and disinterest in further promotions. This made Lieutenant Drocco the ideal springboard in unwittingly helping Bare bolt to the top. Sergeant Bare was still inexperienced, primarily loyal only to himself and very ambitious.

Just as O'Shea made the first call, Drocco and Bare were identifying the van of cholos noisily approaching. "...License No. B26484, it's on. Thanks, John, don't worry."

As Drocco fired up his engine, he was hoping O'Shea and Ellis could handle Rodriguez without back up. Monitoring O'Shea's call to Drocco, Lunsted, driving unmarked car No. 65, made a quick u-turn on Capp Street, while No. 102, the SWAT van, turned down Fifteenth Street toward Capp. Over the phone, Drocco orchestrated the pursuit.

"...Perps heading east on Seventeenth. Unit 65, keep me in sight by a block and a half. Unit 102, follow 65 by a block and a half, at the ready." A block behind the cholos, Drocco gave Sergeant Bare the phone in anticipation of the unexpected. Breathing heavily, Bare held the phone in his left hand, his 9 mm automatic in his right and a 12-gauge shotgun between his knees. Drocco gave him a quick glance. "Relax, Bill, we won't start a war unless we have to. We'll follow them until there are fewer civilians around." Drocco smiled. "Maybe we'll get lucky and catch them off guard."

Suddenly, the worst of the unexpected happened. The cholo van stopped abruptly in the middle of Seventeenth Street, a block off Potrero. People were wandering all over the place, returning from work. Traffic was heavy and cars were beginning to honk. Drocco slowly drove within fifteen feet of the van, when the lookout, Silhouette, opened the passenger door. He jumped out, brandishing an automatic pistol, unbuttoned his coat, unzipped his trousers and leaned against the van.

"Goddammit, he's pissing. These guys want to take on the whole neighborhood."

Drocco grabbed the phone from Bare, who seemed frozen. "All hell's going down. Unit 102, Code Two, Seventeenth between Bryant and Potrero. Unit 65, block Potrero exit, call for more back up, then abandon your car and take cover.

A young Hispanic family walking down Seventeenth from Potrero saw Silhouette urinating on the van. The father, watching with his wife and two children, stopped his family and in typical macho tradition, walked toward the van. "Hey man, whatcha think you're doin'. There's women and chil..."

Silhouette had spun around and shot the father twice in the chest. As he fell backward over the curb, his wife screamed and by-standers started running in all directions. At that point, the cholo van side door slid open.

Drocco couldn't wait the few seconds for the SWAT team. He slammed the throttle to the floor, steered around to the side of the van and hit Silhouette head-on. "Get outta here," Drocco shouted to Sergeant Bare. Bare opened the passenger door, fell to the street and crawled under a parked car. At that moment, Drocco's car window exploded into bits of shard. It was too late for Drocco. No more than a foot away from his car, the cholos were hysterically screaming, laughing and shooting. Reaching for his handgun, he lost most of his head, when over fifty AK-47 rounds splattered the inside of the car. A few seconds later, those precious moments Drocco couldn't risk, two of the SWAT team emptied their automatic clips into the van, killing the driver and cholo leaders.

By that time, thirty police cars jammed the streets. Sergeant Panovich, in charge of the SWAT team, pulled panicked Sergeant Bare from under the parked car, thinking he was one of the cholos; Panovich had come very close to shooting him.

📖 📖 📖

Waiting in their car, O'Shea and Ellis could hear the jackhammer pops of nearby gunfire. It was too soon, O'Shea thought. Something had gone dangerously wrong. Gritting his teeth, O'Shea looked at a restless Ellis, who stared back at O'Shea.

"I'm OK, Loot, let's go."

Ellis wasn't OK.

O'Shea also realized their efforts would be too little, too late. He snapped on the police radio and through shouts and orders, it was apparent half the police force was at the shooting scene or on their way. "Cool it, Paul. The medics and our teams will be here soon."

It was Ellis' time to tear up in anguished frustration. So close, yet too far to aid his comrades.

O'Shea was quietly biting his lip, praying Drocco was OK.

It was several hours later, after Rodriguez was bagged, his house sealed and Ellis was examined at General Hospital, that they were officially advised. O'Shea and Ellis were waiting for some pain pills in the emergency room when Detective Guiliani entered. He knew too well the close friendship between Drocco and O'Shea—a relationship that began in high school. He was also aware of the deep respect and admiration Ellis felt for Drocco.

"Hi, Frank. Lay it on us." O'Shea was dreading the news and trying to be casual. It wasn't working too well. Deep stuttered sighs and lip biting were O'Shea's personal signature of grief.

Sitting down, Guiliani's eyes also said it all. They were glistening red and swollen. Barely controlling his own grief, Guiliani looked at Ellis with a sallow smile, "How ya feeling, Paul?"

"I'll be just fine in a few days, thanks for asking."

Ellis and O'Shea resumed their silence, with pleading eyes searching Guiliani's face for answers. After another pause, Guiliani looked away from them and took a deep, labored breath, then exhaled. "Well, Drocco's dead. He was my boss. I always admired him. Now he's my hero. He was more concerned with saving others than himself. Over the phone he ordered me and Ron to block off the street and take cover away from our car. He knew those cholos with automatic rifles could easily waste us in our car. The cholos stopped their van in the middle of Seventeenth and one of them actually got out to take a piss. Drocco probably knew then they were really crazy and itching to kill somebody. When the pisser shot and killed a bystander, Drocco used his car to off the cholo. He stopped his car less than a foot from the van's sliding door that was opening. Sergeant Bare was apparently scared shitless and Drocco's last words were to order Bare to run for it."

"Drocco knew that even though the SWAT team was seconds behind, the cholos opening the side door could hurt a lot of civilians in seconds. He actually used his car as a shield. He was killed instantly by automatic fire." Guiliani was crying. "The SWAT's shot through the van's back window, killing all three cholos. If Drocco could have waited three more seconds."

Then they all cried in their own deeply personal way. Just tears and silent thoughts.

CHAPTER 10

At the funeral, the Mayor and his entourage of high-ranking officials set aside their political one-liners to express condolences to Drocco's family and close police friends. It was a solemn time for police officers and civilians who had come to pay their respects to a fallen hero. There were lots of sympathetic handshakes, tears, hugs and spontaneous eulogies. Even those police officers who didn't know Drocco were deeply moved by the loss of one of their own; and proudly identified with such a heroic death. It was a traditional police extended family. An indispensable support system, where in time of need, no officer felt alone — except for Sergeant Bare.

Those very few cops who did stop by Bare to give their condolences were less friendly, more shallow and rigidly formal. Their handshakes were briefer and without the firmness and warmth they were offering others. He also realized that none of his fellow officers lingered to chat with him. Poised, as if at attention, Sergeant Bare was standing by himself in a corner of the funeral parlor when O'Shea approached.

"Are you OK, Bill?"

Feeling uneasy in a face-to-face confrontation with one of Drocco's best friends, Sergeant Bare dropped his eyes and strained a smile. "I'm fine, Lieutenant."

Searching for eye contact, O'Shea shouted, "Hey." When Bare looked up, O'Shea added, "Bullshit."

That was enough to easily collapse Bare's floundering pride and stolid posturing. Suddenly his shoulders drooped, eyes watered and his lower lip trembled. "I panicked, Lieutenant, I froze to my seat, I didn't move until Lieutenant Drocco commanded me to get out."

O'Shea clearly understood. "You were afraid, big deal. You were in an extremely dangerous situation that would frighten any cop. Worse, it was your first, and you were sitting next to a man with twenty years more experience and plenty of gun battles to his credit. Drocco knew that. He also knew you wouldn't run. You'd have sat there like a fool and got killed. You retreated under orders. Bill, you couldn't have changed a thing except the length of your life."

Bare wiped his wet face with his sleeve. Then he looked up wide-eyed as if before an older and wiser parent. "Thanks, Lieutenant, what should I do now? I love the police force. Can I ever be trusted? Should I just get a desk job?"

O'Shea held Bare firmly by the shoulders. "Your only problem is too much responsibility too soon. If there's a next dangerous time, you'll be less frightened and more in control. You're still learning, Bill, and you'll be fine in time. And don't forget that most of the cops in here have never used their weapon except on the range, and even fewer were ever faced with a street gunfight. That's no bullshit."

📖 📖 📖

After the burial, O'Shea left the Colma cemetery alone. Driving north on Highway 101, he thought of his heroic football days at San Francisco State, his *semper fi* Marine Corps tour of duty. That's when he was an uptight, kick-ass provost marshal in Japan, while Korea was killing and maiming his Marine buddies. He thought of a solid, righteous, Catholic marriage gone sour and his loving, admiring children whose adult lives had replaced their need for him. Jarred out of his trance by a honking horn, O'Shea discovered he was cruising the Tenderloin, down Turk Street along his beat when he was a rookie. He could taste his near panic the first time he heard gunshots. They were coming from around the corner on Leavenworth.

Slowly he drove by some of the old "gin mills." He could vividly remember feeling hesitant at first, special later, when given free drinks, Christmas presents or a few bucks just to look the other way after hours. Then later, those years in narcotics, countless drug busts, extra money, plenty of booze and lots of prostitutes. In more recent years, his empty house with lonely nights. How many old police buddies blew their brains out after retiring too alone and too drunk? Too many. Drifting toward the present, he thought of the eight Wednesday deaths that still baffled him and his partner. He thought of his friend, Drocco—dead and Mahoney, the asshole—alive. Shit, it was Saturday afternoon and he was ready for a *run*.

A hard, squealing right onto Leavenworth took him to Geary Street. A quick left onto Van Ness and across Market Street, then South Van Ness to Cesar Chavez Street, finally to Mission and he knew there was no turning back. This morning his subconscious must have whispered to take the other car. The invisible, dirt streaked gray Chevy Nova, his obscure transportation when he was on a run. No one ever recognized the '89 Chevy; it just faded into any curb.

He was nearing his own "Alcoholics Anonymous" in the Outer Mission. He had tried AA a few times with similar outcomes. He resented the hypocrisy, mixed with desperation and court orders. Some wanted to socialize, get laid, get support or get their card signed. His own "AA" was a more honest, kind of sarcastic metaphor. It represented a refuge, where he could be an active alcoholic with genuine anonymity for his entire run.

There were several Outer Mission bars on the fringe of South San Francisco. The Fandango, El Maravilloso, Gruta Azul and Las Hermanas were his favorites, primarily because they were unknown to any of his friends or acquaintances. In those clubs, he was known only as a generous loner. He was a self-reliant, formidable looking drunk, who always had money.

Parking his invisible car a couple blocks off Mission, he stuffed his bag of deep frowns, rage, regrets and sorrows in the trunk, along with his badge, shoulder holster and gun. This was his transition period, when O'Shea's soft steady breathing, relaxed smile and twinkling, mischievous eyes mirrored his temporary retreat from stress and pressure. Before closing the Chevy trunk, O'Shea grabbed his shaving kit, then opened an old briefcase. Removing about a thousand dollars, he tucked the wad of bills into his pocket. *That should last me for the whole run*, he thought. This was the briefcase containing over $200,000 in cash he had accumulated through the years. He grinned at the briefcase containing extra perks for being a cop. Then he closed the trunk.

After renting a room in a nearby hotel, O'Shea walked directly to the El Maravilloso. It was dark, lively and typically jammed with blue collar Mexicans. It was a place he could sit unnoticed for hours, watching the patrons dance and listening to the mariachis.

When sober, O'Shea was a shy drinker who thoroughly enjoyed just watching, while drinking. When drunk, however, he liked being noticed as long as he didn't have to interact. That's one of the reasons he chose Mexican bars. He couldn't speak Spanish and most of the patrons couldn't speak English. This was the generous second phase of his run, when he'd buy drinks for the house. Red-faced, O'Shea would sit silently smiling at his drink while patrons waved expressions of gratitude. He liked the friendly waves and grins; yet, lifting his glass with a blushing nod was the extent of his animation and communication. Dulled by hours of drinking and privacy, he didn't want friends, affection or conversation; he simply wanted some attention along with his cherished anonymity.

Arriving at phase two generally required three to four hours of steady drinking, starting with double bourbons on the rocks. He actually sipped the drinks, as if monitoring his intake. O'Shea characteristically swirled the ice cubes with his finger, sipped, swirled and sipped until bourbon and cubes were gone. It's surprising how much bourbon can be consumed in a few hours of slow swirling and sipping.

Bartenders provided a courteous continuous flow of bar bourbon without small talk. One reason, they barely spoke English. The secret to sipping well over a fifth of bourbon in a few hours was O'Shea's consistency. No breaks for food, phones, bathrooms or bar room banter. O'Shea's bladder was as remarkable as his bourbon intake. For most men, such a routine would have toxified them into unconsciousness, while bursting their bladders. O'Shea's stamina was remarkable.

Although there were few external signs of "drunk," his eyes were typically first to go. They seemed a bit out of focus, as if looking through or beyond an object—like glazed-over indifference. Sagging eyelids, however, tended to narrow his clouding, reddened eyes into slits of melancholy. He rarely said a word and his movements were slow, albeit steady.

At this point, O'Shea strangely looked more sad than drunk, or maybe more distant than sad, or simply at peace with himself. Perhaps this was a real glimpse of O'Shea from within, underscoring his need for an occasional run. He often thought that his runs were like being healed from the inside out. A tiny dying ember somewhere within him was fueled by stirred sips of bourbon. Igniting into bursts of brilliance, the ember glowed with a soothing fervor that spread over his body— with each sip. These were warm, analgesic compresses on his aching, guilt-laden memories and painful frustrations. For O'Shea, phase two was a euphoric numb.

In San Francisco, bars are closed from 2:00 a.m. to 6:00 a.m. This gave O'Shea a brief respite he wouldn't have taken otherwise. He would leave one of the clubs by 2:15, return to his room; sleep for a few hours, shower, shave and back to the club by 6:00 a.m. This routine went on for days, until phase two deteriorated into phase three—the finale.

Those bartenders who had served O'Shea's runs before knew when he was on the fade. First signs were his increasingly seedy appearance, sprouts of grayish red whiskers, tangled hair, wrinkled, disheveled clothing, a frozen half-grimace/half-smile and a fixed, vacant stare. Motor coordination was the last to go. When O'Shea could hardly mount a barstool, no one had to tell him it was time. As if sensing collapse, he quietly struggled to his feet and staggered his way back to the hotel, where, malnourished and exhausted, he fell across his bed in stuporous sleep.

CHAPTER 11

"Hey, Ellis, I heard you got back OK." Straining a pasty smile through his wired teeth, Mahoney was uneasily surprised to see O'Shea's partner in his office.

Ellis wasn't smiling. "Yeah. Drocco got killed, a by-stander got killed, my partner got devastated, the so-called suspect got wasted and I got back. But not OK."

Down the hall Officer Logan responded to Ellis' loud anger with poor judgment. Running back to the office, Logan started to pull Ellis by his shoulder. "Back off…"

Before Logan could finish his warning, Ellis spun around, karate-stomped Logan on the right kneecap and nailed him with a single left jab, as Logan lunged forward.

Mahoney was so stunned with shock and rage, he displayed more poor judgment. He went for his gun. Ellis kicked hand and gun into Mahoney's flaccid chest. This left Mahoney gasping for breath and clutching a broken hand.

Holding his own painfully throbbing chest with both hands, Ellis stepped over Logan who was dazed on the floor with a splattered nose and smashed patella. Other police who were gathering at the door stepped aside as Ellis, breathing heavily, left.

In pain and embarrassed, Mahoney glared at the cops still hanging around the door. "What the fusch you lookin' at? Get a ambulance."

Later, on their way to the hospital, Mahoney and Logan knew better than to try charging Ellis with assault. They would not only look like sissies, they were aware an official inquiry into the reason for the assault could expose their reckless plan to set up O'Shea.

📖 📖 📖

It was another Wednesday, a grim reminder to Ellis of the eight violent crimes still unsolved, despite their thorough police work. Glancing at O'Shea's empty desk was an added painful jolt to his jagged memories of those recent events. His partner had been gone since the funeral on Saturday. There had been a brooding, restless quality to O'Shea's grieving that mildly troubled Ellis that day.

Gently stroking his bruised chest with his swollen right hand, he was enveloped in ugly thoughts. He flinched, expecting the magnum impact to again knock him off the porch. He could still feel O'Shea's concern for Drocco and his intense grief when he learned that Drocco was dead. Ellis rediscovered his own rage resulting in his maniacal assaults on Mahoney and Logan. Ellis hadn't been so morbidly preoccupied since his daughter nearly died of pneumonia several years ago. He really missed his partner.

Slumped over his desk that Wednesday morning, Ellis was oblivious to corridor sounds of cops and clerks scurrying back and forth in a hurry to somewhere. He didn't hear the resounding jokes and laughter around the water cooler, the shouts of impatient administrators or detectives calling to their partners to wait up. He was even desensitized to the harsh colognes and cheap perfumes wafting down the corridor, the smell of percolating coffee or the aromas of assorted breakfast take-outs passing by on their way to some other desk.

Then, for no apparent reason, he was aroused out of his gloom to a sense of sheer frustration. Ellis looked around his cubicle at a large calendar on the wall. *Exactly three weeks since we got these cases,* he thought, *and now I've lost my partner.* His eyes wandered back to his desk until he was looking at the eight files neatly stacked at the rear, near pens, pencils, paper clips and his stapler. Staring at the cases, Ellis again sensed a foreboding that somehow they were having an evil effect on everyone who touched them.

Removing the top case file from the stack, he idly began thumbing through the documents and notes. Each page seemed crammed with questions, distracting clues, puzzles, frustrations, tragedies and no answers. Severing the hydraulic brake lines on Carlos Villa's old truck had prompted a diabolical chain reaction: killing Dorothy, a mother;

Melanie, her four-year-old daughter; and later, Jerran, the son and Carlos, both by suicides.

A thorough investigation of Carlos and his surviving wife, Leona, revealed a clear absence of any motives for the crime. No drugs, lovers, rivalries or jealousies; four violent deaths and no answers. *Could the person who cut the brake lines have made the wrong vehicle by mistake?* He wondered. *Maybe,* he reasoned, *but that doesn't account for some pervasive evil affecting all these cases.* Ellis threw the file back on the desk. *If the brakes on Villa's truck had never been cut, Drocco and the by-stander would also be alive, and my partner would be here.*

📖 📖 📖

Ellis was again slumped over his desk in deep thought mainly about his missing partner.

"I can't fine my car." Standing over Ellis' desk was a well-dressed, clean-shaven O'Shea.

Startled out of his slumping posture, Ellis' eyes bulged as his mouth gaped open. Then it registered, he was staring at O'Shea. Suddenly Ellis was bathed in a warm, tingling flood of relief. He just couldn't contain himself. "You son of a bitch, I should have known you were on a run," he happily shrieked while slapping his forehead.

"Now the whole fucking floor knows it," O'Shea replied with less exuberance.

"I'm sorry, John, I guess I got carried away. I wanted to help ya and I didn't know where you were. I didn't know you were, well…you know."

Ah hell, O'Shea signed to himself. He immediately regretted his insensitive sarcasm. "Sometimes I move my mouth before I think. I'm the asshole, Paul. I should have given you some signal I'd be out for a few days. The damn problem is, I generally don't know I'm going on a run until I'm on it. Anyway, thanks for giving a shit."

Those hesitant comments meant more to Ellis than O'Shea could ever imagine.

O'Shea finally broke an awkward silence with a confidential whisper. "I can't find my Chevy Nova. I always take it on a run because it's inconspicuous. That's the trouble with the goddamn car; it's practically invisible.

Ellis was acutely aware of O'Shea's pride and self-reliance. He felt honored when O'Shea even obliquely asked for such a personal favor. He also knew from his narcotics days with O'Shea there was plenty of money stashed in the trunk, probably along with his gun and badge. It was obvious to Ellis that a stolen vehicle report wasn't an option. "Do you still have the keys?"

O'Shea smiled. "Here, Paul, you know I wouldn't ask if..."

Ellis interrupted. "Give me the license number, all of the geographic details you can recall and I'm out of here."

O'Shea divulged information he had never told anyone before. He gave the names of the clubs, his hotel and his habit of parking off the main drag in a no-tow zone.

As Ellis suspected, he had stashed his gun and badge in the trunk, along with his briefcase filled with money, lots of money.

Ellis didn't bother to ask where O'Shea had already looked for the car; and O'Shea knew that information was irrelevant. He could trust his compulsively thorough partner to search in a carefully gridded, methodical way. No further words were necessary for either of them. Ellis grabbed his coat and hurried down the corridor, while O'Shea began checking a stack of memos and phone messages.

Ellis had never been with O'Shea on a run. In fact he'd never seen him drunk. For Ellis, of course, that didn't matter. He had many years experience with his partner's driving and parking habits. He knew O'Shea had parked only once on his most recent run, that he had parked within walking distance from his hotel and that he was sober when he parked.

Ellis wasn't taking any chances of possibly exposing O'Shea's drinking neighborhood. Riding along with a patrol unit to the Outer Mission, he took a Mission Street bus for the final leg of his search. Less than an hour later, Ellis was staring at a 1989 Chevy Nova, parked on a side street three and a half blocks from the hotel. He recognized the car immediately. To Ellis it was so distinctively invisible; it was conspicuous.

Gotcha, he thought.

CHAPTER 12

O'Shea was reading through the Villa file when Ellis returned. As if thoroughly engrossed in the file, he didn't look up. "OK, you're back too soon. Give me the bad news."

Ellis laid a claim check from the gas station across the street, as well as O'Shea's holstered gun and badge on O'Shea's desk. "I could hardly see through the windshield, so the car's being washed and gassed up at the Shell Station."

O'Shea finally looked up. "Everything else still in the trunk?"

"Everything." Ellis smiled.

"Christ, Paul, you're a fucking phenomenon. I owe you big time."

Ellis shot O'Shea a tight-lipped pout of hurt feelings. "Friends don't owe each other, ever."

O'Shea dropped the file on his desk. "Boy I can really jam my mouth up my ass. That isn't even close to what I wanted to say." Standing up, O'Shea looked directly at Ellis. "No one's ever shown me more loyalty than you. I couldn't have a better friend."

Pausing for a moment, O'Shea lowered his voice. "I heard about the number you did on Mahoney and Logan. You saved my ass again, because I probably would have been forced to kill both of them and go to jail. By the way," O'Shea added, "don't even think about official charges against you or unofficial vengeance. There won't be any—I promise!"

O'Shea had made another resolute promise earlier that day. He guaranteed Mahoney there'd be no negotiations, reprieve or compromise if Ellis or his family was ever harmed in the slightest way. He would slowly kill Mahoney by torturing him to death. Mahoney was no fool. He knew O'Shea and believed him.

Restacking the eight files on his desk, O'Shea locked his gun in a side drawer and stuck his badge in his pocket. "Let's get out of here." O'Shea loved to eat, but he didn't care about fancy or expensive food. "We're gonna have dinner at Tommy's Joynt. We'll even take my car, you know the old invisible Chevy. I'm buying because I feel like it; and that's an order from your boss."

📖 📖 📖

During the Wednesday night dinner at Tommy's Joynt, both detectives agreed there was enough evidence for a manslaughter indictment against Robinson. O'Shea was still not completely convinced, but figured it was finally the DA's decision. Besides, then they could start carefully reviewing the other seven cases for overlooked clues and new suspects.

As usual, the food at Tommy's Joynt was cheap and delicious, while the atmosphere was historical, old San Francisco, with wall-filling memorabilia reminding patrons about it's 70 year legacy of fine food and fun. O'Shea had the carved turkey breast, stuffing, mashed potatoes and salad. Ellis, with a spirit of adventure, had the buffalo stew and salad. Both had a great dessert. O'Shea smiled to himself as they dug in.

Downing his chocolate mousse cake in record time, Ellis eyed O'Shea's remaining piece.

O'Shea grinned. "Not a chance, pal."

📖 📖 📖

O'Shea was in the office earlier than usual on Thursday. He wanted his morning routine out of the way, then he could look over the Sutherland case once more before his partner arrived. He should have known better. When O'Shea returned to their cubicle, Ellis was already at his desk jotting down something for the Sutherland file. O'Shea looked at his full cup of coffee, then dropped the Chronicle newspaper on his desk as he glanced at the file. *Oh well,* he thought, *at least I caught the headlines.*

"Morning, Paul. What's up so early? It's not even 8:00 yet."

Ellis kept taking notes without looking up. "Morning, Loot. Thought I'd check the Sutherland case again before we threw it in."

O'Shea shook his head in amazement. "Christ, you're doing it again. Why do you think I came in so early?"

Ellis ignored the question. "While you were getting coffee and taking your Jimmy Brit, I checked last night's messages and memos. There's an M.E. forensic report on Sutherland we haven't read yet."

Picking up the report, O'Shea glanced down at his newspaper. "I haven't had my Jimmy Brit yet."

Ellis continued, "There was also a call from an Officer Blake from the park police. I just called him and this is about what he said." Ellis read from his notes. "On the Wednesday of Sutherland's death, at about 12 noon, Officer Blake was on horse patrol. He stopped in front of the Aquatic Park Marine Museum to let some young kids pet Serendipity, his horse. Looking over the Aquatic Park water, he noticed the usual swimmers. He also noticed two SCUBA divers surfacing from under the schooner anchored near the eastern edge of the Aquatic Park water. Blake watched for a while, mainly because he'd hardly ever noticed divers in that area before. The water's much too murky for recreational diving, which led him to believe they were commercial divers, possibly checking the hull of the old ship. When they re-submerged, however, their occasional flipper splash and air bubbles indicated they were headed toward the buoys where swimmers take their laps. That's when the officer resumed chatting with the children and their parents.

"About ten minutes later he resumed his patrol. Still a bit curious about the divers, the officer idly scanned the Bay as he trotted along the beachfront. That's when he noticed, just for a second, two figures in wet suits carrying tanks and masks. They were moving fast up the beach when they disappeared behind the public restrooms. Officer Blake had considered their Aquatic Park dive and haste a little unusual, but certainly not suspicious enough to look for them any further. He simply forgot about his observations until he read our memo."

O'Shea had been listening carefully, while opening the M.E.'s forensic report. "Guess we have to assume the presence of divers is just another strange coincidence. Oh shit, no we don't." O'Shea was reading the last paragraph of the M.E.'s report. "Are you a SCUBA diver?" O'Shea asked.

"No, but my daughter is into it. In fact, she wants to get me involved. As part of their athletic program, they have SCUBA courses in most high schools now. So why did you ask—as if I didn't know?"

Clearing his throat, O'Shea slipped into his smug, teacher's role. "Remember some of Sutherland's fingernails looked dirty? We even thought Robinson might have been scratched in a struggle. Now I know why Robinson didn't have any scratches." Still in his teaching mode, O'Shea turned toward Ellis with a pause for suspenseful effect. "That's because he didn't kill Sutherland. The stuff under the fingernails was pieces of neoprene foam. Not just any kind of neoprene. It's called closed-cell neoprene. It has millions of tiny nitrogen gas bubbles that provide insulation and high buoyancy. In other words, Paul, it's from a diver's wet suit. Robinson wasn't bullshitting us, he's as innocent as all the other primaries in these goddamn cases. So let's get him out of that shit hole city jail and start again where we left off—wherever that was."

📖 📖 📖

Both detectives needed to see Robinson. O'Shea had his release papers and Ellis had an apology. As usual, they could virtually feel the frantic commotion and nearly taste the stench before entering the big steel door to the city jail.

Robinson had been informed by a deputy that all charges had been dropped and there were no outstanding arrest warrants. He would be released within the hour. When the detectives arrived, the release papers were checked carefully by the watch sergeant, before officially authorizing Robinson's discharge. Ten minutes later Robinson walked through the last cell door, which led to the sergeant's desk and freedom. He was dressed in his own civilian casual clothes and clutched in his arms were two brown bags of personal belongings. All those deep, taut furrows of resistance were gone from his face. He looked relaxed, even humble.

Ellis stood in the background as O'Shea offered a tentative faint smile, while trying to remain professional. "Our investigation finally proved your innocence and frankly, we're both glad."

Robinson's smile was neither tentative nor faint. "I'm glad, too. You guys did your job well and came up with the right answers. I'm grateful because I know some cops who would have tried to nail me just to close the case."

O'Shea's smile broadened. "We don't work that way, we really want to nail the bad guys."

"Have you found the real murderer yet?" asked Robinson.

"No, but we believe it was the SCUBA divers you saw. Anyway, we'll stay with it until we find them."

Dropping his eyes, Robinson slowly shook his head. "You know, after all my hard-assing Harry, I'm sorry he's gone; and I really can't understand who'd want to kill the guy. Ain't that crazy coming from me?"

"Not at all, but now who are you gonna lean on?"

"No one, Lieutenant O'Shea, I've done a lot of thinking in here and I'm too damn old to play gunslinger anymore. I'm hangin' up my guns. I intend to enjoy my wife, my good health and laps at Aquatic Park."

Ellis decided it was safe to move forward. "Can I shake your hand and wish you luck?"

"You sure can, Sergeant, good luck to both of you guys."

All three of them took a deep breath of fresh air and heaved a huge sigh as the big steel door to the city jail slammed shut behind them. After hugging his wife, who had been waiting on the outside steps, Robinson was gone; and O'Shea and Ellis hurried back to their office.

CHAPTER 13

O'Shea and Ellis sat silently at their desks for the rest of the morning and most of the afternoon. Yet again they carefully read and evaluated every document, note and memo in each of the eight files. They were searching for any obscure clues, overlooked suspects, hidden motives or flaws in their own investigative procedures. They were keenly aware that murders are usually performed by persons who somehow benefit from the death. This is the first and most vital lesson in any detective manual or homicide correspondence course. Without smoking guns or eyewitnesses, it's motives that identify suspects, which leads to arrests and convictions.

Heading any traditional menu of motives is some sort of financial gain. The victim dies and the perpetrator gains wealth, preserves wealth or increases wealth; which is generally associated with power or its loss. Another category in the investigative manuals is the so-called *crimes of passion*. In these cases the big payoffs are relief from the torturous pains of betrayal, revenge, jealousy or unrequited love. The faithless, tormenting or conniving victim dies and the perpetrator is no longer spurned, deceived, mocked or, perhaps, threatened.

Then there are the more macabre, unpredictable murders. These are not easily categorized and even more difficult to solve. They are the ones police dread and criminology courses tend to omit. The motives are "helter-skelter," illogical, supernatural, paranormal or delusional. In these cases, the victims have no conspiratorial roll in their deaths. There are no tauntings, betrayals, rejections or intimidations. The victims are just randomly murdered; and the crimes are inexplicable, irrational, demonic and pervasively evil.

Experienced detectives like O'Shea and Ellis were well aware that murders announcing the clearest, unequivocal motives were the puny tip of the proverbial iceberg—the easy ones. They realized as well, that the science of criminology was severely challenged when trying to solve those others—the evil ones. O'Shea and Ellis also knew that indispensable, hard evidence or eye witnesses at the scene of a crime could lead to dead ends when there were no motives.

Both detectives dropped the files they were scanning at the same time. Leaning back in their swivel chairs they slowly stretched their arms over their heads. After heaving deep sighs, they sat silently staring at their desks. Ellis was the first to acknowledge his deep thoughts. "Are you thinking what I'm thinking?"

O'Shea looked over at Ellis. "Probably. We seem to be joined at the hip when it comes to criminal investigations."

Ellis quickly nodded with boyish enthusiasm. "Maybe that's the problem. Most of my detective skills were taught by you. So rather than compliment each other's work, we tend to duplicate it. I'm beginning to feel we need more of our own intuition and less 'by the book' if we're ever going to figure out these cases. I don't think there are motives for these eight murders."

Clearing his throat as if preparing for another lecture, O'Shea got up and paced around the small cubicle. He finally sat on the edge of his desk, with a benign, fatherly gaze at Ellis. "You nailed it dead center, Paul, but think back. As professionals, we have to slowly and methodically eliminate every possible suspect, every lead, every clue and motive. We've been doing that; and after reviewing all of these cases once more, maybe we can begin to say with some certainty all eight are linked to something without rational reason or traditional motives. You know what that conclusion means. All the cases may remain unsolved. But on the other hand, if we're right and solve just one of the eight cases, we might easily solve the other seven. So come on, you know the book well. But you've also got great street savvy and intuitive skills. That's what makes us great detectives."

Ellis' blank expression twisted into a slight grin. "Thanks, boss, glad your summation included me as great."

At that, they both had to smile.

📖　📖　📖

Their strategy was clear and straightforward. Simply start all over again and surgically replicate the first investigation including crime scenes, witnesses and suspects—if any were still alive. Should the conclusions remain the same, the detectives would alter their investigation, by looking for the strange, bizarre and unusual in all the unlikely places. This plan would require less homicide manual, more detective intuition and a lot of luck.

Just as they started to sort cases, however, there was an unexpected telephone call from Judge Hall. A call that would prolong their conventional investigative approach. O'Shea was abruptly reminded that his appointment to Chief of Police was contingent upon Hall's election to mayor of San Francisco.

"Let's have dinner, Jack, say about six at Aqua. Is that alright?"

O'Shea knew his workday with Ellis was over. "Certainly, Judge. What's up?"

"Derrick Hansen called. He has a note for you that may help solve Helen's murder. It's also a fundraiser for me. You'll be introduced to my fans. See you then, Jack." Click.

As much as O'Shea wanted to be Chief of Police, he hated those introductions, when he told the audience what good friends he and Judge Hall were, and what a great guy the Judge was. *Shit,* he thought. He also hated the fancy, overpriced continental cuisine at Aqua. Everything was ala carte and no meal was less than $70 or $80. "Shit," he grumbled. Then he thought of Derrick—"Shit."

"An evening with the high rollers?" Ellis grinned.

"You know I hate that crap. But the Judge may have a new lead on the Hansen case."

Ellis kept grinning. "He also has a chief's job in his briefcase."

O'Shea flipped Ellis a quick middle finger.

"I heard you mumble 'Shit' a couple of times," Ellis added.

"You don't miss a thing. One for Derrick, who I can't stand; one for that expensive artery-clogging food I hate and the one you didn't hear for being coerced into talking to the rich and arrogant. The judge said it's also a goddamn fundraiser for him. So go home to your little family and have a good home-cooked meal. We'll hit it hard tomorrow, it's almost five."

📖 📖 📖

There was the usual array of Armani suits, over tasseled Church shoes, all sorted into circles by price tags, positions and power. As prominent was a rainbow display of Neiman Marcus and Saks Fifth Avenue dresses above the finest Cinderella heels, all hovering near those male clusters of wealth and prestige. Politicians, attorneys, CEO's, all kinds of doctors and just the plain old family rich were nodding and laughing within their tight little cliques of small talk. That's what O'Shea was thinking as he stood self-consciously in a corner of the huge chandeliered reception area, wearing his ten year old Penney's single-breasted suit and half-soled Florsheims.

He could have stood there alone forever if Judge Hall hadn't inadvertently noticed him. Surrounded by an adoring group of prim, pampered and very rich ladies, the judge couldn't miss O'Shea, the only person not embedded in a group.

At six feet, three inches, slender and handsome, Hall was an impressive sight, silver-tongued, with a deep voice that resonated charm and wisdom. "Can you excuse me, ladies? There's some important business I must attend to." The sparkling jeweleried ladies slowly parted, forming a celestial pathway, like glistening meteor dust trailing the massive blazing meteor. As the trail of ladies disbursed to different groups, Judge Hall quickly found Derrick schmoozing with a circle of other prominent attorneys. All the judge needed was a soft, throaty "excuse me," and the circle quickly parted. Beaming a fixed smile of acknowledgment to all of the bobbing heads and gaping mouths, Judge Hall motioned to Derrick, who was already exiting the breeched circle.

"Over there," Hall said dryly, as he shifted to his serious, courtroom demeanor.

Derrick complied with a sober nod and an all-business quick stride.

O'Shea saw them coming and tried to cover his bored expression with a smile. It didn't work.

"This must be terribly boring for you, Jack," was Hall's opening comment, while vigorously shaking O'Shea's hand.

O'Shea offered an uneasy, protocol lie. "Oh, no, Judge, I just don't know many of these people."

"You will," replied Hall. "Especially when you're Chief of the San Francisco Police Department."

O'Shea knew that comment was the carrot, the reminder why he was at the fundraiser in the first place. Shifting his attention to Derrick,

O'Shea changed to a more comfortable, official subject. "Hello, Mr. Hansen. I understand you have some information that might help with our investigation."

Derrick didn't particularly like O'Shea either. Actually, Derrick was a user, not a giver. He really didn't like anyone he couldn't manipulate; and he knew O'Shea wasn't an easy mark. He was aware, however, O'Shea was Hall's stooge and a thorough detective who would follow any lead. "Here's a note I found in Helen's purse a few days ago. The 'Matt' she refers to is the McGuire chauffeur. They have the Seacliff estate adjacent to mine."

O'Shea couldn't help but notice Derrick's snobbish choice of the word "estate." He also realized there was nothing snobbish about the note. Brief, to the point and typed on a memo pad, there was no date.

"Matt, please! No more. It was just a harmless flirtation that got out of hand. I'm sorry, but please leave me alone." There was no signature, which O'Shea conceded to himself was understandable for a woman who needed to avoid signing evidence of her mistake. Looking up at Derrick, O'Shea was about to return the note when Judge Hall softly intervened.

"Keep it for now, Jack. This may be the break you were looking for. Could be she was seduced by this guy, Matt, who may have become her jealous stalker."

Derrick offered a quick follow-up comment. "Gosh, John. I didn't know anything about this. Poor Helen never told me. It might be worth checking out, don't you think?"

"Yeah, we'll definitely look into it." O'Shea answered with a barely veiled frown. *Just don't call me John. I'm not your friend. Don't even call me Jack, you asshole!* O'Shea added, to himself.

Smiling and nodding friendly gestures to the wealthy guests heading toward the dining room, Judge Hall lightly stroked O'Shea's back. "Thanks, Jack. I know you're the best in the business. Why do you think I would need you as Chief?"

O'Shea weakly smiled at both of them while thinking, *I'm beginning to wonder myself. If he needs a political stooge, he'll really be pissed when I'm Chief.*

O'Shea stumbled through an awkward "Aw shucks" type of response, when Hall introduced him during dinner. Still, he was genuinely grateful when the Judge acknowledged to all those prominent guests that, when he was elected Mayor, O'Shea would indeed be the Chief of Police. What O'Shea didn't know was the game of stooge he was about to play.

Derrick had known for over a year that Matt, the chauffeur, was having a sexual fling with Helen. He really didn't care about her extramarital sex. During their marriage he had had plenty of sexual trysts; and in recent years, he made no attempts to conceal them. He had continuously hinted to Helen that they have some kind of open marriage. Of course, he figured that Helen was too proper, old-fashioned and religious to go for such an arrangement. It would be open for him, not her. He was wrong and furious. *How dare she have an affair with a chauffeur*, he fretted. It was an affront to his most precious possession, his ego. Although he had set up Carol Evermore in an apartment where he spent much of his leisure time, he despised Helen's relationship with a mere servant. A few weeks before Helen's death, he became more enraged when he received his private investigator's report.

Matt was more than a mere servant; he was a tough ex-con. Ten years younger than Helen, Matt Diger had served time at Folsom State Prison near Sacramento for the armed robbery of a Safeway supermarket. He had also been convicted of several assault and batteries, resulting in county jail sentences. Both in prison and jail he earned the reputation of "super bad ass." The report answered another gnawing question. Why did the wealthy, highly respected retired investment banker, Dave McGuire, hire an ex-convict as a chauffeur? It was simple and never a dark secret; Matt was family. The maverick son of McGuire's wife, Virginia, from her first marriage, Matt was fiercely loyal to his stepfather. During his last Adult Authority Board hearing, Matt was paroled to Mr. McGuire, who promised to hire and watch over him.

Derrick had been painfully aware there wasn't much he could do about the ex-con, Matt, working for the McGuire family. Dave McGuire would be a formidable opponent against anyone; especially someone like Derrick, with considerably less wealth, no community respect and not a semblance of altruism. In a showdown, the Bay Area community would be on McGuire's side. The death of Helen, however, ironically leveled the playing field. She wasn't available to defend her lowlife lover; and Derrick could practically taste revenge.

It was no neighborhood secret that Matt was occasionally on the Hansen property. Probably their only question was why. The answer could be easily supplied by a few mild clues—like the note, which Derrick reasoned was simply a creative expansion of the truth. The police were under pressure to solve the murder and, with a few subtle nudges, Matt would be their primary suspect.

Judge Hall was provided just enough information to sympathize with his good friend and demand a full investigation. In learning from Derrick about Helen's sexual encounters, Judge Hall assumed Derrick trusted his wife and had been unaware of the affair. He knew that Derrick was somewhat of a womanizer, which didn't matter since it was a macho male thing. He didn't know, however, about Derrick's mistress relationship with his secretary, Carol Evermore, nor was he aware the unsigned note was a fake.

Derrick wasn't sure how far he could go with his friendship with a Superior Court Judge and he wasn't taking any chances of a backfire. In any event, Derrick figured he hadn't planted enough clear evidence in the note to create suspicions about a set-up; and Matt was easily a viable suspect, whom the police wouldn't mind rousting. He was a low life that might be provoked into losing control and doing something stupid, like resisting the authorities. Derrick was satisfied. All he had to do was ignite a small, smoldering suspicion, step aside and the police would do the rest.

CHAPTER 14

By 7:00 a.m. on Friday, O'Shea finished most of his usual in-office, pre-work ritual. Anxious to get an early start, he had again skipped reading his newspaper that was still folded on his desk where he dropped it when he arrived at 6:30.

O'Shea had too much to sort out, just too many thoughts crowding his mind. He was in information overload with no room for any leisure reading. *What the hell am I missing,* he thought. *How did eight fairly routine cases get so damned weird, confusing? Christ, it's more than that; it's some kind of treachery. All those primary suspects with solid motives and solid alibis—solid clues without motives—what the hell was Bigfoot doing in Likert's garage—why did two SCUBA divers kill a nice old guy—how come a freak like Winston got killed, along with a sweet sick lady like Grace? What the hell's going on??*

Draining his third cup of coffee, O'Shea hunched over his desk feeling that crampy knot in the pit of his stomach. Last night's new developments were worse than the coffee he had just drunk. The appearance of Diger, the chauffeur, as a new suspect just didn't fit. O'Shea didn't particularly like Hansen and he trusted him even less. He also had unsettling feelings about his relationship with Judge Hall. Nothing seemed to fit. Half smiling to himself, he thought, B*esides, the chauffeur's motives just aren't vague or evil enough to fit in with these eight cases.*

📖 📖 📖

As O'Shea sat struggling with his obsessive thoughts, Ellis quietly entered their cubicle.

"Morning, Loot."

O'Shea looked up a little startled by Ellis' silent entrance. "Are you OK?" asked O'Shea. "You look different."

Avoiding direct eye contact, Ellis sat down behind his desk. "Robinson is dead," Ellis answered in a lifeless monotone. "Blake from park police called right after you left last night. Apparently Robinson needed to cleanse off the jail stench in his own way. According to Don Dutil, Robinson changed into his trunks and cap about 1:00 p.m. He immediately walked to the Aquatic water, swam to the buoys and started his slow, steady laps. About ten minutes later a powerboat entered from the Bay doing about 25 knots. Motoring in Aquatic Park is prohibited and the marine speed limit is 5 knots. Robinson never saw it coming, John. The boat veered through the buoys where it momentarily lifted out of the water as the hull crushed Robinson's back and the propeller ripped through the top of his head. Officer Blake saw it all. He even shouted a warning to the boat operator. It was too late. Don Dutil and another nearby swimmer were uninjured. The operator was questioned by Blake and the Coast Guard. He said he didn't see the warning signs at the entrance and that he tried to turn when he saw the buoys. His blood alcohol was .10 and he's in the city jail charged with manslaughter."

O'Shea was stunned into rigid, teary-eyed silence. Neither said another word for several minutes. Then Ellis glanced up at O'Shea's eyes. This prompted more silence as Ellis grieved with his partner.

Finally O'Shea slammed his fist on the desk. Ellis flinched, expecting an ear-shattering shout of rage. He was surprised when O'Shea slowly turned to him with a muted, near gentle expression of exasperation. "What a terrible waste. He wasn't out of jail a whole day. Good people and good friends are falling all around us. You're a levelheaded guy, Paul. Is all this just coincidence or our stupidity in missing something or some kind of evil energy?"

Ellis shook his head, "I'm as baffled as you are, John. I couldn't sleep this morning, so I checked the perp through every possible agency. His name is Jimmy Wang, some kind of a rich textile businessman from Vancouver, British Columbia. He has wealthy family and friends in San Francisco. Now grasp this incredible coincidence, or destiny, or evil, or whatever. He has no criminal record in Canada or the U.S., no warrants or prior drunk arrests. I saw him this morning in jail, and he barely speaks English. He said that after he and his family were picked up at the airport, they had a big party at Pier 39 on one of his friends' boats, a 65-foot yacht. He was so happy to see old friends from Mainland China he drank more than he was used to. This was his first vacation in ten years."

"He has a small motorboat in Vancouver; and he was thrilled when one of his friends said he could use their powerboat, a 20 foot Chris Craft, with a 350 cubic inch V8 engine. It was after lunchtime and apparently nobody wanted to go with him. You know, John, the boat would have been too much for him sober; drunk, he was totally overwhelmed. He was used to a nine horsepower outboard, this Chris Craft was a 200 horsepower missile. He didn't know the Bay and probably couldn't read most navigation signs in English either. After nearly hitting the west side of the Aquatic Park pier, he shot into the park trying to stop the boat. He remembers that after hitting something, he managed to locate and close the throttles. He had only been on the boat about ten minutes. His friends, family and witnesses verify his story."

O'Shea sighed deeply and shook his head. "I don't suppose his friends or family knew Robinson."

"So far, John, I found no connection. Neither he nor any of the people he associated with ever had any contact with Robinson, Sutherland or anyone in the other seven cases. This was Mr. Wang's first visit to San Francisco."

O'Shea looked at Ellis with one of his infrequent warm smiles. "You saved me a ton of hassle. We can close out that part of the Sutherland case and get on with our mind-boggling investigation. That poor asshole Wang; he kills a man and ruins his own life during his first visit to San Francisco. It was also probably his first drunk."

Ellis stapled his final Robinson notes to the back of the Sutherland file. "Well, at least Robinson never knew what hit him. I'll bet he would have hated hospitals."

CHAPTER 15

Viewed through a woman's eyes, Matt Diger was a genuine sexual hunk; the type even the most priggish female discretely drools over. He was old Hollywood's tall, silent type with narrow hips, wide shoulders and strong, well-sculptured, chiseled features unveiling a rugged male hero. He could take care of himself and any woman daring enough to let him. His sparkling dark brown eyes complimented his rakish masculinity, while beneath his appearance was an added irresistible message. He was a romantic—deeply passionate, gently caring and intensely loving. Diger was a true lover, more concerned with sexually satisfying his woman than himself. His movements were cat-like graceful, combined with "dirty dancing" sensual. To women, he was their sexual fantasy.

Straight men saw him very differently. In a word, Diger was a threat. Men knew they couldn't compete against such world-class virility. It wasn't simply his sexuality though. He easily charmed women with his boyish sensitivity, wit and sense of humor. This was a package rare in even the best of pimps. As his *coup de grace*, he had no conscience or taboos. He could sleep with any woman, young, old, married, single or engaged, atheist or nun. No man was his sexual competitor. Like overprotective fathers with their beautiful virgin daughters, men would hide their wives, sweethearts, daughters, sisters, even their neighbors' sisters when Diger was on the prowl.

Derrick, the upper class snob, would have probably welcomed some other snob having a sexual liaison with Helen. Yet, when Helen chose Diger, the chauffeur, it was another matter. Derrick hated both of them because his scrawny little ego was placed in jeopardy. *Other nosey snobs*, he thought, *would delight in gossiping about the low life wife who chose a servant.*

Subconsciously, there were other, perhaps more stabbing reasons Derrick resented Diger. He was socioeconomically beneath Derrick and psychosexually he was infinitely superior. Derrick also felt that if he pushed him too hard, Diger could become dangerous.

Still recovering from the shock of Robinson's sudden death, the detectives decided to set aside the Sutherland case for a while. They also agreed to pursue the information from Derrick. Since yesterday, Diger, a chauffeur, had become the hottest suspect in the Hansen case. Actually, Diger was the only suspect in the Hansen case. Although O'Shea had lingering doubts about Derrick's total innocence, there wasn't much he could do about it. Derrick's friendship with Judge Hall was as solid as his alibis. This meant they were virtually herded into focusing all their professional energy and resources on Diger until he was either eliminated or unequivocally incriminated.

📖 📖 📖

Ironically, as the weeks slipped by since the original Wednesday eight were killed, public pressure had slipped as well. The papers were giving the investigation only an occasional D Section flimsy inch or two. No one really seemed to care much anymore about the dead, including surviving friends, relatives and police.

Winston was, at best, a good riddance to all but his lover, Jason, who was comfortably surviving without him. Sadly, Emil had no wife and fortunately no son to grieve for him. All the tears, laughter and small talk of friends and neighbors during his wake had easily finalized his death. Mercifully, Grace Digness was finally awarded infinite peace, after years of mortal pain and suffering. In contrast, since Andre Likert had no admiring fans or broken hearts, his lavish, well-choreographed funeral was an excessive good-bye.

As for beautiful Dorothy Torres, there was no longer any public outcry. The person that caused her death, and later the death of her children, was also dead. Poor old Carlos Villa had always been in the background, always dependable, hard-working, honest and very forgettable. Another easily forgotten victim was Harry Sutherland. He was a likeable old geezer with no one left who really cared. Then there was Officer Nelson's death. It was rapidly fading, along with the military style police funeral. Black, single, and overly ambitious, there really wasn't much about him that inspired police loyalty or the usual cops' demands for vindication when *one of their own* is murdered.

Both detectives also grimly knew that headstones and wilting flowers were about all that was left of the victims and their forever-silent pleas for justice. Yet even their compassion for some of the victims was gradually fading with mounting pressure from superiors. Captain MacInerny was demanding what the Deputy Chief and Chief were mandating. Solve the damn crimes! The detectives also knew there would be no new cases until some of the eight homicides were solved. This promise from their superiors fit one of their major aggravating hunches—if just one of the cases was solved, they were likely to solve the others.

📖 📖 📖

"Lieutenant? It's Captain MacInerny. How are your eight cases coming along? I hate to rag you, but...you know."

O'Shea knew all right. He knew this was an official Friday morning call from his boss who was trying to say in his own timid way that his superiors were demanding results. "Tell the Chief we've made a lot of progress in eliminating practically all suspects. Tell him we're going by the book and have a lead from Judge Hall and Derrick Hansen we intend to thoroughly explore today. Is that good enough, Mac?"

"That's fine, Jack. Thanks." MacInerny was always almost apologetic when demanding results.

Aware of the caller's identity and message, Ellis didn't bother to look up from the cup of creamy, overly sugared coffee he was stirring.

When O'Shea hung up the phone, he smiled at Ellis. "Right on schedule. We couldn't leave without Mac's pep talk. Christ, why don't you try it black some time?" O'Shea added.

Ellis kept stirring. "I really don't like coffee that much. Besides, I'm black enough," he chuckled.

O'Shea shook his head. "Keep working on it, you might get a sense of humor yet."

Ellis slurped his light tan coffee. "I'm tryin', Loot."

"When do we see Diger, the chauffeur?" O'Shea asked.

Ellis grabbed his notes. "Today, anytime between 10:00 a.m. and noon."

Last night, before leaving the office, Ellis had called Dave McGuire to advise him that Diger was a possible suspect in the murder of Helen Hansen. While one of the richest men in the country, McGuire was neither a snob nor a prude. He listened quietly, made no demands and asked no questions that might compromise the investigation. He had quickly agreed to the Diger interview and volunteered to be available himself for questioning if necessary.

Heading down the corridor toward the elevator that leads to the police parking lot, the detectives were rehearsing their interview plan. Suddenly O'Shea felt flushed, sweaty and droopy jawed. There were huge butterfly wings teasing his stomach lining. Then he saw her. Ida was bending beautifully over the drinking fountain, with full ovaled lips pursed to receive the flowing water. *I can't stand it,* he thought.

Noticing the change in O'Shea, Ellis glanced down the corridor toward the water fountain and immediately understood.

As Ida turned from the fountain, she awarded O'Shea with a flirtatious grin. "Hi, Lieutenant. Where are you going in such a rush?"

To O'Shea, her voice was a sensuous melody, which seemed to paralyze his vocal cords and neck muscles. Rigid and unexpressive, O'Shea scurried by Ida without a word.

Ellis slowed down to attempt some damage control. "Howdy, Ida. We're late for our appointment; and the Loot's got some kind of back spasm."

Slightly perplexed, Ida slowly waved with a weak smile as Ellis walked by.

O'Shea was at the elevator, pounding his fists on the wall. "Shit, shit. I totally blew it. I'm a fucking moron."

Ellis caught up with his boss and grabbed him lightly by the shoulder. "Christ, John, she's still looking. Turn around and give her a wave."

Slowly and reluctantly, O'Shea lifted what felt like a 200-pound right arm.

Ida returned a more energetic wave and disappeared down the corridor.

That's when O'Shea groaned and looked at Ellis. "What the hell am I doing? I feel like I'm back in high school."

"It's worse than that, John. You're acting like you're still in elementary school. You're not just my partner and my boss, I trust you with my life. But I haven't the slightest idea why you fall apart with Ida. I don't even know who to blame."

"Blame me. She's just being nice and I can't handle it."

"How about your psychology pal?"

O'Shea strained a grin. "She's not Wunden's type."

Ellis scowled. "I didn't mean it that way."

"I know, but you're right. I'll have to give Jerry a call." Pensively O'Shea added, "Maybe if we just nailed one of these cases—nah, that's not it."

The elevator door finally opened. "Do you want me to drive, Loot?"

"No, I'll drive. At least I can handle that without folding."

CHAPTER 16

Calling McGuire's place a house was like calling the Taj Mahal a studio apartment. There wasn't the slightest evidence of a house within the McGuire's residence, including the servants' quarters. Even estate missed the mark. It had the awesome splendor and elegance of the finest of palaces. Attempting an entrance was like breeching the wall of China. More imposing than any border crossing were the two gilded black metal gates, hinged on either side by towering marble monoliths. Guarding the entrance were crouching black, winged gargoyles atop the marble columns. Their fiery red eyes were ready to scorch any intruder's glance. There were other prying electronic eyes perched everywhere from turrets, all with a bold clear message—we already know you're here.

A bit stunned by the fortress effect, the detectives stopped about ten feet from the gate. O'Shea looked at his partner. "Christ, it's the Berlin wall in drag."

Ellis was still wide-eyed and scanning. "I can't seem to see the top of the gate from the car. Where's the doorbell?"

📖 📖 📖

As the two detectives awaited some acknowledgement of their arrival, they were suddenly enveloped in a high-pitched wailing sound. Then a crisp, unearthly electronic voice whirled its searing message. "Do you have an appointment?"

Searching the gates and wall for some life form, O'Shea finally answered the wall with unusual formality. "This is Lieutenant O'Shea and Sergeant Ellis of the San Francisco Police Department to see Mr. McGuire."

Within seconds the car began to vibrate to the motion of the huge gates rumbling to opposite sides of a driveway that looked more like a highway. Then more sonorous words of Biblical authority. "Please follow the yellow line to the front entrance. Park at the red marker."

O'Shea quickly complied, feeling a bit intimidated and concerned the gates might close, crushing their car at any moment. Following the yellow line, O'Shea mumbled a thought to his partner. "Christ, we're in Oz."

Ellis didn't reply. He was in his speechless, gawking mode.

It was about a two-minute ride to the red sign, with the order, STOP HERE.

Standing by the sign was a pot-bellied, white haired, rosy-cheeked jolly looking old man who could have been the gardener or a stand-in Santa Claus. He was wearing black Frisco jeans, yellow suspenders, a torn gray flannel shirt and old work boots. This was billionaire Dave McGuire. Stripped of all the symbols of power and wealth, McGuire seemed like just a roly-poly, down-home nice little guy.

"Hi, fellas," he shouted, with a broad smile and unabashed wave. "There's a few fixin's for you in the dining room. A little lunch before work will do you good."

Both detectives smiled at McGuire as O'Shea whispered to Ellis, "Look at him, he's the real Wizard of Oz, the guy behind the curtain."

Still in awe, Ellis could only manage a quick, wide-eyed nod.

Following brief introductions and hearty handshakes, McGuire led Ellis and O'Shea through the massive entrance, past a sculptured fountain, an Olympic size swimming pool and even a small gas station adjoining a garage, with a couple of pickup trucks and five expensive vintage or race type cars. Fascinated by the vehicles, Ellis had to stop for a moment.

Finally, they reached the main building. The eleven-foot high twin solid oak portals seemed thick enough to resist any Roman battering ram, while the vestibule, beneath a crystal chandelier of showering lights, was virtually walled with countless original paintings. To the detectives, this mammoth foyer could have been the Louvre. Tripping along the inlaid floors, Ellis whispered to his partner a delayed observation of his own, "Maybe this is Oz."

After a walk of about a half block, they entered the dining room, where a tall, formally clad, distinguished looking man with white gloves and black tuxedo stood erect and silent. As the waiter smoothly drew the chairs under McGuire and the detectives, Ellis gazed down the long mahogany table. *What a bowling alley,* he thought.

O'Shea was thinking about this seemingly unpretentious, simple man who has economically influenced much of the world. He was also thinking about the dining room table. *Christ, it could be one hell of a shuffleboard.*

Those "few fixin's" McGuire had mentioned were beyond their wildest fantasies. At their end of the table was an astonishing assortment of imported hors d'oevres, such as caviar, oysters, anchovies, marinated vegetables and powerfully seasoned escargot, masking the slightest hint of "snail". Thinking it was their entire lunch, the detectives happily stuffed themselves without identifying most of the appetizers. McGuire just nibbled, watched and smiled.

Then came the first course they naively thought was their last. This was a seafood salad with mounds of crab, shrimp and lobster flown in from Maine. Along with a staggering array of the usual salad garnishes were imported Spanish palmettos, German artichoke hearts, Italian olives, French truffles and a variety of exotic salad dressings.

Restuffing themselves, the detectives were about to burst when served additional courses including minestrone soup and fettuccini alfredo. Despite their polite demurs, the food kept coming, they kept eating and McGuire kept smiling. There was even a menu of entrees they never expected. The choices demolished what was left of their resistance. O'Shea devoured a filet mignon; Ellis munched down the Mahi Mahi and McGuire's smile broadened.

The finale was the dessert announced formally by the austere, distinguished looking waiter. "The Baked Alaska will be ready in two minutes."

Downing his last morsel of filet, O'Shea whispered to Ellis. "What's a Baked Alaska?"

"Don't know," Ellis murmured. "Maybe it's some kind of crushed ice and fish."

Were they surprised! Both detectives ravaged the richly delicate dessert. Speechless, they had also almost forgotten why they were there.

McGuire cordially reminded them.

📖 📖 📖

"Matt Diger returned about a half hour ago from running a few errands. He's available whenever you want to question him. I also have a written record of all his work-related activities during the past several months, if that'll help you in your investigation."

Leaning over his full stomach and empty dessert plate, O'Shea reached for McGuire's records with a muffled burp. "That was a real fine meal, Mr. McGuire. I ate more than I should, but what the hell."

Ellis nodded with a grin as he polished off his last mouthful of Baked Alaska. "Me too, Mr. McGuire. Do you happen to have the recipe for that great dessert?"

McGuire laughed. "My chef will be happy to give you one, that is, if you really want to know the calories involved."

Idly scanning the work record as he listened to McGuire, O'Shea's attention peaked with the Wednesday, April 8th entry. Matt Diger had arrived home at 8 p.m. The April 7th entry further indicated the chauffeur had taken the 10 a.m. United Airlines flight to Seattle, Washington, where he delivered and received urgent confidential documents from corporate CEO's. He had also escorted McGuire's five-year-old niece back to San Francisco to stay with her uncle for a few days.

After several more cups of coffee, a few muffled burps, profuse "thank yous" and assurances that an interview with McGuire was unnecessary, the detectives were taken to the library where Matt Diger was waiting. As they followed the butler toward the library, O'Shea unleashed a belch that echoed down the corridor. Red-faced, he subtly gave Ellis one of his sheepish grins. "Well, if it all checks out, Diger's off the hook. He wasn't even in San Francisco when Helen was snuffed."

"I'm not really surprised," said Ellis, trying to ignore the belch. "But since we're here, we might as well get another view of Derrick, Helen and their relationship."

This time, O'Shea managed a more subdued burp. "I agree, let's pump this guy."

As the butler opened the massive library door, Diger was relaxing on a beautiful tapestry couch, reading a handsomely bound copy of H. Rider Haggard's, *Allen Quartermaine*. After casually bookmarking his page, he slowly arose from the couch, placed the book on a shelf and strolled matter-of-factly toward the detectives.

"I'm Matt Diger. I understand you want to see me."

O'Shea nudged Ellis with a quick, wry, knowing wink. Here was a 21st Century Adonis who knew he was an Adonis, who disliked authority and also knew he was innocent, well-alibied and could have some fun toying with these two detectives for a while.

Neither O'Shea nor Ellis was willing to play such a game. For one thing, they were too full. "Hello, Mr. Diger, I'm Lieutenant O'Shea and this is Sergeant Ellis. Please relax. We know you didn't push Mrs. Hansen off the cliff."

Along with a furrowing brow, Diger's eyes narrowed. He was bright and perceptive enough to realize toying with these guys wouldn't work after all.

It was Ellis' turn to further deflate Diger's ploy. "We really don't mean to embarrass you, Mr. Diger, but this note was discovered in Mrs. Hansen's purse a few days after her death." Ellis handed Diger the note, which changed the entire interview process.

After reading the note several times, Diger's comments and demeanor stunned both detectives.

Diger's message began with glistening eyes and an unmistakable tear. "Helen was the only woman I ever really loved, and I'm sure she loved me. At first it was the predator/prey thing. I figured she was very attractive, lonely and vulnerable. I was the big stud ready to pounce on an easy score. But she was so open, straightforward and principled, she actually shamed me out of seducing her. Without trying, she showed me that she was real and genuine; and I was a fraud, a goddamn fake. Just about all my life I was convinced my manhood was connected to my fists and my dick. Later, we had sex because it was the natural thing for two healthy people, not because I hustled her. I learned it was never necessary to impress her, other than with honesty. We leveled with each other about our past and present lives. I learned from her about loyalty and true friendship.

"You know, I would have been content for the rest of my life being her friend and lover, but then she was dead and I was numb. I still am, except for Derrick. That rotten son of a bitch. He was the worst kind of womanizer. He liked them real young, including streetwalkers. He even cheated on Carol, his mistress. You probably didn't know the bastard gave Helen the clap and more recently syphilis. I still haven't talked myself out of wasting that worthless piece of shit."

O'Shea cleared his throat as if apologizing for the interruption.

"Everything we're learning from you and your work records should contradict such a note from Helen."

Diger stared directly into O'Shea's eyes, with a deliberate, almost sinister grin. "Come on, Detective, you're no dummy, you know who wrote the note. In fact, I bet Derrick gave it to you to set me up."

Although O'Shea agreed, he knew better than to openly support Diger's hunches; which might be all he needed to kill Derrick. "If all you say is true, Derrick isn't worth going back to prison for."

Ellis, taking notes, looked up and nodded to Diger.

As Diger clenched all the blood from his fists, his knuckles turned white. "I know the fucker killed her, because he was afraid to take me on, that chicken shit bastard."

Ellis dropped his pen and looked at Diger sympathetically. "He was our primary suspect and, believe me, we checked him and Carol Evermore thoroughly before concluding they couldn't have pushed her."

"Then he must have hired somebody," countered Diger.

"Got any ideas?" O'Shea asked. "Anyone hanging around the Hansen house in recent months, unfamiliar cars or did Helen ever mention anything or anyone unusual?"

Diger's clenched jaw was twitching. "Helen told me Derrick resented her caring for a lowly chauffeur. He hinted there were prominent professionals around who were ready to service her. That's when she got a call at her front door from a Tim Buchholtz, one of Derrick's high roller attorney friends. When Helen told him Derrick wasn't there, the guy asked her if he could come in for coffee. The asshole knew fuckin' well Derrick wasn't home; and she politely told him to get lost."

Ellis again looked up from his notes. "We'll definitely check this Tim guy out. Anything else that may help us and you?"

Diger was calming down a bit. "Some old guy with a dog has been slinking around with the guilts about something. He even called on Helen once."

Ellis had to smile. "Yeah, I think I met the guy."

"There was also the P.G.& E. guy. She said he hit on her and left a little pissed. That was about a week before she…passed."

"He was another dead end," commented O'Shea. "We checked anyone known to have been at her house before she…ah, passed."

Diger offered O'Shea a barely discernable smile. "There was also some buff looking kid, sixteen or seventeen years old, a tall blond

Aryan. We saw him a few times. He was always bouncing a ball and flirting with Helen. Kind of the neighborhood adolescent jerk."

"Yeah, I know." Ellis grinned.

After less than an hour, the detectives were satisfied Diger had been straightforward in telling them all he knew. He kind of reminded them of a young Robinson, yet more psychopathic and certainly more prone to murder. In fact, O'Shea was actually surprised that Diger hadn't already killed or at least confronted Derrick.

On their way out, a brief good-bye to McGuire provided some of the further answers about Diger. McGuire was grateful and relieved to learn that Diger was cooperative and no longer a suspect. He also explained to the detectives that, despite Diger's shaky background, they had developed a strong, trusting relationship. McGuire was confidant Diger would do nothing to disgrace him.

The rest of Friday was spent in their homicide department cubicle re-examining the alibis and activities of the Hansen murder suspects. Ellis learned that the day Helen died, Tim Buchholtz was in Jamaica on one of his many "business" trips with Cassie, his secretary. So much for a Buchholtz possibility.

At 5:30 p.m., O'Shea furtively looked down the hall, scanning the water cooler. Stretching his arms over his head, he heaved a loud yawn. "Do me a favor, Paul, go home to your family and forget the eight until Monday. I promise, I'm out of here after a little more paperwork."

Ellis closed the Hansen file and, without a protest, grabbed his coat. "Take care, boss."

"Yeah," O'Shea replied, continuing to scan the water cooler.

CHAPTER 17

The occasional Saturday drive to Santa Cruz had been a special clandestine treat for Derrick and Carol when Helen was alive. Just a few weeks after her death, the drive south became their regular weekend playtime. A Friday dinner downtown at Aqua was the sumptuous prelude to their Santa Cruz weekend. After dinner, they spent the rest of the night at Derrick's Sea Cliff house.

As a part of the Friday night menu, this was their time for a wild, vicarious sex orgy. Although Derrick could never entice Carol into group or even threesome sex, he did manage a workable compromise. Watching one of his huge supply of pornographic movies, they'd join in mimicking the on-screen sexual antics. This lasted until Derrick was satisfied, which rarely took over ten minutes. Unfortunately for Carol, she rarely climaxed before Derrick lost interest and fell asleep. Carol knew better than to complain to Derrick, so she routinely masturbated herself into an orgasm. Then she'd turn off the X-rated movie, watch the TV news and eventually fall asleep, despite Derrick's abrasive snores.

On this special Saturday morning, Carol and Derrick awakened to a red, shimmering sun that promised a clear, fogless drive along the coast on Highway One. This gleefully encouraged Derrick to take his prized Mercedes 500 SL convertible, the car he had justified buying as a gift for Helen the week before her death. Eager to begin their Saturday trek, they had a quick shower and light breakfast of orange juice, coffee and toast. They were looking forward to their two-hour drive, brunch at the Crow's Nest in Santa Cruz and a relaxing afternoon sunbathing on the deck of Derrick's thirty-six-foot Islander sloop moored at the nearby harbor.

Derrick wasn't much of a sailor. In fact, he had never hoisted a sail; and motoring out of the breakwater for a couple of hundred yards was actually his only real sailing experience. He was, however, a consummate phony who tried to impress his colleagues and clients with stories of his offshore adventures.

"Come on, Sweets," he cheerfully shouted, putting their luggage in the Mercedes trunk. Derrick felt like the sharpest of weekend mariners, with his gold-buttoned blue blazer, scrambled egg visor sailor cap, red silk ascot tucked into his tan silk shirt, white slacks and, of course, deck shoes. Yet, to real sailors in Santa Cruz, Derrick was just another rich jerk.

"One minute," chirped Carol, staring adoringly at the full-length bedroom mirror. To men, she was an undisputed knockout and she made the most of it, with carefully chosen scanty clothes that highlighted the best of her anatomy. This couple was the perfect match—utterly superficial, greedy, self-indulgent and preoccupied with appearance. Even their relationship was an ideal symbiosis. Derrick needed displays, like Carol and his boat, to bolster his shallow identity. Carol needed to associate with men like Derrick, who had money and status. She had learned early in life that her body, as sexual currency, was the talent that clearly overshadowed her meager intelligence—at least to bright, shallow men like Derrick.

Sashaying down the stairs, Carol's graceful undulations were strikingly sensual. *Wowee, she could have been a six-figure model,* Derrick thought, as he waited by the open front door.

Carol watched Derrick's searching eyes and smiled a quiet thought of her own. *Maybe I can't talk too good, but men don't care about that.*

When she reached the door, Derrick leaned forward and stroked her firm inner thighs. "You'll have every guy in Santa Cruz envying me and drooling over you."

Puckering her lips, she smiled coyly. "I know."

As they walked toward the Mercedes parked in the driveway, Carol stopped and looked at Derrick with a fading smile.

"What's the matter?" Derrick asked.

"Is there anything else I should know about Helen's death?"

This time Derrick leaned forward and firmly cupped her face in his hands. "Listen carefully, Sweets. There's really nothing to worry about. We're really in the clear. There's no problem, Sweet Buns."

Carol cuddled close to Derrick as he started the throaty engine and lowered the top. Pulling out of the driveway, Derrick gave Carol a knee pat of reassurance. "Don't worry, it couldn't be better—really."

From Sea Cliff, it was a short drive to Ocean Beach and the Great Highway, where they could avoid most of the weekend city traffic. Reassured and relaxed, Carol was teasing Derrick with her usual station-changing game. Derrick always tuned the car radio to a classical station, and Carol, with a devilish grin, promptly switched to '50's rock and roll. Derrick invariably gave in after his fourth switch, even though he couldn't stand rock and roll. *Anyway,* he thought, *it's a beautiful day, a fine ocean view and a great car. Thanks Helen,* he laughed to himself.

By 10:00 a.m. they were passing through Pacifica and Carol was happily humming out of tune to an old Elvis hit song. Approaching the forested half-mile grade south of Pacifica, traffic was unusually light. That didn't matter to Derrick. Rarely reaching the speed limit, he was a neurotically cautious driver. Checking his rearview mirror, he carefully pulled to the slow lane so any cars coming up behind him could pass safely before the highway narrowed to the two-lane grade. He knew that the next chance to pass was in Montara, another ten miles.

Reaching the top of the grade, the spectacular, rugged coastline burst into view. Derrick was always fascinated with this panorama of the Pacific Ocean. He was also experiencing his usual discomfort. He knew Highway One was narrow and treacherous for the next few miles, especially where it passed Devil's Slide, with its one hundred fifty-foot sheer drop to the ocean. Driving this narrow stretch of road slowly and cautiously was the main reason he let the faster vehicles pass him before the grade. Otherwise, Derrick was always nervous if someone followed him too closely.

Nearing Devil's Slide, Derrick was managing to contentedly enjoy the view, when he noticed the huge tires of an older black three-quarter-ton Dodge Ram pickup a few feet from his rear bumper. "Oh no." He gulped.

Carol was humming along with the rock music when she felt the sharp jolt. The truck had gently rammed the Mercedes trunk lid. "My God, it's pushing us," she cried.

Derrick frantically stood on the brake pedal, Carol screamed and the Mercedes was eased through the guardrail for an exceptional aerial view of Devil's Slide. During the one hundred fifty-foot ride down to the rocky coastline, Carol continued to scream, Derrick desperately clutched the steering wheel and the music blared, *"You ain't nothin' but a hound dog"*.

CHAPTER 18

Driving to the Java House, O'Shea was experiencing one of his increasingly rare good moods. Despite his nagging frustration with the unsolved *stale eight*, he had really enjoyed spending Saturday with his daughters in Sacramento. This was his first weekend in months away from his police cubicle on Bryant Street. Even the acrid after-taste of those cases dissolved with his daughters' delicious dinner and their show of affection.

Both were married and living in the Sacramento area for several years. June and Jenny missed their father, who had generously supported them through college graduation and law school. He had happily given them elaborate weddings and exerted some of his limited influence in helping them obtain much sought-after positions in the State judicial system. During his marriage, O'Shea had been an excellent provider, marginal husband and lousy father. *Oh well*, he debated with himself, *the girls still love me, the boys rely on me when they need to be rescued and the wife grew out of me into an independent woman. Guess it's not too bad for a part-time drunk with more interest in being a cop than a husband and parent.*

It had been a pleasant, reflective Sunday morning drive from Sacramento and O'Shea was now looking forward to seeing Phil Papadopoulos, the Java House owner, and his friend, Jerry Wunden. The South Shore parking lot was filled when he arrived at 10:45. *Hell, it's yuppie day at Phil's*, he thought. Tossing one of his police business cards on the dash, O'Shea parked in the *No Parking* zone directly in front of the Java House. *I don't do this very often*, he reasoned.

Through the Java House crowd O'Shea easily found the big, handlebar mustache, followed by a broad grinning Papadopoulos motioning to him. "I saw you park, you picked a bad day for bullshit. I have a whole crowd of bullshitters here."

O'Shea gave him a firm, Greek-style hug. "Do you have a table for an old friend?"

Papadopoulos pointed to a small table buried near a stack of boxes at the rear of the restaurant. "That's my personal table. It's yours."

O'Shea shook his head. "You know, Phil, you're full of more bullshit than most of your customers." He grinned. "How 'bout the usual grease and coffee. And if you see Dr. Wunden, show him where I'm hidden there behind the boxes."

Scanning the crowd, Papadopoulos dropped his grin. "You should stay away on Sundays, too much bullshit here. If I can find a better table, I'll give it to you."

"Don't sweat it, Phil, that rear table will do fine." Walking back to the table, O'Shea grabbed part of a Sunday paper left on the counter. He had barely sat down when he saw his friend, Wunden, weaving through the crowded tables toward him. O'Shea was glad to see his friend, whom he had called while in Sacramento. He had conceded, after talking to Ellis, that he needed advice about Ida and his irrationally shy, awkward inability to relate to attractive women.

O'Shea leaped up offering a long, firm handshake. "Great to see ya, Jerry, grab a box and sit."

Wunden stood for a moment looking around. "If this table were any further back, we'd be outside."

O'Shea laughed. "As Phil said, this is a bad day for regulars. Anyway, I'm buying, so have a big breakfast."

"Just coffee for me, John. I already ate, but I'll watch you scarf the grease. Now, what's up?"

Even with his good friend, O'Shea felt a bit awkward trying to explain his problem with women in general and with Ida in particular. After twenty minutes of hesitant explanation, between gulps of coffee and mouthfuls of breakfast, O'Shea finally dropped his gaze to the table and silently sat, idly fiddling with his napkin.

"Jesus, John, you look like a kid waiting for the teacher to grade his paper."

Red-faced, O'Shea looked up with a strained smile, "Other than Ellis, my partner, no one knows just how fucked up I am with women.

You know, your advice is really important to me. I trust ya, pal."

Muffling a gaping yawn with his left hand over his mouth, Wunden poured some coffee from the pitcher Papadopoulos had left on the table.

"Am I keeping you up?" O'Shea snickered.

Wunden returned the snicker. "Come on! You know me, John; I don't know why the hell I stifled that one. I could have sucked all of the air out of the Java House." Stretching his arms over his head, Wunden smiled at the ceiling. "I love to yawn. I've been yawning my whole life."

"Alright, Jerry, I get the message. Now what do ya think?"

"I'm going to give you a hundred dollars of professional advice free, as your friend. You can take notes if you want. First of all, when it comes to women, you're not an invalid, retarded or mentally incompetent. You're just an asshole, a real jerk. Ever since I've known you, which takes us back to high school, you've had a double standard for treating males and females. Interacting with men, you've always been super tough, bright and fair. With women, like your ex-wife, Mary, you've expected them to serve you, and if they're the independent, bright, emancipated type you find attractive, you just cave in and avoid them. You never really learned how to deal with attractive, self-assertive women. How many bright, pretty, independent women have you had a relationship with since your divorce?"

O'Shea shrugged. "None. So what do I do?"

"The very thing you've avoided doing—practice, practice, practice. The problem is you don't want them to know you're shy, inexperienced and awkward around them, which is the first thing you should tell them. Once they know, you've eliminated all pressure, there's nothing to hide. So my hundred-dollar advice is to immediately tell Ida that she should know you're too damn shy and clumsy with any woman you find attractive, and you find her attractive. That's it, Pal. No magic pill, no cookbook recipe, just the courage to try something new, and faith in your buddy's advice."

O'Shea was fiddling with his napkin again. "Thanks, Jerry. I'll think about it."

"You guys talk too much." Papadopoulos was standing over their table with another pot of coffee.

Wunden looked up with a facetious sneer. "You know, Phil, we may talk too much, but you bullshit too much."

O'Shea put his hand over his cup, blocking more coffee. "We've been keeping an eye on you, Phil. You wiggle your mustache, flash the little honeys a toothy smile and join in on their little yuppie conversations. I ought to arrest you for excessive bullshit."

"Yeah," added Wunden, "next thing you'll be agreeing with these yuppies that we've never really been gouged by oil companies and that George W. actually got the popular vote."

But Papadopoulos always managed to get the last word. "Bullshit." He grinned as he walked to a nearby table covered with bicycle helmets, gloves and bottled water galore. "Are you skin divers or space people? No coffee for you." He pulled his pot away and all six of the thirty-somethings laughed.

O'Shea shook his head. "Boy, what a world class bullshitter."

"He's the best," countered Wunden as he slowly rose from his chair. "I gotta go, John, I'm going sailing out of Sausalito. Wanna come?"

"No thanks, Jerry. I think I'll just relax here and read the Sunday paper for awhile." O'Shea got up and gave Wunden a long crushing hug. "Thanks again, my friend. I didn't take notes, but I'll really think about your advice."

As Wunden headed for the door, he shouted a good-bye to Papadopoulos, who was deep in talk at a table of young girls. Glancing back at O'Shea, Wunden smiled, pointed at Papadopoulos and mouthed the words, *more bullshit.*

Settling back in his chair between the boxes, O'Shea started sorting through the partial Sunday paper he'd snatched from the counter. One passive, casual perusal of the front-page news section and his relaxing weekend was over. In the lower right hand corner, the heading of a small article abruptly demolished his good mood.

DEVIL'S SLIDE KILLS PROMINENT ATTORNEY

A shot of adrenaline surged through his body as he began reading the article.

"Derrick Hansen was killed instantly when his Mercedes convertible careened off Devil's Slide to the rocks 150 feet below. His death has an ironic and eerie similarity to the death of his wife, Helen, several weeks ago when she fell off a steep cliff near their coastal home in San Francisco. Several witnesses to the Hansen crash believe his car might have been pushed over the side. This underscores the mystery

surrounding these two deaths. In both tragedies, homicide, suicide or accidents are still to be established by the police. Carol Evermore, Mr. Hansen's legal secretary, was also killed."

At that moment, anyone idly looking at O'Shea would have probably run for it. With gnashing teeth, twitching jaw and fiery eyes, he read the article several times. He never liked anything about Derrick, yet he liked the implications of Derrick's death even less. His mind was flooded with ugly possibilities. *Are these two more deaths in some way associated with the eight cases? If the car had been pushed off the cliff, did Diger have something to do with the deaths? If so, did Diger know more than he had admitted? Is McGuire involved? Did Derrick somehow kill Helen? Were we conned by all these people? How's Judge Hall going to react to all this? Does any of this fit the evil aura permeating the eight murders? Or, are these deaths just a rotten coincidence?*

📖 📖 📖

Just ten minutes after reading the article, O'Shea was bounding down the corridor toward his cubicle. Leaving the Java House, the drive to the office had been a blur. Then he remembered, *Aw shit! I forgot to pay Phil.* Nearing his desk, O'Shea saw Ellis bent over his own desk, with phone in one hand and pen in the other, scribbling notes.

"OK, fine, keep us informed and we'll do the same. Thanks." Ellis hung up and noticed O'Shea looking at him bewildered. "Hi, Boss, I read the paper too, you know. I tried to call you about five times then figured you'd get here sooner or later."

O'Shea slumped in his swivel chair with a deep sign. "And I thought I wouldn't bother you until tomorrow. How long have you been here?"

"Oh, a couple of hours and a bunch of phone calls. You OK, John?"

O'Shea sat upright with a grin. "I'm fine. It's just, well this case is so goddamned convoluted, I never know what to expect next. So what do we have beyond the newspaper article?"

Ellis rearranged the pile of papers on his desk. "A couple of sightseers, sitting on a hill above Highway 1 and across from Devil's Slide, saw two versions of the whole crash. It was about 10:10 a.m. They ran to their parked car and called 911 from their cell phone. The

CHP, Pacifica P.D. and the Pacifica Rescue team arrived within five minutes."

"You said two versions?" O'Shea asked impatiently.

"Hold on, Loot, I'll give you all of it."

O'Shea nodded.

"Anyway, the witnesses are in their twenties. They're both students at San Francisco State University. Their parents are rich and the kids have no records. The guy, Fred Wechsler, is a psych major with honors. The gal, Wanda Kepler, is a grad student in sociology, as well as a teaching assistant."

Pausing for a moment, Ellis grinned at O'Shea. "Now for their observations. According to Wechsler, he was enjoying the ocean view, when he inadvertently noticed a bright red convertible moving pretty fast near a sharp turn in the road by Devil's Slide. Close behind the convertible was a darker car or truck. In the convertible, the passenger, probably a woman, and the male driver seemed to be arguing or shouting at each other. They never made the turn. The car shot through the guardrail and began a surrealistic, silent forward roll through the air before disappearing from view. He added it was like an avant-garde silent movie. He never heard the crash. The car just disappeared below the shattered guardrail. Wechsler had further explained he didn't know or remember what happened to the dark vehicle, except that it didn't stop.

"Kepler, on the other hand, was much more observant. She was sitting almost shoulder-to-shoulder with Wechsler, so their vantage points were the same. She was gazing at the panoramic view of the Pacific coast when she heard a screech or scream. Looking down, she saw a bright red convertible with a young blond girl in the passenger's seat and an older man driving. The driver was looking back, where a black Dodge or Chevy pickup was so close, it seemed to be connected to the rear of the convertible. Then the car hit the guardrail and literally flew up in the air and down out of sight. The black pickup accelerated by and disappeared around the turn. She further told police that the black pickup looked old, had big wheels and some sort of a snakelike green object on top of a long antenna she thought was white. Her conclusion was that the convertible was pushed off the road by the pickup.

"Less specifically, Wechsler concluded that the dark vehicle might have been following too closely, made the convertible driver a bit nervous and when he sped up, arguing with the lady passenger, he must have lost control. His vague description of the dark vehicle was that it was big, could have been a pickup, it had big tires, it wasn't new and yes, there was a green thing on the top of some kind of antenna. Neither noticed the license plates of the vehicle."

Ellis grabbed another paper full of notes off the desk. "While the rescue team was climbing down the cliff, the Highway Patrol and Pacifica P.D. interviewed the two, meaning the witnesses' recall was only five or ten minutes after the event. Interviewed separately by the CHP and PPD, the witnesses were considered bright, calm and perceptive, with no evidence of alcohol or drugs. There were also no other witnesses to the event. Any questions about the two versions, Boss?"

Leaning back in his chair, O'Shea slowly shook his head. "I'll try not to ever interrupt you again."

"Don't ever say 'ever', John."

O'Shea threw up his hands, as if surrendering.

"Shall I go on?" asked Ellis.

"It's all yours."

"The police and rescue team were also pretty thorough. Both police agencies concur that the Mercedes went through the guardrail at twenty-five miles an hour and that all four wheels were locked as evidenced by the forty-foot skid marks. There was also about a twenty-foot intermittent, overlapping set of marks of a wider rubber pattern that could suggest a vehicle was pushing the Mercedes from behind. This is a bit speculative, since the rescue team and several other trucks might have skidded along the original skid marks, before the area was blocked off. There is, however, more support for a rear end push. Normally, when cars brake hard, the weight distribution is shifted about 70% to the front wheels. That's why rear brakes last at least three or four times longer than front ones. Anyhow, the Mercedes front and rear skid marks were fairly even. Now for the rescue team's report. It's pretty gory."

"If I raise my hand, can I ask a question?"

"Sure, but just one."

"Did they find any debris on the highway around the skid marks, like broken tail lights or wheel panel dirt. Stuff like that?"

Ellis acknowledged with thumbs up. "In fact, I had asked the same questions, figuring a rear end push might have knocked out tail lights or caused other rear end damage. They found nothing, and the car was so new, there was probably no wheel-well dirt. In any event, they're checking the Mercedes for a rear end push. But that'll be a slow process, since the car was literally smashed to pieces. They collected everything they could find and hauled it into a Pacifica garage. CHP and PPD said they'd call and send their report when finished. One of the rescue workers mentioned that Devil's Slide cliff is just about vertical, which means the Mercedes was airborne all the way down."

O'Shea shook his head. "Christ, it must have been like a plane crash."

"Exactly, the Mercedes nosed over, hit a huge boulder on the shoreline and upside down it practically exploded into pieces. Hansen's head and torso were smashed into his belt area, while Evermore lost her head and both arms by impacting with the windshield frame. They were both I.D.'d by fingerprints, driver's licenses, credit cards and other documents scattered all over. There's no evidence of alcohol or drug use either. That's about all I have for now."

"Jesus Christ, just one more question. How the hell did you get all the information in just a couple of hours?"

"Well, I didn't drive to Pacifica. In fact, I haven't been on Highway 1 near Pacifica or Devil's Slide in years. Besides, you can't beat the telephone and friends. There was also some luck involved. Each person I needed to talk to was available and an old friend of mine is a paramedic, mountain climber, who just happens to work weekends at Pacifica Rescue. When I found out both witnesses were San Francisco State students, I called another friend who is now an assistant dean of student affairs. He helped me verify the credibility of the witnesses. You see, Boss, I also know a few people."

Picking up his phone, O'Shea nodded. "Hell, I should have stayed at the Java House and finished reading my paper."

"I bet you didn't buy it."

O'Shea's face reddened a bit as he rolled his eyes. "OK, here's one for ya. I bet you didn't call McGuire or Diger yet."

Ellis did his own eye rolling and straightened the notes on his desk. "Gee, how'd ya guess? Maybe because I was just too busy with all the preliminary stuff that should've taken all day. By the way, who are you phoning?"

O'Shea looked at the receiver like it didn't belong in his hand. "Oh yeah, who the hell am I calling? Let's talk to Diger before the alibis are well rehearsed. What's his number?"

CHAPTER 19

"Well, hi there, Lieutenant O'Shea. I had a sneaking hunch you'd call. In fact, I thought you might call last night."

Momentarily jolted by McGuire's candid offensive, O'Shea paused for a second before a quick recovery. "We just read about the death of Mr. Hansen a few hours ago and wanted to gather as much information as possible before calling Mr. Diger."

McGuire still managed a cheerful tone. "So, you're assuming it's a homicide."

"We really don't know yet, but the evidence indicates it's very possible."

McGuire's voice hardened. "Well, my reliable sources say causes of the crash are very equivocal, numerous possibilities. In any event, why don't you and Sergeant Ellis drop by for a little brunch and a good chat?"

"That's fine, Mr. McGuire, we'll be there in an hour. And I hope you can round up Diger for another good chat as well."

After a brief pause, McGuire replied crisply, "I'll be looking forward to seeing you and I'll explain about Matt as we eat." Click.

Oh shit, O'Shea thought, *it's hardball time.*

"What's up?" asked Ellis.

O'Shea slowly got up from his chair, wearing a broad, wry smile. "You hungry? We're off to McGuire's fortress. We're not going to get much but slick alibis and some great food."

Ellis grinned. "Sounds worth the ride."

Once again the towering gates, menacing gargoyles, electronic eyes, yellow lines and commanding voices were an intimidating reception. O'Shea grinned at Ellis as they drove through the gates. "The meal will be worth it."

Looking around, Ellis nodded.

At the end of the yellow line, one of the many butlers stood by the *Stop Here* sign. O'Shea nudged Ellis. "No McGuire this time. I guess the gracious, 'aw shucks' host ploy is over."

Ellis was again awed by the statues. "Yes, but I hope the 'aw shucks' great food isn't over."

Following the butler by the service station, Ellis suddenly stopped. "Can you wait for a minute?" he called to the fast moving butler.

"What are you onto?" asked O'Shea.

"Remember those trucks and expensive cars parked in that huge garage? Well, all the doors are closed now, but I clearly remember that one of the trucks was an older black pickup."

"You really don't miss a thing, do you? We'll ask McGuire if we can take a look at his cars."

Ellis motioned the butler to go on. "You know, Loot, how much you wanna bet the pickup's gone? I'm sure it's the same one, because I remember the saguaro man, all green, hanging on top of the long antenna. It was an older truck, kind of out of place with all those new or restored vehicles in the garage. And it had those oversized tires I hate. I'm just about sure I remember thinking it was an older Dodge Ram. Remember, our witness, Kepler's first choice was a Dodge."

O'Shea slowed his pace and looked at Ellis. "What the hell's a saguaro man?"

"When we vacationed in Arizona a couple of years ago, they were in all the gift shops. A little green foam saguaro, you know the national cactus, with the two arms."

"So that's what they call them."

"Yeah, at the top of the metal stem is a cartoon type guy. Now what's the probability of another black pickup with a green thing on top of its antenna?"

O'Shea nodded. "It's pretty low, but certainly possible. The witnesses have two different stories and there's no license number, make or model of the pickup."

"Come on, John," Ellis argued. "At least it's something tangible to confront McGuire and Diger with."

"Absolutely," replied O'Shea as they reached the formidable oak portals to the main house.

Once inside, they were led directly to the dining room, where McGuire was seated, sipping a glass of wine at the foot of the enormous table. McGuire stood up and offered O'Shea and Ellis a noticeably more subdued smile than at their first meeting. "Hi guys, I'm glad you could make it. Come sit down by me."

The entire brunch was rich in patronizing small talk with McGuire, tinged with haughty, snobbish jokes that were full of racial innuendos. The food was equally tasteless and disingenuous. Seated on both sides of McGuire, there was no escape. They were his guests, invited to eat his food and so far, McGuire and the menu were cold and taunting.

The meal began with a small bowl of vichyssoise; a cold soup that both detectives thought needed heating. This was followed by a more liberal serving of raw celery, watercress, broccoli, raw carrots and a few unseasoned escargot that Ellis thought tasted suspiciously like snails or rubber bands. A small scoop of orange sherbet concluded the brunch and McGuire's ramblings. The message, however, was clear; McGuire had no intention of offering further cooperation and could easily outmaneuver the detectives in any investigation.

Donning a grin as cold as the vichyssoise, McGuire gave a sardonic lecture on the epidemic of obesity in the United States, and the necessity of sound dieting for taxpayer supported public servants.

So far there had been no mention of Derrick Hansen's death or Diger's whereabouts. Knowing the gracious "aw shucks" down home routine was over, O'Shea dropped all restraint and shifted to his professional investigation mode. "Thanks for the diet food. Now, is Diger available?"

McGuire had relinquished even a cold grin. "Diger won't be back until sometime tomorrow. I sent him on a business mission to one of my corporate offices in New York yesterday. He left on my Lear jet at 9 a.m. from the San Jose Airport."

"I suppose all of this is verifiable?" O'Shea asked mechanically.

McGuire's reply was not the least bit surprising. "Of course. My pilot and crew will verify his departure and arrival; business associates and hotel clerks will verify his presence in New York."

"How about the flight plan and passenger list?" asked Ellis abruptly, while crunching his last piece of celery.

McGuire quickly turned directly toward Ellis with an impish, narrow-eyed smile. "Why certainly. Everything is covered."

Like a professional chess tournament, O'Shea quickly responded with another move. "Can we meet the Lear jet at the airport when it arrives?"

"Oh, absolutely. I insist." McGuire countered without the slightest hesitancy.

Ellis tried his surprise move. "Can we see your garage?"

"Which one?" McGuire asked with a sneering grin.

"The one we walked by near the sculptures." Ellis answered, now realizing that McGuire most likely had the pick-up covered as well.

"Sure," McGuire said. "Let's go there now."

Arriving at the mammoth garage, one of McGuire's staff opened the seven garage doors simultaneously. From left to right there was a 1998 black Dodge Ram pickup with oversized tires, a red Chevy one-ton pickup with oversized tires, a white 1954 300SL gull-wing Mercedes, a Concourse D'elegance Porsche 911S, a cherry 289 A.C. Cobra and an exquisitely restored XK120 Jaguar convertible. Ellis stared at the treasure of vehicles, then turned to O'Shea and with a deep sigh, to McGuire. "Aren't you missing one, an older black pickup with big wheels, a white antenna with little a green man on top?

McGuire's eyes narrowed to slits. "Do you have the license plate number?"

When Ellis didn't answer, McGuire answered for him. "I suppose that's a 'no'. Then whatcha see is all ya get. If you're referring to a vague description of a phantom truck behind Hansen's car, if it really exists, you won't find it here. I invite you to check with DMV. These are the only pickups I own; and you should know, Diger doesn't own a vehicle."

Silent since they left the main house, O'Shea's head was pounding. *Checkmate*, he thought. *The son of a bitch is going to beat us.* "Thanks for the lunch and your time, Mr. McGuire; and would you tell Mr. Diger to call us when he returns.

Ellis looked at O'Shea searchingly, while McGuire just smiled.

"Nice to see you two again. I'll give Matt your message."

Walking back to the car, Ellis, with head hung low and rounded shoulders, buried his hands in his pockets. "Aw, damn," he muttered.

O'Shea jutted out his jaw, sucked in his stomach and threw back his shoulders. "Hey, Paul," he whispered, looking straight ahead with an erect marching gait, "we're the cops, the authority, remember? We're the good guys. McGuire won a battle, but we'll win the war— maybe, I hope. And stop the goddamn swearing!"

CHAPTER 20

The drive back to the Bryant Street office was a bit solemn, despite O'Shea's pep talk and a brief stop at Jack in the Box for two burgers with fries, to go. Their strategy was clear and certainly necessary—at least the first part. Down the burgers and fries to regain their strength, then verify McGuire's statements. Their first task was quick, tasty and effortless. Not so for the second.

DMV reported having no record of any pickup trucks owned by David McGuire, other than the black 1998 Dodge Ram and the red Chevy one-ton. After examining the black pickup, both detectives were aware that neither of those registered vehicles were suspects.

Although the Dodge pickup fit the general description, including big tires, there weren't any bumper scratches or indications of front-end damage. There was also no evidence that the truck had pushed a red Mercedes 500 SL. Both witnesses had agreed that the truck was older than a 1998 model. McGuire was also registered owner of the 300 SL Gull Wing, 289 Cobra, Porsche 911S, and Jaguar XK120 observed by the detectives while in McGuire's seven-vehicle garage. DMV records further indicated that McGuire owned a beige Rolls Royce convertible, an XKE Jaguar, a 427 Cobra, and a very rare Porsche 907, all stashed somewhere at the same Sea Cliff address. There was no record of any vehicles registered to Matt Diger.

San Jose Air Traffic Control faxed McGuire's Lear Jet flight manifest for the Saturday Derrick Hansen and Carol Evermore died. It included pilot Mark Varnhagen, co-pilot Al Colburn and sole passenger Matt Diger. The destination was New York Kennedy International Airport, enroute to Heathrow International Airport in London, England with return to Kennedy on the following Monday. As expected by the detectives, the New York Hilton Hotel staff and corporate executives verified Diger's arrival that Saturday.

O'Shea sighed through a head-shaking smile. "Christ, he's covered everything."

"Hey, wait a minute," Ellis protested. "McGuire may be the richest guy in the world, but he's not infallible. One of his corporate lackeys, pilots, butlers or whatever is bound to blow McGuire's alibis for Diger under pressure."

Before looking up at Ellis, O'Shea scanned the fax and his notes from their phone calls. "Under what pressure? From us? We're going to re-question or interrogate McGuire's associates, staff, and his whole goddamn army? Then we can launch a campaign against DMV, the San Jose Air Traffic Control and the Hilton Corporation. We should also get a search warrant and go through his estate that's larger than most small towns. We'll check all his garages, guest houses, warehouses, shit houses, sheds for an older black pickup with a green thing dangling from its antenna."

Quietly listening at his desk, Ellis stifled a slight yawn.

"Don't interrupt!"

"Geeze, Boss, I was just yawning. Do you mind if I breathe?"

O'Shea choked back a belly laugh. "Shit, you just blew my great monologue."

Ellis cleared his throat. "Can I have my turn now, OK?"

O'Shea sat back in his swivel chair, hands clasped behind his head. "Sure, but I already know and agree with what you're going to say."

Ellis grimaced. "What are you, a mind reader?"

"Go on," O'Shea replied, rocking back in his chair.

"First, and most important, I actually saw that black three-quarter-ton pickup in McGuire's seven-car garage. I'm pretty sure it was an older, probably late 70's Dodge Ram, and it had a green saguaro man on top of the white antennae. That's a fact."

"Yeah, I know that and I agree."

"Another fact. McGuire deliberately planted a similar black Dodge pickup, figuring we'd assume it was the earlier pickup in his garage, just in case we noticed."

"I already know that and agree," O'Shea repeated.

"Even though the descriptions are vague, the match with the pickup in the garage is too much of a coincidence. It's the same truck."

"I know that, Paul, and again I agree, but so what?"

Ellis glanced around their cubicle with a squinty-eyed frown, as if looking for the person who said that. "So what! We're cops. We've established the murder weapon was on McGuire's property before the crime, and that it's been removed, making Diger our primary. So, it's pretty obvious, we've got to find the pickup."

O'Shea leaned forward offering an empathic nod and soft smile. "You're right again. Now let's go beyond what you, as a good cop, concluded. If McGuire is as rich, sharp and influential as we think he is, the phantom pickup is probably no bigger than a bread basket in some wrecking yard where it sits crushed by one of those compacters. Let's assume the phantom pickup is still a pickup, hidden where we can find it. Isn't it likely the green thing and the front-end damage, if any, are gone? Or, what if McGuire lost his brain and the pickup is easily found intact, including the green thing; and there's even a match of paint on the bumper from the destroyed Mercedes. Who do we arrest? McGuire? Diger? The Butler...or some other staff member who may have fingerprints inside? With no one to identify the driver, no license number, and even a flimsy description of the pickup by the only witnesses, we have no viable case against Diger or McGuire. We also don't have the legions of detectives to find a possible flaw in their alibis. And, you know, Diger just might have been out of town. Any one of a thousand loyal McGuire heavies could have been the driver."

Ellis sat silent and motionless as O'Shea continued.

"There are three other reasons I'm not interested in pursuing the deaths of Hansen and Evermore. For one thing, they're not really our assigned cases, and you know damn well McInerney's going to call telling us to back off because of McGuire's power and no substantial evidence. My instincts also tell me these probable murders have nothing to do with our eight; and finally, I thought Derrick was a fucking asshole."

Ellis gave one more try. "What about Evermore and Judge Hall?"

O'Shea looked pensively at the ceiling. "Trust you to ask the hard ones. Poor, pretty Carol, she was road kill, just along for a free ride that cost her the rest of her life. She was one of those millions of victims who die of poor judgment, of life's endless hazards, of innocence or stupidity, or just grabbing a ride with a Mr. Trouble. You hang around shit long enough and you begin to smell like it."

"Wow, John, you should have been a philosopher. You really feel for that girl."

O'Shea turned away from Ellis and quickly rubbed his eyes. "She was somebody's daughter, like mine or yours. Christ, we all die but no one should get killed; yet thousands of innocent bystanders are killed every minute, all over the world. Carol was one of them."

"How about Hall?"

Clearing his throat, O'Shea straightened up in his chair. "You notice Hall hasn't called. He was a friend of Hansen and McGuire, but he's no fool. If he's got to choose between demanding an investigation that could brush McGuire, or just backing off, it's a no-brainer. Compared to McGuire, Hansen was less than a light weight."

Ellis finally smiled. "You know, Loot, somewhere there are some real flaws in your logic yet I can't even disagree. It all makes sense. Besides we've got more than our hands full with the eight cases."

📖　📖　📖

O'Shea despised unfinished cases, yet he hated even more the frustrations of expending endless hours of energy, skill and plain leg work to develop a circumstantial case that's thrown out of court. Even though he was convinced further investigation of the Hansen/Evermore car deaths would result in overwhelming obstacles and an exasperating dead end, he needed to confirm, off the record, some of the reasoning he had patiently offered his partner.

After persuading Ellis that he really belonged with his family for the remainder of the Sunday, O'Shea was finally alone in his cubicle. His first call was to Captain McInerney, who predictably puttered around his garden on Sundays. McInerney somehow managed to answer his home phone on the first ring. This Sunday was no exception, and O'Shea had to smile as McInerney breathlessly answered.

"Hello, Captain McInerney here."

"O'Shea here. How's the garden coming along, Captain?"

"Oh, O'Shea. Ah, it's fine."

"Sorry to bother you on Sunday, Captain, but I needed to run something by you before further investigating those eight homicide cases. It'll just take a few minutes. O.K.?"

"Ah, sure John."

"Remember Helen Hansen, one of our eight homicide victims who was pushed off a cliff near her home on April 8th? Well, her husband, Derrick, an initial suspect, was killed yesterday, along with his girlfriend, Carol Evermore, when their car was pushed over Devil's Slide. Are you with me so far?"

"Ah, yeah. I know all about it. I've been told there are too many heavies involved. I was going to call you the first thing tomorrow. I was told that, unless you find a smoking gun, leave those two homicides alone. Is that O.K. with you guys?"

O'Shea was relieved. "That's fine, Captain. We've already concluded there're no reliable witnesses or hard evidence, and too many solid alibis. Tomorrow Sergeant Ellis and I'll start a thorough review of any leads connected to our eight homicides. That should satisfy our bosses."

McInerney was also relieved. He knew O'Shea could be a real maverick when he disagreed with the establishment. "That's great. Anything else I should know?"

"No, Captain. We're all covered. Enjoy your plants"

📖 📖 📖

Judge Hall's whereabouts on a Sunday weren't as predictable, yet locating him wasn't too difficult. As an unofficial member of his campaign staff, O'Shea had a confidential, privileged list of phone numbers. His first call was to Hall's home.

"Hello, this is Lieutenant O'Shea. May I speak to Judge Hall please?"

The reply was dryly terse. "Judge Hall is away for the day. You may, however, leave a message at the tone." Although the butler had met O'Shea numerous times over the years, he never acknowledged knowing him or his name.

After hanging up, O'Shea shook his head with the after-thought, *Hell, I don't know his name either.*

O'Shea's second call to the Olympic Club was more rewarding. Generally, the front desk clerk had to page the Judge who was either swimming, playing handball, immersed in the Jacuzzi, showering, or eating in one of their three restaurants. A half hour wait wasn't unusual. This time the Judge was just walking past the front desk when O'Shea called.

"This is Judge Hall."

O'Shea wasn't ready for the brief five-second wait. "Aah, Judge Hall?"

"Yes. Is this O'Shea?"

"Hi, Judge. Yeah, this is O'Shea. I expected the usual long wait. Do you have a part-time job at the front desk?"

Hall wasn't amused. "What do you need, Jack?"

"I'm sorry about Hansen's death. I know he was a good friend of yours."

The intensity of Hall's response was somewhat of a surprise. "Thanks, he was a good friend, but he was also a self-centered womanizer. No one respected him, and just between you and me, I suspected he probably had something to do with Helen's death. Anyway Jack, you've no doubt been advised by now that unless you come up with absolute, clear evidence, stick to your eight cases."

Well that's clear enough, O'Shea thought. "I understand, Judge and there's no indication we'll find any hard evidence."

Hall's voice softened. "If you need any help investigating the eight cases—you know, subpoenas, search warrants or interagency co-operation, I'll be there for you. Incidentally, will you be available in the coming weeks to accompany me on some of my campaign functions?"

O'Shea didn't hesitate. "Of course."

"Great. I'll call you later to discuss logistics on campaign strategies, for both of us. Are you OK with all that?"

O'Shea knew "all that" meant backing off on the Hansen/ Evermore murders and working as Hall's chauffeur during the campaign. "That's fine with me."

"Have a good day, Jack."

O'Shea noticed that during their entire conversation, Judge Hall never mentioned McGuire or Derrick's note, implicating Diger in Helen's murder. Leaning back in his swivel chair, O'Shea grinned at the ceiling. He was doubly relieved. His reasoning to Ellis had been more accurate than he thought. Hall's silence was a clear message to O'Shea that the note from Derrick was no longer relevant, and pursuing Diger as the Devil's Slide suspect would be pointless and self-defeating. Now he could concentrate both on the eight homicides and his one and only shot at Chief of the San Francisco Police Department—thanks to Hall's campaign.

CHAPTER 21

On the way home, O'Shea felt that slight pang of negative insight when he couldn't think of a good reason to actually go home. He was a fine cook with no one to cook for but himself. He was an avid reader, but he'd read every book in his apartment. He loved watching Sunday football games, which were long over until the fall. He had a two-hundred-channel cable set-up for his thirty-inch TV. He was also a classical music buff with a six speaker SONY CD sound system. He just wasn't in the mood for any of it. Then he unleashed one of his reflective smiles. Maybe I'll sit in my big leather chair, watch my knees and fall asleep.

O'Shea finally conceded to himself that he hated Sundays unless he could find some reason to return to his homicide cubicle. He knew too well that the boredom or emptiness of a Sunday teased his ever-present urge for a drink. "Shit," he grumbled as he made a U-turn a block from his apartment building.

After eating alone at Tommy's Joynt, O'Shea went home, sat in his big chair, watched his knees and fell asleep.

📖 📖 📖

Since his divorce, Mondays had become O'Shea's favorite day—kind of a new beginning. The first day of the rest of his life, as the hippies used to say. He needed no excuse to go to work on Monday. It was his first official work day of the week and then it struck him. He'd pretend the eight cases were brand new to him and Ellis. They were transferred to them when a couple of detectives retired, leaving ten pounds of thorough investigation notes and documents that had eliminated all primary suspects and motives. *What a great idea*, O'Shea thought. Start fresh without the encumbrance of the obvious suspects or motives that had relentlessly pointed them in the wrong direction.

It was 7:15 a.m. and O'Shea had already completed most of his morning routine—sipping his first cup of coffee and that relaxing constitutional while reading the Chronicle. He and Ellis could rethink the eight cases, and Derrick Hansen was no longer an issue. For the first time in weeks, O'Shea actually felt unshackled and confident.

"Happy Monday, Paul. Welcome to your other home, you know, the one away from home. I beat you here this morning by twenty minutes. Isn't it ironic? We're supposed to officially start work by 8:00 a.m., five days a week, but both of us feel late for work after 7:30. Christ, what a couple of workaholics."

Ellis dropped his attaché case on his desk, grabbed his coffee cup and stared at O'Shea, a bit puzzled. "Wow, what crawled up your butt? Whatever it was sure ignited something frisky."

O'Shea smiled as he picked up his phone to check for messages. "We just got eight new cases from two retiring detectives."

"Criminy—eight more?"

O'Shea paused for a second with a roguish smirk. "Christ, don't panic. Not literally. These retired cops are just like us—thorough, competent, experienced workaholics with eight cases. In other words, the other two Dicks have done all the vital grunt work that clearly rules out all suspects related to the victims and all of their possible motives. Now we can start where the retirees left off—with none of their biases, frustrations, or mind sets."

Ellis sniffed his cup with yesterday's left over, well-creamed and sugared coffee. "O.K. I get it. Purge the clutter of all the misdirection, wrong turns, tainted expectations and sad memories so we can become uninvolved before becoming freshly involved."

O'Shea nodded his head with one of his wry smiles. "Something like that, I guess."

"Your game may just work, Loot. We've done all the correct investigative procedures, like your fictitious detectives, and all we have is burnout and no arrests."

"No, it's not a game. It's a new strategy, a fresh approach to our nagging riddle; and as you so accurately put it, to provide an antidote for our burn out."

Ellis was about to add another comment when O'Shea hung up the phone, as well as his smile.

"Oh shit, Scotty Harvey died at County Hospital of a possible blood clot, cirrhosis, and all his other ailments. Jason, the fag, is also at County with some kind of pneumonia associated with AIDs. Claims his roommate is Winston's killer."

Downing the last few drops of cold coffee, Ellis began thumbing through his attaché case. "Well, guess this is as good a start as any. I'll try to interview Jason while he's still breathing."

"Thanks, Paul. I've had enough of Jason for a while. I'll go with you. Tuttle, Harvey's old friend, is at County. He could probably use a kind word right now. He's also pretty much recovered and sober, so I might as well re-interview him. Guess we're starting where those retired detectives left off."

"I guess." Ellis smiled.

📖 📖 📖

Neither detective said much during their drive to County Hospital. O'Shea was thinking about Scotty Harvey's primitive, tortured life of abuse, indignities and his utter insignificance. *Yet, there was his loyal friend, Tuttle,* he thought. *Maybe there was some purpose to his existence after all.* O'Shea grinned to himself. *I liked the guy.*

Ellis was shifting thoughts between Beth, his daughter, and Jason, his irritant. Beth was secretly his favorite, even though he expressed his love to his children evenly. She had been mourning the loss of her good friend, Jerran, who had hanged himself at school. Ellis didn't know the circumstance surrounding Jerran's death or that the kid was the sole surviving member of the Dorothy Torres family. He had promised to look into the investigation, but hadn't gotten around to it. In fact, he still didn't know Jerran's last name.

Ellis was also wondering about Jason's AIDS condition, if a mask and rubber gloves were necessary, and if Jason's new information was just another misdirection. *What a way to start a Monday,* he thought.

Approaching County Hospital, both detectives sensed the aroma of early Twentieth Century San Francisco. Leaving the trendy, downtown high rise modern, they entered Potrero Street, with its abundant assortment of very old Victorians. Then, like a Victorian centerfold, loomed the huge red brick buildings with tiers of bay windows under swirling gold gingerbread designs. It was the roaring twenties and both O'Shea and Ellis felt strangely younger as they parked their unmarked car in the hospital's official parking lot.

O'Shea grinned up at the old buildings, remembering his first trip to County Hospital when he was eight years old. He had broken his collarbone playing sandlot football. Still reminiscing, O'Shea looked back at his partner. "Why don't we meet in the staff coffee shop when we're finished?"

Scanning the well-worn marble stairs leading to the main entrance, Ellis whistled softly. "Sure thing, John. Boy, they sure don't build them like this anymore."

O'Shea nodded. "You got that right. Good luck with Jason and don't forget, AIDS isn't contagious unless you fuck him or he bites you."

Ellis tried to ignore the specifics.

After a quick stop at the information desk, Ellis headed for Building A. O'Shea had the long walk to Building D.

Despite O'Shea's crude reassurances, and the mask provided by the ward nurse, Ellis felt a tad vulnerable as he entered the AIDS unit. He didn't know the protective surgical mask was for the patient's protection, not his. Jason was in an intensive care room with one other pneumonia patient. Queasy with fascination by all the tubes and wires terminating in every orifice, Ellis tiptoed up to Jason's bed, half hoping he could leave without arousing him.

"Who are you?" rasped a barely audible voice. Each word had an eerie, slow, strained breathy quality followed by a sigh, like swishing of air, along with a clicking, gurgling sound.

Ellis practically froze in the middle of a step, as if he had been caught red-handed doing something. "I'm Sergeant Ellis of the SFPD. Ah, Lieutenant O'Shea said you had information about Winston's murder."

"Come closer if you want to hear what I have to say. I'm not contagious you know."

Ellis really didn't know. All he wanted to do was get the interview over without catching something. Cautiously leaning over the bed, Ellis forced a smile through his surgical mask. "Just take your time and tell me all you know; and I'll take some notes if you don't mind."

Like air being gradually released from an over-inflated truck tire, Jason's halting, breathy words occupied the next hour. "Hell, why should I mind, I'm dying."

According to Jason, his "roommate" for over five years, Humphrey, paid most of their bills, including the rent, from his earnings as bouncer at the Corned Whole Tavern on Castro Street. Not too bright or attractive, Humphrey was *at least* a good provider, who even cleaned the house and did the laundry. He idolized Jason and his skill in "gracefully eroticizing pain and creating artistic climaxes." Humphrey was the perfect audience. When home from work, he sat in a corner of the room quietly watching each performance, while stroking his massive penis, in anticipation of his occasional participation as an *extra*. Sometimes, Humphrey's "elephant-sized cock" was used when "fist fucking" wasn't painfully satisfying enough for Jason's partner. Jason added that Humphrey loved "butt fucking."

Jason's breathing became more labored, with a quickening sound of the mechanical pump and a louder, shriller sound of rushing air. He was obviously becoming agitated as he recounted Humphrey's treachery. Humphrey never told Jason that he had full-blown AIDS, nor did he ever tell him that he hated the "freak bitch," Winston. About a week ago, when Jason started feeling ill, Humphrey sobbingly confessed that he had AIDS, which was probably why Jason was so sick. He also admitted to "sanding" the jar of lubricating gel used to ease the initial penetration of Winston's anal aperture.

He wanted to cause internal bleeding that might severely damage Winston's sexual activity and appetite. The scheme backfired by stimulating Winston's libido, while sending several of Jason's other partners to the hospital.

"Humphrey wanted to kill Bill. He finally did." Those were Jason's last comments as the gushing air and rapid clicking merged into a high-pitched whistle. Ellis quickly closed his notebook, back stepped toward the door and ran down the hall in search of a nurse.

📖 📖 📖

O'Shea's interview with Tuttle was less dramatic and much less stressful. When O'Shea finally found the right ward, Ron Tuttle was sitting on his bed reading the Chronicle funnies, with an I.V. stuck in his arm. As O'Shea approached, Tuttle looked up wide-eyed with a noticeable flinch, as if expecting a slap or worse. He instantly felt a mixture of sympathy for Tuttle and anger at a police image that easily intimidated old street drunks.

"Hi, Mr. Tuttle, remember me? I'm Jack O'Shea, a friend of

Scotty Harvey. I'm also one of the good guy cops." O'Shea tried to speak softly and gently. "I'm terribly sorry about the loss of your best friend, Scotty."

Tuttle's wide eyes reddened, then drooped with tears. "I remember. You were nice to Scotty and me. You never rousted us or hit us. You gave Scotty five dollars once."

O'Shea nodded. "Mind if I close the curtain for a little privacy?"

Still droopy-eyed, with tears dripping from his chin, he nodded back.

Avoiding the slightest show of aggression, O'Shea sat as far as he could from Tuttle at the foot of the bed. "Anything I can get you?"

Tuttle strained a slight smile. "No thanks, I'm OK."

O'Shea was thrilled that Tuttle was thoroughly sober and pretty well oriented. Just maybe he could learn something about the Officer Nelson crime scene before it was mauled over by those hair-brained cops. "Can you remember anything about that night in the old Embarcadero freeway rubble when you saw the guy lying under a blanket with his head crushed by a big rock?"

Tuttle looked up with a blank stare while wiping the tears from his chin.

O'Shea slowly and softly repeated the question.

Tuttle paused for a minute, clasped his hands in front of his face, closed his eyes, and sighed deeply. "We'd come back from Sixth Street. We hustled a few bucks on Sixth and had some drinks. We was looking for a place to roll out our blankets; some shelter. There was a loud, weird noise, kinda like a watermelon hitting the ground from way up in the air." Tuttle paused again and looked at O'Shea. " Is that what you want to know?"

O'Shea reached over with a smile and patted Tuttle on the leg. "You're doing great. That's exactly what I want to know. Everything you can remember about that night."

"We heard laughing and voices in the direction of the watermelon sound. Like kids at a party."

"Kids? A party?" O'Shea quickly asked. "Can you explain?"

"They said something like 'what a blast man…blood sport…we did it…what a rush.' They said 'we did it' a few times. Then they started hooting or howling. Weird noises. Scotty and me hid until we heard running and the sounds getting farther away. A little later, maybe ten minutes, or a little more, we snuck around and saw something like a body and a big piece of cement. Then the bright lights, lots of noise, shouting. We knew they was cops. They grabbed us and asked why we did it. When I said we didn't do nothin', they punched us, knocked us down. We woke up in a police car."

O'Shea was amazed at the clarity of Tuttle's recall and the amount of information. "Were the cops' voices the same as the earlier voices you heard?"

O'Shea was pleased with Tuttle's unequivocal reply. "Oh, no. The first voices were like wild kids, not mad cops."

O'Shea stuffed the notebook in his pocket and looked up at Tuttle with a soft smile. "When is the hospital releasing you?"

"Maybe tomorrow, sir. They gave me some pills for seizures and the nurse said another drink and I'm dead."

O'Shea knew that for Tuttle, it was years too late for warnings or sermons. "Where will you go when you're released?"

Tuttle sat quietly for several minutes fiddling with his blanket. Then through red, watery eyes he strained a look at O'Shea. "I don't know. The streets I guess. I ain't got no friends now."

O'Shea was aware that Tuttle had SSI benefits of about $600 per month. He also knew that the Salvation Army was his representative payee, because Tuttle couldn't manage money. Tuttle and Harvey hadn't been near the Salvation Army in months. They simply couldn't handle the restrictions and the structure, despite the shelter of a sleeping room and meals.

O'Shea got up from the foot of the bed, deep in thought about Tuttle's options. Slowly pulling back the long white curtain, he realized that Tuttle could die on the streets a lot quicker and freer than in some regimented facility. Reaching into his pocket, O'Shea gave Tuttle an impassioned smile. "Here's thirty-eight bucks. All I've got on me. When you get out of here, enjoy yourself while you can."

Tuttle grasped the money in both hands. "God bless you, sir."

📖 📖 📖

O'Shea found Ellis munching on a tuna sandwich in the hospital staff coffee shop. "How'd it go?" he asked.

"I think he died while talking to me. I must have spent twenty minutes in the rest room washing up."

"Christ, Paul, what the hell did you do? Rip off your mask and gloves and give the guy CPR?"

Ellis blushed. "No, I summoned a nurse and left. Anyway, rather than a deathbed confession, I think it was deathbed revenge. He was convinced Humphrey, his roomy, gave him AIDS. Now I've got to check out Humphrey, even though I doubt he's part of our eight."

"Remember, we're starting new."

"Yeah, I know." Ellis wasn't looking forward to the Corned Whole or another interview with someone with AIDS. "How did your interview go?"

O'Shea avoided discussing his compassion for Tuttle or the $38. "Tuttle was amazingly well-oriented for an old, burned-out drunk. He and Scotty apparently heard youthful laughter, a whooping it up, even howling after the loud sound of a squashed watermelon, which was no doubt Nelson's head. This may be our first new case lead. Possibly a couple of drunk college kids. Maybe a hazing or something. It was most likely a spur of the moment act that will haunt them forever."

Ellis swallowed the last of his tuna sandwich while thoughtfully gazing at the ceiling. "I wonder what a couple of young drunks were doing out there, and how did they elude the cops and how spontaneous is a huge rock that would be hard for two strong sober guys to lift?"

O'Shea looked over his shoulder at Ellis as he headed for the sandwich tray. "That's why you're a good cop, lots of good questions. By the way, loan me a Pedro." When O'Shea returned with two ham and cheese sandwiches, Russian fries, and coffee, his scowl told Ellis there was something else on his mind.

"What's the matter, John?"

"I was thinking about those asshole cops who beat the shit out of Tuttle and Scotty, mangled evidence and didn't find a couple of drunk, loud-mouth kids."

"How's Tuttle?"

Still scowling, O'Shea dropped the sandwich he was about to eat. "He'll be dead in a week or two. When we get back, I gotta talk to Sullivan and find out what the hell went on that Wednesday night."

Ellis nodded. "Eat your pile of food, Loot. We've both got a lot to do when we get back."

CHAPTER 22

Sean Sullivan had walked a beat along the San Francisco waterfront for over twenty years. He finally made Sergeant a few years ago; which wasn't a particularly enviable promotion. He received a moderate pay raise and an unspectacular reassignment as supervisor of waterfront beat cops. Sullivan didn't mind. He had those laid back, mild-mannered qualities of an easygoing follower with minimal ambition and mundane interests. As a high school kid, then cop, his main activity and interest was always wandering the waterfront, where he'd wave at longshoremen, merchant marines and old folks walking their dogs. Now, although more confined to the precinct office, he was still able to cruise the Embarcadero, stopping to chat with a new group of beat cops, younger dog walkers and plenty of roller-bladders and skateboarders.

The newer beat cops politely tolerated him. The older ones were just tolerant, without the politeness. He was one of the old historical dinosaurs the new breed didn't take too seriously. Nevertheless, at 6'3", with square, prominent jaw, thick grayish black hair, and an imposing angled profile, Sullivan had a "MacArthuresk" appearance that invited respect from other cops. At fifty-five, his broad shoulders and narrow hips helped bolster his impressive image, while his soft-spoken casual demeanor and flourishing potbelly tended to soften that formidable first impression.

"Hi, Sergeant Sullivan. Got a few minutes?" O'Shea didn't know Sullivan well enough to start out too palsey or assie, especially since he wasn't quite sure what role Sullivan played in the Officer Nelson fiasco.

"Well, I haven't seen you since Lieutenant Drocco's funeral. How are you, Lieutenant? Sure I've got plenty of time. Gee whiz, after all these years on the force, we've never really had a good talk. Here, have a seat."

O'Shea was already hoping Sullivan wasn't an active part of the Nelson debacle. *He seems like a nice enough guy*, he thought. O'Shea had never been in the new Embarcadero Precinct on Townsend Street. He had vague memories of the original Third Street station that resembled something out of an old Dracula movie. The new station was third millennium slick and efficient. No more of the dungeon look. It was brightly lighted, with thick bulletproof glass partitions, video cameras all over the place, intercoms for visitors and large well-ventilated actual offices for staff. O'Shea even noticed the glaring absence of cubicles.

Seated in a comfortable, overstuffed chair, O'Shea scanned the huge, private room with a slight taste of envy. "It's so damned crowded on Bryant, my office is a partitioned off, small area we call the cubicles." O'Shea wasn't prepared for Sullivan's sympathy.

"I've heard, and you're homicide, where you need plenty of privacy to really concentrate. I feel guilty with all this room and not much to concentrate on. I wish we could trade."

O'Shea chuckled to himself, *Christ, I bet he really means it.*

"How about a cup of coffee, Lieutenant. It's the good stuff. I make it myself."

O'Shea had smelled the fresh coffee aroma wafting around the room when he entered. He finally spotted it—an old solid marble coffee table obscured behind Sullivan's big mahogany desk. On the table was everything any good household needed to serve guests. "Sure, just black. Where're the crumpets?" O'Shea added wryly.

Sullivan laughed. "This ain't Scotland Yard, but we do have glazed donuts."

"Yeah, I'll handle one of those. And call me Jack." O'Shea was actually relaxing his usual guard when dealing with cops he didn't know well. Pulverizing his second donut in three gargantuan bites, O'Shea licked his fingers and gulped some coffee, while deciding to ask the questions in a more folksy, casual manner than planned.

Sullivan listened carefully to O'Shea's questions about the night Officer Nelson was murdered. He even took a few notes, before thoughtfully squinting up at the ceiling with a deeply wrinkled frown. Sullivan was neither casual nor indifferent about the homicide of one of his police officers. "I was wondering when you'd get around to our investigation, or our screw up."

O'Shea was again relieved by Sullivan's candor.

"I suppose I'm responsible for the whole botched mess," he began. "I was assigned by my watch commander, Lieutenant Pettit, to set up the surveillance. Although the Chief ordered it, I later figured out that the assignment trickled down to me because no one really cared about the torched derelict, finding the perp, or, in the end, Officer Bob Nelson. I assigned Officer Mike Haggarty as backup because he's one of the more reliable, quick-thinking, new beat cops working the Embarcadero. The veteran officers wanted nothing to do with it, and you know, Lieutenant, it probably didn't matter. Officer Haggarty did his job."

"What were the actual orders given to Nelson and Haggarty?" asked O'Shea.

Sullivan looked over the contents of a confidential folder he had removed from his filing cabinet. "Their watch started at twenty-four hundred hours. Officer Nelson, bundled in old heavy clothes and blankets, pretended to be asleep on the ground between some of the concrete rubble from the demolished freeway. Officer Nelson was never more than ten feet from a dirt access road leading to the Embarcadero Boulevard, just a block away. Before Officer Haggarty parked his patrol car, he knew exactly where Nelson was lying and could be there in about twenty seconds. Several other patrol cars were ready to respond immediately at Officer Haggarty's order with an ETA of less than five minutes."

Sullivan dropped the folder for a moment and looked almost pleadingly at O'Shea. "No one, including me, figured the person or persons who torched the old homeless drunk would repeat it, let alone in the same area. It was a million to one shot. Anyway, Officer Nelson had on flame-retardant underclothes and hood. Even if torched with gasoline, it was estimated by the Nomex manufacturer of the cloth that he could survive for at least forty seconds."

"What about contingencies, the *what if all goes wrong* plans? I'm sorry, Sean. I'm getting ahead of you."

Sullivan poured himself more coffee. "Another shot of coffee, Lieutenant?"

"Thanks."

Pouring the coffee, Sullivan gave O'Shea a quick, uneasy glance. "Yes, those contingencies," he said ruefully. "We should have had visual contact with Officer Nelson at all times. I blew it."

O'Shea set his coffee cup precariously on the arm of his chair and waved both hands, as if flagging down a train. "Hey, hold on. Stop slapping yourself around with the *what if's* and *should of's*. Hindsight is always 20/20. It was standard procedure and I'll bet your superiors OK'd your plan. I'll even lay you odds they told you a visual would have been overkill."

Still looking somewhat pensive, Sullivan slowly nodded. "I suppose you're right, Lieutenant. All the top brass figured the plan was fine for such a low probability event. I guess I take the death of an officer under my orders more seriously than most."

O'Shea grabbed his teetering cup, and half-smiled with a tight-lipped hint of emerging impatience. "Yeah, I know. The best of strategies are lousy when they don't work and an officer is killed. Tell me the rest of it."

Sullivan looked through his report again. "Officer Nelson was killed the fourth night of the stake-out. He was instructed to call in to Officer Haggarty on the hour, with optional calls by either officer if anything seemed suspicious. About ten minutes after his 2:00 a.m. call, Officer Nelson called Haggarty, saying he heard some laughing and talking twenty-five or thirty feet from him. Officer Haggarty offered to investigate, but Nelson told him to wait since the sounds were fading and seemed more playful than threatening.

"About 2:30 a.m., Haggarty thought he heard a howling in the distance, but wasn't sure of the direction. At 3:02 a.m., Haggarty called Officer Nelson. With no reply, Officer Haggarty followed procedure swiftly and thoroughly. While driving the short distance to the stakeout site, he alerted four patrol cars to the area, without Christmas lights or sirens. They were further instructed to approach cautiously in four separate directions as a perimeter to block possible perps' exit. Haggarty was over Officer Nelson's body in less than thirty seconds after his unanswered call.

"Once he concluded Officer Nelson's head was totally crushed, he contacted me. As acting watch commander, I promptly called the coroner's office and paramedics, more standard procedure in the suspected death of an officer. I also dispatched any other nearby units to cordon off the area as back up. It was 3:05 a.m., the time of my major investigative blunder." Sullivan laid down the folder, picked up his coffee cup, set it back on the desk, and stared at the wall.

"Go on," O'Shea urged him more gently.

Sullivan glanced at O'Shea, cleared his throat and grabbed the folder. "Seems like the whole graveyard shift of mainly rookie cops thought this was their big chance for action. Officer Haggarty only had a few minutes to study the crime scene before the first units arrived. He managed to record seeing multiple running type shoe prints around the body, and two extremely large impressions between the rubble that looked like giant's footprints. That was all he could record before he was practically blinded by the headlights of three of the four cruisers that were supposed to establish a perimeter.

"That's when Haggarty also noticed the two old winos, but before he could reach them, the patrol officers, with guns drawn, had knocked them down and dragged them to a cruiser. Cops were apparently running all over the place, and when six of the so-called backup units arrived, the officers were all adrenalined up, thinking they were in the center of a riot scene. In fact, one of the cruisers almost drove over Officer Nelson's body, which was spared by the quick thinking of Officer Haggarty. He slammed his hands and arms across the hood while screaming at the driver. Haggarty got two broken toes in the mêlée, and was taken to Emergency by the paramedics.

"When I arrived at 3:10, the area was so trampled, a bulldozer couldn't have done any better to eliminate evidence. There were fourteen patrol cars, the Coroner's van, and a paramedic ambulance that treated Haggarty. Twenty-four police officers were jammed together in and around their units. Of course, all the headlights were on, and from a distance the area looked like a night game at PacBell Park. Some of the cops were wandering with guns drawn; others were asking what happened, and some were just chatting with friends they hadn't seen since the Academy. It's amazing no one got shot."

Sullivan again dropped the folder and looked at O'Shea with a tentative guffaw as if not quite sure about O'Shea's reaction. "I'm telling you all this because you deserve to know everything. It was a disastrous combination of inexperience, incompetence, lack of super-vision, complacency and indifference from the top on down. You know, Lieutenant, when I drove up, it was instantly obvious that a goddamned elephant could have escaped undetected. Most of the officers hadn't even noticed Nelson's body until it was bagged by the Coroner. One unit even backed into the side of another unit, and two other cruisers had extensive undercarriage damage after crashing into large boulders from the Embarcadero demolition."

O'Shea was feeling those pangs of impatience again, yet he could also sympathize. "Sounds like a nightmare. Can we get back to the evidence? What about those big footprints, the running shoes, or anything else?"

"That's the problem. Most of my report is about how we lost the evidence. Officer Haggarty is really the only person who actually saw the untrampled evidence. Let me call him in. He's on desk duty for a while longer."

By old Irish cop standards, Haggarty wasn't traditional looking. O'Shea was a bit surprised. He expected the over six foot, rugged-looking stereotypical Irish cop, especially after Sullivan's impressive description. As Haggarty entered Sullivan's office, O'Shea couldn't help thinking he was meeting a new age of pretty cops. At barely 5'5", Haggarty had a cherubic round face with soft delicate features, flaming red hair, dimpled red cheeks, dabs of scattered freckles across his pug nose, and full cupid lips. *Jesus,* O'Shea thought, *he's a blushing teenager.*

As Haggarty explained his observations in detail, O'Shea was also impressed with his professionalism. His report was clear, tightly written and unembellished, along with a refreshing show of objectivity. This was a no-nonsense guy who said it like it was. He began by saying he would stick closely to his notes since reliance on memory has a tendency to distort the truth.

O'Shea agreed.

Haggarty was articulate, calm and thorough as he described his cursory examination of Nelson's body and the immediate area, his calls and an interrupted attempt to more closely re-examine the crime scene. Initially, he had noticed the running shoe prints and the impressions of two enormous footprints in the sandy rubble; but when he returned to more carefully examine all possible evidence, the patrol cars arrived with blinding lights and trampling feet.

O'Shea didn't bother asking why he hadn't attempted to stop them from stomping the crime scene. After all, Haggarty wasn't in charge. He was just another beat cop. "Can you give me a rough estimate of foot sizes?" asked O'Shea.

"The running shoes weren't unusually large or small—not children's or giant's. I would have remembered that. The two other footprints were really large. They could have easily held up an eight foot body."

O'Shea scanned the notes he had scribbled. "I think you used the words 'footprints' and 'shoeprints'. Do you mean the big ones were like bare feet?"

"Not really, Lieutenant, now that you mention it, I mean the large prints were unclear and could have been either bare feet or shoes."

"Anything else that might help our investigation?"

Haggarty paused for a moment, searching through his notes. "I noticed a long metal pole, like a hurricane fence post lying in the rumble near Officer Nelson's body, but by then vehicles and police officers had invalidated the whole area, including myself."

O'Shea looked at Sullivan, then Haggarty. "What do you mean?"

"Well, I suppose I should have tried to restore some order. At least keep them off the immediate crime scene, but I just stood around watching."

O'Shea nodded. "Under the circumstances, you did fine, Mike. Anything else?"

Haggarty glanced at Sullivan as if looking for permission to continue.

Sullivan smiled with a slow nod. "One more thing may be relevant. The block of concrete that killed Officer Nelson weighted two hundred twelve pounds. Maybe there is a giant out there."

Driving back to his Bryant Street office, O'Shea decided he liked both cops.

📖 📖 📖

Ellis parked on Seventeenth Street, with a two-block walk to the Corned Whole on Castro. His dry mouth and nervous stomach provided first-hand knowledge of how O'Shea felt at the Full Load Bar on Castro, when he had interviewed Jason.

Hoping Humphrey wasn't there yet, Ellis pushed on the Old Western swinging doors. He was half expecting it was too early for Humphrey to be working. So, he was looking forward to hastily giving his card to the manager, with a quick, friendly retreat. He was wrong. One step through the swinging doors, and a brief adjustment to the dim lighting was all it took. His wishful thinking crumbled as he spotted Humphrey standing at the end of the long, dingy, crowded bar. No one else on Castro could have been Humphrey. At 6'9", he had monstrous arms, gigantic, lantern-jawed head, with huge flaring nostrils and shoulders as broad and bulging as some distant mountain range. Ellis' mouth dropped open in stunned awe. *My God*, he thought. *He not only looks* strong *as an ox, he looks like one.*

Ellis imagined he was running the gauntlet as he anxiously slithered his way to the end of the sixty-foot bar. He passed waving, laughing, winking, puckering, even sneering men of all sizes, shapes and ages. He felt like a displayed, on-sale pork chop while trying to ignore the prods and pats, by focusing on the huge *ox* at the end of the bar.

His target seemed to grow with each uneasy step, until Ellis was standing under an overhang of massive, pulsating chest supporting an outcropping of craggy, undulating chin. *Good God*, he shuddered to himself. *He's more mountain than ox.*

Just then, noticing Ellis' incredulous stare, Humphrey looked down with a smile. "Isth there thumthing I can help you with?"

The stark contrast of high-pitched, lispy voice attached to Frankenstein monster's body was almost too much for Ellis. He had been sucked into a surreal dream where he didn't belong. He flashed his badge as some sort of protective garlic or cross. It worked. He was again a cop in a gay bar.

"I'm Sergeant Ellis of the San Francisco Police Department. Can we go somewhere and talk?"

Without asking why, Humphrey quickly complied. "Thertainly. Let'th go outhide. I don't thtart working until five."

Walking back down the bar was easy. Ellis simply followed behind Humphrey, who carved a three-foot wide swath of peace and quiet. Once outside, Humphrey led the way to a nearby side street.

Humphrey was an easy interview with a straightforward, glaringly different story. He was Jason's actual roommate, not lover. He was tired of the cramped space in Jason's apartment and recently decided to move in with another friend, Cecil Lombardy, who had a large house in Pacifica. Humphrey was also tired of Jason's nightly sex orgies, and no, he didn't have AIDS. Another emphatic *no* was when asked about owning a gun of any kind.

Ellis also asked about the National Guard, another *no*, and his relationship with Winston.

Humphrey liked him. "He wath kinda freaky looking like me," he said.

"Do you remember where you were on the Wednesday·Winston was killed?"

Supplying corroborative names, addresses, and phone numbers,

Humphrey told about his week's stay with relatives and friends in Oxnard, California, for his father's funeral.

Why didn't I ask him that first? Ellis thought. After thanking Humphrey for his cooperation and a handshake that covered most of Ellis' arm, there was just one more question. "Forgive my curiosity, but what size shoe do you wear?"

Humphrey laughed. "Thize 20."

Ellis walked away shaking his head. *Now why did I ask that?*

📖 📖 📖

When Ellis returned from the Corned Whole, O'Shea was half out of his desk chair watching Ida and her posterior disappear down the corridor. O'Shea grabbed a file and slinked into his chair when he noticed Ellis enter their cubicle from the other direction.

Ellis dropped his attaché case on his desk with an unabashed grin. "How's Ida doing?"

Not looking up, O'Shea busily opened the file. "I don't know," he answered with a show of indifference disputed by his reddening Irish face.

"She passed right by you. Didn't you two say anything?"

Shaking his head, O'Shea stared blankly at the file he replaced on his desk. "Not a word. She went zipping by with a big smile. I didn't have time to think, so I froze. Shit, I didn't even smile back. When it comes to women, I'm a retarded loser."

Realizing the time for levity was over, Ellis changed the subject. "Loot! I'll never kid you again about the gay scene. I almost panicked when I entered the Corned Whole Bar. Yeah, I even flashed my badge to ward off the, umm, bad karma that might get me."

That comment seemed to be what O'Shea needed to clear the air and his low mood. "Did it work?" he asked with his own unabashed grin.

"Well, it helped. At least I got through it without calling for back-up." They both laughed and Ellis finally sat down behind his desk, quietly assured that his lieutenant and friend was OK.

As Ellis wrote up his findings, he explained to O'Shea in detail the entire scenario from the swinging doors to the size 20 shoes.

O'Shea was as baffled as Ellis about the shoe size question. "Do we have some kind of telepathy? I learn about two giant footprints at the Nelson crime scene and you check Humphrey's shoe size. What's going on?"

"Maybe I remembered the huge footprint in Likert's garage. I don't know. Guess it really doesn't matter. I doubt if Humphrey had anything to do with our eight cases, and once I confirm his alibis, I'll know it. Cripes, I know it already. Right before I left him, he showed me a Public Health certificate dated last week, verifying an HIV/AIDS free test."

When Ellis finished explaining his report, O'Shea concurred with the conclusions. He did, however, have one additional question. "If Humphrey is 6'9" with size 20's, how big a shoe does an eight-footer wear?"

Unsure if O'Shea was serious or joking, Ellis tried a little of both. "Well, what I've gleaned from all this is that Sasquatch lives; and Humphrey is just another gay giant with a lisp."

O'Shea paused for a moment as he stared affectionately at Ellis. "You know, Paul, you're beginning to grow a real sense of humor."

"I've always had it. You're just beginning to understand it."

O'Shea thumbed through his newspaper. "You've got a point. Let's see how you handle this one. See this full-page ad in the paper about the Russian circus that's been here a couple months? They have an 8'1" giant they call Big Foot. Should we check him out? The circus is even on the Embarcadero by the demolished freeway."

Ellis got up and looked at the ad over O'Shea's shoulder. "I don't know about their Big Foot, but I'd sure like to go to the circus. Beth's been bugging me about going for the past month, but look at the tickets. Forty-five dollars for the cheapest seats."

Turning back toward Ellis, O'Shea closed the paper. "I'll pop for tickets for your whole family if you check Big Foot's feet and alibis."

Still not certain if O'Shea was serious, Ellis was ready to call his bluff. "You're on, Loot. How about this weekend?"

"Fine," replied O'Shea. He wasn't bluffing. "The footprints in Likert's garage and the Embarcadero are twenty-five inches long. The connection is kindergarten obvious and more obviously remote. But if he were the perp, we'd be laughed out of the state for failing to check the obvious."

Ellis vigorously nodded. "I agree. Is it really OK if I take my whole family?"

"Not your pets," O'Shea insisted with a smile.

With the Circus tickets confirmed, Ellis changed the subject before O'Shea might change his mind. "Did you break any knuckles talking to Sergeant Sullivan?"

"Actually, he's not a bad guy. Who could have possibly predicted a one in a million probability murder of a staked-out cop, killed by a two hundred twelve pound piece of concrete. Haggarty, Nelson's backup, also seemed to do his best to cover the evidence at the crime scene. Christ, it was a stampede of very green, rookie beat cops who tripped all over themselves in confusion and inexperience. It's all in my report.

"Bottom line is, a few clues were recorded by Haggarty before the onslaught of cops. Running shoe type sneaker prints of average size near the body. Two twenty-five-inch footprints, that could be shoe prints, also near the area where Nelson's head was crushed. Haggarty heard laughter and howling. Tuttle, one of the old winos, corroborated the laughter, howling and added a few phrases like 'blood sport', 'what a blast' and 'we did it'. Could have been college or high school kids. But there's no spring break yet. Kids at 2:30 in the morning, party time, huge footprints, extremely heavy weapon. The clues are bizarre, Paul. Anyway, that's what we've got."

Ellis slowly shook his head as he looked over the report. "I don't know why, but I'm convinced something strange ties all eight cases together."

O'Shea slumped deeper in his chair. "Yeah, me too."

φ   φ   φ

Elvin Streichner, Jr. received the German equivalent of a Bachelor of Science degree at age twelve, while athletically, he was considered one of the top high bar gymnasts in Europe. Then, like vengeful mockery of his genetic gifts, his body was suddenly a tortured, wasting mass of twitching, stabbing muscular cramps along with mind-twisting self-pity crafted into rage.

Less than a month before his thirteenth birthday, Streichner had succumbed to Infantile Paralysis. Family visions of Olympic medals, national idolatry, of their son becoming the Aryan paragon or world leader, all crumbled into a single burning drive—to keep him alive.

For eight months he was confined to an *Iron Lung*, which he ambivalently revered as his *tubular breathing coffin*. Had it not been for the wealth, influence and devotion of his parents, he would have died. Only the rich could afford the round-the-clock medical care, and only his parents could satisfy his ravenous need to fortify his mind with knowledge. As his legs shriveled, his mind amplified. After his release from the respirator, he spent virtually all of his time, bound to a wheelchair, reading scholarly books and journals on mysticism, medicine, physical sciences, metaphysics, astronomy and astrology. Streichner read in seven languages, and with a photographic memory, plus exquisite abstract thinking, there was no subject he couldn't master. Not just in knowledge, but transforming what he learned into practice.

Through fierce determination and keen mental focus, he learned how to endure his intense pain without medications. Combining Western concentration with Eastern meditation, he began shifting pervasive felt pain to more tolerable body parts. First to his hand, then his index finger, a fingernail, and the *coup de grace*—to objects outside his body; a chair, a lamp, a cup, and finally, the ultimate transfer—to a housefly, killing it instantly. Following that experience, Streichner's mystical growth was beyond incredible. Whatever his body had surrendered, his mind conquered—telepathy, psycho kinesis, clairvoyance and psychic-persuasion.

He also returned to school, dabbling in biomechanics and other complex subjects. Four years after he had succumbed to polio, Streichner earned his first Ph.D. degree, in physics. His dissertation was related to electromechanical stimulation of atrophied muscle groups. In addition to a Ph.D., his complex research project earned him simulated walking on his own. He was still seventeen.

Then another mind-tormenting tragedy. On a full-mooned April evening, a week past his eighteenth birthday, both parents were killed on the Autobahn when rear-ended by a drunk traveling at over one hundred fifteen miles per hour. A professional soccer star with politically powerful parents, the young drunk was uninjured. He later received a light probation sentence. Elvin was emotionally devastated and choking on renewed bitterness.

Six months after the funeral and mock trial of the celebrity athlete, Elvin sold all inherited properties except the two-foot diameter silver pentacle his mother had given him on his eighteenth birthday. Renouncing Germany and all its toxic memories, Elvin headed for Canada.

CHAPTER 23

After making some calls to eliminate a few more alibis and a pile of paperwork, Ellis happily headed home with his circus surprise. As he drove leisurely in the slow lane on Lincoln Avenue, an enraged SUV driver who had been tailgating six inches from Ellis' bumper, shot by, blasting his horn and thrusting a defiant middle finger. Ellis just grinned back.

True, he enjoyed all the challenges of his job, but most important he was a devoted family man. Home was Elizabeth, his comely, 5'1" wife whose beauty blossomed as she moved with the grace of a ballerina and a smile that could eclipse the sun. At least he thought so.

Home was also his three children. Beth, the oldest at fifteen, was the mature, responsible one. He knew she was fiercely loyal to family and friends, while her big, glistening saucer eyes, baby smooth light brown skin, serene smile and fluid movements matched an inner sweetness and compassion.

Thinking of his boys, Ellis kept grinning, reminded that they were spewing fresh signs of growth every day. Chris, at thirteen, was the family's promising athlete, struggling to maintain a "C" average. Mark, in contrast, was the eleven-year-old family scholar and video game whiz. All the kids did have one interest in common; they loved animals, including dogs, cats, parakeets and turtles rescued from the local SPCA. Those were some of the reasons Ellis' work always came in second behind his family.

Wearing a deeply engraved smile all over his face, he drove the rest of the way home reminded of more reasons.

◫ ◫ ◫

Opening the front door, he was greeted by one of the most mouth-watering aromas in his entire world. It was beef stroganoff night. Following the richly scented trail, Ellis salivated his way into the kitchen. There, Elizabeth was deftly browning strips of lean beef in a huge caldron sizzling with special herbs, onions, mushrooms and an overpowering abundance of fresh, crushed garlic. The beef broth and sour cream were waiting on the sidelines as a final touch. Below her exuberant stirs, were firm, well-sculptured hips rotating sensually to a flamenco guitar rendition of Malaguena, one of their favorites. "Hi, sweetie," he said. "Boy, I can't wait."

Stirring the last strip of beef into the thickening recipe, Elizabeth tangoed backwards until her protruding hips were rhythmically gyrating against Ellis' crotch. "You can't wait for what?" she asked as she wiggled.

Ellis gently massaged her braless breasts as he pulled her closer, swaying with the music. "Gee, now I'm not sure. I thought I was talking about the stroganoff."

Slowly turning around, Elizabeth laughed her way into their usual welcome home hugs and kisses.

Another pleasant ritual was greeting his kids, if he could find them. Mark and Chris were in the adolescent *Oh hi, Dad* mode, unless they needed something. This Monday evening neither son needed anything. Mark was slouching on the living room couch, buried in a book. "How you doing, Mark?"

He casually answered without looking up. "Oh hi, Dad."

Ellis found Chris on his bed, arms behind his head, listening to techno music through earphones. Before he could speak, Chris looked up. "Oh hi, Dad."

Beth was just the opposite of her brothers. No matter what she was doing when Ellis came home, she always greeted her dad with an affectionate hug and a synopsis of her day's activities. Today was a little different. The hug and synopsis were longer, more emotional. Beth was setting the dining room table when Ellis entered.

Arms out-stretched he offered her his usual big smile. "How was your day, Honey?"

That's all she needed to plunge into her father's arms with a shower of tears she had been holding back most of the day. "Oh Daddy," she sobbed, "I really had a hard time dealing with today."

Ellis held her tightly, recognizing that she openly needed him.

Beth rested her head on his chest, and after several minutes of tears, sniffles and nose bubbles, she leaned back, looking up at her father. "Thanks, Daddy. Oh, your shirt. It's soaking wet."

Wiping her face with his sleeve, he slowly hugged her again. "Those are your tears and snot. I wouldn't trade them for the world. Now, tell me all about your rotten day, and we'll figure out how to fix it. OK?"

Ellis poked his head into the kitchen to ask for a dinner delay.

Elizabeth, lowering the flame under the stroganoff, already knew. "You just let me know when you want to eat. I'll get the boys to help with the salad."

As they sat facing each other in Ellis' work den, Beth blew her nose. "Well, Daddy," she began slowly. "Our school held a fund raising rally today to help defray the cost of burying Jerran, his mother and little sister. Jerran's uncle, Dan, was the only surviving relative. Even though he couldn't afford it, he arranged for the funerals and accepted all the bills."

Ellis flushed with the word *Jerran*. He had forgotten the assurance he gave Beth that he'd look into Jerran's death. Although he had found the name of the investigating detective last week, he hadn't called him. Even worse was a gnawing premonition. There was something ominous, doubly tragic about the unusual name Jerran. While never meeting the boy, he knew Beth had a close friend with shared interests in becoming physicians. She once told him that Jerran needed to help others, and they would some day open a free clinic for the poor.

Ellis felt he had let her down. "No excuse, Honey. I just plain forgot to follow up on Jerran's death. He was found hanging in the boys' gym, right? I got the name of the PD investigator last week. A guy named Jim Tashima. That's all I remember before my brain shut down." Ellis looked at his daughter with a sheepish smile.

Beth smiled back sympathetically. "Gosh, Daddy, I understand. I just wish that was all there was to this."

"Go on."

"He was such a caring person. When his mother was hit by a car and killed, Jerran was devastated; and when his little sister died of her injuries, I saw him only once more before his death. It was only in the hall between classes. He looked more grim, or maybe resolute, than sad. He said he had decided to take care of business and he'd tell me about it later."

The instant Beth mentioned mother and little daughter killed by a car, Ellis' vague sense of dread was painfully clear. He had to interrupt. "I'm sorry, what was their last name, for the record?"

"Torres, Dorothy, and his little sister was Melody."

What a macabre coincidence, or was it, he wondered. "Honey, I need to know everything Jerran told you after his mother's and sister's deaths. You know I can't tell you about my cases, but I *can* tell you that the crash that killed them has something to do with one of our investigations. For example, you said car. Did Jerran use that word?"

Beth blew her nose again and cleared her throat. "I guess to me, car is kind of a generic term for vehicle. Jerran didn't say car, he said 'old pick-up'. After he learned about his mother's death, he didn't say much to anybody. He was out of school for two days; and when he returned he seemed to stay by himself. His eyes were always swollen and red. It was obvious he was in deep grief. I did hug him once with expressions of my sympathy. I knew I couldn't interfere with his grieving, so I told him to just tell me if he needed me. He never did." Beth paused, then wiped away more tears. "I'm sorry."

Ellis tried a big, casual grin. "You're doing fine. I wish I had your memory for details. Most people can't remember what they had for breakfast. Speaking of food, how about taking a break with beef stroganoff?"

"I'll bet you're starving, Daddy."

By 7:30 all the stroganoff, salad and sourdough bread were gone, and the boys were helping Elizabeth clear the table. Ellis and daughter were back in the work den.

"Did Jerran seem like the kind of boy who would take his own life?"

Beth was shaking her head before Ellis finished the sentence. "Not at all. He was a devoted Catholic with life long plans to help others. He loved science and learning. He was just showing understandable grief for his mother."

"What about when his sister, Melody, died. Did he seem different?"

Closing her eyes, Beth dried another tear. "Yes, Daddy, there was a difference."

To Ellis, his daughter seemed a bit more hesitant. "You mentioned that he was resolute and was going to take care of business. By resolute, do you mean determined?"

"Yes, um, kind of. Like resolved. As if he had decided he must do something and then everything would be better. He was much calmer. No tears, and he was going to tell me later. He couldn't have been planning suicide if he were going to tell me something later."

Jotting down a few notes, Ellis leaned forward, patting her shoulder. "Makes sense to me too. He was calmly resolved. He had things to do and he'd tell you about them later. Doesn't sound suicidal to me. I'll bounce this off O'Shea's psych friend. Now, hang in there, Honey, you're doing fine. If it wasn't suicide, the police will have to determine who killed him and why."

"I have no idea who or why. I just know it wasn't suicide. He was an honor student, the top in all his classes, and so helpful, even humble. No one could dislike him."

Ellis had underlined the word *could*. "Do you know of any occasion when someone argued with him or when he mentioned a dispute with someone, even a difference of opinion?"

Beth sat thinking for several minutes. "I know this is important, and I can't think of a thing. Almost nothing really."

"Tell me about the *almost nothing really*."

Beth grinned. "Well, he was apparently a great all-around athlete in grammar school, especially baseball. Mr. Crites, the baseball coach, wanted Jerran to join the team and got some of the school's best athletes to try to persuade him. He always refused, which created kind of a civil resentment by the jocks. But they seemed to just leave him alone and it never seemed to bother Jerran."

Ellis clicked his pen closed and gazed at his daughter for a moment. "I haven't forgotten what you said earlier. So, what else happened today?"

Tears welled up and spilled down her cheeks. "Someone broke into my locker and left a message in chalk. It said 'Leave it alone.' It could only be one thing. The whole school, including the faculty, has decided Jerran's death was a suicide. I keep disagreeing. Most people know Jerran and I were close. So they seem to understand. Some say it's nonsense and others just walk away."

Now Ellis was concerned. This was his angel who had never harmed a fly. "Has anyone made even the slightest warning, threat or friendly advice to stop expressing your opinion?"

"Well, only one, Daddy. Mr. Boyd, the history teacher."

CHAPTER 24

Ellis had been waiting for O'Shea since 7:00 a.m. He just sat, slumped over his desk, grasping one of the unopened eight files, while obsessing over those fiendish bits and pieces that never seem to fit. Death pressure on Helen's back, big foot, Boyd, saguaro man, headless cop, howls, road kill, SCUBA, fist fucking, murder, suicide, angels, demons, alibis, innocence, evils, angels—Beth.

"Christ, Paul, what is this, a contest?" Standing over his desk with newspaper tucked under his arm, O'Shea grinned down at the top of Ellis' head. "It's only 7:15. Are you going for my job or were you evicted?" O'Shea took a closer look at his partner. "Hey, pal. What's up?"

This was what Ellis was waiting for, a time to confer with his boss as a friend. He detailed everything Beth had told him, his own doubts about the cause of Jerran's death, Tashima's negligence, Dick Boyd's warning to Beth and his efforts to comfort her. "I promised Beth we would find out what really happened to Jerran, and who broke into her locker. I also told her to just keep a low profile for now. Will you back me?"

O'Shea massaged Ellis' sagging shoulders reassuringly. "Don't you ever doubt that for a moment. Besides, I'm as pissed as you about Tashima; and we're not going to let anyone mess with your daughter. Give me a few minutes for my jimmy brit and coffee. I'll cut the rest of my routine." O'Shea scanned the front page, dumped the paper in the trashcan and scurried down the corridor toward the toilet.

Reminded of their friendship, Ellis sat up, smiled, grabbed the police directory and found Tashima's number.

◫ ◫ ◫

Entering Tashima's cubicle, a floor below, Ellis was astonished into momentary silence. Seated erectly on top of his desk was Buddha, or at least his look-alike. Legs crossed under a near perfectly round, massive belly with matching body, pudgy hands out-stretched, palms out, Tashima slowly opened his eyes. "Good morning," he whispered gently. "My morning prayer before I start the day. I'm Jim Tashima. How can I help you?"

Ellis furtively glanced at his watch. It was 7:55 a.m., and he had an inner urge to either apologize or laugh. He bit his tongue. "I'm really sorry I interrupted you before work. I'm Sergeant Paul Ellis from upstairs, homicide."

Tashima nodded slowly, peacefully with a soulful smile. Agilely alighting from his desktop, he sat behind his desk, gesturing for Ellis to sit down.

Ellis noticed that, other than the one additional chair, there was nothing else within the standard sized cubicle.

Tashima grinned knowingly with a childlike giggle. "My partner, Mary Purvis, is down the hall. In here, I could barely squeeze by her desk without knocking something over."

Ellis was beginning to feel a near spiritual quality to Tashima's mannerisms. An unpretentious calm that made Tashima the most unlikely looking and acting cop on the force. Ellis leaned forward with a smiling nod. "Well, anyway, you got a private cubicle out of it."

"Yes, I guess it is a blessing in disguise. Mary also has her own space. I think we even get along much better now. We talk a lot over the phone, and we eat most of our lunches together. It's such a pleasant way to discuss cases."

I'll bet, Ellis thought, looking at Tashima stuffed in his chair. By now, Ellis was so disarmed, he again practically apologized when bringing up the Torres case. "Do you know my partner, Lieutenant O'Shea? We still fit tolerably well in our cubicle. But I agree. It's a little too much togetherness."

Tashima's expressive, pancake face happily rolled and twisted with another giggle. "I've never met him but he has an outstanding reputation as an excellent detective."

"He's the best," Ellis proudly proclaimed. "Well, we've been investigating the death of Dorothy Torres and Melody, her youngest child. Then, recently we discovered that Mrs. Torres had a teenage boy named Jerran." Softening any hint of challenge, Ellis added, "We didn't know, or overlooked the fact that Jerran was her son, until we learned of his death at Polytechnic."

As he listened carefully, Tashima thumbed through a pile of files until he found the Ramsey case.

"Golly, we're all police detectives, for the same department, one floor apart and I never associated our case with any of yours." Tashima looked up from the opened file with wide-eyed bewilderment. "How could this happen? We knew you fellows were working on eight deaths; even that one of them involved a vehicular fatality. I remember perusing the names of victims. I guess Torres just never connected."

Ellis found it easy to commiserate with his gentle explanation. He was still wondering, however, how all the juvenile detectives missed the Torres connection. *On the other hand*, he thought, *how did we miss it?*

As if he had read his thoughts, Tashima answered. "You know, Sergeant Ellis, we need to develop some method of cross-referencing or cross-indexing names. Polytechnic High admission files list Jerran's last name as Ramsey, and I guess it never occurred to me his deceased mother had used her maiden name. We even interviewed Jerran's uncle, Dan Torres. Even then the two last names never came up."

Tashima had really gotten Ellis' attention. "So Jerran was registered at school with the name Ramsey?"

"That's right Sergeant, Jerran used his father's last name at school, even though his mother didn't. I would imagine she was terribly hurt when her husband deserted the family for another woman. That would probably be enough reason to drop his name."

It was all making sense to Ellis. "Oh, I agree. Poor lady, despite her apparent strong ethnic loyalties, she probably felt her son would have more favorable opportunities throughout his life with a non-Hispanic name. On the other hand," Ellis added with a sardonic smile, "there's still some job and school preferences for minorities."

Tashima gave an agreeing nod, and Ellis was thinking if he were more at ease, he'd fall asleep. Any blaming or friction never had a chance to develop.

"Well, Jim, no matter how long we're in this business, we learn something. This was one of those one-in-a-million oversights.

Nobody's fault unless we're all supposed to be perfect."

Tashima giggled. "I'm certainly not."

Slowly moving his arms away from his body, palms out, Ellis tried a slow saintly smile. "Thank you, Jim."

The two detectives exchanged copies of their reports, then sat together for over an hour comparing the separate findings. Ellis told Tashima all about Beth's friendship with Jerran, his curious comments the day before he died, the note in her vandalized locker and Boyd's warning.

Ellis was ecstatic to learn that Sam Eng, baby-faced undercover cop, had been assigned to the school. Sergeant Tashima also explained that he doubted Jerran had committed suicide, and that Dick Boyd was assisting juvenile cops by stashing Eng in some of his classes.

Ellis had to ask one more question before leaving. "Say Jim, what religion do you practice? Are you a Buddhist, Hindu, or Muslim?"

Tashima giggled again. "I'm a Methodist."

"Oh."

📖 📖 📖

One flight of stairs, and Ellis was just in time to spot O'Shea watching Ida down the corridor. She was bent over, posterior well displayed, and pouring coffee. Ellis slipped into his desk chair, still unnoticed by O'Shea. No more joking, prodding, even acknowledging the Ida dilemma Ellis promised himself.

"Oh, how long have you been back, buddy?"

Busily flipping through the Torres file, as if thoroughly engrossed, Ellis waited a few seconds, then glanced up, ignoring O'Shea's question. "Hi, John. Boy, we sure misread Tashima. He's a life replica of Buddha. He even gives off a Buddha sort of aura."

Relieved that Ellis hadn't noticed his ogling or at least hadn't mentioned it, O'Shea casually shot back to his desk. "Oh yeah? Tell me about him."

Ellis passed O'Shea the copy of Tashima's notes, while going over how the absence of departmental communication occurred, Eng's high school stake out, Boyd's participation, and increased police agreement that Jerran was murdered.

O'Shea listened quietly without his usual interruptions, probably because he actually liked what he heard. "You know, I've never met Tashima. One of these days I'm going the drop down to juvy homicide, introduce myself, and apologize to him for thinking he was an asshole." O'Shea, still smirking, gave Ellis back the Tashima notes and some of his own.

As Ellis scanned the new material, O'Shea explained his call to Boyd just after Ellis went to see Tashima. He had been relieved when Boyd told him about his efforts to work with the stakeout, his personal belief that Jerran was murdered, and his concern for Beth's safety, especially knowing she was Ellis' daughter.

O'Shea had also given Dr. Wunden a call about Jerran's demeanor and comments to Beth a day before he died. Explaining this second call, O'Shea admitted he wasn't as satisfied with the outcome. "I suppose Jerry couldn't give me the definite conclusions I wanted. He listened carefully when I told him about Jerran's talk with Beth and his death the next day. Then he reminded me that emotionally devastated persons frequently become calm and determined before committing suicide. They no longer had to face turmoil, no more emotional pain. There was a clear way out, a *final solution*."

Now Ellis was jotting down a few notes for his personal psych file. "So, Dr. Wunden is saying when a depressed person suddenly shows a calm resolve, it's not necessarily progress or improvement. It might be a clear, comfortable decision to die?"

"That's the rub. Like Jerry always points out, all behavioral stuff is in probabilities, no certainties. So, any good shrink would tell us that there's only a high probability Jerran offed himself. But wait, take a few more notes. Wunden added that Jerran's comments about *taking care of business* and telling Beth about it later, could mean he was really resolved to deal with some unfinished situation in his life unrelated to suicide."

Ellis dropped his pen. "How about an indirect suicide, you know, like those suicidal perps who deliberately provoke a cop into killing them?"

O'Shea gave Ellis a slow, head shaking grin. "You beat me to it. That's about what Jerry said. The possibility that Jerran knew something dangerous and, if dealt with, would get him killed. Jerry also said that Jerran's promise to tell your daughter about it later, could have obviously meant, provided he was still alive. He was leaving his fate in the hands of providence."

"Good God, John. Regardless of who killed Jerran, we have another death somehow associated with our eight cases. How many is that since we got them?"

Thumbing through the phone messages since last night, O'Shea didn't need to calculate or even look up. "Eleven unless you count the four dead cholos, the bystander, Drocco and Rodriquez. That's seventeen. No, wait a minute." O'Shea reread the phone message in his hand. "Eighteen."

"Now what?" asked Ellis.

O'Shea looked at Ellis with a deep sigh. Coroner's office says Terry Digness died of probable carbon monoxide poisoning. He was found by a neighbor, in his closed garage with the motor running. These eight cases are like some fucking virus that snuffs anyone near them. I'm beginning to wonder how *we've* lasted this long."

Ellis snapped his head up, eyeing O'Shea with a glower.

"Hold on, Paul. Just kidding about the last part. But the rest is true. Other than the Mahoney set up, all the dead were, at one time, suspects, relatives, or both."

Ellis reached for the message. "That's better, we have enough negative energy around these eight without including ourselves."

O'Shea knew what was on Ellis' mind. "Eng's a good cop and Boyd's tough and loyal. They'll take good care of Beth."

CHAPTER 25

Beth reluctantly followed her dad's advice to keep her opinions a secret. Since Jerran's funeral, this was the first school day she hadn't openly announced to anyone her utter disagreement with the suicide theory. Of course, it was Monday and she had only been back to school a few hours. By lunchtime, her secrecy resolve was starting to deflate. She felt alone and in need of someone to confide in. Beth knew there was no one more understanding and loyal than Connie Wong, her best friend.

Connie was the delightful embodiment of those enchanting Chinese dolls in oriental gift shops throughout the world. A petite five feet tall, her sheer presence tended to slack jaws and invite all kinds of awes and wows. Despite the stunning appearance of these two fifteen-year-olds together, both seemed oblivious to low whistles and broad smiles. Their relationship had nothing to do with appearances. They had been sharing their innermost secrets since they dissected their first frog together. That was in their ninth grade science class when they both got sick smelling formaldehyde for the first time.

Beth quietly decided that her dearest friend was the only exception to the promise that she would keep her opinion of Jerran's death to herself. *After all,* she reasoned, *Connie already knows my position on Jerran's death.* Yet, even such a slight compromise was a bit troubling to Beth. For her, the tiniest dents in a promise were betrayals. This meant that, if asked about the death of Jerran, she was compelled to give her honest opinion. She just wouldn't bring it up anymore. *Fair enough*, she thought.

Their routine spring schedule was eating at the old, run down, barracks-style school cafeteria practically every day before track practice. Both were members of the half-mile relay team, but for Beth, the relay was just a warm-up. Her most grueling event was the mile run.

Their forty-five minute lunches together were as vital as the track sessions. Typical of their usual lunch schedule was an early arrival at the cafeteria to ensure being first in line when it opened at 11:30 a.m.

Once they filled their trays, they hurried to claim their favorite small table near the exit. Although most students paid as they left, the two girls put their trays on the table, grabbed their bills and paid the cashier before eating. This way, they could make a fast getaway to the gym before the long lines formed at the cashier. While eating, they chatted about classes, homework, exams, the cutest boys, the prettiest girls and the best teachers in school.

This Monday, their mutual friend Jerran was part of the dessert conversation. Beth said, "You know, I talked to my dad after my locker was vandalized last week."

Connie leaned forward in a gesture of secrecy as she downed her last gulp of orange juice. "What did he say about the warning?"

"Well, he said he would watch over me and thoroughly investigate Jerran's death. In the meantime he suggests I not talk about it."

Still leaning over their table, Connie was listening carefully while eyeing Beth's untouched carton of orange juice. "What did your dad say about Mr. Boyd?"

"He didn't, but Mr. Boyd is a good friend of Mr. O'Shea, so I know dad will talk to him."

Connie sat back in her chair lightly shaking her empty carton. "You haven't even opened your juice."

Beth grinned as she handed the orange juice to Connie. "Funny, I just don't want any today. Guess I should have gotten a soda."

Connie smiled back as she folded open the spout and downed all the juice. "Thanks, I was really thirsty."

Finishing her chocolate cake without any liquid, however, was becoming a real challenge for Beth. "My mouth is going to glue shut if I don't get some water." Returning a few minutes later with a paper cup of water, Beth checked her watch. "We've got about ten minutes."

Connie didn't reply. She was starring vacantly through Beth, with a yellowish drool oozing from the sides of her mouth.

"Connie! What's the matter?" Before she could repeat her concern, Connie started twitching, followed by convulsions, knocking her tray off the table. Beth practically dove across the table, screaming, "Somebody call 911," as she grabbed her friend by the shoulders to prevent her from falling off her chair. Gently laying Connie on the floor, Beth kept screaming for help. She also held her thrashing body firmly until the convulsions subsided. Beth could barely feel Connie's pulse and her breathing was so shallow she began CPR.

Fortunately, the paramedics arrived within three minutes, and a relieved Beth stood aside as the medics checked vital signs and applied oxygen. As they carried Connie to the awaiting ambulance, one of the medics whispered to Beth. "Your friend is unconscious, but we think she'll be fine. You did good."

📖 📖 📖

Beth just had to call Connie's family, even though she knew it was the school's responsibility. The mother, Sue, worked for the City as an architect in the newly renovated Ferry Building at the foot of Market Street. Connie's father, George, was a city attorney at City Hall.

She chose to call Sue first. A receptionist, who could barely speak English, told Beth that Mrs. Wong was at lunch. No, the receptionist didn't know where she ate or when she'd return. Beth left a message.

She had better luck with the father. He actually answered his own phone. A mild-mannered, gracious man, he listened quietly, thanked Beth for the call, and then explained he had been informed by a school counselor. Connie's physician had already been advised, and she was being transferred to Kaiser Hospital. Mr. Wong also assured Beth that Connie was in stable condition. He was just about to meet Mrs. Wong in front of the Ferry building. They were on their way to the hospital. He thanked her again.

📖 📖 📖

Still upset, but relieved, Beth went to the girls' gym, which was one of the newest buildings at Polytechnic. She changed to her sweats and ran across Frederick Street to the oval half-mile track, with its inner-grassed field, all beneath the towering football stadium, ghostly quiet until the fall. Brimming with aspiring athletes, the inner field was swarming with activity. There were designated areas for shot putters, pole-vaulters, discus and javelin throwers, broad jumpers and high jumpers.

The track was also jammed with more sweat-suited groups of student athletes. Dotting the inner field and track was a scattering of coaches and trainers.

Hurdlers were practice-skimming a few hurdles, while sprinters carefully positioned themselves on starting blocks before catapulting down the track. Other groups of runners were doing their stretching exercises, vigorous calisthenics, and pre-event warm-ups. This was it. Everyone was vying for a spot on the team, and only four more days before final selections.

Beth was assured a place in the mile event and on the half-mile relay team. She was physiologically a natural athlete, and psychologically a gift to any coach. She gave one hundred percent of herself to whatever sport she entered.

After a prolonged series of exercises, Beth trotted to her place on the track where she would practice receiving the baton from Margo Watson, a senior and veteran relay runner. Standing alone in the middle of the track, Beth was waiting for Watson's start by their coach, when she noticed a student approaching from the stands.

Slowly jogging up to her, he smilingly commented, "Connie's fine. Don't worry and good luck with your practice."

Then, high above the bustle of student athletes, was a vaguely familiar sizzling, whistling sound. Beth saw it coming with only enough time to shout, "look out" to the friendly student. Missing Beth by a couple of feet, the javelin tore through the shoulder blade of Sam Eng. The steel point and long shaft, approaching missile velocity, literally pinned him to the track like some medieval fallen gladiator.

For the second time in a few hours, Beth was screaming for 911 and medical assistance, as Eng quietly stared at Beth with a wide-eyed, grimacing expression of shock and pain.

CHAPTER 26

From O'Shea's professional vantage point, knowing Jerran was the son of Dorothy Torres, one of their eight cases, really didn't make too much difference. It simply added to the expanding death toll and one more investigation that wasn't one of theirs. As a consequence, he was as determined as ever to start anew, to redefine their approach. It was time to painstakingly examine all the physical evidence—to really start over.

From Ellis' personal viewpoint, Jerran had been a friend of his daughter, and even though Jerran's death was a juvenile case only cursorily related to the eight, Beth was possibly in danger because of his death. Protecting her was his first priority.

Hunched over his desk, O'Shea began the arduous task of reviewing crime scene reports in the aging files. Sensing his partner's present dilemma, however, O'Shea glanced over at Ellis talking on the phone. Tapping his desk, O'Shea whispered. "When you're through, go to Poly and monitor their investigation for today."

Ellis nodded while listening carefully to the phone voice. After another five minutes of uh-huh's along with hectic note taking, he eased the phone onto its hook.

"What's up?" O'Shea asked, again buried in a file.

Ellis slowly shook his head as he looked over his notes. "Seems like every time we start over, something pulls us back with new bait."

O'Shea dropped his file. "Are you saying we've got a new suspect for one of the eight?"

Ellis' head shifted to a slow nod. "Looks that way. We never did factor in an actual interview with the San Francisco National Guard Armory other than determining our suspects weren't members." He paused, fumbling with his notes. "I should have gone to the armory after we knew Winston was shot with an Army issue .22 bullet."

"If anybody screwed up, I did. Remember? I gave you your assignments."

"Yeah, Loot, but you always rely on me to use my own judgment to expand our investigation or pursue possibilities."

O'Shea's face was beginning to flush with a tinge of impatience. "OK then, how did we both fuck up?"

Ellis held back a grin. "That was Captain Wilson, in charge of ordinance at the armory. I must have asked our forensic lab to check with the armory about matching slugs and casings. Well, according to the captain, it's a perfect match, and on April 1st, a week before Winston's death, the Armory was burglarized."

Turning toward Ellis, O'Shea leaned across his desk. "Go on. Now you've really got my attention."

"Well, three skinheads in orange and black jackets broke into the ordinance section of the armory and removed six target .22 caliber rifles with scopes, and about five hundred rounds of .22 long bullets. Two of the three got away in a van; the third was shot and killed by two on-duty National Guardsmen. The dead skinhead was identified as Richard Mueller, twenty-four years old. He had a record for participation in white supremacy rallies that turned violent. He's a member of a gang called the 'Trickers.' They reportedly hate everybody, especially gays. The two that escaped are unknown. They got away with four of the six rifles and plenty of ammo. The van was also unidentified other than dark and an older model. No plate I.D."

O'Shea had jotted down a couple of questions. "Didn't some witness mention a similar type jacketed person pausing over Winston's body?"

"I think so. But there were so many witnesses with a ton of vague descriptions in that busy area. Remember? We thought the info too confusing to be helpful."

O'Shea found the original police report in the Winston file. "Here it is. By an Officer Brady. Says an elderly woman saw the body lying on the sidewalk, with several people just standing and looking. No description of the gawkers, but she remembered two guys walking through the rapidly forming crowd. They looked down at the body, nodded to each other and walked off. They were both wearing 'black jackets with red or yellow sleeves'. She couldn't remember if they were carrying anything. Did the captain give you a description of the dead guys jacket?"

"Sure did," said Ellis, reburied in his notes. "A black jacket with orange sleeves. He's also faxing us their complete report. Apparently the Feds are working on the heist. They've interviewed several Trickers. All were well alibied and no rifles or bullets found yet, as of yesterday."

As Ellis talked, O'Shea began leaning back in his chair, staring at the ceiling—his thinking posture. "You know, this may be our new beginning after all. That first day of the rest of the investigation. We've been examining each of the eight separately, looking for victim related suspects and motives." Pausing for a moment, O'Shea looked over at Ellis, with a slower, more reflective explanation. "You know the hunch we've both had about missing something? Maybe all, or at least some of our eight cases are related. A one day serial killer or killers."

Ellis slowly nodded in hesitant agreement. "You mean, maybe the Trickers killed some of our victims? They sure hate gays, Hispanics, cops, blacks, probably even rich women like Helen. Anyway, maybe it's worth a new approach. Although in some ways it complicates the cases. Now we've got to sort out the serials from the others."

O'Shea smiled back, snapping his spine with a prolonged arm stretch. "Not really. We just have to go over all the physical evidence with a microscope and a new mind set that focuses on case similarities as well as differences. That way, we're less likely to overlook what we weren't looking for before. Got it?"

Ellis laughed. "Got it, Loot—I think"

"So, go to your kid's school. I know where most of your head is right now, I'll take care of everything here and fill you in tomorrow."

Ellis was already up. "Thanks."

📖 📖 📖

Once O'Shea had scrutinized all the faxed information on the bungled armory heist, he had a vague sensation, like the onset of an adrenalin rush.

Leaning way back in his swivel chair, staring at the ceiling, he imagined the arrest of the Trickers, with mounds of irrefutable evidence leading to clear convictions in all eight cases. Motives unique to each case would be unnecessary. They had ballistic matches, fingerprints, shoe print matches, license plates and tape recordings. How about eyewitnesses, confessions, DNA? *Christ*, he thought, *what a high that would be.*

Unfortunately, still on the verge of exuberance, his call to FBI Agent Ramos quickly ruptured his fantasy. An alert Daly City cruiser noticed an older model Ford van, fitting the description of the FBI bulletin. Rear plate was covered in mud, which gave the officers added reason to pursue.

Agent Ramos further explained that the cruiser followed the van, while awaiting backup, which arrived in three minutes. As the driver attempted to escape the five chasing cruisers, the van went through a boulevard intersection at an estimated speed of sixty miles per hour, directly into the side of a fifty-four foot trailer, missing the tractor by a few feet. The impact sheered off the top of the van and the occupants' heads. Both were wearing black jackets with orange sleeves. An armory bag used in the burglary to carry the stolen bullets was found in the van, which verified the identity of the van and the two Trickers. However, no weapons or bullets were discovered. The FBI was closing the case, concluding it was highly unlikely the rifles would be found unless eventually used in a crime.

"Shit," O'Shea muttered under his breath. "Do you have any other evidence?"

Anticipating the question, Agent Ramos quickly replied. "No hard evidence, just two names. Peter Mueller, Richard's brother and Karl Schwass. Both were members of the Trickers, according to earlier questioning of other Trickers. No other information was available."

"Shit," mumbled O'Shea again as he thanked Ramos for the update.

The FBI agent apparently heard the last mumble. "Sorry we couldn't help you wrap up your old ones. We'll fax you the updated report in a few minutes."

"Thanks again," O'Shea added. *Shit.*

O'Shea had to agree with Ramos, realizing that further efforts to find the rifles and bullets would be more wasted time. *So much for positive physical evidence against the Trickers,* he thought.

On the other hand, still arguing with himself, *the Trickers could be solid suspects in several of our eight, which jogs us out of our one-motive-per-case rut. Some of our victims were probably killed "just because," like bystanders.*

📖 📖 📖

Half an hour later, O'Shea was standing near the edge of the cliff where Helen had fallen to her death over three weeks earlier. After talking with Ramos, he just had to get out of the cubicle for a while. He wasn't quite sure why he returned to the first crime scene. *Maybe the beautiful view,* he thought.

The San Francisco Bay was ablaze with the high afternoon sun. A light breeze ruffled the waters into sparkling, golden-flecked twinkles that vanished and reappeared like millions of hide and seek fireflies. This lively hippity-hop twinkling showered the bay with such a spangled array of brilliance; the bridge was truly golden, at least for a while.

Just a mile from the bay's entrance lurked an awesome sight familiar and exciting to O'Shea. It was an eighty-five story, ten-mile long amorphous wall of chilling vapors oozing its way toward the bay. A silent colossus of rolling, swirling, writhing fog, shrouded everything in its path with dreary, cold shades of gray. O'Shea inhaled deeply. "God, I love fog," he murmured.

Peacefully viewing the panorama, he thought of Helen's last minutes. Then he heard the clear, unmistakable crunching of gravel behind him. The noise jolted him out of his reveries. He quickly spun around to face a sniffing little Yorkshire terrier.

"Come Mozart," shouted a delicate, female voice. Standing on the sidewalk, about twenty-five feet away from O'Shea was a little gray-haired lady bundled in a fluffy bathrobe, bandana tied under her chin, and running shoes.

O'Shea had to smile, thinking if that were my Grandma, she would have been wearing house slippers. Grandma was holding the handle of one of those retractable leashes that extent to twenty-five feet. Mozart had maxed out his line, and Grandma was trying to reel him in.

"Damned dog," she hollered to O'Shea. "He can't just stay on the street beside me. He's always wandering to the end of this gadget."

O'Shea waved at the old lady. "I know what you mean. Dogs love to explore."

Mozart grunted a head-shaking sniff. As he waddled back to the sidewalk, Grandma waved goodbye to O'Shea. Then it dawned on him. No one could have snuck up on Helen. That gravel is like a siren announcing someone's presence. She must have either known the person, or didn't feel threatened. Maybe a neighbor, small person, little old lady. *Or,* he thought, *maybe suicide.*

"Shit," he shouted down to the rugged coastline.

Despite a near month-old crime scene, the cop in O'Shea glanced around where Helen had taken her last few steps. He noticed a candy wrapper, partially buried in the sand, a couple of Tecate bottle caps, even a crumpled paper that he picked up. It was a flyer announcing the opening of a new pizza restaurant on Clement Street. Grand opening last week. *Just what Clement needs,* he thought, *another pizza place.*

Still using his shoe as a backhoe in the sand, O'Shea noticed a round reddish object, about the size of a dime, with a black letter "E" in the middle. The reverse side was thick with sand. *Probably the adhesive side,* he figured. Turning it over a few times, O'Shea realized it was a thin plastic disk, maybe from some game. Each time he was about to toss it in the sand with the rest of the objects, he hesitated. Then looked at it again. *Why am I hanging on to this?* he wondered. Stuffing the disk in his pocket, O'Shea felt the drastic drop in temperature on Helen's cliff. The ghostly fog had obscured the sun and shadowed the bay in churning, dreary grays. He turned up his collar, took one more look at the paling bay and headed for his car.

CHAPTER 27

On his way to Polytechnic, Ellis heard the 911 response, dispatching ambulances and patrol cars to the school. For the first time in his police career, he hit the siren and began speeding through stop signs and heavy traffic. Ellis wasn't exactly the best driver on the force. Actually, he was one of the worst. It was well known that his partners chose to walk when Ellis was assigned to drive.

Barely in control of his thoughts and his speeding undercover car, he probably looked more like a maniac than a detective. Up Seventeenth Street, a skidding, curb-pounding, hubcap-popping right onto Stanyan Street, a near collision with a milk truck through Parnassus, and another bouncing, skidding, curb slamming left turn onto Frederick Street. There were just two more blurred, white knuckled, teeth grinding blocks to go. Drenched in sweat and adrenalin, he finally skidded over a curb to a panic sidewalk stop. *Whew!* He made it in one piece! The car even survived fairly well. Wheel alignment and a couple of hubcaps were all it needed.

Ellis had heard over the police radio that a female student and a police officer had been injured. He had immediately thought it was his daughter and Eng; and of course, during his hysterical drive, he didn't know that he was only half right. When Ellis screeched to a stop, he could see an ambulance, with EMT's about to close the rear doors. Clawing at his door handle, Ellis pushed it open as he almost catapulted himself onto the street. Half way out the car, he was flung back into the driver's seat. He had forgotten to release his seat belt.

Untangling himself from his car, Ellis sprinted across the street shouting to the ambulance pulling slowly away from the curb. He was just in time to taste a blast of diesel exhaust and an ear-slapping siren. Emotionally exhausted, with streaks of glistening sweat dripping off his chin and ears, labored, heavy breathing, and a torn coat suggested to bystanders that Ellis was a victim the ambulance forgot.

"Are you all right?" asked a concerned looking man, quickly approaching Ellis.

"I think my daughter and a police officer were in that ambulance."

The concerned looking man offered a sympathetic smile. "I don't think you're Mr. Wong. His daughter was taken to the hospital about a half hour ago. You must be Sergeant Ellis. Your daughter's fine. She had the misfortune of being a witness to two traumatic events separated by a couple hours. She was with Connie Wong when she had a seizure, and about an hour later Detective Eng was pierced through the shoulder with a javelin, while talking with Beth."

Ellis heaved a deep sigh of relief. "How are they? Connie and Eng."

"They'll both make it fine, and your daughter is with a school counselor before her next class."

Ellis had calmed down sufficiently to vaguely recall the man with all the information. "I really appreciate your help. I guess you've figured by now that Beth's very precious to me."

"I can see why. She's the most mature kid I've ever met. She stayed by both victims offering support and encouragement until the medics arrived. Witnesses also said she remained perfectly calm while other students were screaming. She's also a beauty."

Ellis squinted a cocked-head grin at the man. "You're a police officer. Didn't you work vice years ago? Wagner? Wilf Wagner?"

He laughed. "I wondered when you'd remember. It was our first plain clothes assignments. We played Tenderloin bums for about a year. God, we were beginning to think we were bums."

Ellis grabbed Wagner's hand with both of his in a vigorous handshake. "Sure, we used to share the same office over on Kearny Street with twenty other guys. Oh, and don't forget Hunter's Point. Seems to me, we were both reassigned there and then we lost contact."

Wagner couldn't restrain a hardy chuckle. "You were much better suited for undercover in Hunter's Point. I got a real taste of skin prejudice there. Don't you remember? I was the only honky on our team."

Ellis stared at him with a warm smile. "You know, Wilf, you were always color-blind."

"So were you. Those were tough days for both of us."

Wagner was a tall, slender, craggy faced, ruggedly handsome detective, who entered the police force shortly before Ellis applied. Seeing Ellis again prompted a flashback to their earlier days together. He remembered it was a time of black and white gangs, burning ghettos, uneasy school integrations and discrimination lawsuits. A time when blacks were still called *niggers* by the young and angry, or *Negroes* by the old and insular.

Wagner also flashed on his own plight during his rookie years. Although gays were creeping out of the closet, they were still a social irritant. The medical community regarded them as *homosexuals*, while San Franciscans typically referred to them as *fags, queers, fairies*, or *cherries*. These attitudinal perceptions of minorities were more openly blatant and ugly in the police department. Police brass even resented educated cops. Education still meant *pussy* behaviors like non-violence, compassion and understanding. Still reflecting on the past, Wagner inwardly beamed, remembering that he was one of the earliest openly gay cops. To make matters even more challenging, he was well educated with a bachelor's degree from San Francisco State University. *How did I ever survive those years?* He thought.

Ellis had always admired Wagner's courage and dogged stubbornness in staying with the department, despite dead cats, threatening notes and other unspeakable objects in his locker, and virtually no partners to back him on the streets. Today, he's a legend and hero to other gays.

After a little more mutual reminiscing, an exchange of phone numbers and promises to get together for dinner, they were pleased to learn that they would be working together, at least for the day. Sergeant Wagner, a juvenile division detective for over ten years, had been assigned a week earlier by Lieutenant McDonald, his partner, to evaluate the Jerran Ramsey case. He was also informed by Sergeant Tashima that Sergeant Ellis had an interest in contributing to the ongoing investigation.

📖 📖 📖

On their way to the boy's gym, Ellis stopped by the counselor's office, where a brief chat with Beth convinced him she was okay. Relieved, he assured her that Jerran's case would remain open until cause of death was clearly established. Wagner further promised Beth another undercover cop would be at the school by the next day.

He added reassuringly, "I think you're right, Beth, there's still no solid evidence of suicide."

Ellis nodded. "Don't worry, honey. Sergeant Wagner's good at his job. In fact, I am too."

For the first time that day, Beth's cheeks dimpled into a smile.

As they left the office, Beth's eyes followed them out the door. "Thank you both."

📔 📔 📔

Entering the gym, Ellis was reminded of his high school athletic days—that pervasive aroma of dirty socks, jocks and sweaty young bodies, mixed with hints of strong disinfectants.

Wagner grinned, watching Ellis sniff the heavy air. "You'd think after all these years the odors would have changed."

Ellis nodded.

The Poly gymnasiums were situated on either side of the school, boys' on the west and girls' on the east. Both were separated from the main building and were unusually large for a high school. Except for urinals in the boys' gym and shower stalls with doors in the girls, both gyms were identical. There were three doors into the boys' locker room. The detectives entered the gym through the side door in an alley between school classrooms and the gym. This door led through the locker room to the boys' bathroom. Access to the other two doors was gained from the main archway entrance.

After touring the entire locker room, the detectives entered the gym through the door at the north end of the room. The other door, at the southwest corner, was to the entrance archway.

Ellis stopped after a couple of steps. Wagner waited, realizing that Ellis wanted an overall orientation of the gym.

"How often do they buff the floors?" Ellis asked.

"Every Sunday evening. Then no one is permitted on the floor until Monday."

"Was the gym opened yesterday?"

"Yes it was. What are you thinking?"

Ellis was trying to scuff the floor with the side of his sneaker.

"Well, nothing much. It's still pretty free of sole marks. I can mark it easily with my shoe bottoms. Are there certain kinds of soles not permitted in here?"

Wagner looked down at his leather shoes. "You got me. No leather shoes are allowed." Raising his hands with a boyish grin, he lifted his shoe for Ellis. "I confess. The school also encourages white rubber soled gym shoes, but it's not a rule because some black soles don't scuff and some kids can't afford the white sole shoes. So, I guess the rule has to be flexible."

"You broke the law, but I'll accept a bribe, like a cup of coffee after we finish here."

Wagner removed his shoes. "I'll go for that."

Standing by the main entrance door, Ellis marveled at how the yellowish sheen on the highly polished and buffed gym floor created a depth effect. The lines forming the basketball court seemed to be floating atop a clear pool of olive oil. "My God," Ellis remarked. "Those janitors must buff these hardwood floors to death. It looks surreal."

Wagner, also looking over the gym, slowly nodded. "Sometimes on a Monday, if the lighting is just right, it looks to me like you could jump in and splash around on the court."

📖 📖 📖

Both detectives stood silently for several minutes while Wagner let Ellis look over the rest of the gym. On the north wall, opposite the main entrance, were retractable bleachers eight tiers high; and when retracted, there was ample space for gymnastic mats and equipment use. Ellis also noticed the emergency doors on either side of the bleachers. When opened, Wagner explained, they emitted a shrill alarm.

The west wall was a storage area for folding chairs, fifteen mats, two vaulting horses, two sets of parallel bars, high bar, and balancing beams, all of which could be quickly wheeled to the practice area or performance area on the basketball court. There were ten vertical climbing ropes suspended from the rafters by a pulley, and to be lowered over the basketball court when needed. The east wall was blank, except for an eight-inch steam pipe originating in the locker room and exiting through the north wall. The pipe paralleled the entire west wall, with a six-inch clearance and sturdy brackets bracing the pipe every ten feet.

"Is that where Jerran was found hanging?" asked Ellis.

"Right, about eighteen feet out from the southwest corner. Come on, I'll show you." Beneath the pipe, Wagner pointed to the exact spot where Jerran's belt was lashed.

"How high?"

Wagner opened his notebook. "Eight feet even. I think I know where you're going, so let me give you the rest. Jerran was 5'8", with a seventeen-inch arm reach above his head. His *Sergeant's Jump Test* was another eleven inches. That was his best."

Ellis jotted down some figures in his notebook. "So, in a full stretch and best jump, Jerran could reach eight feet two inches. Then he could have grabbed the pipe, hung with one arm, lapped the belt over the pipe, threaded it through the belt buckle, wrapped it around his neck and twisted the belt into a half hitch."

Ellis stood silently looking up at the pipe. Reaching over his head, he stretched his right arm toward the pipe until his bone sockets groaned. Simulating the *Sergeant's Jump Test*, Ellis marked his reach with the tips of his fingers. Then he crouched, knees bent, arms straight back, and head up, with intense concentration. He sprang upward, slapping the wall an inch below the pipe. A scant six-inch leap. "Yeah, sure. I'm an inch taller and I couldn't have done it in my athletic prime. I'd have collapsed after about a minute hanging by one arm. Why would he even try here? There are a million easier ways to off yourself. And why the gym? None of this fits suicide so far."

Wagner patted Ellis on the back. "You'll get no argument out of me."

Ellis asked, "What kind of shoes was Jerran wearing?"

Wagner again glanced at his notes. "The sneakers were the black sole kind that mark easily."

Ellis knew Wagner was a professional. Yet he was treating him like some rookie. "Why don't you give me all you've got? You guys obviously knew what you were doing."

Wagner bowed slowly with a grin. "Jerran's body was discovered at 7:15 a.m. by Mark Crites, the track coach, and three students who were with him. All coaches have keys to the main entrance and their offices. Crites wisely kept the visibly upset kids at the main door, instructing them to call 911. He walked gingerly along the south wall, then up along the west wall where he was quickly satisfied Jerran was dead. He was stiff as a board. Except for Crite's footprints, the gym

THE ULTIMATE EVIL   ▪   189

floor was absolutely clean. Folding chairs and other equipment were in place at the other end of the gym, all doors had been locked and the janitor swears no bodies were hanging when he buffed and locked up at 10:00 p.m. Sunday. No locks, including panic hardware and emergency doors, had the slightest evidence of tampering.

"Two forensically trained coroner attendants removed Jerran's body using two ladders." Wagner handed Ellis copies of the attendants' and Medical Examiner's reports. "The gist of their reports is no physical evidence of tissue damage or death by anything other than the belt. The trachea was crushed beneath the pressure of the belt and he was internally clean. No drugs, sedatives, or any reason for death other than suffocation due to a crushed windpipe. There weren't any other marks or bruises on his body. All his clothes, including his shorts, were clean—even his new looking 'Members Only' jacket. You'll also notice in the forensic report that his shoes were neatly and firmly tied, hair combed, hands and fingernails clean. Time of death estimated at between 9:00 p.m. Sunday and 3:00 a.m. Monday. Oh yeah, Paul, no witnesses."

Ellis sat on the floor under the pipe. Scribbling notes and perusing the reports, he looked over at Wagner who had decided to sit as well. "So Wilf, what are your conclusions at this point?"

Wagner leaned against the wall, legs crossed, looking around the gym as if searching for something. "I personally believe Jerran was murdered, even though I have no solid ideas how he got up there. He couldn't do it by himself, and there's no present indication of force. There were absolutely no footprints, so, unless he or they could fly, we still don't know how he got there. Even an eight foot giant would have left prints." Wagner looked at Ellis with a shoulder-hunching smile. "Big prints. I guess for me and the team of investigators, the kid was somehow killed but there's no hard evidence either way. I suppose that's one reason we welcome another opinion."

Ellis stuck his notebook in his pocket, laid the reports on the floor, tucked his knees under his chin and stared at the shimmering floor. "Guess you mean me. Well, my partner, Lieutenant O'Shea, has often said that *the absence of evidence isn't necessarily evidence of absence.*"

Ellis glanced up at the pipe, then at Wagner. "If you agree with that, there're plenty of inferences from the absence of evidence in this case. First, there's no way Jerran could have killed himself in the gym. Second, dead or alive, he didn't manage to wrap around that pipe alone. Third, the M.E.'s report tells us Jerran was drug free and in no way resisted the strangulation. In fact, he permitted it. Forth, he must have been unconscious or dead before he was dangled from the pipe. Remember, forensic medicine is still an art. Fifth, there were several perps, or," he winced, "one giant." Then he looked at Wagner. "Are those pretty much your conclusions so far?"

Looking over the notes he had just written, Wagner slowly nodded. "You're still the same logical, methodical guy. And yes, I agree."

"Wilf, even in the Tenderloin you were methodical. We might have both been rookie plain clothes, but I learned a lot from you. I've been lucky to work with some good cops. My partner, O'Shea, is the best."

Wagner offered Ellis a soft, empathic stare. "I've been hearing for years that he's either loved and respected or hated and mistrusted."

Ellis stared at the pipe again. "That's true. I'm one that loves the guy."

Wagner nodded eagerly. "Me too, then."

They both laughed.

📖 📖 📖

"How about some more of that *absence of evidence.* Did the perps fly in with the body or just rematerialize, like in Star Wars?"

Ellis smiled, looking down at Wagner's socks. "I suspect they took off their shoes, or maybe they buffed the floor on their way out."

Wagner turned beet red, slapped his forehead, and beat the floor with his fists, like bongo drums. "Crap. I'd better turn in my sleuth badge. That's like searching for a bullet entry wound around the hole in the victim's forehead."

In rhythm with Wagner, Ellis lightly pounded his fists on the floor. "I suppose that's the trouble with the obvious. It's like *white noise.* After a while it's so taken for granted you forget about it."

Wagner stopped drumming. "I should have listened more carefully to an old, uneducated mechanic friend of mine. One piece of advice was, if your car stops running, don't lift the hood until you check the gas gauge." He paused reflectively. "Anything else you think we might have missed?"

"Well, you already know there's a ton of loose ends, like key access to the gym, the choice of the gym with all its logistic problems, the absence of a struggle and," Ellis added, giving Wagner a wide-eyed glance, "Who done it? I even wonder why Jerran had his shoes on. That would suggest he was carried in. You know, one of these reports says he was left-handed. Are there any close-up shots of his shoes?"

Wagner flipped through his file. "In the office we've got multiple pictures of every inch of his body and clothing before he was let down."

"That's great," said Ellis. "I learned from a magician years ago how to tell, by looking, if shoe laces were tied by a left or right-handed person. If a right-handed person tied Jerran's laces, the end of one lace would be facing down and to the right. I've got a whole list of ways to tell. So, if a left-hander tied the shoes, Jerran probably did them himself. But if the tie is right-handed, it provides a very different scenario, with additional questions."

Wagner was writing again. "That's a new one I've got to learn. I'll fax you all the shoe pictures. Fax me your findings and teach me how. OK?"

"I might even show you some slight of hand." Ellis sat silently for a moment, almost uneasily, before searchingly staring at Wagner. "Now I've got a question that's been bugging me."

Wagner sensed the change in mood. "I'm ready."

"Well, your investigators essentially concluded homicide. Then you were assigned to review everything again and you agreed with the first conclusions. Now, I'm welcomed to take another shot at it. In the meantime, my kid has been derided and threatened because of her opinion about Jerran's death. The same opinion the police have. What's going on?"

Wagner returned the eye contact with a straightforward reply. "I'm not really sure, but it's time to find out. Lieutenant McDonald, my partner, told me to reinvestigate because the case had to be air tight, especially if homicide was the conclusion. When I showed my report to McDonald, concluding it was a homicide, he said something to the effect that the evidence was *ragged*. You know, he's always respected my professional judgment before. But ragged? That irritated the hell out of me. Let's find out what's going on."

They both got up from the gym floor with another look at the pipe eight feet over their heads.

CHAPTER 28

Lieutenant Ray McDonald was quietly annoyed when Wagner called. He was bogged down in Tuesday afternoon paper work, and didn't need an urgent conference with Sergeant Ellis. Nevertheless, he was a sycophant of sorts who never directly argued with any of his colleagues, especially superiors and competent partners. He knew too well that the police department was a complex morass of politics, and that after thirty years of service, he was still too mediocre to advance on merit alone. He had learned to passively align himself with the winners.

McDonald was even mediocre looking—at 5'6", one hundred thirty-five pounds soaking wet, pale complexion, balding pate, pinched features and ever thickening glasses. As an authority figure, he had rarely been taken seriously by civilians, colleagues or for that matter, suspects. He was grateful that his badge, gun and obsequious demeanor had moved him a little beyond the obscurity he expected out of life.

So, awaiting his exceptionally bright, self-sufficient partner and Sergeant Ellis, an equally competent detective, McDonald cleared his desk and *put on a happy face*.

📖 📖 📖

Wagner entered the office with a sober face, more intense than usual. "Hi Lieutenant, this is Sergeant Paul Ellis. Sorry to cut into your paperwork, but we need to talk."

Flashing one of his pretentious smiles, McDonald rose half way out of his desk chair and extended a hand toward Ellis. While vigorously shaking Ellis' hand, he nodded with equal vigor. "I've been looking forward to meeting you for a lot of years, but you know, we detectives in juvenile hardly ever get upstairs."

Ellis returned a more subdued smile. "Nice to meet you, Lieutenant."

Wagner grabbed a couple of chairs and slid them close to McDonald's desk.

"Oh, I apologize," blurted McDonald. "Please sit down, Sergeants. Would you like some coffee?"

Both detectives declined.

Wagner then leaned forward, placing his file and notebook on the edge of McDonald's desk. "As you know, Ray, the initial investigation, which was comprehensive, concluded that Jerran's death was a high probability homicide. My follow-up investigation arrived at the same conclusion. Now, Sergeant Ellis has carefully re-examined the site, physical evidence and all reports, including forensics. His conclusions are the same. It's time to begin the second phase of the investigation. To find the perps before the evidence is ice cold. It's also time to advise the papers and school principal of our findings.

McDonald fumbled with a few papers on his desk. "Well, ah, do you think the phrase *high probability* is enough to label this a homicide?"

Wagner had been through this vague passive resistance earlier. "Enough is enough, Ray. You know as well as I that high probability findings are always enough. Especially when the high probability is murder. Otherwise we'd never get around to catching the bad guys."

Ellis quietly watched the interaction, feeling satisfied with Wagner's tenable logic and assertiveness. This, however, seemed the right time for his added reasoning. "If I may add my two cents worth, I totally agree with Wilf. It would have been virtually impossible for Jerran to kill himself. You realize, Lieutenant, that a suicide finding closes this case, which would be a serious oversight. Another aspect of this case that really bugs me is the premature police announcement that the death was a suicide. It not only thwarted the investigation, it was not true. For some unknown reason, it also put my daughter in danger as the only one at her school not calling it suicide."

"Besides," Wagner protested, "that announcement may have

gotten Detective Eng seriously injured. So, what's really going on? Who the hell's responsible for this feet dragging?"

Lieutenant McDonald searched his desk, perhaps hoping to find an answer pleasing to everyone. Then he leaned forward, clasping his hands on the desk while staring blankly between both detectives. *They're absolutely right*, he thought. *They have the courage to take a stand. I've been a damned sponge. Hell, I'll never advance beyond Lieutenant. Anyway, I can retire anytime I want.*

Looking up at both detectives he smiled. "It all started with Thelma Caruthers."

With head scratching frowns, both detectives glanced at each other, then at McDonald.

"Thelma who?" they asked in unison.

Sitting up straight, with direct eye contact, he was prepared to run the gauntlet for the first time in his career. McDonald cleared his throat.

📖 📖 📖

"She was affectionately, and sometimes mockingly, called *Aunt Thelma* by old money San Franciscans and politicians. Her granddaddy made mountains of money in gambling and whoring when our city was still loose and frisky. Then her father, J. J. Caruthers, poured his inheritance into seemingly more respectable, sometimes shady land development projects. Needless to say, by the time her dad died, Thelma, spinster and only child, was one of the richest and politically most influential people in our city."

Wagner shrugged, while Ellis yawned.

"I still never heard of her," grumbled Wagner.

"Me neither." Ellis frowned.

"Aunt Thelma was a philanthropist with the guilts. She was the first to openly admit that her wealth was an outgrowth of ruthless, amoral relatives who had stepped on and over lots of good people. She used to say one of her goals in life was to return her inheritance to San Francisco before she died.

"Every charity, hospital, library, animal shelter and politician held out their hands and she gave to them all. All she wanted in return was some recognition. There was nothing anonymous about her donations. She liked medals, plaques, stuff like that with big thank you's on them."

"Oh yeah, didn't she die recently?" asked Wagner. "I actually remember reading something about her."

Ellis rapidly nodded his head. "It's finally dawning on me. Didn't she also expect something to be named after her?"

"Exactly, that's where I'm going with this long explanation. Stan Burton, our esteemed mayor, probably owes his election results to Aunt Thelma. They were neighbors when Burton was the city attorney. She, of course, lived in the Caruthers' Nob Hill mansion. Burton lived down the street in a nice two story old Victorian. Well, she liked his liberal political views and shrewd political savvy. I suppose in some ways Burton's street smarts and hustle reminded her of her Grandpa and Dad. Anyway, when Burton ran for mayor on a shoestring, Thelma blank-checked his campaign."

Wagner grinned at McDonald. "What did she want from Burton, besides his body?"

"I don't know about his body, but she did want a high school named after her."

Ellis nudged Wagner. "Now I remember. When she died, Mayor Burton said that because of her philanthropy to San Francisco, Polytechnic High would be renamed Thelma Caruthers High, when rebuilt."

McDonald gave a genuine smile. "You got it, Paul. Burton had promised Thelma the renaming of Polytechnic. He expected it to be condemned within a year or two, and other land developers, who are now backing his re-election, are panting over the present Polytechnic property. They want to build a big apartment complex there to accommodate the ever expanding UC Medical Center up the hill."

"So," added Wagner, "a new group of sharks are circling."

"Boy, are they, and Burton is frantic to have the developers in his pocket and the promise to Thelma fulfilled before the election. Our mayor is a real barracuda himself, and everything is sliding his way. He has most of the Board of Supervisors in his pocket too."

"Didn't he appoint most of them?" asked Ellis.

McDonald was on a moral run and there was no stopping him. "He certainly did, including Dean Parker, the District 9 supervisor where Polytechnic is located. The supervisors had voted unanimously to rebuild the school in the Western Addition. No problem. That is until Ed Matson, an active alumnus from the '30's demanded public hearings, and was instrumental in organizing the alumni and getting sufficient signatures to place it on an emergency ballot in June."

Wagner was chuckling to himself as he headed for their coffee pot. "Coffee, Paul?"

Ellis nodded. "Thanks, I'll get it."

As Ellis prepared his milky, sugared coffee, Wagner shook his head knowingly. "Burton must have fumed when someone stood up to him."

"Matson even hired engineers to prove the fiscal feasibility of renovating the old school. So, Burton needs all the influence and arguments he could acquire to show voters Polytechnic needs more than a new location. It needs a new name and a more positive, scholastic image."

Ellis was starting to fume. "Are you telling us, Lieutenant, that a homicide finding has been delayed because it somehow doesn't mesh with Burton's political deals?"

McDonald couldn't help but grin. "You're getting it."

Wagner cut in. "Why would the mayor want it to look like a suicide? Seems to me if he's looking for negative press against Poly, he'd be pushing for homicide."

McDonald could hardly contain himself. "Exactly."

Though a bit puzzled, Wagner was enjoying his partner's strange transformation.

McDonald was beaming. "Chief Hoel has been apprising our mayor of everything connected with Jerran's death. Burton probably already knows of your conclusions, Paul. Anyway, even though he's agreed all along that Jerran was probably murdered, his handlers advised him to hold off on the homicide announcement to the papers until a couple weeks before the special election. In that way, the public will get the full impact of negative press against Polytechnic just before voting. That strategy will also legitimize Burton's discrediting the school as being as dangerous and worn out as its buildings."

Both Ellis and Wagner were shaking their heads.

"How did you learn of all this and why didn't you tell me, Ray?"

"Orders from the brass. They knew, as usual, I could be trusted to do whatever they say, and that you were too independent. Kind of a maverick that shouldn't know what was going on. You see, there's a real pecking order and you guys, or guys like O'Shea, aren't part of it. Starting with the mayor, there are seven supervisors, including Stanton, Chief Glenn Hoel, Superintendent of Schools Jeff Wilton, Deputy Chief Jean Parker, a bunch of watch commanders, and on down the chain. Magdalene Belotti, the Polytechnic principal, also marches to Burton's drummers."

McDonald added a little pensively, "So there you are."

Ellis looked at McDonald searchingly. "I really appreciate your honesty and integrity, Lieutenant. But, why are you telling us all this? If I may, what has changed you?"

McDonald stared at his partner and Ellis for nearly a minute before answering. "It's about time, isn't it? "

Both detectives sat quietly stunned as McDonald casually picked up his phone, dialed a number and asked for Ron Skoggins, Chronicle police reporter. Giving his name, he told the reporter that Jerran's death was officially a homicide and for public information. After hanging up he offered a weak smile. "Well that's it, the new me."

Wagner got up and leaned across McDonald's desk with his arm outstretched. "I'm proud to have you as my partner and my boss."

As they shook hands, Ellis added, "Thanks, Lieutenant. I truly admire your courage."

For McDonald, this was the most gratifying moment of his life.

📖 📖 📖

Ellis and Wagner enjoyed their speedy, silent drive back to Poly-technic. The principal, Magdalena Belotti, had reluctantly agreed to wait for them. But, before she hung up on Wagner, without a good-bye, she insisted they arrive before 5:00 p.m. It was 4:30 when they left the Bryant Street office.

Both detectives were too relieved and pleased with the events of the last few hours to permit the principal's negative energy to affect them.

Ellis had called Beth at home just before they left Lieutenant McDonald's office. *What a great kid*, he thought. He would drive her to the hospital later in the evening to see her friend, Connie, while he saw Detective Eng. He would also have good news for Beth. Jerran's death had officially been ruled homicide.

Wagner was thinking about Lieutenant McDonald. He actually liked him, despite his inability to stand up for his partner. *Now*, he thought, *We'll make a fine team.*

Arriving at Polytechnic, the detectives ran up the stairs and down the hall of the administration building, just as the principal, attaché case in hand, was walking out the door. It was 5:01 p.m.

📖 📖 📖

Ms. Belotti was a tall, slender, elegantly attractive, feminist who looked markedly younger than her forty-three years. Her very expensive, Neiman Marcus navy blue, wool worsted suit was all business and strictly unisex. Her jet-black hair, pulled straight back in a bun, effectively wrenched all hints of softness from her face. Even her use of makeup was severe. Her sharp, heavy eye brow lines, thinly painted lips, and a light facial powder provided a mask-like effect that managed to camouflage any traces of warmth or femininity. To her, being called pretty was an insult. Opening the door for her or calling her honey may be life threatening.

She had taken a law course from Mayor Burton during his city attorney days. Sensing he would rise to political prominence, she submitted to his advances, purely as a career aid. The affair was brief but the friendship lasting. Recognizing their mutually ruthless drive for power, they could be useful allies.

As an English teacher at the swanky, Altamont Private School, Ms. Belotti had tirelessly campaigned for Burton in his first run for mayor. Her efforts paid off. He was her advocate, and principal of Polytechnic High was a rest stop on her way to a city supervisor appointment.

📖 📖 📖

Still in good moods, the detectives waved at Ms. Belotti, who was unaffectionately known as *Vampira* by the students. Ellis had met her briefly at a few school functions. He also knew her nickname. Each time he saw her, he couldn't help feeling she might drain the blood from his neck.

"Hi, Ms. Belotti. Sorry we're late."

Not knowing the principal, Wagner glanced at his watch, as he whispered to Ellis. "Hell, it's only one minute after five."

Ellis gave Wagner an elbow nudge. "May we talk in your office? It's important."

Ms Belotti shot both of the detectives one of her stern principal glances. "I'll give you ten minutes."

Lightly grabbing his neck, he stroked his carotid arteries. "That will be fine," he replied softly. Following Ms Belotti into her office, he nudged Wagner with a whisper. "You start the talking."

The principal sat stiffly behind her huge desk with hands firmly clasped, thin pursed lips and what seemed like a fixed frown. Staring unblinkingly at the detectives seated in front of her desk, she said nothing. The message, however, was clear. *Get going. You're being timed!*

Wagner telegraphically reviewed the day's events, the medical condition of both victims, and finally, the protracted investigation of Jerran's death.

"Since all investigators agree Jerran was most likely murdered, it's vital you hold an assembly tomorrow to advise students of these official findings, and to let them know the police will be surveiling the school until the crime is solved. It would also help to give students my name and juvenile division hot line number in case they know anything related to the homicide."

Ms. Belotti was shaking her head before Wagner finished. "Has this announcement been cleared by the mayor?"

Wagner looked at Ellis with a puzzled expression before replying, "I really don't know."

Continuing to frown, she tersely decreed her position. "There'll be no assembly until approved by the mayor."

Wagner lost his patience and his good mood. "Ms. Belotti, I don't know if your problem is related to penis-envy or premature menopause and I don't care. This is police business not political strategy. We don't need the mayor's approval to investigate a crime or protect students. I intend to return tomorrow morning with some uniformed officers; and if there's no assembly, we'll have one at noon with bull horns and leaflets, advising all students and teachers of the homicide finding and that the principal wouldn't cooperate in warning the students."

Belotti's eyes narrowed into an acetylene glare of flaming fury. Then she sat back half smirking. "We'll see about that."

Ellis had lost his good mood, as well. "You know, Ms. Belotti, my daughter's life was probably in danger because she spoke out against suicide and you rebuked her for it. Tomorrow you can make amends by an assembly, or we'll do it for you. Goodbye. Our time is up."

Without another word from anyone, both detectives left the principal's office.

□ □ □

It was nearly 6:00 p.m. when Ellis made it back to his office cubicle. A half filled cup of icy cold coffee and an absence of case files all over O'Shea's desk suggested his partner had left for the day.

Checking his message spindle, Ellis found several. Three from Beth, assuring him she was OK. There was one from Belotti's office, canceling their 5 o'clock appointment. *Sure glad I didn't get that one*, he mused, *next time it's garlic and a cross.*

There was one from their computer wiz, June Zimmerman in Identifications. "Have some information on Lula Rogoff, St Mary's Hos."

Who's Lula Rogoff? he wondered.

Ellis respected Zimmerman's dogged efficiency. She rivaled the FBI in checking backgrounds, crosschecking names, even fingerprint matching. On the other hand, her stingy messages were a real pain. Kind of abbreviated computer talk, he thought. Then it hit him; June had apparently learned something significant about the on-duty staff in the Grace Digness homicide. Zimmerman would be his first call in the morning.

His last message was from O'Shea. "Learned a few things on the Hansen cliff. No big deal until tomorrow. Glad Beth's fine, her friend is recovering, and Eng's making it. Fill me in tomorrow. Try to come in late for a change. Like 8:00 a.m. Go home! —O'Shea"

Ellis grinned, locked his desk, and took his boss' advice.

CHAPTER 29

Oozing into the city, the fog was beginning its eerie tumble over rooftops that were all jammed together like successive thickets of dominoes. As the drifting, murky vapors squeezed through the narrow spaces between houses, O'Shea scanned the rows of buildings. To him, they seemed to ominously spill gaseous fingers down walls, permeating archways and finally splashing onto the streets. The sun was a filtered haze of lost warmth and shadowless gloom. He had never lost his enchantment with the city's ever-changing micro-climates.

O'Shea had left the Sea Cliff area a half hour earlier with no definite plan other than an eventual dinner. Ever since his uniformed patrol car days, he enjoyed just aimlessly cruising through the city.

Driving up Turk Street, he thought of his rookie cop beat days in the Tenderloin when he rousted every other person because they all looked suspicious. He recalled the pathetically too young or too old street prostitutes, the jive-ass pimps, the winos and those shifty little groups of drug pushers. They were still center stage. He shook his head, thinking nothing had changed.

Turning right onto Leavenworth Street, a *LIVE NUDES* sign over one of the many Tenderloin clubs sent a sickening jolt of current to the pit of his stomach. Not because there's anything foreboding about live nudes. It was the color of the sign, orange with black letters. He had flashed on the plastic disk with the "E" that he found at the cliff.

O'Shea pulled over to the curb, and removed the little object buried in his pocket. Again he had a fretful feeling that the plastic circle had some strange significance. *Maybe it's a logo,* he thought, *part of a kids game, like Monopoly, or a child's spelling game. Maybe a puzzle part, ah shit.*

His thoughts were interrupted by a light tapping on his window. Glancing to his left, O'Shea was starring at a pretty, grinning, overly made-up face about an inch from the window. *Christ,* he sighed, *she could almost be my granddaughter, if I had one.*

"Hi, honey. You looking for something?"

Shaking his head, O'Shea glowered at her, with a backhand flick as if he were shooing away a fly. Immediately shifting to a bored expression, the young hooker sashayed down the street. Watching her disappear around the corner, O'Shea was thinking, *She's so damned new, she can't even spot a cop in an unmarked car. Hasn't she learned anything?*

📖 📖 📖

Still preoccupied with the disk, O'Shea left the Tenderloin and headed for an office supply store. No longer in his cruising mode, he increased the speed to his usual twenty miles per hour. He found an OfficeMax on Van Ness Avenue that might be able to identify the disk. No luck. The first clerk he asked gave him a flat *no.* The store manager was a bit more expansive. It wasn't a part of any computer game he'd ever seen, and there was nothing in the store that resembled it. Casually shifting into his salesman mode, the manager added that the store could easily reproduce the disk in about the same color with a black "E". He explained that they do business cards, logos, and all kinds of other special orders on paper, cardboard or plastic.

"Thanks for the information," O'Shea replied, thinking, *No wonder this guy's a manager.* O'Shea had two final questions he needed to ask for no discernable reason. He flashed his badge to hopefully get a more direct answer without the sales pitch. "Were such orders sent to some outside printer?"

"No, like all other office supply/computer stores, all the work is done here."

"Do you keep records that include a description of the order, with name and address of the buyer?"

Another *no,* with an explanation that just the price is listed since the work is done there immediately. The manager agreed, however, that a descriptive work order would be completed if the job were left overnight.

O'Shea's final question was met with another *No.*

"Work orders are destroyed when a job's completed."

Again thanking the manager, O'Shea wondered, *Why the hell did I ask all those questions? What is it with this disk? It was probably lying there for years.* O'Shea carefully slid the little disk between business cards in his badge wallet. "Oh, the hell with it," he mumbled.

📖   📖   📖

Back in the car, he decided to eat at nearby Tommy's Joynt on Van Ness and Geary. At 6:30, Tommy's Joynt was mobbed as usual with the dinner crowd. O'Shea parked half a block away in a red zone, one of the privileges of the job in a city with three times as many cars as parking places. After placing a business card on the dashboard along with an SFPD placard, he strolled the twenty-five steps to the end of the food line that was restlessly trailing out the entrance like an old shaggy dog's tail.

O'Shea wasn't a line buff. Actually, he hated lines. Over three people awaiting a table or ticket to a movie was, to O'Shea, a line. In this case, however, he needed to talk with Paola, the cocktail waitress with six kids, ranging from age three to eighteen or one every three years. Besides, he reasoned, he was hungry, and Hauf Brau lines moved pretty fast. So, gritting his teeth, he impatiently tolerated standing in line behind a small mountain of a guy with two fat children hanging on to the guy's coat. Grinding his teeth harder, he anticipated a slow trudging wait behind a guy who would order half the remaining entrees for himself and the other half for his fat kids. O'Shea was happily wrong. When they reached the servers, the guy ordered a plain turkey sandwich on wheat bread and coffee. *The kids have probably already eaten at McDonalds,* he thought.

O'Shea could finally relax his jaw muscles. He ordered the roast beef dinner with string beans, mashed potatoes, gravy, potato salad, sourdough bread and coffee. All for $6.75, which was another reason he liked Tommy's Joynt. *Food is cheap!*

The price of food at Tommy's Joynt matched its funky, old time décor. It was a huge place, loaded with artifacts. O'Shea loved it all, including the Gold Rush vintage mahogany bar he no longer patronized. It was too popular to cops.

Standing in the milling crowd with a seven-pound tray of food and no table, O'Shea knew the contest well. Only rule was no physical contact with a competitor who was also looking for a table. Everything else goes. First, spot a table with customers about to leave as evidenced by the subtle clues that took years of experience to assess. Second, anticipate their barely perceptible departure movements, then go for it.

O'Shea had spotted a small, obscure table near the back stairs leading to the restrooms. He was ready, but so was a couple who also had their eyes on the table. No sweat, O'Shea figured. He not only had a three-step lead, he noticed the seated customers' slight twitchy, muscle flexing—a dead give away that the guy was about to get up. O'Shea was right, and before the customer had fully cleared his chair, O'Shea had staked his claim by placing his tray on the edge of the table. "Hi." O'Shea smiled to the guy who was shaking his head in annoyance as he left. O'Shea also caught scowling glances from the couple he beat. *Gottcha*, he snickered, *I won!*

Clearing a space for his tray, he stacked the remaining dirty dishes and cleaned the table with some paper napkins. He was ready for his $6.75 feast.

"Hello, Jack. How about some more coffee?" Half way through his meal, O'Shea was glad to see Paola, whom he hadn't noticed earlier.

"Oh sure. Say when you got a minute, I've got something to show you."

Paola arched her brows with a devilish grin. "What do have in mind?"

Even though he had known her for years, O'Shea blanched a little. "It's a little disk that may be part of a game or something. With all your kids, I thought you might recognize it."

In her forties, Paola was exceptionally pretty, with an equally alluring, well-proportioned, sensuous body. She was constantly the object of dirty jokes and sexual innuendos, which she cheerfully tolerated, for the good of tips. Yet, so different from most men, especially cops, O'Shea had never hit on her. She rightfully assumed it was a combination of his bashfulness and respect for her marriage. She liked both reasons, and when she liked a customer, she enjoyed chatting with them regardless the demands of business.

After filling O'Shea's cup, she placed her tray of drinks and coffee pot on the table, as if she had nothing but time. "Let me see the disk."

Retrieving it from his wallet, O'Shea almost reverently stared at the disk before handing it to her.

She spent a solid minute examining both sides of the disk while she paused a few times as if trying to place it. Finally, "No, Jack, with all the toys, games, puzzles and computer software we've gotten the kids, this is a new one on me. Where'd you get it?"

As she returned the disk, O'Shea smiled thinly. "Oh, in the sand. Thanks, Paola."

She nodded, grabbed the tray and pot and disappeared into the crowd of customers.

As he finished his meal and last drop of coffee, O'Shea noticed the back of a person wearing an orange jacket with black sleeves. Feeling another jolt of adrenalin, O'Shea jumped up and weaved his way through the mob that blocked full view of the jacket. Then he saw it was a guy on his way out.

"Hey," O'Shea shouted. "You with the orange and black jacket."

A no-neck, bulldog looking guy, instantly spun around. "What do ya want?" he growled. There was a large logo stitched in black across the front of his huge jacket: "San Francisco Rollerblades".

Oh shit, O'Shea winced to himself. "I'm sorry, I thought you were with a club called *The Trickers*."

The guys jaw relaxed a bit. "Nah," he muttered, shaking his head.

O'Shea stood flat-footed for a moment, as he watched the bulldog spin around and swagger out the entrance.

A few hours later, while sitting in his living room watching the TV news, he took another look at the small orange disk with the black letter "E".

"Christ, Helen," he whispered, "did that prick of a husband off you? Why didn't you just kill the son of a bitch? He deserved it. Hell, he died anyway."

📖 📖 📖

Usually, a visit to the hospital wasn't a gala event for the Ellis family. This evening, however, was one of those rare exceptions. After seeing Connie Wong and Sam Eng at Kaiser Hospital, they were off to the circus. Ellis just couldn't wait any longer for the surprise. It had been a traumatic few days for all of them, including his two boys. They adored their sister even though they didn't show it in words.

At dinner, when Ellis had told his unusually subdued family about an evening at the circus, their mood swing was electrifying.

Elizabeth squeezed Paul's hand until his knuckles cracked. She knew they all needed a fun respite.

Beth leaped up, and practically strangled her dad with a hug. "Thank you so much, Dad. It's a real circus without animals."

The two boys cheered in the background. "All right! Hey, great! Tonight, really?"

Ellis and his wife hadn't been to a circus since their childhoods. The boys had never been to one, and Beth had gone to a disappointing Barnum and Bailey Circus with her seventh grade class. She couldn't bear to see the animals in bondage. Her parents agreed.

After dishes, it took a record breaking ten minutes of scurrying, to get the whole family in the car.

At Kaiser, Ellis joined the rest of his family in Connie's room before seeing Detective Eng. Connie was propped up in bed, partially concealed by a room-filling, iridescent array of flowers. The fresh, rich colors and fragrant aromas complimented her youthful beauty as she hugged and smiled her way through the whole family.

Before Ellis left the room, he checked with Connie's nurse. She told him Connie had ingested a powerful barbiturate, probably from her carton of orange juice, and that her high normal blood pressure no doubt contributed to her quick recovery. Her blood pressure on the way to the hospital was a dangerously low 65/30.

Ellis was thinking of Beth's low normal blood pressure when he asked the nurse. "What if Miss Wong had low blood pressure before the barbiturate?"

She replied softly, in confidence. "Well, that's for the doctor to say, but personally, she might have died before she got here."

📖 📖 📖

Sam Eng, the twenty-three year old detective who looked fourteen, was also sitting up in bed. He was reading Homer's *Iliad*. Other than mummifying, shingled layers of bandage around his right arm and shoulder, he seemed fine. Closing his book, Eng looked at his sole bouquet of flowers, then at Ellis. "Thanks, Sergeant Ellis. I really appreciate the flowers."

Ellis looked down at the book and grinned. "I'm glad you like them. It was Elizabeth's idea. How you feeling, when do you get out of here, and what's this with Homer?"

Eng laughed as he put the book on his nightstand. "Well, I feel great. Just a little stiff. The Doc said it was a clean skewer beneath the shoulder joint that missed bone, major blood vessels, and any vitals. The javelin went through nothing but flesh and tissue. Since I live alone, they'll keep me here an extra couple of days. I'll be out of here by the weekend. Now, about the book. Well, sitting in on a literature class, the other students were assigned to read both the *Iliad* and the *Odyssey*. I probably hated Homer when I was a real high school student, but since I was supposed to be a student, I started rereading the *Iliad*. And you know what, Sergeant, it's really interesting."

Ellis sat on the edge of Eng's bed, nodding with a smirk. "You know, Sam, looking over some of Beth's reading assignments, I've been doing the same thing. Reading some of the classics I couldn't stand in high school."

Eng covered, in detail, how he was pinned to the ground by a javelin when less than two feet from Beth. He recalled no pain, "...Since I was probably in shock."

When Ellis asked about the javelin thrower, Eng told him an initial investigation report would be in his office tomorrow. Highlighting some of the report, he said that one of the initial investigators said all student javelins had been accounted for, and that none of those practicing were possible suspects. No wild throws.

"You know, Sergeant," Eng added, "they said the guy must have been a giant, judging by the estimated velocity of the javelin."

God, more giant clues, Ellis thought. "Interesting," he said.

CHAPTER 30

Down Mariposa Street, right on Third Street, over the China Basin drawbridge, and onto the Embarcadero, that was where Ellis announced to his family, "About a quarter mile and we're there."

Five pairs of eyes were scanning both sides of the Embarcadero's Herb Caen Lane, an area that was once the center of world shipping, then called the Waterfront.

"Look!" shouted Elizabeth. Their response was a chorus of *Wow's*. About a hundred yards down the boulevard was a hundred fifty acre opened pier that had years ago lost its mammoth warehouse to bulldozers. Then it was, "Pier 32." Now it was a city event area over the water, and for the next week, it was *The Russian Circus,* a place promising to thrill anyone—who could afford it.

The entire area was ablaze with colorful, undulating spotlights, swaying search lights, and red, blue and white strobe lights, lining both sides of the block long entrance way. Mark noticed first. "Gosh Mom, it looks like an Airport runway."

He got one "uh huh" from his dad, as the family's eyes bounced all over the place. There was so much to see.

The tent alone was spectacular. As long as three city blocks and seven-stories high, it was a dynamic white whale, speckled with thousands of silver leaf scales. The Bay winds, along with the dazzling play of lights, created an illusion of flowing movement, power and the magic of Moby Dick. The white whale's tail, trailing gracefully downward from the main body, swayed with the winds and thrashed with the changing splashes of light. To anyone with even a little imagination it was indeed a lively Moby Dick whose gaping mouth gobbled up the audience as they entered the main entrance.

It was an evening of oohes, aahs and wows that thrilled the whole family. There were jugglers galore, up close and personal clowns, fire eaters warming the cool breeze, sword swallowers riding unicycles, ten-feet tall trolls who scared Mark until he finally figured out they were on stilts. "All this," Paul marveled, "and we haven't gone inside yet."

So delighted with his family's soaring mood swing, Ellis bought the second best seats at $69 apiece. At $105 for the front row, he just couldn't part with any more generosity. When they found their seats, about six feet above and fifteen feet behind the front row, he grinned almost triumphantly. *Second best is a better vantage point than the front row.* Better still, was his family's wide-eyed smiles as they clutched their $30 worth of cotton candy, nachos, hot dogs, root beers, and onion rings. Typically the cool, blasé teenagers, Chris and Mark were jumping out of their seats, screaming, laughing, and eating. Elizabeth and Beth, on either side of Paul, practically ripped his arms off in excitement. And Paul? Every time he glanced at his wife and kids' happy faces, he couldn't stop beaming. *Thanks boss*, he grinned.

Inside, under the Big Top, the fascinated family had quickly realized that the outside entertainment was just a tasty hors d'oevre. The main meal was in Moby Dick's stomach.

Sixty feet above the crowd were trapeze artists with incredible feats of flight, twists, summersaults and one arm catches. Below were beautiful precision dancers seemingly locked together as one. There were musclemen taking cannonball shots in the stomach, magician illusionists, vanishing large sections of the audience in a cloud of golden smoke, thirty foot high platform divers splashing into a three foot pool of water, and gymnastic acts that would astound Olympic athletes. Throughout the multiple performances, there was a periodic sight that triggered gasps from all spectators.

It was Ellis' errant benefactor, *Gazaba le Terrible*. At eight feet four inches, he was billed as the tallest man in the world. Dressed in a silver space suit, helmet and all, he wandered the arena shaking his clinched fist at the audience. Occasionally he left the arena, or walked to the $105 front row seats and stared menacingly as the audience screamed. Even Sergeant Ellis was amazed. *My God, it is a real giant*, he thought, *with feet to match*.

It was one of those enchanting evenings the Ellis' would long remember, sharing with each other their favorite acts and most thrilling moments. Ellis would also never forget his interview with Gazaba the Terrible.

Sitting down in his dressing room, he towered over Ellis, who thought the giant's feet looked like a pair of chaise lounges, with a head the size of a twenty-five pound watermelon. Observing the giant and listening to his handler, a Russian physician, however, was sad.

Orphaned and sickly from birth, he was hospitalized during most of his childhood. At nineteen, his legs could barely carry his massive body. He was in constant pain and his space suit effectively concealed his leg braces, permitting him to walk for about ten minutes before sitting down. Looking up at the giant's mournful eyes, his handler clasped one of the huge, bony hands, explaining, that was why Gazaba frequently left the arena during the two and a half hour show. The essentially disabled giant was also mildly retarded and his shoe length was a surprising eighteen inches, much smaller than they appeared. Thanking the physician and circus managers, Ellis promised them confidentiality, as he patted Gazaba on the knee.

Rejoining his exuberant family, Ellis turned on a quick smile while thinking what a dismal ending to such a happy night.

CHAPTER 31

Looking down at the note under a little statue on his desk, O'Shea did one of his slow head-shaking grins. *Christ, it's only 7:30*, he thought. Reading the note, his grin expanded into a broad smile.

"Thanks, John. It was a night the whole family will never forget. Here's the giant, *Gazaba the Terrible*. Not as big as we expected."

O'Shea chuckled as he picked up the five-inch tall statue. Seeing Ellis returning with a cup of coffee, O'Shea examined the Gazaba statue carefully. "Hell," he shouted, "his feet couldn't be over a half inch long. Naw, he's not our giant."

Sitting himself on the edge of O'Shea's desk, Ellis reached over and squeezed his boss's shoulder. "You can't imagine how happy you made my family and me."

O'Shea put the statue on the corner of his desk, glancing at his partner. "Just don't kiss me."

"That I can't promise."

O'Shea looked slightly startled. "Christ, Paul. You're developing a wild sense of humor; it better be humor." He smiled. "Now, what did the tickets cost you?"

"Not what you said they'd cost." After pausing a few moments, Ellis grabbed his coffee cup and sat at his desk. "The cheapest tickets were $45."

"I didn't ask you that." O'Shea loudly interrupted.

Ellis threw up his hands. "Let me finish, will ya? I got the second best tickets for $69 apiece."

O'Shea got up with his newspaper and coffee cup. "I gotta take my *brit* and get some coffee. When I return, I want to know why you were too goddamned chincy to buy your family the best tickets."

Somewhat puzzled, Ellis scratched his head as he watched O'Shea disappear down the corridor.

By 8:00 a.m., O'Shea reappeared with his full coffee cup and a tight-lipped grimace. "Well?" he asked.

"God, Loot, are you serious? The top tickets cost $105, and the ones I bought gave us as good or better view."

Sipping his hot coffee, O'Shea softened his tone. "I screwed up. I'd forgotten to tell you to buy the best tickets in the house. PD budget can afford them."

"I did get the best, John."

"Great." O'Shea grinned. "Just fill out the voucher with $345 plus fifty bucks for meals. I know how your kids scarf, and don't even think of kissing me."

"OK, I promise."

"Alright, now what do you say we stop farting around and get some work done?"

Grabbing an expense voucher from their filing cabinet, Ellis immediately started justifying the circus trip. He told O'Shea about the interview with the giant's handler/physician, Gazaba's enfeebled physical condition, debilitating health, his mild retardation and minimal language development.

"Besides," Ellis added, "his shoe length is only eighteen inches."

O'Shea nodded. "No big deal. That's what I figured. At least we've officially eliminated a suspect. Anyway, I read the report on Eng. This poor bastard, Gazaba, wouldn't have had the strength to chuck a javelin over his shoes. Our giant, whoever or whatever it is, is big, powerful, and the sucker's invisible."

Dropping the completed voucher in the out box, Ellis resugared his half-cup of milky white coffee. "Did you read the forensic report on Beth's friend, Connie Wong?"

O'Shea shook his head. "You get here so goddamned early, I never get a chance to read anything."

"Well," Ellis explained, "I also learned a lot last night talking to Wong and her nurse. Someone at the school wanted to kill my kid. Maybe to keep her from demanding a homicide investigation of Jerran's death."

O'Shea dropped one of his files on the desk, and leaned forward.

"Go on," he said.

"A powerful barbiturate was injected into Beth's orange juice carton. It's also a drug to lower blood pressure. Fortunately, Beth gave her carton to Connie Wong, a kid whose normal blood pressure is high enough to offset any of the barbiturate blood pressure reducing effects. But my daughter's pressure is normally low enough that the drug could have killed her."

Ellis continued uninterrupted. "It's also highly likely the javelin throw was meant for Beth, and Eng got in the way. On the positive side, a little arm-twisting of Poly's principal by Sergeant Wagner and me got an assembly this morning, which is going on right now. Wagner called just before you came in. He'll be telling the whole student body about the homicide conclusions, ongoing investigation and undercover cops planted at the school. That should eliminate any further attacks on Beth."

O'Shea was immersed in thought, leaning back, staring blankly at the ceiling. "You know, even though this isn't our case, it's one of your kids, and something doesn't make a hell of a lot of sense. Jerran was obviously murdered with an amateurish effort to make it look like a suicide. Beth wasn't going for it. If the perps were trying to avoid a school investigation, why in the hell would they try to kill Beth? Christ, two deaths of kids from the same school within a month would insure a police investigation. It's got to be something else."

Looking over the medical report, O'Shea continued. "Generally, such an overdose of barbiturates isn't lethal. Just makes you weird-out or sick as hell. I doubt if the perp knew about Beth's blood pressure, and the super stud, invisible giant or whatever the hell it is, missed by a couple feet with the javelin. You know, I think they wanted to scare your kid, not kill her, and they sure as hell didn't want to spotlight Poly as *Murder Incorporated*."

Ellis gave a slight grin. "As usual, I gotta agree with you when I evaluate what happened as a cop, not a father.

O'Shea inadvertently did a double take while glancing down the hall to the coffee machine. Watching Ida's firm, curvaceous posterior as she bent low over the coffee pot, he silently stared for a moment. "Ah...OK then, we can get back to our own investigation."

Ellis noticed the double take. "Great, so why don't you get another cup of coffee first."

Clearing his throat, O'Shea, grabbed his cup. "Might as well. Do you want a refill?"

"I'm fine."

Just as O'Shea hit the hallway at a full gallop, Ida, with a cup of coffee in each hand, swayed her hips down the side corridor. When O'Shea reached the coffee machine, she was nowhere in sight. *Oh well*, he figured, *I wasn't ready for a pitch anyway.* Returning to their cubicle, O'Shea unobtrusively slipped into his chair.

After a minute, Ellis broke the awkward silence. "Can I get you a cup of coffee?"

Glancing at his empty cup, O'Shea looked up with a feeble smile. "Oh, no thanks. I drink too much of the crap. Keeps me awake all night."

It was obvious to Ellis that his partner still wasn't ready to discuss Ida. "There's a memo here from Zimmerman. I'm sure glad she's persistent. I was supposed to call her this morning"

"There's still a lot of morning," O'Shea interjected.

"It's a long memo. She discovered, through computer checks and cross checks, that a Lula Rogoff, who was on duty when Grace Digness was killed, had been arrested twice. The first time was in St. Paul, Minnesota in 1987 and again in Kansas City, Missouri in 1995, for second-degree murder. Both times she was a registered nurse, accused of killing a terminally ill, elderly patient. Despite pretty solid evidence, she was acquitted each time. She was certified as a nurse's aide in California a few years ago, and she's been working at St. Mary's Hospital for seven months."

Half listening, O'Shea glanced at the Hansen file, then absently removed the little disk from his badge wallet. "Christ, here we go again. Every time we're going to carefully re-examine all physical evidence, we get a new suspect, or something."

Folding the paper into a glider, Ellis floated the memo onto O'Shea's desk. "I know what you're thinking. I still believe these deaths are somehow connected, especially with a hate gang like the Trickers possibly linked to one of our eight. But, it's also very possible some are independent homicides that happened to occur the same day as the others."

Massaging the disk like some lucky charm, O'Shea ignored the glider's landing. "Yeah, you're right, this is another one that has to be checked out thoroughly. Let's hope this isn't another waste of time."

"Well, this sounds like a solid lead, Loot."

Still fiddling with the little disk, O'Shea grinned faintly. "OK, OK! It's all standard procedure. Guess I'm just tired of dead ends. So, go get 'em. I'll hang out here for awhile, rechecking our evidence against a one perp theory."

Ellis gathered up his notes and the Digness file. "I'll go to ID first, talk with Zimmerman. Then re-interview hospital staff, Rogoff and, you know, standard procedure. Incidentally, what's that thing you keep fooling with? Can I see it?"

Almost begrudgingly, as if losing his talisman, O'Shea handed the disk to his partner. "I found it in the sand, on Helen Hansen's cliff. It's got an 'E' on it."

Ellis spent a silent minute flipping the disk over, staring at and examining both sides. "You know, I've seen another one like this, but I don't think it had the same letter."

"From one of your kids games maybe?"

"No, I get the feeling it has something to do with the cases. I can't remember which, it just seemed odd at the time, and I remember it was the color of the Trickers' jackets."

Suddenly O'Shea seemed re-energized. Slapping his forehead with the palm of his left hand, while quickly reaching for the disk with his right, he gave Ellis some rapid blinks and head shakes, as if regaining consciousness. "Thanks partner. Now I know why I've been hanging onto this thing. There's something like it in the effects of one of the eight. I saw it somewhere. Maybe it's in the property room! Paul, you've got a memory like a goddamn elephant. Christ, I could kiss you."

Ellis gave an exaggerated sneer. "Yuk, no thanks. I guess I know where you'll spend the morning."

"You got it. Let's get out of here."

φ φ φ

By age twenty-three, with associate professor status, Elvin Streichner also received his second Ph.D. at the University of Montreal, this one in chemistry. During his first five years there, he demonstrated his academic genius with over twenty scientific publications. He was marveled as a scholar, yet shunned socially. Assigned principally to the Physics Department, Streichner was initially disliked and later despised by many of his colleagues, some of whom feared him, while others considered him *strange*. In class, he was so strict and demanding, especially with star athletes, students avoided enrolling in his classes. It was also rumored that, following a shouting argument with a full professor in an adjoining office, the professor walked up to the sixth floor and leaped to his death.

Four years later, with trustees barely tolerating him and colleagues ignoring him, Streichner justified his position by working alone in research, while publishing more for the school than any five professors. He might have worked there until pensioned, if he hadn't clashed severely with the university chancellor. It was an argument over one of his forthcoming publications. The chancellor vehemently disagreed with the paper's conclusions, which contradicted earlier research by the previous head of the physics department, who was now the chancellor. As usual, he was absolutely right scientifically and absolutely wrong interpersonally. He threatened the chancellor with black magic justice, a strategy that ended his Canadian professional career. He still hadn't gotten the hang of professional decorum or just getting along with others.

His mountain of publications in prestigious scientific journals, together with numerous awards, won him a Harvard University faculty position, without Canadian references. He also recognized a need for mastery of another subject he had never thought necessary.

While traveling down Canada into the United States, he purchased a variety of psychology books on social skills training. By the time he arrived at Harvard, he had absorbed the contents of fifteen psychology texts and pop-self help books on winning friends, developing interpersonal skills, and the practical use of *operant conditioning* with positive reinforcement in daily social interactions. He was ready!

CHAPTER 32

During his drive to St. Mary's Hospital, Ellis thought about June Zimmerman. She was 6'1", with a scrawny hundred eighteen pound body; shaped like PVC pipe, buck teeth, receding chin and big, hawkish nose. A spinster, at age thirty-eight, she was too tall, too skinny, too ugly and too awkward to those who didn't know her. To her departmental peers, she was too smart, too reliable, too efficient and much too indispensable. To the cops who needed her skills, however, her appearance never mattered. She was simply the best. *Bless her heart*, Ellis thought.

He learned from her that fifty-five year old Lula Rogoff had been a registered nurse in three states including Ohio, Missouri, and Minnesota. Other than the two murder charges, she had no malpractice complaints in any states. In fact, nurse supervisors had consistently regarded her performance as superior, with excellent nursing skills, and a markedly cooperative, uncomplaining attitude. She was also extremely compassionate and couldn't bear to see her patients suffering. She had also been exceptionally precise in administering medications prescribed by an attending physician.

The only exceptions to her exemplary record were the two cancer patients who died of Morphine overdoses on her shift. In both cases, Rogoff had reportedly complained to her supervisors that the patients needed a higher level of self-administered Morphine. Eight years apart, both of her requests were denied, and the patients overdosed the nights she had complained.

Despite plenty of circumstantial evidence, there was reasonable doubt by both juries. Morphine drips were not one hundred percent reliable, and in their eighties, both patients were painfully on the verge of death. These considerations apparently encouraged both juries to give Rogoff the benefit of any doubt.

Pulling into the St. Mary's Hospital official parking lot, Ellis felt well fortified with plenty of solid information. Yet, even though he could legitimately approach Rogoff as a primary suspect, it was far from a slam-dunk fit. *Oh well*, he thought.

📖 📖 📖

Arriving unannounced, Ellis couldn't have planned the visit better. It happened to be a Wednesday, the same day of the week Grace Digness had died, and remarkably, the staff on duty that day, was still working together in the ICU. Equally fortunate, there were only two patients in the twenty-bed unit, which resulted in a slow pace with few staff distractions during interviews with Ellis.

Since the detectives had pretty much initially assumed Terry Digness had killed his wife, the earlier perfunctory interviews with some of the on-duty staff had been brief. Ellis hadn't even met the nurses' aides. He had figured it wasn't necessary, since the head nurse, Eloise Pardee, an elegant-looking black woman, had vouched for their whereabouts. Also not important at the time, Pardee had no way of knowing exactly where the aides were, nor had the detectives clearly established Pardee's whereabouts.

The only person at the nurses' station nearest Digness' room was Janice Hanna, one of the ICU nurses. Candice Craven, the other ICU nurse, was clearly alibied on a break in the staff dining room at the time of Grace's death. Ellis also learned from Zimmerman that all of the staff, except Rogoff, had unblemished work records and not as much as a traffic ticket arrest record.

Another good fortune for Ellis was the head nurse's open cooperation and her own thorough record keeping. Reviewing her nurses' station records during the half hour bracketing Digness' death, the two nurses' aides were either in rooms 123 or 125, changing beds. Nurse Craven was on her break, Nurse Hanna was covering the station where she could receive visitors, answer the phone, and monitor the TV screens of vital signs. Head Nurse Pardee was actually consulting with Evelyn Harrison, M.D. in the doctor's office, well down an adjoining corridor.

During his interview with nurse Hanna, a cheerful, ten year ICU veteran of St. Mary's Hospital, Ellis knew she obviously had no alibi. She had been alone at the station and immediately hit the alarm, as she tried to resuscitate Digness. There was still no tenable reason to consider her a suspect. She again stated there had been no visitors while she was at the station. She did acknowledge, however, that while doing paper work at the desk, someone could have slipped by unnoticed. As she stated during the first interview, she did see Mr. Digness tearfully running from his wife's room about a half hour before she discovered the victim's body.

Ellis interviewed the nurses' aides last. Marilynn Garcia confirmed the head nurse's notes. She was working with Lula Rogoff making beds and tidying up rooms when they both heard about the Digness death. Ellis quietly felt relieved with Rogoff's firm alibi. Like Terry Digness, Rogoff's personality profile contradicted violence of the kind evident in the Digness murder. Without an alibi, however, Ellis would have had a tough time eliminating her as a suspect. It was well known that the DA's office considered prior arrests, regardless of convictions, as much more convincing evidence than behavioral portraits. They would have wanted the detectives to keep pressing her for a slip up in her story.

When Ellis finally met Lula Rogoff near the nurses' station, he was doubly ecstatic that she was no longer a suspect. *It's uncanny*, he thought. *She looks like everybody's mother, right down to the apron. God, she's my mother with a white face, and how could I have ever interrogated Mom.* Still gawking at her from a distance, he tried to figure out why she exuded such a comforting radiance. She was kind of average everything, with short graying brown hair in a net, little wire-rimmed half glasses on a chain, pug nosed, round pudgy face with the slightest trace of makeup, and a moderately short, plumping body.

Once he introduced himself, however, he realized why. Her motherly, unpretentious appearance matched her totally natural openness and gentle interest in others. Ellis felt she listened to him as if he were the most important person in the universe. "It's really my pleasure meeting you, ma'am. Can I ask you one question?"

She smiled and nodded permission. "Of course, what would you like to know?"

He smiled back a bit self-consciously. "Um, I was just wondering why you're not working as a registered nurse. You're apparently so well-qualified."

She replied softly, almost soothingly and without the slightest hesitation. "After all the negative publicity and doubts about my professional conduct in the past, I thought it might be a problem to obtain a California license. I love working with those who need help. So being a nurses' aide is just fine."

Ellis knew she was aware he had checked her background, which for some strange reason embarrassed him a little. "I'm glad we have nice people like you helping others."

She seemed to recognize his last comment as a subtle apology. "Thank you, Sergeant Ellis, you're a good man."

This time Ellis was relieved at the loss of a suspect.

📖 📖 📖

Before leaving ICU, Ellis wandered into the unoccupied room where Grace Digness had expired. He sat in the single chair in the corner, staring at the empty bed, blank TV screen, silent monitors and sterile, white walls. Stroking his chin, Ellis relaxed into deep thought. *Now we're satisfied the staff didn't do it. Neither did Terry Digness, and Grace was too weak to kill herself.* He smiled with a new thought. *The giant would have been spotted before he hit the room. How could anyone slip in and out of this room without being seen? Something's missing.* With an inward chuckle, he thought of O'Shea's sense of humor as he whispered out loud, "The killer's missing."

Slipping back into sober thoughts, Ellis examined the physical evidence in his mind's eye. *Nothing, no prints, struggle, hair samples, fibers, smudges, missing items, or witnesses.* Anticipating a headache, he decided to leave. Waving goodbye to the head nurse alone at the nurses' station, Ellis stopped for no apparent reason. *Just one more try,* he thought.

"I'm sorry. I was just thinking that we might have overlooked something in the Digness room. Maybe something you or the aides found after we left."

Slightly protruding her lower lip, Mrs. Pardee rolled her eyes upward for a few moments. "As a matter of fact, after cleaning the room, Marilynn and Lula did have a few items they put in a bag in case one of you returned." Reaching under a counter, she came up with a brown paper bag she quickly handed to Ellis. The top was stapled and on the side was a scribbled note. "Grace Digness Deceased 4/8/02 For SFPD Misc. items."

Tearing open the top of the bag, Ellis glanced at the head nurse with a boyish smile. "Do you mind if I pour the contents on the counter?"

She grinned. "Go right ahead. I won't tell."

A small pile of stuff fell all over the counter. *Wow*, Ellis thought, *didn't forensics bother to take anything other than Mrs. Digness?* Donning a latex glove, Ellis sifted through an empty Kleenex box, partially empty bottles of aspirin, Motrin, Tylenol with codeine, paper clips, and two paperback novels. As he fanned the pages of the first book, a local laundromat business card went flying. *Probably used as a bookmark*, he figured. The other book was brand new and empty. Ellis looked at Mrs. Pardee. "I suppose she died before her husband could read this one to her."

She nodded reverently.

Heaving a light sigh of disappointment, Ellis took one fast peek into the empty bag. There on the bottom was a little round object wedged in a paper clip.

CHAPTER 33

Headed for the property room, O'Shea was urged back to his desk by the demanding ring of his phone. It was Captain McInerney, who was generally the bearer of bad news. This wasn't the hopeful exception. Timidly, he asked if O'Shea would come to Chief Hoel's office.

"When?"

After a minute pause and a muffled coughing sound, O'Shea got an apologetic answer. "Is right now OK?"

"Do I really have a choice?"

Following another pause. "Well, no. I guess not."

"Don't sweat it, Captain, you're just the messenger."

"Thanks, Jack."

Heading out the door again, he grumbled. "Now what? Shit, it's not even 9:00 yet."

The receptionist was expecting him, and as he entered the chief's office, he knew the *now what* wasn't going to be friendly. Behind his mahogany desk, the chief, in a well-tailored uniform, was already leaning forward with a teeth-clinching glower.

Stan Burton, the mayor, seated in a comfortable leather chair to the chief's left, was less dramatic—just a cold stare.

To the right of the chief's desk was another soft leather chair occupied by Polytechnic's principal, Ms. Belotti. She was contemptuously smirking. Although O'Shea had never met her, he had a pretty good idea who she was and why he was there.

The mayor was a tall, broad-shouldered, handsome politician. He hated O'Shea for his out-spoken disagreements with many of his policies, and O'Shea's allegiance to mayoral candidate, Hall.

Short, chubby Chief Hoel hated O'Shea for obvious reasons. Not only was Hoel appointed by the mayor, but O'Shea wanted his job. They were indisputable opposites. Hoel was a politician, a bright company lackey, who had advanced from one desk to another, never challenging superiors while generally functioning as their cheerleader. Since his first year as a rookie he had never worked in the field, yet now, as chief, he knew an effective police department needed front line cops like O'Shea—provided they didn't threaten his job.

As O'Shea's boss, Hoel was the first to speak. "Have a seat," he said, pointing to an old folding metal chair directly in front of his desk.

In many ways O'Shea was a rebel, but certainly not a fool. He knew there was enough political power in the office to fire half of San Francisco. He quickly and quietly sat down.

"It's police policy that any disagreements with other city agencies must be cleared with superiors prior to any action against another city agency. You're aware of that policy, Lieutenant?"

"Yes, I am, Chief."

Hoel rose off his chair and leaned forward over his desk with a more downward view of O'Shea. "Then why didn't you go through proper channels before demanding that the principal of Polytechnic have an immediate police-inspired assembly, despite her disagreement? You have your own cases to deal with. This was a juvenile division matter."

O'Shea knew better than to start an argument. He was outgunned. So, as a compromise, he offered an explanation. "I'm sure you know, Chief, that my partner, Sergeant Ellis, was authorized by Lieutenant McDonald to investigate the death of student Jerran Ramsey, and that Sergeant Ellis' daughter had been threatened, which was related to the death. As you also know, I'm Sergeant Ellis' superior, which I assumed legitimized authorizing his participation in such an assembly. It was my judgment that students were in danger, as evidenced by the threatening note, the poisoning of one student and the potentially fatal injury of an undercover detective during a school function. Police policy to protect and warn citizens who are possibly in danger, in my judgment as Sergeant Ellis' superior officer, was sufficient reason to disregard an interagency dispute in favor of our police mission."

Glancing at all three, O'Shea added a token dash of contrition. "I certainly apologize if it inconvenienced anyone."

That son of a bitch, Hoel thought, *he's covered all bases*. "Next time, let your top brass know what's going on. If there's a danger in a school, the entire police force should be alerted."

O'Shea knew the chief's reply was pathetic. There were no such mandates. He also knew this harsh last word was for the mayor's benefit.

"Anything else, Chief?"

Glancing at the bored looking mayor, Hoel thought for a moment. "If there's no progress on your current cases in a few more weeks, I'll transfer them to some other detectives. That's all."

O'Shea knew that was more posturing crap. As he got up from the hard seat, he casually nodded to each person. "OK, Chief, Mayor, Ms. Principal." Closing the door behind him, he had the last smirk. *It's the three stooges*, he thought.

O'Shea really needed a cup of coffee. Returning to his office, he looked around for a moment, realizing the cramped little cubicle was kind of a refuge. *Maybe more of a home than my apartment*, he sighed. Picking up his coffee cup, a souvenir from a long ago trip to Hawaii, he reminisced about the wife and family he once had. *Christ*, he thought, *did I screw that up*. Heading for the coffee machine, he scanned the cubicle with another thought—*Oh well. Shit.*

O'Shea hadn't noticed Ida on her way to the coffee machine down the side corridor. Nearly colliding, they brushed each other as they sidestepped their way to the coffee pot. Ida greeted O'Shea with a warm smile. Inches away, she made no effort to move.

O'Shea was bathing in her feminine fragrance when he blurted out, "Would you have dinner with me some evening?"

"I'd love to."

O'Shea was stunned by his spontaneous request and her quick reply.

"Tonight?"

"Sure." She grinned, still inches away.

Incredulous, he welcomed his fantasy. "Seven o'clock all right?"

She lightly squeezed his upper arm, which he instinctively flexed. "Fine."

O'Shea got her address and scurried back to his cubicle with an empty coffee cup. Almost panting, he sat down at his desk. Then it dawned on him. Throwing his hands up in the air, he closed his eyes and shook his head. "Jesus Christ," he wailed, "it's not a dream. She's going out with this old fart. I did it."

O'Shea cheerfully hummed his way down to the property room, where the sergeant in charge couldn't understand why any cop would smile in such a grim, dirty area.

O'Shea started with Villa. Nothing but blood stained Torres clothes, several inhalers, a matchbook, couple of ballpoint pens, an address book and a notebook with appointments Carlos never made. He carefully examined the items several times without finding another disk. Then, looking at the piles of musty property, O'Shea whispered to himself, *I'd better get out of here before I lose my great mood.*

📖 📖 📖

Reaching his office, O'Shea glanced down the hall at the coffee machine. *I've really got a date with her. YES!* He snickered to himself.

Ellis hung up his phone just as O'Shea, wearing an impish grin, entered their inner office cubicle. "Wow, John, did you win the lottery?"

This time, O'Shea had no intention of stifling his feelings with a friend. He kept grinning. "I hope it's only that obvious to you. Are you ready for the news?"

Ellis leaned forward with a wide-eyed smile. "Lay it on me."

"I'm taking Ida to dinner tonight, and you know, it's not just the date. That by itself is great. It's that I overcame a stupid fear of being rejected, and by somebody I really didn't even know. Without brooding about it, I just met her at the coffee pot, asked her out and she said yes. If she had said no, I'd still have my nuts. You can't lose a relationship you never had. Right?"

Ellis had listened carefully with a deep smile. "I'm really proud of you. I know how overwhelming it is to deal with some irrational fear. I never told you, but I'm terrified of bees. I've never had a bad sting and I'm still terrified. It's a real phobia. Anyway, you did it. No matter how the date goes, you conquered a fear."

"Thanks, pal. It's not just a gorgeous gal, half my age. Well, that's part of it."

Ellis gave O'Shea a quizzical frown. "Really?" They both laughed.

Noticing the pile of notes on Ellis' desk, O'Shea got up grabbing both coffee cups. "Guess it's work time. I'll get the coffee. Christ, I can actually stroll down to the machine without a knot in my stomach."

Ellis nodded. "Wish I could say the same about bees."

"That's my next project." O'Shea winked.

◫ ◫ ◫

As he reviewed his notes, Ellis stirred his cup of thick, white coffee while O'Shea shook his head in amazement. Ellis looked up at his partner. "Don't say it."

"I won't," O'Shea quickly replied, holding back a laugh. "What ya got?"

"I'll start with the call from Sergeant Wagner. Lieutenant MacDonald's retiring next week."

"Did he have a choice?" asked O'Shea.

Ellis grimaced. "Sure, back in uniform working the graveyard in the city jail. The one time in his career he righteously defies the chief, he's an outcast."

"I figured as much. I was hot-seated this morning by the three stooges. The mayor, the chief and the principal. They were all pissed because none of us sucked up. The chief and Ms. Principal take turns burying their nose eight inches up the mayor's ass, and it's all power politics. Nothing to do with police work."

Sipping his white coffee, Ellis nodded. "Knowing you, Loot, I'm surprised they didn't try to fire you."

"They would in a heartbeat if they could. They hate my guts, but with nothing substantial against me, they can't do squat. In the old days, they could summarily get rid of me. But now, with gay rights, minority rights, women's rights, and old fart's rights, you have to burn down city hall before they can fire you."

Ellis was shaking his head. "But they can screw you around, try to force you out. Like Lieutenant MacDonald."

O'Shea grinned. "You see, Paul, once you've rolled over or sucked up, they got ya. MacDonald could change but they wouldn't tolerate it. Remember, he was one of them, which makes him some kind of a traitor. Whether he knew it or not, he was one of their gang, and once a member, you can't quit."

Ellis added another spoonful of sugar to his coffee. "Is that why the chief hasn't rousted Wagner and me?"

O'Shea shook his head with a sigh as he watched Ellis down his white, sugar coffee.

"Don't say it," Ellis snapped.

Wide-eyed, O'Shea threw up his hands. "Say what? Anyway, you guys never joined the suck-ass club, and you're fine detectives. But remember, if the chief or his cronies ever catch you guys violating any rules of conduct, they won't hesitate to crucify your asses. They just protect their own as long as they stay their own."

Ellis leaned back in a deep stretch. "You know me, John. Guess I'm too straight to ever be busted."

O'Shea shook his head vigorously. "I don't want to get you paranoid, but don't ever count on your honesty and integrity in this business. Always watch your back. These bastards look for ways to set up those they don't like. Got it?"

Ellis narrowed his eyes with a frown. "Hey, wake up, it's me, your partner. I'm no maverick like you, but I'm sure as hell no trick. After narcotics, why do you think I still wanted you as my homicide partner and mentor, huh? Because you're the very best and the worst all combined into my friend. Remember, I'm the guy who doesn't miss a thing. I know what's going on. Half the department's gunning for you. So, I don't just watch my back, I'm always watching your back."

Sighing deeply, O'Shea sat back, silently staring within himself, then at Ellis.

"John, sometimes I don't say what I mean. Wunden would probably say I'm projecting my own paranoia onto you."

O'Shea paused. "I'd trust you with my life anytime. You're the best, with no *worst* except for your bullshit coffee and weird sense of humor."

That comment brought a brief exchange of faint smiles. Clearing his throat, O'Shea glanced thoughtfully at his partner. "Guess I just worry about you more than I should. Christ, you can take care of yourself."

Ellis nodded with a soft smile. "I guess I needed to hear all that. Let's just keep watching each others back, and when are we going to the Java House?"

O'Shea grabbed several files from his desk and waved them at Ellis. "When we get the bad guys, whoever the hell they are."

Ellis slammed his fist lightly on his desk. "I can sure live with that, Loot."

"How about a refill, Paul. What is it? Eight drops of coffee, a quart of cream, and three pounds of sugar?

Ellis grabbed his cup with both hands. "Stay put. I'll get both of ours. I can't have you hanging around the coffee pot anymore. You've got to leave a few females for the other bachelors."

O'Shea gave Ellis a jutting jaw nod. "Not bad. There's a sense of humor in there, somewhere."

When Ellis returned, O'Shea ignored the napkin over his partner's cup. "Any honeys waiting for me at the machine?'

Ellis handed O'Shea his cup, with a smirk. "Yeah, Loot, they're lining up."

"Tell them I'm busy. They'll have to come back later."

"I have a better idea. Let's do some work."

O'Shea shrugged and blew on his steaming coffee. "Hell, why not."

Ellis was already reviewing his notes.

O'Shea picked up a file, then, glancing at Ellis he dropped it. "How's Beth doing?"

"I'm glad you asked. That's our next topic."

📖 📖 📖

"Beth's fine for a couple reasons. She's tough, resilient and her friend, Connie Wong and Eng are recovering nicely. She also got another note. This time on her locker, not in it."

O'Shea interrupted. "Is that supposed to be good?"

Ellis heaved a heavy sigh. "Geeeeze, will you let me finish?"

O'Shea nodded with a puckish grin. "Sorry!"

"I got kinda mixed feelings about the note. Beth's relieved and it's a lot better than the first one. Maybe being a cop makes you paranoid. Anyhow, I'll read it to you:

> *Oh whitish night,*
> *Your date is right,*
> *So don't be blue,*
> *We won't hurt you.*"

Ellis looked at O'Shea with wide-eyed silence.

"Seems like the assembly might have scared somebody into backing off."

"Only problem with that is the timing. She found the note first thing in the morning, before the assembly."

O'Shea grunted. "Well, before I run my mouth, why don't you give me the whole picture and your opinion."

"Oh, OK. Remember, the first note was a warning in chalk on the inside of her locker. This time, it was a typed note in an envelope, taped to the outside of the locker door. Could have been messages from two separate people. The *we* in the second note obviously suggests more than one person. Maybe some students who felt sorry for her, or maybe an apology from the first perps who, even before the rally, decided to back off before someone got seriously dead. Lots of maybes."

O'Shea agreed with a nod. "I guess we're troubled by the same thing. Why the four line limerick, or whatever the hell it is? It's a weird note with little puzzles, which gives it a sinister spin. Freaky. Or maybe today's high school kids are just freaky."

Ellis was nodding frantically. "Boy, you got my concerns exactly. Instead of cryptic poetry, why didn't students just offer her their support? Or, if afraid of getting involved, just a clear message that they're on her side. And yes, there are some weird kids in most high schools. The schools just promote them each year rather than trying to justify expelling them. Students also have children's rights groups and indignant parents."

"I sure as hell won't interfere if you want to work with juvy for a while. But personally, I think Beth is in no immediate danger. I also think Wagner is a good cop who'll keep you posted. And, there are our own eight cases. You call it, Paul."

Ellis smiled. "What do you say we get on with our cases. OK?"

CHAPTER 34

O'Shea's good mood stumbled when Ellis told him all about the elimination of the nurses' aide, Rogoff, as a suspect. In one sense, he was glad because she seemed like a fine woman. On the other hand, he realized that everyone in the hospital known to be near the Digness' room was also alibied. Another case with no suspects left and no witnesses to a crime. *Now what*, he thought.

Downing their third cup of coffee, Ellis was ready to share the information that would send O'Shea's mood and enthusiasm soaring into the stratosphere. "Oh, by the way," he started, "before I left the hospital, I went through a bag of stuff the nurses' aides collected from the Digness room after her death, and look what I found."

Reaching over his desk, Ellis handed his partner a dime size orange and black disk with the letter "R" in the middle.

"Holy Jesus H. Christ. Why didn't you tell me hours ago?"

Ellis came close to giggling. "I wanted to save it for dessert."

O'Shea took the other disk from his desk drawer, compared the two and grinned. "Yes!" Turning toward Ellis, he held up both disks. "Look, partner. You've made my day."

Ellis shook his head with a broad smile. "No, John. Ida made your day. This just makes it even better."

O'Shea nodded as he examined both disks. "I sure as hell can't argue that. Think about it. We've been busting our humps investigating the traditional suspects. Derrick Hansen, poor old Terry Digness, Lula Rogoff. All that's sound detective procedure, and now we have some evidence for our gut hunch of something really rotten out there. Incidentally, yesterday you mentioned seeing a disk before you knew about the hospital one. Right?"

Thumbing through a stack of police color photos, Ellis took a closer look at one. "Right, this one is the third disk. I pulled these pictures from the photo lab. They're of Villa's wrecked truck."

O'Shea was up like a rocket, leaning over Ellis' shoulder. "Yeah, I remember looking through these."

Ellis held up a photo close-up of the passenger side front windshield, which had been cracked on impact. "Look right here, underneath the AAA decal at the lower right hand corner. See there, between those cracks?"

Searching for a few moments, O'Shea slowly began nodding his head. "Christ, you've got eyes like a goddamned eagle. It's an orange and black disk just like the others. I can't make out the letter. Possibly an 'S'?"

"I wasn't sure either, but when I called impound, one of the mechanics verified the letter 'S'."

Still staring at the photo, O'Shea looked at Ellis. "How the hell did you store that little disk in your memory bank? How the fuck did you even care to notice? It meant nothing at the time. I don't remember seeing it, and if I did, I probably figured it was something related to AAA or parking.

A little embarrassed, Ellis absently restacked the other photos, with a slight guffaw. "You've always said to look for stuff no one else would notice or understand. I thought it might eventually have some significance. It was something I had never seen before."

O'Shea couldn't stop blowing deep sighs, while shaking his head, and staring at the photo. "I'll be a son of a bitch. That's three out of eight. It's a mind blower. The death of little old Grace Digness is somehow linked to the death of young, wealthy Helen Hansen and the probable attempted murder of hard working Carlos Villa. They couldn't be more different. Christ, even locations—Sea Cliff, St Mary's Hospital and the outer Mission. Who planted them and how? Shit, I gotta sit down."

Still holding the photo, O'Shea returned to his desk, as Ellis looked over at his boss. "The *how* doesn't seem to be a big deal, Loot. It's the *who* that's the toughie. The Villa disk was on the outside of the windshield, easily placed there after the break lines were cut. The perp with the cajones to kill Grace Digness could have easily dropped the disk on her bed. Finding Helen's disk in the sand was incredible luck. Keeping it was plain, uncanny cop intuition. The perp probably slapped it on her back when she was pushed and it fell off."

O'Shea nodded in agreement. "Either that or the killer stuck it on a rock or something near the edge of the cliff and we all missed it. Anyway, you're right. It would be easy to plant, so finding out *why* is sure more important than *how*."

Leaning back in his chair, O'Shea stared at the ceiling for a moment. "Damn it. Even with just these three, there are a lot of dead people who probably had nothing to do with any of this."

"And you know, Loot, I'll bet we may find a few more of these disks now that we know what we're looking for."

O'Shea picked up the two and held them up by the overhead light, as if examining some precious stones. "I've been thinking the same thing since you mentioned number two. Christ, I'm like a kid with new toys. When can we get number three over here?"

Ellis laughed. "It's on its way. When I called impound, they took it off the windshield, marked it and are sending it over by a uniform."

O'Shea slipped the two disks in an envelope. "Now I know why you're my partner. If you want to get me pissed, just try to transfer out of here."

"Not a chance." Ellis watched O'Shea gently place the disk envelope in his lower left hand drawer, special evidence section in the rear. "You know, I have a sneaking hunch what our strategy is."

O'Shea took another look at the color photo with the "S" disk. "You got it. First we tear into all the property of the remaining five, then we re-interview anyone remotely connected to the crime scenes. We've gotta roust the Trickers. The .22 bullets they stole were the same Armory type used to kill Winston, and their colors are orange and black. We'll need some backup on that one. And last, if there're no disks or solid perps, we scour the crime scenes ourselves. Is that what you had in mind?"

Ellis rubbed his hands together. "Oh boy. It'll be like a big Easter egg hunt."

O'Shea gave an exaggerated eye roll. "That's about a D+. You gotta keep working on that sense of humor."

"Another thing, John. Those letters just might end up a word or acronym, you know, like SFPD. The three letters we've got now spell the verb *to be* in Spanish. Elizabeth and I are taking a neighborhood Spanish course, and *SER* is one of the first verbs we learned. Want me to conjugate it for you?"

O'Shea rolled his eyes again. "No, but I was thinking the same thing, about possible words and acronyms. We just gotta find all the letters first."

Ellis rubbed his hands together again. "Then we can play SCRABBLE!"

"About a C-."

📖 📖 📖

An indispensable, yet irritable, part of detective work has traditionally been paper work. All that changed with the advent of computers, a technological boon to police departments and a nightmare for detectives, especially the computer illiterate older ones like O'Shea and Ellis. One scrawny little three by three diskette could store five filing cabinets of data, provided it could be processed into a computer. Only high-ranking police officers have their own computer savvy secretaries.

O'Shea and Ellis decided they had delayed long enough. Grabbing some ready-made sandwiches from the truck vender on Bryant Street, they returned to their office, intending to computerize all of last month's case progress reports, arrest summaries, interagency or departmental contacts, vehicle mileage, expense vouchers, etc. This tortuous labor took considerable time, since each month they had to start over, figuring out how to work their computer. Neither detective used computers at home. O'Shea didn't have one or want one; and Ellis never played with the awesome computer he had bought for his kids. Anyway, it was always in use.

While Ellis reviewed the computer manual, O'Shea sorted a two-inch pile of paper for processing. That's when they both noticed a tall, broad-shouldered, husky, uniformed police officer standing quietly at the cubicle entrance. His/her gender was unclear to the detectives. It could have been a ruggedly handsome male or female. The prominent, square jaw, unplucked bushy eyebrows, thin lips, and the absence of any makeup, argued *male*. Yet, the hint of breasts, sandwiched between huge shoulders and big hips, said *female*.

"Lieutenant O'Shea and Sergeant Ellis?" The voice was a low-pitched Lauren Bacall. Definitely female.

"Hi. I'm O'Shea. This is Sergeant Ellis."

Remaining at the cubicle entrance, she smiled with a nod. "Pleased to meet both of you. I have an envelope from the impound garage." Stepping slowly and quite gracefully into the cubicle, she handed the envelope to O'Shea.

Ripping open the top, O'Shea removed the little disk, taped to an index card with the number 27 and a scribbled signature. Slowly, gently he rolled the edge of the little disk between his index finger and thumb. Then he turned to Ellis. "It's the same, with an 'S'." O'Shea carefully placed the disk at the back of his drawer with the other two. "Thank you, Officer," he smiled. "I don't think we've ever met."

Smiling back at O'Shea, the officer also acknowledged Ellis with a polite nod. "I'm Officer Jill Hasselburg, I've been on the police force for nearly two years. I have, ah, worked all over, but this is my first time up here."

Both detectives found her voice calm and soothing, despite her strong, gladiator appearance.

Ellis leaned over his chair, extending his hand. "Well, it has been our pleasure meeting you. Lots of luck in your career." He could feel the strength in her firm grip. Ellis also knew it wasn't a challenging grip. She was simply strong.

Continuing the handshake, Officer Hasselburg dipped her head at O'Shea with a warm, courteous smile. "I've heard a great deal about both of you from my uncle. Permit me to say that I really admire you two."

Ellis replied with an embarrassed grin and a more vigorous handshake.

O'Shea just blushed. "Who's your uncle? We may know him."

Easing her hand from Ellis' hand-pumping action, she removed an envelope from her back pocket. "My uncle is Captain McInerney. I stopped by his office before coming here, and he asked me to give you this letter."

O'Shea read the hand-written letter aloud. "I have taken the liberty, as your friend and immediate superior, to assign Officer Hasselburg to your unit. The brass keeps telling me you and Sergeant Ellis are getting nowhere, and they intend to assign one of their own to assist you. You know what that means. I actually talked them into doing my own assigning. Although she's my niece, she is very capable, a fast learner, and she can be trusted. I wanted her to learn from the best. She's loyal, Jack, and you need all the help you can get to watch your back."

After glancing at each other with a few nods, grimaces and head shakes, both detectives sat in expressionless silence for a few minutes. Standing awkwardly in the entranceway, Officer Hasselburg chewed on her lower lip. O'Shea finally broke the uneasy silence. "Do you have any computer savvy?"

Officer Hasselburg exhaled through her sagging mouth, curling upward with a slight sigh of relief. "Oh, yes sir, Lieutenant. I was practically raised with computers. My first one had only a few megabytes. Now my data storage is in gigabytes.

Ellis smiled, while wondering, *what's a gigabyte?*

O'Shea nodded. *Whatever the hell that means,* he thought. "Knowing that you'll be our computer expert and general grunt, are you still willing to work with us?" O'Shea asked.

"I would consider it an honor."

Both detectives grinned.

"In that case," O'Shea said, "why don't you grab a cup of coffee at the lunch wagon? I haven't talked to Captain McInerney or Sergeant Ellis, for that matter."

Hasselburg beamed. "I really understand. Is a half hour long enough?"

"That'll be fine," replied O'Shea.

📖 📖 📖

Captain McInerney preferred memos and letters to direct confrontations. Yet, when O'Shea called, he readily agreed to see the detectives in his office. O'Shea knew Bruce McInerney was one of his few higher-ranking loyal friends. He further realized McInerney was powerless to take on any of his enemies. The top ranking cops and most of the lower ranks just didn't take the captain seriously. This meant that in a showdown against O'Shea or Ellis, McInerney wouldn't be able to protect them, or their jobs. O'Shea didn't care, because more importantly, McInerney would never betray them in any way. Besides, he was still a heroic legend, an icon to be left alone, especially by the brass.

Captain McInerney greeted them with hearty handshakes, and a fawning eagerness. "Boy it's sure good to see you two. We haven't had a chance to sit and chat for some time. Come on, sit down."

As the detectives sat on a comfortable leather couch, McInerney opened a folding metal chair and sat beside them. "How are the cases coming?"

Looking around the office, O'Shea slowing nodded. "We've got some new evidence. It's beginning to come together. It's good to see you too, Captain."

Ellis nodded in smiling agreement.

After a slightly awkward silence, O'Shea eased into their reason for meeting. "I didn't even know you had a niece. She seems like a nice kid."

McInerney leaned forward in his chair, clearing his throat as if about to give a speech. "She's great, Jack; smart as a whip, loyal to her uncle's friends, and strong as an ox. She respects you guys, wants to learn from the best. She's a career cop, serious about the job and a quick study. You guys got your hands full with eight tough cases, and the top brass and some detectives are hoping you'll blow it. You need all the help and loyalty you can get. She's also a computer whiz." McInerney added with a childlike smile, "You'd be doing me a favor."

The two detectives soberly looked at each other with subtle nods before turning toward McInerney. He was still leaning forward, wide-eyed and motionless.

O'Shea broke into a grin. "Well, Bruce, we'll take your niece on as a favor to you, and for her computer skills, which is a favor to us. Anyhow, the last thing we want is a helper who's really working for the brass."

Ellis added, "You're one of the few ranks we can trust."

McInerney sat back in his metal chair, folding his hands in his lap. "Thanks guys. Jill will be a true asset and loyal just to you two. She could even teach you how to operate your computers."

"No thanks," they quickly replied with rapid head shakes.

📖 📖 📖

The remaining fifteen minutes in McInerney's office was a more relaxed, kicked back reunion of old friends. They promised to have dinner once a month just "for old times," and the detectives promised to look after McInerney's niece. They all knew the monthly dinners were wishful courtesies; a promise they'd never get around to, even though it would have been nice. They also knew they would keep their promise to protect McInerney's niece. When the detectives left McInerney with their sincere handshakes, back pats, and assurances, he folded his metal chair, returned to his big oak desk and cried.

CHAPTER 35

Officer Jill Hasselburg was waiting in the hall when the detectives returned. Leaning against the wall with head bowed, she glanced up with a nervous, lip-biting smile. "Did I come back too early?" she asked almost inaudibly.

"Relax, you're in," grinned O'Shea. "Unless you want to sit on one of our desks, grab a chair from somewhere and come on in."

As they walked by McInerney's thrilled niece, Ellis patted her on the shoulder. "Welcome, Officer Jill Hasselburg."

Fighting back the embarrassment of tears, she retreated down the hall. "Thank you. I'm going to get a chair, somewhere."

Back in their cubicle, O'Shea removed the three disks from his drawer before surveying their office space. "Christ, Paul. We'll have to give the kid a lot of outside work. There's no room for even another real small desk."

"Come on, we're not here all the time either. We can put her chair, if she finds one, in that corner. It'll just fit."

Fingering the disks, O'Shea laughed. "Hell, you or I'll probably be sitting in the corner so she can use the computer."

Ellis gave O'Shea a joshing sneer. "I'd be in the corner."

O'Shea carefully returned the disks to their envelope and drawer, with a quick glance at his partner. "Only when you're bad."

"If that were the criterion, Loot, you know who'd be there most of the time."

O'Shea grinned. "Can I take my disks with me?"

"No, but I'll help you get some more. Why don't we hit the property room for a while? We'll leave Hasselburg her first memo."

"Let's do it," O'Shea replied. "Tell her to answer the phones, sweep the floors, review all eight cases and load the computer with our paper work."

"Anything else? How about varnishing the desks."

O'Shea slowly looked around their cubicle. "Let's see. Just tell her to kick back, relax and get us a bigger place to flop before we return from the property room in about an hour."

📖 📖 📖

On their way, it dawned on O'Shea that Sergeant Flanagan was on duty. Routinely, the two detectives tried to avoid Flanagan. Both his appearance and demeanor were as grim and dirty as the property room. He was the regular sergeant in charge, and a legend of sorts. They figured he had probably been there since the '06 earthquake. In fact, he looked like earthquake damage. In his early sixties, he looked like a ghoulish ninety-year-old, with a brown, sputum-stained mouth wrapped around a piece of unraveling, wet blackish tobacco that was once a cigar.

In the center of his pinched, wrinkled face was a shriveled, pointed nose, sagging toward his stubbled, droopy chin. His sunken, zombie-like, bloodshot eyes highlighted his ghoulish appearance, while his faded uniform, food stained shirt, frayed pockets, and poorly fitting, soiled trousers suggested undercover work—maybe as a bum or disaster victim.

These were Flanagan's most pleasing features. It was his mannerisms that really annoyed the detectives. No one using the property room, including Flanagan's morning alternate, Sergeant Kitchen, had ever seen him smile, grin or even guffaw. Descriptions of his fixed expression varied from brooding, angry, ghoulish and miserable, to grim. Equally strange was Flanagan's anonymity. He was never seen outside the property room. He seemed to just appear and disappear, five days a week, from noon to 9:00 p.m.

When the detectives arrived, Flanagan was seated seemingly comatose behind the counter. Ellis offered a friendly wake-up gesture. "Hi, Sergeant."

Flanagan rose from his chair and slammed a clipboard on the counter. "Fill this out and sign," was his dry, squinty, unblinking response.

As Ellis filled out the sign-in sheet, O'Shea, still in a good mood, decided to test Flanagan's limits. Leaning over into his sour face, O'Shea tried to tickle him with a wide-eyed, near comical smile. "Boy, it's good to see you, Sergeant, how've you been? Seen any good movies lately?"

Without the slightest change in his sour expression, Flanagan handed O'Shea another clipboard. "You didn't complete this earlier for Sergeant Kitchen. You gotta sign here."

How the hell did this son of a bitch recognize me, O'Shea thought? *He's never looked directly at me and we've never talked.*

As O'Shea signed the form, Ellis gave him a nudging whisper. "Great job, John. You really got a rise out of him."

The shrill buzzer jolted the detectives into a sprint for the property room door. Once the buzzer stopped, the door relocked, and neither O'Shea nor Ellis wanted to bother Flanagan again.

"Yea, we made it! Who do we check first?"

Catching his breath, O'Shea scanned his list. "Let's give Nelson a try."

Two full baskets of Officer Nelson's bloodied belongings were found on shelf seven of row fifteen, exactly where Flanagan said they would be. Reaching for one of the baskets, O'Shea shot Ellis a wry grin. "How the hell does he know where all this crap is? He never misses. Maybe he's a worn out humanoid."

"I don't think robots are that nasty," Ellis replied, struggling with the second basket.

O'Shea gave Ellis a slow nod. "Not bad. That's a B+."

Along the rear wall of the musty property room were several old, dented metal tables with historical San Francisco graffiti. Some of the scratches were of the classical *fuck you—eat shit* variety. Others were assorted dates, indicating that the tables were at least fifty years old.

Both detectives had ceased to notice the etchings long ago. To them they were just autopsy platforms with remnants of violent crimes, retired cops and forgotten victims.

Sifting through the clothes worn in violent death is never pleasant—worse when you knew or knew *of* the victim; doubly worse when the head was instantly flattened, sending internal fluids gushing out of any bodily orifice. There were dried stains, lumps, and flakes of feces, blood, urine and mucus everywhere. Putrid odors of all kinds were nauseatingly aroused every time O'Shea or Ellis unfolded a piece of Nelson's clothes to the musty air. After a half hour of searching clothes and sleeping bag, their soiled latex gloves turned brownish green, and dry, foul tasting mouths, pleaded for a time out.

O'Shea was first to repack a basket. "It's not in this stuff. I even checked the basket in case it fell out of the clothes."

Carefully examining Officer Nelson's wallet, Ellis wiped the sweat off his forehead with the back of his wrist. "Yeah. That's it for me, too. I've been through it all. There's no disk here."

O'Shea impatiently checked his watch. "Damn it all, I thought it might be easy. You know, like a disk in every basket until it spells out the name of the killer."

Ellis picked up the last item in the second basket. Removing the radiotelephone from its leather holder, he grinned at O'Shea. "You can't say we're not thorough. Anyway, now we know it's not here. Another turned over stone."

"You got that right. I'm a little short on patience and rotten smells. Anyway, that should have been the toughest for us. Christ, poor bastard was probably freezing his buns off. He must have been wearing twenty pounds of clothes."

Repacking the second basket, Ellis removed his grimy latex gloves. "Do you want to wash up and give one more a try?"

O'Shea delayed answering as he removed his gloves with an irritated headshake and wrinkled nose. "Shit. What a glamorous life, huh? OK, let's sterilize ourselves first and then try Sutherland. Shouldn't be much property and he wasn't mangled."

📖 📖 📖

It took the two detectives fifteen minutes of soap scrubs and mouth washes to feel detoxed. Another fifteen minutes was necessary for basket returns, unblinking scrutiny by Sergeant Flanagan, and more forms before they returned to the old metal table. This time there was only one small plastic box with five small items that turned out to be six.

Ellis painstakingly examined Sutherland's bathing suit while O'Shea scanned the swim goggles like a jeweler with a rare gem.

"Nothing," they both said almost simultaneously.

"At least it's all clean stuff," O'Shea remarked, as he picked up Sutherland's red swim cap. Ellis was about to reach for the neoprene swim shoes when O'Shea practically burst his ear drum. "Holy shit. I don't believe it. Look, Paul, there it is like a goddamned logo. A little black and orange disk, stuck to the front, or maybe back of Sutherland's cap. I don't know which is which. Look! It's a 'T'."

Taking the cap from O'Shea, Ellis took a closer look. "No wonder it wasn't on the property list. Everyone probably thought it was part of the swim cap."

Grabbing the cap back from Ellis, O'Shea nodded. "No shit. I'd have missed it if I hadn't seen the others. I would have assumed the 'T' stood for *Trimwear*. You know, those ads that say, *Trimwear: the best of swimwear*."

Following a mild tug of war, Ellis eased the cap from O'Shea's grasp. "I've probably heard that commercial a thousand times. By the way, the disk is on the back of the cap. It's tapered longer in the back, to cover the ears."

O'Shea stelthfully pulled the cap from Ellis' hands. "Is it OK if I do the surgical removal?"

"You found the first one. That's gotta entitle you to some honors. But do we have forensic photos of the disk on the cap?"

O'Shea flopped the cap on the table with a sigh. "Ah hell. I'm not sure. They're so jammed, they probably haven't had time."

Ellis reached for his coat lying across a chair. Out of an inside pocket came a small, throwaway Kodak flash camera.

Propping up the cap with Sutherland's swimsuit stuffed inside, O'Shea stepped back. "You're always blowing me out. What else you got in that coat? A dark room?"

Ellis aimed his cardboard camera at the cap. "No, Loot, just a dark pocket."

"Your humor is back to D's."

Ignoring O'Shea's last remark, Ellis photographed the puffed-up cap from every conceivable direction.

By then, O'Shea had sat down in one of the old folding chairs. "Christ, that's enough! Don't you think twelve goddamned pictures of a stuffed red cap is at least mild overkill?"

Ellis swung the camera around and clicked one at O'Shea heaving a cavernous yawn.

Holding a bored expression, O'Shea gave Ellis his middle finger. "You little prick."

Ellis gave a crooked grin, replaced the camera in his coat, and carefully examined the swim shoes. "Just in case there's an extra disk."

Repacking the plastic box, O'Shea grabbed the second swim shoe. "Wouldn't that be a bitch if we started finding more than one of these disks? That might push me over the edge."

Ignoring the last comment, Ellis tossed the shoe into the plastic box. "None here."

O'Shea dropped the second shoe in the box. "Nothing there either. I think one per victim is the most we'll get."

Picking up the box, Ellis shot a playful jab at O'Shea's shoulder. "I sure hope so. Wouldn't want my partner to go over the edge."

Heading back to the entrance in silence, Ellis stopped for a moment. "Are you up to another victim search or is the 'T' enough for today?"

O'Shea fingered the "T" in his pocket. "Hell, why not? We're on a roll. Maybe we'll get lucky again." Removing the disk from his pocket, O'Shea glanced at Ellis with sober reflection. "Do you know what the four letters spell?

Ellis thought for a moment. "Probably lots of those words used in crossword puzzles, or other Spanish words. How about SERT, the candy mint?"

Cautiously slipping the disk back in his pocket, O'Shea nodded, with a strangely gentle tolerance. "Not bad, except Cert is spelled with a 'C', the 'S' goes at the end. They also spell REST. Did you know that there are twenty-four different word combinations in just four lousy letters?"

Still holding the plastic box, Ellis was becoming a bit impatient. "I do now. I even know how to spell Certs. So, what's the point?"

O'Shea laid a condescending hand on Ellis' shoulder. "A little patience, Paul. In higher mathematics dealing with probability theory, they're called permutations and combinations. Did you know that if we find a fifth letter, it jumps to a hundred twenty different arrangements?"

Shifting the plastic box to his left arm, Ellis threw back his head with an eye roll. "I was terrible in math. So where are you going with this quiz?"

Sticking to his calm, patient demeanor, O'Shea offered a sympathetic smile along with a soft, slow monologue. "Hang on, my friend. Do you have any idea how many different ways you can order just three more letters, making a total of eight?"

"No, John."

"Guess."

"No."

O'Shea offered a slow nod of acceptance. "Let me explain. If we find a disk for each of our eight, we employ the simple factorial eight mathematical formula to determine how many arrangements are possible. Would you like to know the formula?"

"No, John."

"Would you like to know the answer?"

Shifting the plastic box back to his right arm, Ellis heaved a deep sigh. "I bet you're going to tell me."

O'Shea paused, then beamed. "Forty thousand, three hundred twenty."

This managed to jolt Ellis out of his impatience. "Come on. You mean there's over forty thousand ways to arrange eight letters? Are you putting me on?"

O'Shea continued to beam as he took his ballpoint pen and notebook from his pocket. "Here, I'll show you how."

Ellis began scurrying down the aisle with O'Shea in hot pursuit. "I don't want to learn how," he shouted. "I hate math. The number's incredible and I believe you. Now let's look for number five."

As Ellis reached the Sergeant's desk at the property room entrance, O'Shea was a few paces behind, devilishly waving his notebook. "It's just a matter of multiplying each product of the number of letters..."

Ellis slammed the box on the counter. "I give up," he interrupted. "Please, no more. Which victim's property do you want?"

O'Shea's impish smirk vanished as Sergeant Flanagan suddenly appeared behind his desk through a side door.

"Are you through?" Flanagan asked icily, while again seeming to look between the detectives.

Shifting to his professional, austere mode, O'Shea obediently picked up the clipboard before being told. "No, Sergeant. We're returning this one and we'll be needing one on Winston."

Ellis practically curtsied while handing Flanagan the plastic box.

Noticing Ellis' acquiescence, O'Shea choked back a laugh, not knowing if his partner was trying to be funny.

After another thorough examination of the clip-boarded form by Flanagan, the detectives located Winston's property. Back at the metal table, O'Shea smiled at Ellis. "If you were subtlety screwing with the Sarg back there, you get an A."

Ellis shrugged with a puzzled look and O'Shea shook his head.

"Forget it. Let's see what we can find."

The one basket was a welcomed relief after Nelson's two heavy ones loaded with clothes. They knew, however, the Winston basket wouldn't be quick and easy like the Sutherland plastic box. At least Winston's upper clothes, examined by O'Shea, were clean except for bloodstains on the shirt and jacket collar.

Ellis wasn't surprised or pleased to find the victim's trousers and under shorts soiled with remnants of feces and urine. Pockets contained a lighter, less than a dollar in change, white capsules, a few condoms, a pack of cigarettes, and a pocketknife. Both detectives repeated their careful search of all the items, including every inch of clothing, socks, the cigarette pack, change, even the bottle of pills— probably Amyl Nitrite. Nothing, until the cowboy boots. O'Shea took the right, Ellis the left.

O'Shea was assiduously examining the inside of his boot when Ellis did a lottery winning leap into the air. "Bingo. *It's mine; all mine precious.* I found it so it's mine," he shouted with a shuffling, quick step dance around the metal table.

"Pretty good," O'Shea smirked. "That's a solid B, especially your impersonation of Tolkien's Gollum and Michael Jackson. Now, where is it?"

A little winded, Ellis gave a breathless smile, and handing O'Shea the cowboy boot. "Check the inside, front part of the heel." Then he added, "I didn't know you read the *Hobbits.*"

Carefully pulling the orange and black disk off the inner heel, O'Shea patiently scrutinized the fifth letter. Then he quickly glanced at Ellis before again staring at the disk. "Nice going. Now we've got an 'I'." As O'Shea pocketed the disk, he began a brief, self-absorbed monologue. "Number five, another victim of the disk gang, whoever they are. A hundred twenty ways to arrange the letters. One more motiveless murder." Recovering from his preoccupations, he helped his partner repack Winston's property. "By the way Paul, The sixties hippies loved the Hobbits. Remember, *Froto Lives?* I think they even had bumper stickers."

Ellis sat on the table and closed his eyes. "That really brings back some old memories. Of course, I remember. I thought I was one of them for awhile."

"A Hobbit?" asked O'Shea.

Ellis opened his eyes. "No John, a hippie."

O'Shea laughed.

📖 📖 📖

It was 4:30 when the detectives finally returned to the corridor leading to the homicide offices. Both felt a little guilty leaving Officer Hasselburg alone so long on her first day.

Entering the doorway, O'Shea heaved a deep sigh. "Oh well, at least she had time to find a chair and relax awhile." O'Shea hardly finished his comment, when he slammed into the back of Ellis. He had suddenly stopped in the aisle, near their cubicle. Puzzled, Ellis scanned the area with head shaking blinks.

Also puzzled, O'Shea glanced back to make sure they had entered the right door. "This doesn't look right. Where the hell are we, in the Twilight Zone?"

Ellis broke into a full-cheek grin. Sitting at a third desk in an expanded cubicle was Officer Hasselburg, typing away on their relocated computer. "Our office is still here, just a lot bigger."

O'Shea stuck his head through the entranceway, scanned the new area, and gave Hasselburg an eye squinting smirk. "Holy Christ. What happened? How did you do it? We suggested a chair and you give us a whole new office."

Misreading O'Shea's smirk as a sneer, Hasselburg blanched. "Oh, my God. It just dawned on me. Maybe you didn't want an office change. I can change it back if you want."

Ellis quickly wormed his way in front of O'Shea. "Hey, we've been trying to get this office enlarged for years, and you did it in a couple hours. We're grateful, right, Loot?"

O'Shea broke into a vigorous nod and smiled. "Absolutely, change it back and you're fired!"

Officer Hasselburg blushed shyly. "Well, first I realized you two would end up resenting me if we were all crammed into your tiny space. Then I went down the aisle in both directions. I discovered that next to the last office cubicle on the right was six feet of useless space. My uncle did the rest. He got me a desk, chair and building maintenance to give the south end cubicle a wall, move two partitions, and give your partition the extra six feet."

Both detectives crowded around her desk, and O'Shea extended his hand. "You're not just a computer whiz. You got grit. You got initiative, and you got some juice around here. Thanks."

Hasselburg shook O'Shea's hand, followed by another hearty

handshake with Ellis. "I'll even share some of the computer work with you," Ellis offered a bit hesitantly.

"That's not necessary, Sergeant. By noon tomorrow, all your paper work will be on diskettes. Then it'll be easy to keep up."

Both detectives awkwardly smiled at her in amazement. O'Shea broke the brief silence. "Anything we can do for you?"

Hasselburg slowly shook her head. "Thank you, Lieutenant, but I'm not into paybacks. I'm just so grateful you've accepted me to work for you. That's all the payback I need."

The detectives' silence echoed their embarrassment as they slinked back to their desks. Searching for something witty or nice to say, Ellis smiled faintly at Hasselburg. *Just be honest*, he thought. "Glad to have you with us, Jill. We're really not used to cops offering so much help for nothing other than to learn."

Hasselburg shut down the computer, locked some papers in one of her drawers, and clasped her hands on the desk. "This is my career and I'll work hard, go that extra mile as my payback to learn our business. Is that a fair exchange?"

Scanning their new spacious cubicle, O'Shea leaned back in his swivel chair, with a fatherly smile. "That's more than fair. I just hope you don't get disappointed. You've already shown us what you offer. I'm not sure we can teach you what you're looking for."

"You already are. I don't expect you to teach me. I learn from being involved in your work. Loading all your notes and stuff into the computer is teaching me more than I imagined about investigation procedures, trial and error, turning over every stone, patience and frustration. I've also learned all about the eight cases from Captain McInerney. The way you painstakingly eliminate suspects, and search for those disks."

Both detectives glanced at each other with slacked jaws. O'Shea finally replied. "Then you know there's nothing routine about these cases. They're very strange. They seem to keep showing us the obvious that take us to dead ends. It's like the eight are mocking standard detective procedures. Our careful elimination of suspects, the many deaths during our investigation, even our disappointments and frustrations have convinced both of us that there's something devilishly different about these cases. So, our new approach begins with a review of everything. All the property, the crime scenes, giants, gangs and disks. At this point we only know with certainty that at least five of the cases are associated with the disks. This also indicates that despite the utter lack of any other similarity between these murders, they are somehow connected."

Ellis was rapidly nodding in agreement. "We've also figured out that since by-the-book, conventional procedure keeps showing us there's something else going on, we're willing to rely more and more on intuition. Even if we find a disk for each victim, our hunch is that we may reach another dead end. But we still have to turn over ever rock, and that is time consuming."

Hasselburg knew what Ellis was hinting. "What sort of time consuming leg work do you want me to do?"

Ellis began with the need to search all belongings of the remaining three victims for possible disks.

As Ellis started to tell her about the Trickers and a list of gang members to be interviewed, O'Shea slipped the two additional disks into their envelope before quickly locking his desk drawer, then cheerfully said, "You're in good hands, Jill. I have an—ah, urgent appointment this evening, so if you don't mind, I'll see you two tomorrow."

Ellis gave his partner a thumbs up. "Go get 'em, Loot."

CHAPTER 36

The sound of the apartment buzzer triggered a weird punching sensation behind O'Shea's rib cage. *Shit,* he thought, *is that my heart?* Just as he grabbed the doorknob, the buzzer stopped. *Shit,* n*ow she'll think I'm a klutz.*

On his second attempt, O'Shea dove for the knob, sending him stumbling into the foyer. He was glad Ida's one bedroom apartment was on the 3rd floor. The walk up three flights would buy him some time to stop that weird thumping. *Shit!* he thought, *I'll be panting by the time I reach her door.* Then he noticed the elevator. The ride up was mercifully slow, giving him time to reduce his heart rate, wipe his perspiring brow and mind rehearse his initial approach.

Suave and debonair? Hell no. I wouldn't know how. Casual, indifferent? Naw, she'd see through that in a minute. Strong, silent? Christ, she doesn't want a goddamn Neanderthal. Just as the elevator opened on the third floor, he flashed on another thought. *Fatherly? Oh shit,* he thought. *She'd probably go for that one.*

O'Shea cautiously stepped into the hall in moderate panic, with dry mouth, thumps, and an intense urge to urinate or run for it. Spotting a female head from an opened door down the hall, O'Shea took a deep breath, and pulled back his shoulders. *Too late for the retreat. What the hell, get it over with.* Those were his final thoughts before the forty-foot walk to the head, resting on female shoulders, which seemed hinged to the door jam. At fifteen feet, the head was clearer. It was Ida, and as she glided into the hall O'Shea momentarily froze. Pelted with ambivalent thoughts, he moved forward more cautiously, to get a better look. *My God, she looks so young out of uniform. What the hell am I, a child molester? Yeah, fatherly would be the best approach. I could easily be her father—or grandfather? Shit.*

Standing ten feet away and closing was lively brown hair and a radiant smile adorning full lips, bright blue eyes, satin smooth skin, and perfect features, together creating a *Teen Magazine* cover girl. The sensuous, womanly body was still there, but more tender, innocent, virginous without the bulky police garb. Her breasts, beneath a white blouse, were firm, erect, well-sculptured, not a trace of sag. Working his way down her body, O'Shea's eyes scanned her blue mini skirt. *Even below the waist she looks so young,* he thought. The missing police utility belt narrowed her waist and recontoured her hips into something more supple, more svelte. *Christ, she could be a high school cheerleader.*

Ida's rosy cheeks were dimpled with a happy smile. "Hi, Lieutenant O'Shea. You're right on time."

O'Shea's slightly frowning, stilted reply, wasn't quite what Ida had expected. "Good evening. We're not on duty, so why don't you try calling me Jack."

Overlooking his apparent testiness, Ida kept smiling. "Thanks, Jack. Now I know what you're called when you're not working. Would you like to see my place before we eat?"

O'Shea managed a faint smile. "Sure, why not," he mumbled.

Still sending a warm, natural smile, Ida lightly gripped his shoulder and maneuvered him into her small entry hall. After an awkward minute, she broke the silence with a cheerful monologue about her divorce, her love of police work, her pint sized apartment and her pet hamsters.

While following Ida on her tour, O'Shea noticed out of the corner of his eye, strange and furry somethings darting across the floor. Trying to remain cool and casual, he didn't mention it, but he was glad she had.

Ida's apartment was indeed cozy small, sparsely furnished, yet displayed a rich assortment of paintings and photos covering most of the available wall space. The bedroom was all queen size bed, with barely enough room to open the closet door or dinky nightstand drawer. A leather couch and chair virtually overwhelmed the living room with its two end tables and tiny glass coffee table stuffed in the remaining floor space. There was also a nineteen-inch television hanging precariously from a wall swivel, as in *Motel 6.*

The kitchen was at least user-friendly. Everything, including stove, sink, cabinets and breakfast bar could easily be reached without moving one's feet. Like the rest of the apartment, the bathroom was a downsized version. It had a full-sized toilet, wedged against a trailer-sized shower stall on the right and a one-quart capacity sink with matching cabinet on the left. Leg room wasn't an option.

It didn't take long before O'Shea was back in the small entrance hall, furtively searching for those little fur balls.

Waiting for him to comment about her apartment, Ida finally squelched another uncomfortable silence. "Would you like to sit in the living room for a while before we go?"

O'Shea nodded.

Sensing he might crack a shin against her coffee table, Ida quickly slid it toward the wall. Bad idea she realized. O'Shea cracked his shin anyway. Heading for the more distant chair, he walked into the table propelled by her foot.

O'Shea winced and Ida cringed. "Oh, Jack. I'm so sorry. I thought you were going to sit on the coach. Are you OK?"

Before answering, O'Shea limped to the chair. "Yeah, I'm OK," he sighed.

Ida sat on the couch, starring at O'Shea, clasping her hands on her lap. There wasn't much melody left in her voice. "Are you really OK?"

"Yes."

"Do you have second thoughts about our date?"

O'Shea shook his head, straining a smile.

"Why did you ask me out, Jack?"

O'Shea wasn't ready to deal with a confrontational woman who looked like a high school cheerleader. "Why don't we have dinner and we can talk about it. Are you hungry?"

Ida kept starring inquiringly at him, wondering what attracted her to this crusty old cop. She knew he was resented or feared by over half of the police department. Yet, at the corridor coffee pot, she had seen something shy and sensitive beneath his rugged, craggy face. She relaxed into a warmer smile. "I sure am. Where shall we go?"

Christ, he thought, *I damned near blew it before dinner.* "What kind of food do you like?" He smiled.

"I like all kinds. Especially spicy."

Neither a gourmet nor high roller, O'Shea was relieved that she wasn't interested in those trendy yuppie expensive French restaurants. "How about Mexican?"

"Great, I love Mexican."

O'Shea had three favorites. The Roosevelt Tamale Parlor on Twenty-fourth Street had great food, cheap prices and lousy service. The La Barca Room on Lombard had great food, average prices and great service, and The El Sombrero in Ghirardelli Square had great food, high prices and good service. "Would you like to try Roosevelt Tamale Parlor?" he asked. "It's in the Mexican section on Twenty-fourth Street. The enchiladas and tamales are great. It's like going to Tijuana."

"I've never been there and it sounds interesting. I've never even been to Tijuana, so this will be a preview for me."

O'Shea felt more at ease knowing she didn't expect one of those fancy restaurants. During dinner, he was even more impressed by her robust appetite as she polished off two enchiladas, beans, rice and half dozen tortillas. *Just like my daughters,* he thought.

Following her second beer, his fourth cup of coffee, and the usual first date superficial small talk, they sat smiling at each other, feeling a little more comfortable. Finally, O'Shea tried easing into her earlier sobering question with one of his own. "What happened to your marriage?"

Ida's eyes narrowed, all traces of smile dissolved. Flashing on the last six months of her stormy marriage, she took a swig from her beer bottle. Then she leaned across the table at O'Shea. "You really want to know?"

O'Shea feigned a casual grin. "Only if you want to tell me."

She hesitated just long enough to modulate her rapid, high-pitched voice into a slow breathy rasp. "He was a womanizing, bullying, alcoholic son of a bitch. He's also a cop."

"Guess you can't get much clearer than that. Do I know him?"

"He works the Northern Station on Fillmore. Sergeant Ben Drake. I met him at the Academy. He was one of the small arms instructors."

"He still is," O'Shea said with a slight frown. He remembered reviewing Drake's file during his oral interview three months ago. He had been one of three sergeants before an oral panel for promotion to lieutenant. O'Shea acknowledged to her that he was the only one of four panel members who disliked Drake instantly. He was the type of cop O'Shea never got along with. His file clearly portrayed Drake as an arrogant weight lifter who worshiped guns, force and power. He hung out with other macho cops who thrived on controlling instead of serving the people. O'Shea had told Drake, during his interview, that he wouldn't endorse a promotion. "We're not the best of friends," O'Shea added.

Ida sat back with another smile. "Yes, I know. That's one of the reasons I like you. You say what you think. Because of you, Ben is still a sergeant and I'm grateful. You weren't bullied or impressed by his SWAT Team mentality." Suddenly, on the verge of tears, Ida slide her hands across the table. Her glistening, reddened eyes reminded O'Shea of his youngest daughter, Sandra. *I used to hurt her feelings so damned easily*, he thought.

O'Shea grabbed both of Ida's hands and stared into her tear-filled eyes. "He must have really hurt you."

This unexpected show of tender concern released a flood of tears Ida had been restraining for too long. Through closed-eye sobs, she attempted a weak smile.

"It's really hard to keep a well-centered, stable cop image when you know that not too far beneath that role is a sensitive woman. I managed pretty well, even when he punched me like he was fighting some thug. But working in a man's macho world, I almost lost it after I left him."

O'Shea listened quietly while his sexual impulses dwindled. *Shit,* he thought, *I'm doing the fatherly. This isn't the time to think about patting her sweet ass.* "You almost lost it?" he asked, as he leaned back in his chair.

Deep in thought, she sat back, wiped her eyes with her napkin, and blew her nose. "I guess I had assumed he would shield me from all the other cops. They were constantly telling dirty jokes or checking my breasts or butt."

Oh shit, he thought.

"But when I couldn't take his drunken abuse and walked out, Ben told his buddies it was all my fault. He spread the word that I was a rotten screw, a lesbian, and an all around bitch. That was last year when the whole department was either shunning me, mocking me, or hitting on me more aggressively. Some of the gals even became too sympathetic, if you know what I mean."

Shifting to a fatherly role was almost too easy for O'Shea. *Christ, sex with her now would be incest*, he thought. He leaned far enough forward to lightly pat her hand resting on the table. "I never heard of any rumors about you. None of the cops I know ever mentioned it.

Must have been Drake's little gang of assholes."

Ida dried a few more tears, squeezed O'Shea's hands and smiled gratefully. "You're probably right. When I started working all over the department, rumors, hits, dirty looks and the rest of the hustles seemed to die away. I have to tell you though. Ben threatened that if I dated another cop, he'd take care of both of us."

O'Shea slowly eased back in his chair and drank the last few drops of his coffee. "Am I your first test run?" he asked.

She took a swig of beer. "Well. I suppose so. You're the first cop I've dated since I left him."

Oh shit, he thought. "I guess I should take that as a compliment." O'Shea paused, wrestling with his next question. "I'm kinda curious. Um, why me?"

Ida stared down at the table, before replying. "For a lot of reasons. Seems like you're not intimidated by macho cops, you treat people fairly, you've always been nice to me and I don't feel like just a sex object with you."

O'Shea barely restrained an eye roll as he thought to himself. *Shit, that's it. I'm the father figure.* "Waiter, some more coffee, and a beer for the lady."

📖 📖 📖

Four beers and seven cups of coffee later, Ida was experiencing a satisfying catharsis that often accompanies a mellow glow and a good, empathic listener like O'Shea. Once she had detailed her torrid romance with Drake, and her tumultuous marriage, there was no stopping her. She was on a roll.

While O'Shea munched on a couple orders of tortilla chips with Pico de Gallo, Ida unloaded her entire sex life, consecutively, beginning at age thirteen. Remarkably, O'Shea noted, she vividly remembered each nuance, starting with the eighteen-year-old neighbor, followed by a string of junior high classmates, her first orgasm with a thirty-year-old high school math teacher, other students' trysts, more neighbors, college friends, and back to Ben.

O'Shea also learned all about her family history as the youngest of four girls, solid middle-class parents, two years of college, and her goal since adolescence to be a police officer. He learned that her last name was Elster and four beers were all she could handle.

After steadily unloading for two hours, Ida was happily on the brink of word slurring, when she carefully stood up, grinned, and scanned the dining room. "I need a toilet." She grinned, looking down at O'Shea.

Pointing to the rear door, he was amazed at her bladder control. "Through that door, but watch it. There's one step down before the floor levels off." He watched Ida maneuver gracefully around tables and through the door, where she slipped, caught herself, and glanced back with a wave.

O'Shea waved back, thinking what a sweet kid she was, and how he enjoyed her company, even if he were a father figure. Thanks to Ida, he had breached the lonely rut that unwittingly isolated him since his divorce. It had been months since he had dinner with a woman, any woman. He had even conned himself into believing work was all he needed as a substitute social life. Remain on the job as if indispensable, grab something to eat on the way home, watch TV, then to bed. *Oh, yeah*, he thought, *when that routine doesn't work, get lost on a run.*

It no longer mattered to O'Shea why Ida was there. All he knew for sure was it felt good.

Scrolling through his past, made it all even clearer. Raised in an Irish Catholic family, O'Shea had learned early on that women were proper, moral, efficient domestic managers, religious procreators and incubators. Women were wives and mothers.

O'Shea was finally learning that the negative side of these traditions was a major part of his problem. Wives and mothers made lousy companions and boringly predictable sex partners. *They're all Virgin Marys*, he lamented.

Still waiting for Ida, his thoughts turned to Mary, devoted Catholic wife for thirty years. She had been equally well trained in conservative religious traditions. He could clearly remember their high school romance of passionate petting, fondling her full, gorgeous beasts and trudging home nursing aching testicles. That went on for three erotically agonizing years until married, when they finally had permission to consummate their sexual passions. He never forgot that first married night when he ejaculated in Mary's hand. She was just trying to help him find the mark.

His dutiful little wife would do anything to please him. She just didn't know how. Neither did he. "Christ," he mumbled to himself, "I've never felt self-reliant with women—just wives, mothers, daughters, and whores." *They're easy*, he thought.

Just then, Ida flashed a deep dimpled smile as she approached their table. O'Shea rocketed to his feet, returned the smile while exhaling a gratifying sigh to himself. *My God, I'm actually comfortable with this woman.* Extending his arms, he hugged her affectionately. "You know, Ida. You're a fine person. I'm not sure what's happened but it feels good. Are you OK now?"

Ida wasn't sure what he was talking about, and it didn't matter. Wrapped in his strong arms, she felt secure. Looking up at him, Ida's head was clear, "Thank you, Jack. No date has ever called me a fine person." With tears streaming down her smiling cheeks, she was also experiencing a rare feeling. "Gosh, I really feel comfortable with you."

📖 📖 📖

The drive back to Ida's apartment was mutually supportive of their silence. It wasn't a panting silence of impending lust. It was a profound quiet, ironically reflecting both of their past relationships. Each simply wanted a companion who might some day become a trusted friend. O'Shea was too old and too traditionally Catholic. Ida was too bruised and too vulnerable to young studs, especially cops.

When they arrived at Ida's apartment, O'Shea shifted to neutral, set the hand brake and looked fondly at her. "I probably didn't say it too clearly back at the restaurant, so if you got a few minutes, let me explain."

"Jack, I've got all the time in the world. Why don't you turn off the engine?"

O'Shea complied with a roguish grin and not a hint of uneasiness. "I almost blew it earlier because I didn't know how to handle a date with a pretty, single, young, independent woman with a sexy figure. I was uptight and almost angry. Not at you, at myself for being such an asshole. You represented all those attractive women in my life I ran from in fear and resentment." O'Shea paused soberly before offering another roguish grin. "And now, for some strange reason, I'm comfortable with you, and boy it feels so great. You just may become my first woman friend. Is that OK with you?"

Ida looked at O'Shea adoringly. "Oh, Jack, I'd love to be your friend. I'm really tired of performing for men."

O'Shea was thrilled by her last comment. "I'm tired of believing I'm supposed to perform for women. Let's make a deal. No performances, no expectations. Just relax and be friends, which means being good to each other."

She vigorously nodded. "What a refreshing change that will be. Let's see where it takes us."

Shaking hands on their friendship, O'Shea leaned over and kissed her lightly on the cheek.

As he pulled back, Ida grabbed his lapels, pulled him to her mouth and kissed him hard on the lips. "Now I have a question. Do you have time to revisit my apartment for a cup of coffee?"

This time, O'Shea gratefully stayed for nearly an hour, drinking coffee, sharing their pasts, and sitting comfortably close on the couch. He was even getting used to an occasional pair of fur balls, darting under chairs.

It was Ida who closed the narrow gap between them. Resting her head on his shoulder, she looked up just as O'Shea glanced down at her. For the next ten minutes, no words were required. Aware that he was starring at her lips, she slowly moistened them with her tongue.

O'Shea was flabbergasted that sex could be part of their friendship pact. Staring hang-jawed at the friendly invitation, he hesitated. *Oh, what the hell*, he thought. Within seconds, they were locked in hungry, passionate foreplay. Tongues probed mouths, hands explored bodies, movements quickened, and heavy breathing changed to panting.

Undressing was frantic, as bra straps snapped, flies unzipped, buttons popped and shoes went flying, Clothes were everywhere. Both were ready, they thought, until Ida gently reached her hands between O'Shea's thighs, to guide him into her. As she groped searchingly, she glanced downward, then up at O'Shea.

"Aaaw," she lamented with a deep sigh.

ꆆ ꆆ ꆆ

Driving back to his apartment, O'Shea had plenty to think about. He had lost an erection and found a female friend. The anomaly kept him smiling all the way home. Instead of mourning his limp penis, he was savoring the discovery of Ida, female and friend, his first.

He thought about his embarrassment and frustration when a hooker couldn't get a rise out of him. Of course, those were business deals that cost him two hundred dollars whether or not he rose to the occasion. To make matters even worse, he was usually drunk.

The few other women in his past, including his ex-wife were not friends; they treated him like a lover, meaning he was expected to perform on demand. Even sober, this was too much of a challenge. That's when performance anxieties frequently took over, preventing him from getting it up.

But all that's changed now, he thought with a grin. Like a couple of real pals, he and Ida joked about the rise and fall of his *wang*. They agreed that Ida's attack probably scared it away, and when O'Shea assured her *it was no big deal*, Ida glanced at his crotch, adding, "You got that right."

They both roared.

When he arrived home, O'Shea smiled into his bathroom mirror thinking, *You're not bad for an old fart*. He slept well that night.

CHAPTER 37

After O'Shea left for his date with Ida, Ellis spent several hours with Hasselburg, getting acquainted and trading knowledge. He even received a crash course in computer savvy, while Hasselburg learned about alibied suspects, giants, disks, their endless frustrations with the eight cases and the Trickers. His last comment prompted her to tell him all about her best friend, Sharon Kruger, whose younger brother, Brad, belonged to the Trickers.

Hasselburg explained that when she learned earlier about the club's possible connection to some of the eight homicides, she warned Sharon to get her brother out of the club. Brad had insisted to his sister, however, that the Trickers were just a party club. He then called Hasselburg, explaining that Howard Kantner, their new president, welcomed members' friends to their meetings, even if they were cops. Brad had also told her that Trickers involved in the .22 heist, or any violence, were renegades acting alone. He added that all those *renegades* lost their club membership.

"I learned all this last week," Hasselburg explained to Ellis, "and when I informed my uncle, he said it could be useful to your investigation."

Both detectives knew that Trickers ranged in age from fourteen to twenty-five, and that those who were students attended primarily Poly, Lincoln and Galileo High Schools. They didn't know much else about them other than their orange and black jackets. The SFPD gang detail knew only of the Armory robbery. They had no earlier reason to investigate them.

Ellis realized that having Hasselburg attend one of the meetings as a member's guest could really help their investigation. *This could also be good practice for her in criminal investigation work,* he thought. It was safe, worthwhile and sanctioned by their boss, Captain McInerney. He'd run it by O'Shea in the morning.

📖 📖 📖

Thursday morning, Ellis was on the computer when O'Shea arrived at their cubicle. O'Shea roamed the cubicle for a few moments. Pausing over the computer, he smiled down at his partner. "We can actually take a few steps without smashing into something. How you doing?"

Ellis wasn't used to a smiling O'Shea at 7:45 a.m., especially before his morning routine. "I'm fine, John. Just practicing what Officer Hasselburg taught me. It's amazing the amount of information she put in the computer."

Looking up at O'Shea's soft smile, Ellis grinned back. "I've got a sneaking hunch things worked out well last night."

O'Shea's smile became a boyish smirk. "Beyond my wildest dreams and I didn't even get laid. More important, it didn't bother me. I actually liked being with Ida as a companion, a friend. By the end of the night with her, I didn't feel shy, uneasy or locked into some tough-ass role. It was like being with a pal who happened to also be a woman. How does that grab ya?"

Holding back an urge to shower his good friend with congratulations, Ellis tried to remain casually impressed. "It's about time. You might become a renaissance man if you're not careful." He was thinking, *boy, I hope it lasts.*

Picking up his coffee cup and newspaper, O'Shea headed down the hall, cheerfully shouting back at Ellis. "When I'm Chief, you'll be *my* renaissance man and anything else you want. It's Jimmy Brit time."

📖 📖 📖

When O'Shea returned twenty minutes later, he dropped his newspaper in Ellis' lap and placed his coffee cup on his desk, while idly noticing that Hasselburg's desk was empty. It didn't matter much. It was just 8 a.m., and he was still appreciating their expanded cubicle.

"I'm cooking dinner for Ida at her place tonight. She doesn't know I'm a master cook."

Exploring the front page, Ellis didn't bother looking up. "Am I invited?"

"Not this time, pal. But I am one hell of good cook, right?"

Still perusing the front page, Ellis nodded, with a thumbs up.

O'Shea loved to cook, especially for his few close friends. "I take it that's an absolute *yes*. By the way, did Hasselburg get sick of us already?"

Dropping the newspaper in the wastebasket, Ellis looked at him with an expression of mild concern.

O'Shea's grin started to fade. "What's up, Paul?"

Ellis explained in detail the previous evenings conversation with Hasselburg, her willingness to accompany her girlfriend's brother to a Trickers meeting, and McInerney's endorsement of her plan. "Hasselburg phoned and left a message after we left that the Trickers meeting was at Sigmund Stern Grove last night," Ellis added, furtively glancing at the empty desk. "So much for talking it over with you."

O'Shea lost all of his grin. "What time was she going to report for work today?"

"There was no change, she knew we started at eight."

"No calls?"

"On your desk. Just the ones from Judge Hall and Captain McInerney."

O'Shea checked his memos and watch. "Well, it's only 8:10. Let's wait another five minutes before we freak out. But I bet she's like you. Better early than on time. Shit, I'd better call McInerney now."

He didn't have to. Seconds later O'Shea dove for the phone on the first ring.

"McInerney here. Hasselburg's in SF General, room 308. Can you go over there?"

O'Shea motioned Ellis to listen on his extension. "I'll leave after I hang up. Give me a quick rundown."

McInerney paused for a moment as he cleared his throat. "Mounted Patrol Officers found her tied in a tree about twenty-five feet off the ground in Golden Gate Park. Firemen got her down using a ladder truck. She was groggy like she'd been drugged. They I.D.'d her and called me five minutes ago."

"We're on it and outta here. Hang in there, we'll keep you posted."

Twenty-five minutes later O'Shea and Ellis were in hospital room

308 staring down at Hasselburg. They were relieved when she gave a sheepish smile, assuring them she was fine. "There are no physical injuries. My mind's clearing again. I feel awful with embarrassment."

Ellis was reminded of his partner's endearing side, when O'Shea bent over the bed and lightly stroked Hasselburg's forehead. "You must have had one hell of a night."

O'Shea's gentle comment set off a downpour of tears, prompting Ellis to move two chairs next to Hasselburg's bed. "I bet you've got plenty to tell John and me, so if it's OK, we'll sit by you and listen."

Handing Hasselburg the box of Kleenex from the nightstand, O'Shea added, "We're going to be with you as long as it takes to know everything that happened."

Drying her eyes, Hasselburg stared at the two detectives. "I guess the tears are my gratitude for the way you're both treating me. I was afraid you might be mad at me. But you *are* like family. My uncle's right. You're not just good inspectors, you're good humans."

Embarrassed, both detectives handled their *aw shucks* feelings in different ways. Ellis grabbed his notebook and pen. O'Shea got up briefly to look out the window, commenting softly "Gee, you got a nice view of the parking lot." Returning to his chair, he patted Hasselburg on the arm. "Now, what happened?"

Hasselburg began with the dinner at Sharon's house. After eating, she learned from Brad of the Trickers meeting in an hour. Having known Brad for several years as her best friend's shy, baggy pants, teenage brother, she had no reason to mistrust him. It was an impromptu opportunity to gain information about the Trickers that might help her new bosses in their investigation.

Sharon, a senior at San Francisco State University, stayed at home to complete a class assignment. She had never attended any of her brother's club meetings and wasn't interested.

They arrived at Sigmund Stern Grove on Nineteenth Avenue and Sloat Boulevard at 7:30 p.m. Rap music was blaring as they drove to the parking lot, and by the time they walked the fifty yards to the outside meeting area, the music was ear-shattering loud. Hasselburg remembered the crush of guys in orange and black jackets, dancing, prancing, shouting and cavorting. All were in their teens and twenties; and many of the jacketed members were with females.

There were several tables with coffee, huge canisters of soft drinks, mineral water and beer. The atmosphere was boisterous but friendly. When introduced to Howard Kantner, the Trickers new president, he seemed cordial, mild-mannered and pleasant, despite his awesome size and muscular body. He must have been about 6'7", she figured.

Hasselburg further explained that she met several of Brad's friends. Two of them, Al Hoffner and Pete Baker, were Trickers, in Brad's sophomore homeroom at Polytechnic. Both seemed pretty much like typical teenage party boys—boyish looking and happy-go-lucky.

Brad also introduced her to a couple of Poly seniors he seemed to admire as *very intelligent and cool*. Karl Schwartz was the tall handsome one with a sarcastic sense of humor. Erick Taggart was small, wiry and less vocal, with an engaging smile and some dirty jokes. Both were guests and members of a Poly club called the Alchemists.

Hasselburg leaned back in silence, peering at the ceiling as if in deep thought. "The rest is strangely fuzzy or fragmented," she finally added.

"Would you like something to drink?" Ellis asked.

Hasselburg lay quiet for another moment before answering. "You know, I do recall having a couple glasses of Diet Coke. I walked around the party area while Brad was again talking to Al and Pete. The music was so loud I couldn't really carry on a conversation with anyone. I remember smiling and people smiling back at me. I think I intended to leave. That's it, the next thing I remember, I was high up in a tree. Then I was rescued." With a puzzled, frowning smile, Hasselburg nodded slowly to both detectives. "That's all I know."

O'Shea handed her a glass of water. "Jesus, Jill. For someone who was drugged, you've got an incredible memory. Christ, I can't remember the first name of most people I met an hour ago."

Ellis leaned forward showing her his three pages of notes. "Boy, I expected a taste, and you give us a whole meal. So, can we assume Brad stayed at the meeting?"

Before Hasselburg could reply, O'Shea interrupted. "And that you actually left before the big snooze?"

Hasselburg heaved a grinning sigh. "That's what makes my usually photographic recall strange. I just know I wandered around by myself for awhile, then *the big snooze*, as you put it."

Ellis reviewed his notes. "Well, let me run it by you and we'll try to fill in the gaps. As far as you know, you intended to tell Brad you were leaving, then head for your car. You don't actually remember telling him or entering your car. You did drink a Diet Coke, chatted with five people that Brad had introduced you to and wandered around by yourself for a while.

"Your doctor says you had consumed some kind of a Barbiturate cocktail with a pinch of Diazepam and Chlorpromazine. Whoever spiked your Cokes knew his chemistry. He or she didn't want to kill you. The amounts of Phenobarbital, Valium and Thorazine were just enough to slip you into a hypnotic sleep that was apparently so gradual you never knew it happened. You must have peacefully passed out, ending up in a Golden Gate Park tree. The most viable scenario between your unconsciousness and the tree is that someone helped you to your car and drove you to the tree while someone else followed you in another car. Your car was neatly parked at the curb about forty feet from the big tree. The keys were in the ignition. So, we'll have forensics check your car for any obscure little things like prints that shouldn't be there. Want to add anything, John?"

O'Shea had a few notes of his own, hastily written on the back of his electric bill. "I agree with Paul. No one was trying to kill you. That would have been a cinch compared to what happened. They sure as hell didn't want to engage the police department with a cop's death. As usual in this case, they wanted to frustrate us, confuse us. Christ, they're good at it. I say *they* because there is obviously more than one person involved in all this. Don't you dare assume any blame. No way you could have beat this alone. You've reviewed enough of our investigation of the eight cases to see how we've been constantly misdirected or out-maneuvered. We can't even prove you were *mickied* at the Grove. They keep throwing us a few obvious clues or suspects, and then kick us square in the ass. There's something sinister out there that crushes cops with two hundred twelve pound rocks, leaves twenty-five inch foot prints, skewers another cop with an inhuman javelin toss of missile velocity, hangs a kid high on a gym pipe, and parks our new partner in a tree. I could go on but you get the picture.

"Now, as detectives, we've got to go through the standard routine and interview all the obvious suspects, including your best friend's kid brother, and six months ago I wouldn't have dared mention what I'm about to say."

Noticing Ellis' quickening nod, O'Shea grinned. "We sort of read each others minds, Jill. Why don't you finish what I was going to say?" He nodded at Ellis.

Ellis slowly turned toward Hasselburg. "In this case, as we go by the book we've learned over and over that the obvious keeps leading us down dark mysterious paths to nowhere. The Trickers clues are everywhere. Every time I see black and orange, I kinda cringe, yet in our experience with the eight, there's a good possibility these clues might lead us nowhere."

Now O'Shea was nodding. "You took the words right out of my mouth, partner. We'll keep turning over our proverbial rocks until we score, knowing that all these new leads could be more smoke and mirrors—and more deaths. These cases are like a toxic vapor that offs people who just happen by. Jill, you were one of the lucky ones. So was Ellis' daughter. They didn't even take your gun or badge; we checked."

"So did I when I came to," Hasselburg quickly added. "They didn't take a thing except my pride. I could see my car from up in the tree."

O'Shea shook his head. "No, Jill. I don't think they were screwing with you as much as they were mocking all of us. You keep your pride; and Paul and I'll try to keep ours."

Hasselburg managed a pensive smile. " Thanks, Lieutenant. I guess I needed some assurance that I'm worth another chance."

Ellis chimed in. "That was never an issue. What amazes me is how they can savagely kill some and completely protect others, like you. Your car wasn't even slightly damaged."

It was O'Shea's turn. "They're not just super clever, they're arrogant, evil and, goddamn it, baffling. There are no motives for any of the eight cases, and finally we know that at least five of the eight are connected."

Hasselburg looked at both detectives during the brief silence before responding. "From what I've learned so far, don't we know there's a link only because someone's telling us?"

"Great point, Jill," O'Shea acknowledged. "That's what makes this even more frustrating and sinister. Somebody doesn't want us to throw it in and bury this in the inactives."

"John's got it right," Ellis added. "I don't think I've ever felt this impotent on a case. We've been methodically investigating eight deaths, getting nowhere and now someone tells us to try harder and more creatively."

As O'Shea nodded, he got up and replaced his chair by a wall. "Get some rest, Jill. We'll see you tomorrow." Then with a grin, he added, "Eight sharp and don't be late."

After sliding his chair back, Ellis patted her on the shoulder. "What time are they discharging you?"

"Later this afternoon. I can come by the office then."

Ellis smiled. "Eight o'clock sharp—tomorrow."

On their way down the hospital corridor, the detectives met up with Captain McInerney and Sharon Kruger. O'Shea greeted his superior with a message he needed to hear. "She's getting out of here this afternoon. Her pride's hurt a little. Nothing else."

McInerney looked older than usual and exhausted. "It's my fault. I shouldn't have encouraged her to go without checking with you first. You could have given her instructions and wired her or...."

O'Shea interrupted with a smirk. "Hold on, Captain. None of us could have anticipated this. Christ sake. It was just an open meeting. Not an espionage mission. If I had known, I would have let her go anyway. She went as Officer Hasselburg and friend of Brad Kruger, all true. No CIA crap."

"Anyway, Jack, I've got ten uniforms rounding up all those at the meeting who so much as walked by her."

"Leave Sharon's brother, Brad, and the two other Poly guys, Karl and Erick, to us. OK?"

McInerney managed a grin. "They're already in interview rooms, waiting for you two. All those we've detained think they're material witnesses. None of them are booked but we informally took their pictures through a one way, and prints from sanitized glasses of soft drinks. They're no dummies, so we've got to do the interviews before all we hear are lawyers."

O'Shea noticed Sharon, with eyes uneasily lowered, standing next to Captain McInerney. "Why don't you go see your friend? I'll bet she's looking forward to seeing you."

Sharon slowly looked up at O'Shea through red, misty eyes. "Thank you. Is that OK Captain McInerney?"

"Of course. Get going." McInerney watched her scurry down the corridor before looking back at his two detectives. "I forgot Sharon was standing behind me. Thanks, Jack, for the nudge.

O'Shea was thinking about the amorphous killers out there somewhere, probably plotting the next deception. "Let's go find some of the bad ones, Paul, We'll keep you posted, Bruce. Tell the uniforms to send us their reports as soon as possible."

CHAPTER 38

Returning to their Bryant Street office, a memo on O'Shea's desk from McInerney advised the detectives where they'd find Brad Kruger and his two Poly companions, all waiting in separate interview rooms downing soft drinks.

Both detectives interviewed Brad first, and it quickly became obvious he wasn't part of any inner, sinister circle. He was an easily accessible, eager to please fifteen-year-old who actually admired authority. They both noticed a twinkle in his eyes that seemed to belie any deception. Although a bright, honor roll nerd, with a broad fund of scholarly knowledge, he had none of the social skills required for peer recognition. Brad was always the messenger and never part of the message. He was also a joiner who needed a group identity since he still hadn't found his own.

At Polytechnic High School, he was a proud member of the Science Club, the Honor Society and the Chess Club. These member-ships offered him some sense of belonging, but he really wanted an invitation into the more prestigious groups like the Block "P" Society, the Omega's or the Alchemists. These were highly selective clubs requiring athletic or intellectual achievement of juniors and seniors, by invitation only. He wasn't there yet, but hoped his two friends would sponsor him before they graduated.

Brad had an excellent memory and a boyish eagerness to help with the investigation. He recalled introducing Hasselburg to the Trickers' president, his classmates Al and Pete, and school seniors Karl and

Erick, whom he considered special friends. By about 8:30 p.m., he noticed Hasselburg drift into the crowd. That was fine with him. He had expected her to interact with others since she was there to check out the Trickers. After rejoining Pete and Al, they chatted, watched the dancing, especially the girls, for a while. At about 9:30, he looked around for Hasselburg, and when he couldn't find her, he went to the parking lot. Her car was gone, so he assumed she had gotten tired and left. On his way back to the music, he saw Karl and Erick dancing with some pretty girls. Karl waved and offered him a ride home. He finally left with Karl and Erick at about 10:30. The detectives also learned that Brad joined the Trickers two months earlier because of their orange and black jackets, open enrollment and monthly parties.

"Now I can invite my friends to our club activities," he explained. He was referring to Karl and Erick. Aside from being elected officers in Poly's Honor Society, they were members of the Alchemists, popular with the girls, and "well, just real cool," he added.

When the detectives thanked him for his help, Brad's hazel eyes sparkled with pride. Shaking hands with O'Shea and Ellis, Brad hesitated for a few seconds before conjuring the courage to ask an important question. "Do you think I could be a Junior Police cadet?"

Ellis smiled. "Certainly, when you're sixteen."

O'Shea nodded. "You would be a big help while you're in school. But with your grades, you'll end up in a real profession, like doctor or scientist.

As Brad walked off, he slowly looked back at the detectives. "I'm sorry. I shoulda walked Officer Hasselburg to her car when she left."

📖 📖 📖

The interviews with Brad's friends were neither pleasant nor particularly productive. To Karl and Erick, Brad wasn't a friend. He was just a *kid* they met in Honor Society, intelligent but a *clod*.

O'Shea arbitrarily choose to interview Karl, while Ellis saw Erick in another room.

Karl was just about everything O'Shea found annoying in youth. Well over six feet tall, with blond hair, square jawed good looks, and a perpetual bored sneer, all Karl needed was a Nazi uniform to resemble those hated super race Aryans in old WWII movies. It didn't take O'Shea long to realize he was no match for Karl's quick, slashing repartee and skillful manipulation of words. O'Shea had to struggle for every bit of information, and still ended up with nothing worthwhile.

"Hi, I'm Lieutenant O'Shea. Thanks for waiting."

"Are you inferring that I had a choice?"

"Well, we really do need to question witnesses."

"I'm a witness? To what? A meeting? Or are you asking if I were a witness to something?"

O'Shea changed the subject. "Where are you from?"

"Since this isn't a friendly chat, I'll take you literally. I'm from my parents."

After an hour, O'Shea learned little more than Karl's address, about his first and only invitation to a Trickers meeting, his oblivion to any unusual activities there and his drive home with his friend, Erick and *the kid*, Brad at about 11 p.m. He was even more oblique about his school activities. O'Shea was delighted to watch him leave.

Ellis, down the hall, had a similar experience with Erick, who, he thought, could have been Baron Von Stroheim's double, including arrogant jutting chin, multiple smirks, plenty of smilingly sarcastic verbal zingers and little else. His replies to Ellis' questions boiled down to meeting Hasselburg, noticing nothing suspicious, chatting with Howard Kantner, the Trickers' president, about the club's activities, wandering around listening to music and leaving with Karl, who gave Brad a ride home at 11 p.m.

📖　📖　📖

Walking back to their cubicle, the detectives were silently preoccupied with their throbbing, inner frustrations. With clues, suspects and motives again collapsing around them, they were feeling more like victims than investigators.

Staring at Hasselburg's empty desk, Ellis broke the silence. "We can't seem to protect our own, let alone solve the eight cases. What's going on?"

O'Shea, wrestling with similar thoughts, leaned back in his chair, closed his eyes and sighed. "I wish the hell I knew. This sounds like horseshit coming from me, but I've got a gnawing hunch we need, more than ever, to be patient. We're getting closer, Paul, I can almost taste it. We've just gotta keep at it. Do you know what I mean?"

"I guess I've got the same premonition. I wanted to hear it from you. We're closing in and I haven't the slightest idea who we're closing in on. I've got a hunch though, that finding three more disks will help."

"That's exactly what I was thinking. Let me return Judge Hall's call, then we'll have a quick lunch, and it's back to the disk hunt in the cesspool."

Ellis glanced at the computer on the new desk. "She's only been here a couple of days and I appreciate her. She's not just willing to learn, she's tough. Comes to in a tree this morning, drugged out, and she was ready to work this afternoon."

Picking up the phone, O'Shea looked up. "Yeah, we lucked out. She's a quick study, loyal and a computer whiz."

Judge Hall's reply to O'Shea's return call was predictably curt, fast and ingratiating, like an admiral to a seaman second class. "Hello, Jack. It's good to hear from you. How are your cases coming?"

"We're making some progress."

"Fine, I hope you're available a week from this Friday, in the evening."

O'Shea flashed on his gold trimmed uniform with the Chief's stars. "Of course, Judge."

Hall's voice relaxed a bit. "That's fine. It's a major fundraiser at the St Francis. You'll enjoy it. Gourmet food and many celebrities endorsing my candidacy."

Shit, O'Shea thought. "I'll be looking forward to it," he said.

"As the next Chief of Police, you can introduce me before my speech. One of my staff will fill you in early next week. Thanks, Jack." (*Click*)

Listening to the dial tone, O'Shea gritted his teeth at Ellis as he slammed down the phone. "I'm a goddamn lackey and I don't even like the guy."

Ellis offered a consoling grin. "Keep thinking *Chief*."

"Yep, I know. Let's get out of here. How about some grease—a Whopper and fries. Then we'll do disks. OK?"

Grabbing his coat, Ellis hit the corridor shouting, "It's grease time."

📖 📖 📖

Still munching a few stray fries, the detectives agreed to do the *needle in the haystack* disk search where Officer Nelson died. They both figured finding a dime-sized disk at a stale outdoor crime scene was unlikely. Arriving at the site, they knew it was impossible. A twenty-mile-an-hour wind humming through the demolished freeway rubble sent clouds of dust bouncing in swirls, around and over piles of rocks. Ellis thought they looked like little dirt devils, while O'Shea thought they might as well leave. Even the yellow police tape was shredded, eliminating much of the exact crime scene perimeter.

Through the howling winds, O'Shea shouted at Ellis, who was already on his knees, looking between slabs of concrete. "It's hopeless. If it was here, it ain't now; it's probably in Sausalito. Christ, this wind could move boulders."

Ellis poked his head over the rubble. "Come on, Loot. Like the lottery, you can't win unless you play."

Shit, O'Shea grumbled to himself. "We'll play for a half hour."

Ellis was hoping that such a small, light object might have been blown between the slabs of cement, where it might stay secure forever, or until the heavy equipment removed the debris. Working outward from the spot where Nelson's head was crushed, Ellis carefully sifted through drifting dirt piles while examining every crevice and cranny. O'Shea, however, just stood nearby, rubbing his sand blown eyes and half heartedly scanning the area.

"Wow," Ellis snorted, "the urine smell down here is powerful enough to bleach my lungs, what's left of them."

"I know what you mean," O'Shea bellowed. "I'm smelling it up here in the wind." Feeling a bit guilty, O'Shea bent down to join the search when he noticed an orange spot on a piece of pipe. The six-foot pipe was resting on a slab of rock near his feet. Grabbing the pipe just below the little spot, O'Shea slid it closer. "Holy shit," he shouted.

Ellis leaped to his feet, in time to watch O'Shea's jaw take a long slow drop that quickly curled into a broad grin, as he gently wiped the pipe with his sleeve. O'Shea looked up at Ellis with a stare of disbelief. "Look! It's stuck to this pole. Another 'R'." Prying the orange and black disk off the pole, O'Shea handed it to his partner. "It's been waiting for us for three weeks. That's six out of eight. I'll be a son of a bitch; this blows me out. What do you think, partner?"

"I think you've got the eyes of an eagle. I kind of didn't really expect this one. Nelson was a cop, undercover. There's not even a slim motive in this one."

O'Shea plucked the disk out of Ellis' hand. "That's the point. Maybe they're all connected by their randomness—some other type of motive or reason that has nothing to do with the victims. Isn't that where we've been headed the last few weeks? Down some strange maze, where *they* or *it* want to take us."

"It makes me cringe, John. It's like we're not really in control. We just have to keep following, wherever."

Seemingly indifferent to Ellis' comment, O'Shea rolled the disk between his fingers. "Another 'R'. What the hell do the six spell? Who cares? There's going to be eight. They'll spell something that gives us an answer or some more bullshit."

Ellis snatched the disk from O'Shea's fingers to get his attention. "What makes you so certain there'll be two more?"

"When you have six of eight events occur in a roll, the probability of the remaining two occurring is way better than chance. So, I'll bet on the full eight."

Ellis gave the disk back with a wry smile. "I can't argue with a math whiz. How many arrangements of eight letters did you say? Over forty thousand?"

O'Shea returned the wry smile. "That's pure math probability stuff. If it's a message, I doubt it'll be a *nonsense syllable*. It'll be a word or words. That eliminates most combinations and permutations. And you know, I think the three of us are savvy enough to figure it out when the time comes."

Returning the "R" disk to his partner, Ellis wiped some of the blowing dirt from his eyes. "I'm glad you included Hasselburg. She has that youthful intelligence we started losing a few years back. By the way, did you know that the word Trickers has all six letters?"

O'Shea pocketed the "R" with a snicker. "Christ, Paul, I've been tracking that possibility since Helen's Sea Cliff 'E'. Every time we found another letter I knew Trickers was still a possibility. Let's get out of here, I'm tired of shouting in the wind.

📖 📖 📖

The detectives spent most of the next two hours in the dreary surrounds of the property room. Sergeant Flanagan was his usual officious, dry, nasty self and the boxes of clothes reeked of death. There was no pay-off this time. Nothing. After a quick, overly optimistic scan of Likert and Anderson's belongings, the detectives carefully re-examined every item, including the property boxes.

With a deep sigh, O'Shea turned a sock inside out for the third time. It was the last Anderson item. "Shit. I should of known the last two wouldn't be easy."

Ellis placed his last item, a right shoe, into Likert's property box. "Nothing, John. Nothing. But I guess those were at least a few more rocks we needed to turn over."

"Yeah. Now we definitely know the disks aren't here, and you know what that means."

Dumping his latex gloves in the wastebasket, Ellis carefully picked up his coat with thumb and index finger. "After I sterilize myself, I'm on my way to Likert's garage."

"Thanks, Pal. We know where Anderson died but not where he was poisoned. That means I've got to search his house and call Bender. Maybe, like the hospital, his office has something."

Ellis nodded. "When I finish up, I'll give you a hand, if you haven't had any luck."

After dolefully trudging back to Sergeant Flanagan with the two boxes, the disappointed detectives hit the bathroom for their usual surgical scrub down. Then they separated for the rest of the day. As O'Shea went back to their cubicle to make a few calls, Ellis headed for Likert's house.

Even though O'Shea was grateful for his emerging friendship with Ida and was looking forward to cooking a meal for her, he was feeling a tad restricted. He was used to non-stop pursuits of a certain aspect of an investigation until completed, even if it took most of the night. It was 4:00 p.m., but it only allowed him three more hours of searching until Ida was expecting him for dinner. Thinking it over, he reconsidered. *Knock it off you asshole. She'd understand if you cancelled. The truth is you don't want to.*

📖 📖 📖

Knowing a search of Anderson's house might be an all-nighter, he decided to call his friend, Bender, first.

Bender was just about out the door of his office when O'Shea called.

"Mr. Bender, there's a call from an O'Shea. Do you want to take it?"

Grabbing the phone from the receptionist, Bender nodded a thanks. "How you doing, Pal? Ready for some more Java House grease?"

"Give me a couple weeks to unclog my veins and you're on. For now, these eight cases are jamming the shit out of me."

Hanging over the receptionist's desk, Bender learned about the six out of a possible eight dime-sized, orange and black disks; and the possibility someone might have discovered such an item in the DA's office where Anderson died. Bender didn't waste a moment. "Hang on." After asking the receptionist, three DA's, and two secretaries still in the office, Bender contacted the janitor on duty the day Anderson died.

"You still awake, John?"

O'Shea didn't mind the fifteen minute wait. He knew Bender would check every possibility before answering.

"Sorry, buddy, no one remembers anything remotely resembling a disk, including both the receptionist and janitor working that Wednesday."

O'Shea knew it was a long shot. "Thanks, pal. I really didn't expect it to be there. Next stop is Anderson's house. I'll call you in a week or so when the alligators stop snapping at my ass."

"Why Emil's house?" Bender asked. "We know his kid didn't poison him."

O'Shea was also wondering why. "Guess I'm desperate. I've gotta eliminate every possible disk location."

Bender motioned the receptionist to bring him their Anderson file. "I think his message that day said he would grab a bite before coming over here. Yes! It's in his file."

O'Shea felt an adrenaline rush. "Christ, Dick. You're something else. How the hell did I miss that possibility? I'll check all the eateries near his house and store for starters."

Bender didn't respond for a moment. "You still there?" O'Shea asked.

"I just remembered, Emil mentioning Aaron's Creamery on Irving, near his house. We used to have great shakes there as kids. Emil apparently kept in touch with Aaron all these years."

"Thanks, Dick. It's sure worth a shot. Later, OK?"

"Good luck, Pal."

O'Shea was again fully charged and ready to go. *The hell with the phone*, he thought. *I can be on Irving in ten minutes*. He grabbed any excuse to cruise the city. In less than five minutes, O'Shea was cruising along a crowded, weekday Mission Street, onto hectic Market, over the jammed Seventeenth Street hill to Stanyan Street, his childhood stomping grounds, like a spiral staircase leading down to the past. From there on, the ride triggered a kaleidoscope of familiar visions, young sounds and very old memories.

As he passed Grattan Street, he could practically hear the screaming, laughing, shouting kids in the Grattan Grammar School playground. He could hear his friends, even himself. Then he slowed for his left turn onto Parnassus. That's about where he broke his leg when his bicycle slammed into the side of a car. Dick Boyd held him until an ambulance came. Cresting Parnassus, he remembered the roar of the Kezar Stadium crowds below. He'd just scored a touchdown against Washington High. His Sacred Heart teammate, Ginella, slapped him on the ass as they ran back to the huddle. San Francisco was O'Shea's city, and he loved cruising its streets.

It was at Irving and Seventh Avenue, however, where O'Shea finally climbed back to the present. That's when it dawned on him that he didn't have the Creamery's Irving Street address. *Oh well*, he grunted to himself, *I'll just cruise Irving 'til I find it.* A block later, between Eighth and Ninth, he spotted it. There was Aaron's Creamery, sandwiched between a grocery store and a dry cleaner. A grin spread all over his face as he parked his car in the nearest red zone.

Opening the door to the creamery, O'Shea let himself regress to age sixteen for a few moments. The white plastic counter with tall wire-back stools supporting black vinyl seats hadn't changed. Neither had the mirrored wall behind the counter, nor the metal milk shake containers, and those upright, metal machines that whirled the rich contents into thick shakes.

Suddenly the reflection of an old man hunched over the counter jarred O'Shea's daydream.

"Hi, can I help you?" It was a pleasant voice from a craggy-faced, gray-haired, scrawny man with thick wire glasses, Frisco jeans, and rolled-up shirtsleeves. He was holding a mop and wearing a crinkly smile that seemed to trace the deep lines in his face.

I'll bet he's been smiling most of his long life, O'Shea thought. "I'm sorry to bother you. I guess you're closed and cleaning up."

The smiling face broadened its smile. "Hey that's OK. I'm always cleaning up, and since I'm here, I keep the place open after lunch, in case someone wants a cup of coffee. Would you like a cup?"

O'Shea relaxed. "I'd really appreciate that. You must be Aaron. Boy, this place has been here awhile."

Placing a cup of coffee in front of O'Shea, Aaron sat at the counter next to him. "For seventy-two years. Hell, I've been here for forty years. It used to be my dad's place."

The two native San Franciscans chatted for a good fifteen minutes before O'Shea formally introduced himself and his questions. "I'm Jack O'Shea with the San Francisco Police Department. I was hoping you could help me learn more about your friend, Emil Anderson, and his death."

Aaron dropped his eyes and his smile. "We were friends for a long time. I knew his beautiful wife, and his useless son. They're dead too. God, what a tragic family. Emil had breakfast here the day he died." Aaron added with a thin smile. "I didn't think my food was that bad."

O'Shea countered with a gratis grin. "Let me fill you in on all we know. When Mr. Anderson left here on that Wednesday, he went to the DA's Office. He died there about twenty minutes later. He was poisoned on PCP. We figure he ingested the poison an hour or so before death. At home or, well, could have happened here."

Aaron was stunned. "My God! Here?"

O'Shea smiled reassuringly. "It's got nothing to do with you or, for that matter, your food. It's just a possibility, and before we tear his house apart for clues, I thought I might as well come here on the off chance you remember something, anything."

Aaron spent the next five minutes recalling Emil's nervousness that day, his light meal at his usual small table by the window, the crowded breakfast trade, and his abrupt departure before collecting change from the ten-dollar bill he left on the table. "I've still got the ten. Kind of a memento," he said. "Oh yeah, strange, there was a little reddish plastic round thing left on top of the ten-dollar bill."

Trying hard to maintain some semblance of composure, O'Shea shouted, "WHAT? Do you still have it?"

A little startled by the exuberance, Aaron quickly got up and headed for the cash register. "I think it's here with the ten. Uh huh. Here it is."

O'Shea was up like a flash, leaning over Aaron's shoulder at the cash register. "Can I see it?" O'Shea politely requested while plucking the disk from Aaron's fingers. *Number seven;* he smiled almost fiendishly to himself. "See that Aaron? It's the letter 'C', a big help in our investigation. O'Shea shook Aaron's hand with the enthusiasm of a long lost brother. Heading for the door with the disk safely tucked away, O'Shea glanced back. "Thanks again for your help. Let's have coffee one of these days."

Still somewhat bewildered, smiling Aaron waved back as O'Shea disappeared out the door. "Sure."

📖 📖 📖

For well over an hour, Ellis had eyeballed virtually every inch of Likert's TR-4A. Earlier, when Mrs. Likert opened the garage door, Ellis was optimistic. The crime scene was still intact, except that any smell of death had been scrubbed away with sinus-clearing Clorox, topped with Lysol. Nothing had been moved except André's crushed body and the weight of the car's front end, now resting on blocks. The front wheels were still lying flat on either side of the car, and the giant footprint remained prominent and puzzling.

Hoping to get lucky, Ellis had started with the windshield. Not a trace. From there it was all down hill. Down to the dashboard, the instruments, steering wheel, seats, side panels, floor panels, gearshift, hand brake, clutch and brake pedals. After examining the car's body, trunk, engine compartment and the two front wheels, Ellis headed for the dreaded under carriage. As he worked his way under the front suspension, he felt so vulnerable. He thought of Likert's moment of terror before two thousand pounds of front end crushed his chest. *Did Likert see the giant's feet?* he wondered. *How about Officer Nelson's giant? It must have been terrifying*, he thought. Ellis uneasily spent another half hour under the car with no luck. Wiggling out the back end of the car, he struggled to his feet. The worst of his search was over, and the giant didn't get him.

Breathing some clean air outside the garage, he flashed on the possibility that the Clorox scrubbing might have washed the disk away. He decided he had done enough for one day. He'd return tomorrow with Officer Hasselburg.

Somewhat disheartened, Ellis returned to the garage for one more quick peek. After a few minutes, he wondered why he was frowning as he stood by the front of the TR-4A. Then another look around and it hit him. "Where the hell's the floor jack?" he asked the garage.

Mrs. Likert opened the side door. "Is that you, Sergeant?"

Ellis looked over at the door with a smiling wave. "Ah, yes Ma'am. I was just thinking out loud." Ellis found it in the far corner of the garage. He figured it was moved after blocking the front end of the car to remove Likert's body. At about five feet, Ellis spotted the disk, midway up the handle. Plucking it off the handle, he shouted, "It's a 'K'."

Mrs. Likert opened the side door. "Did you call, Sergeant?"

Ellis kept staring at the disk. "Sorry, Ma'am. I'm finished here. Thank you so much."

📖 📖 📖

When O'Shea arrived at Ida's, tired and a little late, he was happily surprised that she was doing the cooking. The dinner was delicious. She wasn't just a real pal, Ida was a fine cook, up on current events and able to hold her own when discussing such sensitive subjects as religion and politics. She also had a great sense of humor. O'Shea genuinely enjoyed her company. He was even getting used to those little critters darting under chairs. Of course, he was in another good mood that rapidly shifted to a great mood with his partner's brief message: "Found the 'K'!"

Laughing and joking, he and Ida cheerfully cleaned the kitchen together. Such a joint effort was unheard of when he was married, even when in a good mood.

A walk to Blockbuster Video followed clean-up. Then, seated on the couch, hand-in-hand, they watched a highly acclaimed, avant-garde movie they both hated. While the endless credits cascaded down the screen, Ida gave a noisy raspberry. "I don't get it."

O'Shea rasberried back. "I not only don't get it, I couldn't stand it."

Staring idly at the blank screen, O'Shea felt warm, moist lips gently kissing his neck. Still slightly bruised by his first inept performance, he tried an indifferent glance at Ida. It didn't work. Her smooth, delicate features formed an impish grin that said it all. This time his hesitation was barely noticed. *Oh, what the hell*, he thought, *the worst she can say is "aaaw."*

Locked in deep searching kisses, their undressing bordered on the barbaric, as clothes went flying. Lying naked together on the couch, Ida straddled O'Shea, who happily leaned back, attacking both of her erect nipples with his mouth. Playfully stroking his knees, Ida began sliding her hand up his inner thigh. She didn't have far to go—"Wow!"

CHAPTER 39

Judge Arnold Hall was admired, idolized, resented, or even hated by those who knew him. These intense opinions were as unequivocal as his predictably linear rise to the summit of judicial and political prosperity. Genetically, he had plenty going for him. For openers, he was destined to be tall, bright, handsome and charismatic. That was a good start, but what propelled him over the top was another birth gift, his *volition*. He was born with an ample supply of that elusive ability to self-start, stay focused and never quit. This provided him with unwavering self-discipline. Once he set a goal, his course was resolutely a straight burst of brilliance to the target. No distractions along the way. No detours. For Judge Hall, the shortest distance between two points was always a straight line, tilted upward. That meteoric ascent, however, was soon to change.

It had been an unexpectedly slow day in Judge Hall's Superior Courtroom. Kidnapping trials involving a child victim, a defendant father, and a hysterical mother generally take forever to reach a verdict. For Hall, a no-contest plea to Child Abduction changed more than his rigorous schedule. It changed his destiny.

Jurors were dismissed, attorneys re-stuffed their attaché cases, the defendant went to jail and a hysterical mother, with sobbing child, went home. Back in his office by 11:00 a.m., Judge Hall signed the usual pile of documents, warrants, and subpoenas. By noon, he had managed to clear his desk and calendar for the rest of the day.

On his way home, he decided to stop by the Le Central Bistro for lunch—another unpredicted tampering with fate. He hadn't eaten in this four-star restaurant in months. He rarely had the time for lunch during the week. So this was a real treat for him.

Judge Hall loved sipping one of their very dry martinis before his Boéuf Bourguignon menu favorite was served. Well known by the maître d', the Judge was escorted to a special table for six, reserved for dignitaries. Sipping his martini, he thought of his flourishing mayoral candidacy, his convincing speeches, and the support of *practically* every agency and union in San Francisco. *Practically*, he repeated to himself. Despite numerous calls by his campaign staff, he still hadn't heard from the powerful Teamsters Union or the Waiters and Bartenders Union.

While scanning the dining room, he mentally rehearsed the campaign phone calls he'd make at home, after lunch. That's when he noticed Raymond O'Reilly, President of the Bartender's Union. A veteran opportunist, Judge Hall sprang into action. Leaping to his feet, he headed for the restroom, which happened to be directly behind O'Reilly and his two companions. Halfway by them, Hall slammed to a theatrical stop, as if he had just recognized an old friend.

"Well, I'll be damned, it's Ray. How are you, Ray? It's Judge Hall. I haven't seen you in a long time." Hall hadn't seen O'Reilly at anytime, which didn't matter. He figured O'Reilly's busy schedule would provide reasonable doubt about their earlier meetings. Hall was right.

"Good to see you again, Judge. How are you?"

Hall was already patting O'Reilly on the back, while acknowledging the two companions with an automatic, head-nodding smile. "Why don't you fellows join me? There's plenty of room at my table."

Although O'Reilly was one of Hall's silent resenters, he was also a politician who never burned his bridges. "Well thanks, Judge. We'll join you if I can buy you a drink."

Hall pondered the offer for a few seconds, knowing that part of his success strategy was a one-martini limit at lunch. He gallantly gestured toward his table. "Why thank you," he replied. Chipping away at destiny, Hall's course was sliding downward, beyond the point of no return.

These three men represented a substantial block of votes, maybe even a guaranteed win. To decline an additional drink was out of the question.

Caught up in promoting himself as a regular guy, Hall also got caught up in a drinker's friendly *buy a round* whirlpool. O'Reilly buys a round, setting the good cheer in motion. Not to be out-done, his friend Joe buys another round, which persuades their friend Pete to buy a third round. Hall's now had three martinis over his avowed limit. Worse, he's lost track of his discipline, as well as the number of drinks. By that time Hall no longer cared that his lunch amounted to four green olives, increasingly slurred small talk, and his turn to buy another round.

After the fatal fifth, his new acquaintances fell all over the special table, waving, shouting and backslapping their way out the door. Hall was once again alone, dizzily trying to remember what he was doing there.

Even the waiter sensed Hall's impending doom if he had any more drinks. "Here's your Boeuf Bourguignon, Judge. The kitchen was about to close. I hope you don't mind."

Hall looked up with a glassy-eyed smile, again remembering why he was at the restaurant. "Oh yesss. I'm, ahhh, ready to eat somesing. I'm, ahhh, thanks you."

Paradoxically, eating some of his lunch sealed his fate. He was beginning to feel less strangely dizzy, more in control. *No need for a taxi*, he thought, *I'm fine now.*

Staggering around the nearby parking lot, it took Judge Hall a while to locate his Mercedes. Once in his car, he was again beaming with confidence and optimism through glazed eyes. West on California, and north on Twenty-fifth Avenue would take him to his Sea Cliff home in less than twenty minutes. *I've driven it a million times*, he reasoned, *no problem.*

He was probably right, provided he had stayed on California Street, but booze has a way of altering the simplest plans. North on Van Ness, Hall realized he had unwittingly overshot California Street. Turning left onto Lombard and another left onto Gough, he was again headed for California. Nearing the crest of the steep Gough Street hill, Judge Hall was driving faster than usual. That's when he decided to call O'Shea about another fundraiser he should attend. The decision was Judge Hall's final detour.

Glancing down for one disastrous second, he punched in O'Shea's code number. Simultaneously, a six-year-old girl stepped off the curb. Obeying her parents, she was walking her bicycle across the Washington/Gough intersection, safely within the crosswalk. The sound of impact was unmistakable. A solid thud, scraping metal, dull bumping thuds, more scraping sounds, a squashing noise, then silence until he looked through his rearview mirror. He could hear the screams of people, along with the screaming shock wave through his nervous system. He had run over a child and bicycle.

Panicked into shock, Hall kept going. In a dreamy nightmare of terror, he crazily drove a high speed twenty blocks of tire screeching left and right turns until he skidded to a stop at the Marina Greens, off Scott Street. The dream was over. Soaked in adrenalin, Hall was sufficiently sober and alert to grasp what had happened.

He had just killed a child and fled the scene of the crime, with a blood alcohol no doubt well beyond the legal California limit. As he regained his logical, rational thinking mode, he knew it was no longer an accident scene. It was a crime scene. The *hit and run* was witnessed by at least a dozen people, and by now, it was highly likely his license plate number was in the possession of the police department. He had hit the child in the safety of a crosswalk while drunk. That's manslaughter and jail time. It also foretold the end of his Superior Court judgeship and his mayoral candidacy. There would be lawsuits, financial ruin and disgrace.

While staring blindly into the choppy San Francisco Bay waters, Hall made his calm decision. It was 3:30 p.m. A right turn onto Marina Boulevard led inextricably to the Golden Gate Bridge. As if in a peaceful trance, Judge Hall was cruising Doyle Drive. Passing the Presidio, then merging with Highway 1. When he drove by the southbound tollgates, the Judge slowed to twenty miles per hour to forever imprint the panoramic view of the entire Bay. Halfway across, he turned on his emergency lights, eased the Mercedes to a stop, left his car through the passenger door and stepped onto the pedestrian walkway. Before hundreds of stunned observers, he walked to the guardrail, climbed over and dove out into the *view*. The plunge was two hundred forty-nine feet, the highest point on the bridge. His body was never recovered.

φ   φ   φ

At twenty-eight, with two Ph.D.'s and a hundred twenty-five scientific publications, Streichner was graciously welcomed to Harvard as another boy wonder. He was more comfortable in a school where geniuses trip over each other in the halls, and he was convinced his greatness would be recognized there. He was indeed ready—so he thought. Although finally separated from the haunting, jeering presence of super athletes, he soon found himself being swept away in an avalanche of super erudite scholars within a setting demanding consecutive publications. There was plenty of competition between faculty for honors.

Since virtually all the faculty was brilliant, the best offices, research grants, graduate assistants and teaching assignments were based on that amorphous, something else, sarcastically referred to as the *good old boy network*. This was one of several concepts he was unprepared for. His newly acquired social skills provided him with a positive reputation as likeable, congenial, etc., but he quickly learned that the well-established political enclave was impervious to new-comers without tenure, which could take at least ten years to achieve. Streichner had known since age thirteen he could never physically compete with, or even challenge, peers. Gradually, that didn't matter as he discovered that he could easily compensate for his physical inadequacies with his intellectual and mystical powers.

His university teaching experiences, however, had provided another cruel, albeit priceless lesson. Competing for popularity, prestigious status, even acceptance in a university setting, required more than his intellectual and psychic talents. He was an outsider, and no amount of scholarly publications would make him an insider. He realized that, while working in universities, his brilliance would always invite applause, admiration, even fear—without acceptance. He still didn't seem to belong anywhere, nor did he know how to belong. This flaw, in contrast to his uncanny abilities, resulted in another tragic argument with a colleague. Shortly after the argument, the colleague ran to his office and hanged himself.

So, at thirty-one, he disappeared from the cloistered university setting. He had been at Harvard for over a year, yet no one had known him. His plan was to travel the world in search of a better fit. Somewhere, he thought, that promised him respect, acceptance, maybe even love. His odyssey carried him to Tibetan monks, Hindu gurus, Buddhist temples, voodoo shamans, wizard and psychic studies, and international *think tanks*.

In ten years of travel, Elvin Streichner, Jr. hadn't found whatever he was looking for, probably because he didn't know that salvation was hidden within his smoldering, unconscious torment. All he knew was his weariness from travel. That's when he decided to settle in the first city to appear in his mind's eye as random geographic co-ordinates. They were latitude 38 north, longitude 122 west. Two days later he flew to San Francisco, California. His only possessions consisted of a suitcase of clothes, an attaché case of research papers and the beautiful sterling silver pentacle his mother had given him.

CHAPTER 40

O'Shea awoke from an unusually deep, pleasant sleep with a smug grin happily carved all over his face. He had spent a memorable evening with Ida. They shared great conversation, a delicious dinner and he had a reawakening of his dormant libido. He wasn't impotent after all, and as an added gift, he had a disk for each murder.

At last, he reasoned, there was irrevocable proof that investigating each case separately had been a frustrating, yet very necessary, waste of time. Those had been the unavoidable steps leading to the disks. O'Shea smirked.

Downing a glass of cranberry juice from his refrigerator, O'Shea's smile drooped for a few moments. *Now what do we do*, he thought. *The eight disks spell Trickers. But is that a clue or decoy; or is the real clue buried in the thousands of permutations and combinations of the eight letters? Is someone telling us something or screwing us around?*

"Christ," he sighed aloud, "the disk hunt's over and we're still no closer. And what about the goddamned giant?"

Shifting his thoughts to Ida, his Viagra-free virility and a fresh approach to the eight, O'Shea smiled.

Perked up again, he reflected on his solid backing for Chief of Police, his loyal friends, albeit few, and no showdowns with his enemies in a couple of weeks.

On his way to work, he stopped at his local grocery store where he bought a Chronicle. Tucking it under his arm, he grinned his way around the store, picking up a plant for Jill's desk, and a bag of Ellis' favorite donuts.

When O'Shea returned to his car, he secured the plant and donuts on the floor, glanced at the headline, and instantly felt the power of words rip through his smile along with his future. *"JUDGE HALL COMMITS SUICIDE"*

Since 8:00 a.m., Jill Hasselburg and Paul Ellis had sat silently waiting for O'Shea. Recovered from her tree episode, Hasselburg was on her way to work when she learned of Hall's death. Awhile earlier that morning, Ellis found out in the corridor as he approached their cubicle. One of Sergeant Mahoney's uniformed pals hurried by with a defiant grin. "O'Shea's suck-up, Hall, took a dive off the GG!"

When Hasselburg arrived at 7:30 a.m., Ellis strained a smile. "I'm glad you're back, Jill. Are you OK now?"

There wasn't a thing tentative about Hasselburg's natural smile. "Gosh, Sergeant Ellis, I was ready to work last night. Just tell me where I should start. Anywhere except, you know, up a tree."

Ellis worked up another faint smile, while shifting to his pressing concern. "Did you hear about Judge Hall's suicide?"

Hasselburg dropped her smile. Even though unaware of its implications, she sensed it was a serious change in conversation. "Yes. I heard it over the radio on my way here. He was a friend of Lieutenant O'Shea, wasn't he?"

Ellis glanced away from her in case his own distress was showing. "No, they weren't friends. Judge Hall was O'Shea's hope for the future. He represented a solution for my friend."

Hasselburg quickly understood the effects of Hall's death on her partners. "Oh, God, I didn't realize. I'm so sorry."

Ellis explained in confidence O'Shea's stressful divorce after twenty-five years of marriage, his loneliness, his *runs*, the many cops who resented his *in your face* independence, and Judge Hall's promising mayoral candidacy. "O'Shea was counting on the Chief of Police appointment when Hall was elected in November. He believed it was his salvation. He thought he could then make everything right in the department and his life."

Hasselburg was genuinely moved by Ellis' barely audible eulogy. "I guess I envy you guys. I've always admired loyalty and friendship. How do such bonds develop between people?"

Ellis' sighing smile was more spontaneous. "You haven't been alive long enough to know. It takes a long time to discover you have a real, bona fide friend who will protect you, listen to you, teach you, even lie for you if necessary. But don't you worry, Jill. You have all the necessary qualities of a loyal friend. By the way, I appreciate your respect for rank and experience, but you're our partner and you've earned the right to call me Paul."

Hasselburg blanched, avoiding eye contact. "I'll try."

"You'll be amazed at how much you learn from people you can't stand. That's provided you don't close up. Everybody can teach us something."

Hasselburg looked at him thoughtfully. Then she noticed Ellis drop his eyes and his smile. O'Shea hadn't shown yet.

It was 8:20 a.m. when Hasselburg finally severed the silence with her worries. "Do you think Lieutenant O'Shea will come in today?"

Ellis, staring blankly at one of the Trickers interrogation reports, had been thinking the same question. "He's always early. I doubt it."

Hasselburg hesitated for a minute before asking a question she needed to know. "Would he harm himself because of this?"

Glancing at her, Ellis shook his head reassuringly. "If you mean is he suicidal like Judge Hall, don't worry, he isn't. We've all got a breaking point and this is well below his. Besides, if backed against the wall, homicide would be his last solution, not suicide."

"Should we try to find him, at least call his apartment?" Hasselburg asked.

Ellis gave an impatient grin. "He doesn't need rescuing. He'd let me know before that. He may go on a run, and I've got to wait it out until he's ready to return. In the meantime, O'Shea will expect us to continue with our investigation like a couple of professionals."

Hasselburg got the message. In his own gentle way, Ellis had told her to back off.

"I'm ready, Sergeant,—uh, Paul. What do you want me to do?"

Leafing through the Trickers' interrogation notes, Ellis placed the stack neatly on his desk. "Just kick back, relax and listen while I bring you up to speed on all the people we questioned at the Trickers meeting, any new developments in the original eight cases and where we go from here. OK?"

She gave an exuberant nod. "Shall I take notes?"

"Not necessary. You can download all of our written stuff later." He winked. Ellis began with the disks. Like O'Shea, he was delighted with their possession of the eight disks.

"The positive news is the link between the cases. One disk per case definitely suggests one motive, probably one perpetrator, and the eight letters spell *Trickers,* which becomes the central focus of our investigation. Of course, there are literally thousands of ways those eight letters could be arranged, and so far none of the Trickers we've interviewed are viable suspects. So, we still can't rule out other possibilities.

"There's another factor that contradicts solid police investigative methodology. It's called intuition, or hunch, or just a consistent feeling, and the longer you've been in this business, the more cops tend to rely on it. O'Shea and I share the same hunch on this case." He gulped, scanned their cubicle almost irritably, and then continued in a near whisper.

"There's something strange, sinister about these murders that seems to keep laughing at us. Seems as if we never get it right. We keep following leads and end up in the wrong direction. Maybe that's why we're not quite prepared to celebrate the eight letters. Anyway, Jill, now you're a part of this. Remember what O'Shea said yesterday? Well, I agree. I doubt if your tree adventure had anything to do with you personally. I think it was a demonstration of their power over the police." Ellis slowly shook his head. "You were no threat. It was just another hint of something weird, like giants, or goblins, or how about wizards. I have no idea yet. All I do know is we've still got to follow every lead or hunch, no matter where it takes us."

Hasselburg sat wide-eyed and open-mouthed as Ellis paused to collect the interrogation notes. "I figured these cases were really tough from what Captain McInerney told me," she said. "I guess I didn't really grasp what Lieutenant O'Shea explained. God, I just didn't realize how mind-boggling these cases are."

Still thinking about his partner and giants, Ellis offered no comment. Instead, he spent the next fifteen minutes carefully summarizing all the interrogation notes. He assured Hasselburg that Brad, her best friend's brother, wasn't a suspect. Neither were Brad's recalcitrant, smart-ass friends, Karl and Erick. She also learned from Ellis that police interrogations of anyone near her during the party came up with no leads, which he felt wasn't surprising. Ellis highlighted Captain McInerney's interviews with Howard Kantner, the club's president, and Brad's two Trickers Poly classmates. Again, no hints of involvement in Hasselburg's abduction—nothing.

Handing Hasselburg the stack of interrogation reports, Ellis asked if she had anything to add about the evening.

"Well," she said, "my mind's cleared a lot since yesterday. Yes, I do remember more. Pete Baker and Al Hoffman are kinda like Brad—very typical high school sophomores. Lots of teenage jargon, self-conscious cheers when cute girls walked by, not much substance yet, but respectful. They asked all sorts of questions about the duties of a police officer, and talked a little about their interest in the Secret Service or FBI. I remember thinking when they walked off that they're a couple of nice, awkward kids who view their Trickers membership as a chance to party."

Ellis was carefully taking notes. "Sounds like my two boys. Didn't mean to interrupt. Go on."

Hasselburg thumbed through the reports until she saw Karl and Erick's names. "Boy, what a difference. The other two Poly guys were arrogant jerks. Karl Schwartz, the taller one, couldn't stop talking about how bright he was. An IQ of 160, he said. Although swigging a beer and taking advantage of the party, he referred to the Trickers as a bunch of uneducated, beer drinking illiterates. He even suggested that cops weren't bright enough to find worthwhile jobs. Erick Taggart seemed a little less arrogant, probably because he let Karl do most of the talking. Nonetheless, he was a jerk too. After agreeing with his pal that cops weren't too bright, he started asking questions about the Police Academy and my qualifying scores on the range. That was his entrée to boast about his expert scores and his invitation to the national rifle marksman finals in June. He also bragged about his straight A's at Polytechnic. I was really glad when they walked off to the dance area."

Hasselburg paused for a moment collecting her thoughts. "There's one thing that puzzles me. Yesterday, when Brad visited me with his sister, we, of course, discussed the Trickers' party and Brad's friends. He tended to agree that Karl and Erick were a little arrogant, but he admitted admiring them because of their genius and achievements. I remember Brad introducing me to them, as his sister's best friend and his ride home. When I asked him how he finally got home, he said Karl and Erick offered him a ride. That wasn't a red flag until Brad absently added that Karl shouted from the dance floor an offer to drive him home, shortly after Brad discovered that my car was gone. Now, could be he had inadvertently mentioned it to Karl or Erick, or maybe they saw me leave. It's also possible someone else at the party told them the cop had left. Then again, they could have been involved in my abduction."

"Another possibility," added Ellis, "is that you were so out of it, maybe feeling out of control, that you instinctively ran for the safety of your car when you couldn't immediately find Brad. In your condition a lot of people could have noticed you leave. You might have even shouted a goodbye to Karl or a frantic request he tell Brad you were leaving. In any case, it's sure worth checking all these possibilities out. Nice goin', partner."

$\square$ $\square$ $\square$

Riveted to his newspaper, O'Shea re-read the article three times. He was desperately searching for the punch line, an April fool gotcha, a retraction, anything to make it go away. There wasn't anything. Judge Hall was dead, along with O'Shea's professional life. "You son of a bitch," he snarled. "If you were alive I'd kill you."

Suddenly his future was as ominous as the blackening clouds forming overhead. *Another late April storm coming in*, he thought, *and there's nothing I can do about that either.* O'Shea felt thunder brewing in his stomach. Tingling hail pelting his insides. Aching, stinging, gut-wrenching breakers of turbulence washing over his lungs. He could barely breath. Then he heard the rain drumming heavily over the top of his car, his hood, his windshield, the streets. He groaned. *The storm is everywhere. In me, out there. Goddammit.*

"Hall is dead," he yelled over the blustery downpour. "Long live O'Shea."

Sitting in his car, shrouded in newspaper, he listened to the rain slow a bit to a mournful dirge, rhythmically drumming on the roof and in his head. As more thoughts scrolled by, he sank deeper in his seat, buried in his own raging storm. An old gunslinger dethroned before his reign. From chief to court jester. His back was now an easy target, a bull's eye with a well-centered "L", for loser. "Shit, shit, shit," he hissed through grinding teeth. "What now?"

Like in a time warp, over an hour of grieving, brooding and raging had flickered by in what seemed like seconds.

The driving rain had slacked to a slight pitter-patter. O'Shea liked the softer beat. Watching the pure droplets sliding in irregular patterns down his windshield, he felt becalmed, safely empty. It was like being caught in the beguiling eye of a hurricane. Of course, he knew the calm wouldn't last long before the next onslaught. Deciding it was time to formulate a quick plan, O'Shea smirked. It was time for a *run*. He knew the Gruta Azul was already open and he had his invisible Nova.

His mind seemed to be in trance-like cruise control as he smoothly drove his Chevy Nova down Oak Street. Turning left onto Laguna, O'Shea eased along the Hayes Valley streets robotically, responding to everything in his path, while seeing nothing. After a few blocks, he glided across Market to Guerrero, then left on Seventeenth to the narrow Shotwell Street. He was in the Mission District, within four blocks of his target.

The rain had thinned to a swirling mist when he parked his car. Hunched over the steering wheel, he couldn't move. For the first time in decades of danger, he was paralyzed with fear. The calm was wearing off, and the short walk to the Gruta Azul seemed nearly overwhelming. *I'll never make it*, he thought. *The storm will hit again.* Looking up at the menacing black skies, he shuttered.

"Christ," he shouted, "it ain't goin' away. Hall is dead, my career's dead and I feel dead." O'Shea stared vacantly down the narrow street for most of an hour before the blast of a passing paramedic unit jarred him out of his stupor.

Taking a closer, conscious look at the street flooded him with haunting memories. He remembered the stakeout in a nearby alley, Drocco's death, Mahoney's consecutive broken jaws, Devil's Slide, giants, the taunts of the unsolved eight. The disks, and his brief bid for Chief of Police. At least his mind was clear again. It was time for that drink.

Through deep sighs of despair, O'Shea neatly folded the crumpled paper and placed it on the rear seat floor along with the doughnuts and plant. Once outside the car, he shivered at the cold dreary skies, locked the doors, placed his gun and badge in the trunk and removed some "run money" from the old briefcase.

Walking down Shotwell, he had no further interest in eye contact with anyone, conversations or checking into a hotel. He just wanted to sit alone at the bar and drink. Yet, there was really no hurry. He was only a few blocks from his anonymity. Anyway, what were the alternatives?

Approaching the corner of Shotwell and Seventeenth Streets, O'Shea heard an unmistakably abrasive noise coming his way. He glanced up just in time to side step the first of two teenage skateboarders whizzing around the corner at top speed. Mud from the earlier rains, oozed onto the sidewalk from a nearby construction site. The first kid managed to avoid the mud that O'Shea had quickly maneuvered through. The other kid, clad in a red and black Poly jacket, wasn't so lucky. Sliding through the mud like a beached surfer, the skateboard hit a piece of two-by-four, catapulting the teenager into a leg-flailing lift off, climaxed by a spectacular somersaulting sprawl, face down in the mud. Struggling to his feet, the kid resembled a giant mud dauber with eyes that flickered on and off. Behind him was his upside-down skateboard embedded in mud. In front was his white and green-jacketed buddy, pointing and laughing.

Wiping some of the mud off his shoes, O'Shea was in no mood for rowdy teenagers, skateboarders, puckish laughter or mud.

"Oh, fuck you, Al," the Poly kid shouted as he scraped several pounds of mud off his face. Al kept laughing and pointing, while the Poly kid looked around for his skateboard, which was now directly in front of O'Shea. Pulling it from the mud by the wheels, O'Shea irritably lobbed it to the Poly kid, splashing more black goo on the teenager's leg. Sensing the crotchety old man was really pissed, both kids skated off grumbling obscenities at O'Shea.

Glancing down at his shoes, his brows arched to record heights as his eyes bulged beyond their sockets. He simply couldn't believe what he saw, but there it was—a clearly delineated reprieve. Etched in the mud a few feet in front of him was the same giant footprint he and his partner had seen outlined in André Likert's garage. The light bulb exploding over his head erupted into a shower of white brilliance that embraced him with a long overdue message.

"There is no giant," O'Shea bellowed as he ran up Shotwell in search of the skateboarders. He was in luck. The two kids had stopped on Shotwell near Fifteenth. The Poly kid was trying to clean more mud off his face and clothes when O'Shea closed in.

"Hey man. We didn't do nothin'," shouted Al with the green and white jacket.

Looking up, the Poly teenager, encased in mud, grabbed his skateboard as a weapon. "Yeah. Don't fuck with us, man."

Raising his hands over his head, O'Shea had to laugh. "I come in peace. All I want to know is the brand name of your skateboard. I want to get one for my son." He happily lied.

Both teenagers immediately relaxed. They loved talking skateboards, and within a few minutes O'Shea knew all about their *Banana Zapper* board. Yellow was the only color; and since they were shorter and narrower than the more popular brands, the *Banana Zapper* boards were more difficult to control. O'Shea even learned that Surfer's Corner in Burlingame and Skater's Warehouse in San Francisco, were the only two Bay Area stores that sold the board. *More good luck*, he thought. *Only two stores to check, and fewer kids probably bought them.* A quick thanks, followed by a couple of high fives, and O'Shea was dashing back down Shotwell.

Breathing heavily, he swiftly opened his trunk, grabbed gun and badge, returned the money and slammed the truck in one blurred motion. Sliding into the front seat of his Nova, he slowed his pace to a hesitation when he reached behind his seat for the doughnuts and plant. The folded newspaper lying on the rear floor was another gut-wrenching reminder. Judge Hall had thrown himself and O'Shea's career off the Golden Gate Bridge. "That dirty bastard," he grimaced. "It's time for a drink." But O'Shea felt paralyzed again. He just slouched in the front seat, mourning his future.

Then he heard that harsh, scrapping sound of a skateboarder. Glancing down the street, he saw another teenager scooting along on one of the full sized, more popular skateboards. Just then, the sun peered through the parting dark grays skies. Glancing toward the Mission Street bars, O'Shea slowly shook his head into a huge grin. *Not this time!*

CHAPTER 41

It was 10:30 a.m. and still no O'Shea. The cubicle was ominously dark and quiet, as if it were somberly awaiting his return. His partners still hadn't turned on the cubicle lights. Hasselburg sat in semidarkness, idly scrolling through the April 8th crime reports, while Ellis stared at the eight disks he had arranged in a row on his desk. Neither had spoken in over an hour. They both realized there was nothing else to say. Their only choice was to work, worry and hope he was all right. Ellis had glumly assumed his partner wasn't going to make it for several days at least. *He would have been here by now*, he thought.

Standing in the entrance to their cubicle was a pursed-lipped, scowling O'Shea clutching a bag of donuts and a potted plant. "Christ, What are you doing? Having a goddamn séance in here, or a wake?" Breaking into a full-face grin, O'Shea turned on the overhead lights and tossed the bag of donuts at Ellis who caught it with a deep sigh of relief.

As O'Shea placed the plant on Hasselburg's desk, she couldn't contain her concern. Leaping out of her chair, she gave him a bear hug that practically lifted him off the ground. "God, we were really worried." Recovering a tad of composure, she added, "I'm sorry Lieutenant, but what would I tell my uncle if we lost you?"

"Or found you up a tree," Ellis added. Knowing well O'Shea's uneasiness with open displays of affection, Ellis was trying to subdue his own feelings with a bit of humor. He was more than a little puzzled by O'Shea's smiles and gifts. *My God,* he wondered, *does he know of*

Hall's suicide?

"Thanks for the donuts, John."

Hasselburg chimed in as she sat down at the computer. "Thank you, Lieutenant, for the beautiful plant."

For an awkward minute, O'Shea said nothing, while Ellis and Hasselburg sat quietly starring at him. Standing erect with chest and chin out, legs spread, and arms behind his back, like a tenured professor or seasoned general, O'Shea smugly nodded to his small audience. "Don't worry, I know. Hall's dead, I'm fine, and there's no Big Foot." Darting glances at his partners, O'Shea silently maintained his smug posturing as if waiting for a hand raising response.

Ellis was first to reply. "Loot, you never cease to amaze me. Hall takes a dive and you're all puffed up and cheerful. What's really up? I at least expected a run and a lost car."

O'Shea dropped his eyes with a more timid smiling nod. Then, after a short pause, he looked up at his friend. "Thanks for the straight shots at your old partner."

Glancing at a wide-eyed Hasselburg, he broadened his smile. "Hey, you're one of us now. You might as well learn about your partners' weaknesses as well as our strengths."

She sighed. "Thanks."

O'Shea stared tenderly at his partners before explaining his opening remarks. "Yeah, I was on my way to a prolonged drunk. I felt stymied by the eight cases, pissed off at my ex, my kids, everything. On top of all that, I put my future in the hands of a guy I didn't like or respect. He set me up then dumped me. When I found out this morning the son of a bitch offed himself, I wanted to strangle the bastard. I blamed him for my failings and all the sleaze in my life. Then I met the *Banana Zapper*."

O'Shea waited for a reaction, and he got it. "A Banana what?" his partners shouted.

"Let me grab some coffee and one of those donuts, and I'll give you the whole nine yards." Returning with a full cup, O'Shea sat with his partners.

After all three tore into the bag of donuts, Ellis broke the slurping, munching sounds. "You got these chocolate cake donuts at Happy Donuts. Geeze, they're good."

Once O'Shea downed three glazed in rapid succession, he continued explaining how his drive to the Mission district for a run turned into some sort of epiphany. He described the two high school kids, the mud spill and the fairly rare Banana Zapper skateboard that leaves a twenty-five-inch shoe print when upside down in mud.

Ellis couldn't contain himself any longer. "That wasn't a foot print in Likert's garage, it was a skateboard. Probably a kid's."

O'Shea was on a roll. "You got it. You know, that single discovery somehow cut me loose from Hall, politics and all that shit. I'm a cop— I'll be a cop until I croak. I'm not a politician and police chiefs are politicians. I'm a detective, and one of our worst nightmares is being hopelessly stuck, mired in confusion, and our greatest thrill is solving the unsolvable. Christ, when I flashed on the Banana Zapper print, I felt a rush and sure as hell didn't need booze to dull the feeling. It was like a revelation that opened all kinds of new possibilities. We're finally in the right room; all we've gotta do now is collect all the pieces."

Finishing his coffee, O'Shea leaned over Ellis' desk and picked up an "S" disk. "You know something else? Not only are these eight cases connected, I wouldn't be at all surprised if the perps are a bunch of kids." Still toying with the disk, O'Shea held it up, toward his partners. "Evidence. But isn't it amazing how expectations influence what we see? We got so caught up in the Armory heist, the .22's and the Trickers; these disks became Trickers' orange and black colors. But look at the colors more objectively. To me it looks more coral than a clear orange. Kind of between a red and orange."

Hasselburg raised her hand with a show of urgency. O'Shea glanced at Ellis with a wry wink. "Jesus, Jill. Just butt in. This isn't a classroom."

Hasselburg looked at both detectives with a slight flush of embarrassment. "I'm sorry. Guess I got carried away with your, ah, lecture"

Ellis nodded supportively to her as O'Shea replied with a guffaw. "You busted me, Jill. Sorry."

"No, Lieutenant, remember, I'm still taking courses at San Francisco State, so I kind of expect lectures. You understand, I hope."

Unwittingly, O'Shea slowly stroked his chin like some thoughtful professor. "I see what you mean. Go on."

"Well, I never said anything, but when I first saw the disks, to me, they were kind of a salmon or red and black. Now, listening to you two since I've been here, they've become, well, more orange."

O'Shea slowly nodded. "So I take it we agree the disks aren't necessarily orange and black?"

"You think it may be Poly students?" Hasselburg asked O'Shea.

"Not necessarily. It could still be teenage Trickers, or even a gang of kids we don't know about because we haven't been looking for a bunch of kids. Maybe a lot of schools are involved. At least we're finally on the right track."

Watching his two partners, O'Shea thought for a moment about their frustrations since assigned the eight cases. "I hope," he added.

Ellis jotted down a few notes while sorting through his partner's comments. "My gut's starting to tell me the same thing, especially after Jill's latest recall about the Tricker's party. It has the rotten flavor of a well-orchestrated prank."

"What else did you remember?" O'Shea quickly asked her.

"Karl Schwartz and Erick Taggart could have been involved in, or at least been aware I would end up in a tree." Hasselburg explained Schwartz's offer to drive Brad home before Brad was aware she was gone. She also cautioned her partners that the Poly boys could have found out in more innocent ways.

"We've gotta reinterview both of those little shits," O'Shea replied.

Ellis agreed. "You know, Loot, when I read these crime reports over, school kids seem to keep emerging from the background. They just didn't seem relevant before."

O'Shea nodded. "I overlooked kids too. Students are sprinkled in most of our reports. They're all over the city, like part of the landscape. So I didn't pay much attention. Remember? We had all those solid suspects." O'Shea glanced at Hasselburg, squirming in her seat. "You don't have to raise your hand. Just interrupt." He grinned.

"Thanks. As you know, since I joined these investigations only recently, I guess I view the deaths a little differently. When I started working with you guys, you had already pretty much exhausted your suspects and individual case-related motives. What I'm getting at is, once motives are eliminated, these separate cases have kind of a depraved fraternity hazing quality to them. Using Paul's word, like they were some kind of terrible pranks. Does that make any sense?"

Ellis was thinking about their earlier weeks of frustration. "It wouldn't have several weeks ago, but it's beginning to make a lot of sense now."

O'Shea interrupted. "'Blood sport.' 'We did it.' 'What a rush.' That's what Tuttle and Harvey, those poor old drunks, heard right after Nelson's death. Kids laughing."

Searching through the reports on the computer, Hasselburg stopped at Winston. "And that lady who witnessed two kids in jackets, probably black and orange or red, leaning over Winston's body after he was shot."

O'Shea interrupted again. "Yeah, and the café on Irving, where Anderson was probably poisoned, was apparently loaded with high school kids. Come to think of it, when Villa lost his brakes, wasn't there mention in one of the reports of a few kids at or near a bus stop in the vicinity of the truck?"

Ellis was frantically leafing through the Villa file. "Boy, you got that right, John. There were reports from a couple of witnesses who heard the crash, and reports from uniforms in a cruiser that arrived a few minutes after the crash. They all agree that there were high school kids all over that Guererro/Mission area at that time of the morning. In fact, the crowd around the crash was about half kids. Of course, no one witnessed anything other than the sound of a crash."

Hasselburg was reviewing the same case notes on the computer, until she scrolled by the Torres coroner's report and the report about Jerran's unsolved murder. She stopped scrolling and squirmed again in her chair before twisting her face into a puzzled expression.

O'Shea noticed. "OK, Jill, what's up?"

Hasselburg looked up with an uncertain smile. "You two already know this, but I guess it's worth mentioning again. When I first read all the reports, I never connected the proximity of Jerran's address to the crash of Villa's truck. Jerran and his family lived a half a block from Villa's home."

O'Shea gave Ellis a sheepish glance. "Christ. I got so caught up in usual suspects, Jerran's address didn't matter. How about you, Paul?"

"To me, he was Beth's friend who lost his mother, his sister, and then himself. Except for Beth, most thought he committed suicide. Beth was right. The poor kid was murdered, and somehow it's all linked to Villa's crash, the disk and teenagers. And bless your heart, Jill, you keep coming up with fresh observations and ideas. I knew the Torres and Villa addresses, but to me, Jerran was always a tragic victim, maybe partly because of my daughter. Anyway, now I see that living so closely to Villa, Jerran could have witnessed the death of his mother, which for some reason, he kept to himself."

O'Shea abruptly added, "Or the kid could have spotted some kids he knew fooling with the truck brakes. Jesus, can you imagine his rage in later learning that his mom and sister ended up dead because of some juvenile prank?"

"That's sure a possibility. What do you think, Jill?" Ellis asked, noticing her hand wandering upwards off the desk.

"Here's another scenario of outlandish coincidence and karma. What if Jerran was part of the hazing or whatever, and tampered with the brakes of Villa's truck that ended up killing his mom and sister."

Both detectives looked at Hasselburg with raised eyebrows. "Christ, what a story that would make," added O'Shea. "Yet, it's a possibility."

"And a real Greek tragedy," Ellis added. "It has an Oedipal or even Faustian aroma. What a movie it would make."

"Wait a minute, you guys, are you making fun of me? It's just another possibility, that's all.

"Hey we're on a roll. Do we all agree it's highly probable that teenagers did the brake number on Villa's truck?"

After some vigorous nodding by both partners, O'Shea continued. "And you can bet your ass that Likert's giant is another kid. Agreed?"

More vigorous nods.

"OK, there's a high probability that kids were involved in Anderson, Winston, Likert, Villa and Nelson's cases. That's five out of eight. Any other probable shoe-in's?"

Wrinkling her nose into a frown, Hasselburg stopped scrolling. "Well…" she murmured.

"Well what?" O'Shea countered.

"I agree all eight cases are related. The disks tell us that pretty clearly. And teenagers seem the most likely suspects. But we don't have any eye witnesses. The MO is also curiously different in the Villa case. Cutting brake lines on a pickup doesn't insure the driver will be killed. No mortal human could have anticipated Villa's subsequent suicide, let alone the death of Dorothy Torres and her daughter. There's also no indication of any kids on the hospital floor when Grace Digness was killed. Just maybe there are a few adults involved as well." Ellis was about to join in with his ideas, when Hasselburg, seeing it coming, quickly added, "There's something else. How did someone lift that big block of concrete that killed Officer Nelson?" Flinging an index finger up to her lips, she caught O'Shea about to interrupt. "Just a couple more things," she whispered. "Who is powerful enough to send a javelin through Officer Eng, and how did I end up high in a tree?"

O'Shea managed to beat Ellis out of his eager reply. "That's exactly what we need, a fresh view with critical questions. Because of the disks, I still think it's all teenagers, but damn it, you're right. No eye witnesses to the crimes; just kids noticed around the crime scenes, except at the hospital, on the cliff, and in the water at Aquatic Park."

O'Shea's pause gave Ellis his chance to comment. "Ever since the Park Ranger reported spotting those two SCUBA divers, I filed youth somewhere in my mind as real possibles. Lots of kids dive in the park. I think some have practice sessions out there."

"That's six out of eight, Paul. Why didn't you tell me that before? Don't answer. I know. Both our heads were stuck in primary suspects. Robinson was our slam-dunk perp. Kids were just around. Hell, they're always around."

Realizing he and O'Shea were beginning to dominate the conversation, Ellis turned toward Hasselburg. "What do you think, Jill?"

"I guess I think we now need all the solid evidence we can get. Thanks to your reports, I've had the benefit of all your investigative skills. I've read every report several times, and I can probably see more clearly than you two, where we are right now, without being burdened with all your earlier suspects."

O'Shea couldn't help but nod. "That's precisely why we welcome your input. Right, Paul?"

"Absolutely."

When Hasselburg started to open her mouth, O'Shea continued as if thinking out loud. "Yeah, I'm still stumped by some things. Things that you mentioned. That javelin thrown at Eng, the two hundred twelve-pound slab of concrete on Nelson's head, both cops. And you, also a cop, found high in a tree. No witnesses, no leads, no specific suspects left. Anything else?"

Ellis smiled at Hasselburg. "I can't fault or answer Jill's other questions. Yes, there may still be adult perps, especially in the Digness murder. And, we haven't totally eliminated giants or something with superhuman strength."

Leaning back in his swivel chair, with hands clasped behind his head, O'Shea stared at the ceiling, deep in thought, as Ellis and Hasselburg waited. "All right, here's where we are, what we know." O'Shea had jotted down a few of his own notes, on the back of his phone bill. "All the crimes are connected. The disks tell us that. Each crime was no doubt committed by a different person. Times, locations and MO's argue against some maniac serial killer. There are definitely teenagers involved in many of the eight crimes, but as of now, not necessarily all eight. The perp's age or ages are too speculative in a few of these cases because there're no witnesses. Could be a gang, club, fraternity, or a loose group of friends involved in the eight. Best bet so far is the Trickers because of the Armory heist, Jill's tree snooze and the colors. But the Trickers aren't an absolute, since the orange could be a red. And yes, Paul, something with superhuman strength still can't be ruled out for the three cop victims. Now, did I miss anything? Oh yeah, Hall's dead and I don't give a shit about the chief's job."

Ellis glanced at Hasselburg, who was recording all but O'Shea's last comments on the computer. "Well, since your Banana Zapper discovery, we've got some leads that were kinda overlooked earlier. Mainly juveniles, probably with no motives related to the victims. There's a good chance the victims were just in the wrong place at the right time."

Hasselburg stopped typing. "Or the right place at the wrong time."

Clutching his notes, O'Shea flew forward in his chair, and gave both of his partners an unblinking stare that said he was about to make an announcement.

"Either way, most of the victims probably weren't even known by the killers. At least not personally. You know, I'll bet the motives had squat to do with the victims and plenty to do with the opportunity."

Hasselburg was back at the computer, pounding away, along with rapid nods.

"For five or six of the cases I agree." Ellis joined in with a nodding wink to Hasselburg.

"Ok," O'Shea snapped. "If we pretty much agree on what we know and where we are, where do we go from here on?"

Ellis raised his hand and waved his notebook, while O'Shea gave a frowning grin.

"Jesus, Paul, you too?"

Ellis nodded a broad smile. "Come on, Jill's a great influence."

"Go on."

"Well, for openers we've got to re-interview Brad and the four other Poly kids and everyone else at the Trickers shindig, for obvious reasons. We've also got to re-canvas all crime scenes for new suspects, especially juveniles, and establish if there are really superhumans or just more Banana Zappers."

During a ten second pause, Hasselburg's hand floated upward, as

O'Shea heaved a deep sigh. "Jesus Christ, Jill, you don't need to do that."

Hasselburg dropped her hand and her eyelids. "Sorry, Lieutenant. I think it's important to reread every initial police report, when crime sites and any observations were still fresh. We may view all those details a bit differently now."

Ellis raised his hand again.

"Enough," O'Shea shouted. "Just interrupt."

Ellis saluted. "OK, Lieutenant, sir. I agree with her. Even though we've got to keep going back to the crime scenes, the only way to return to the initial crime scene is in those initial reports. I nominate Jill for the job. After three weeks, I doubt we could be as objective as she is."

"I second that one." O'Shea smirked.

Both detectives turned toward Hasselburg, who was smiling. "This might surprise you, but I really don't mind. In fact, I enjoy going over original reports. It makes me feel like I just got there after the crime. I'll get right to it."

Needing to make a few more comments, O'Shea raised his hand as he stood up. "Christ, you got me doing it. Before we get hoppin', I just wanted to say; well—you're one of the main reasons I'm not getting shit-faced today. One more thing. These were probably all innocent victims of opportunity, randomly killed because they were available. And that's pure evil. Anyway, you're family, and I'm not drunk. Any questions?"

Both partners shook their heads.

CHAPTER 42

"Watch your back, John."

Despite the warning, O'Shea was thrilled that Ida had called. *Perfect timing,* he thought. He and his partners had just finished their brain storming session, and each had an assignment, Hasselburg on the computer, Ellis to interview Brad Kruger at Polytechnic and O'Shea to the stores that carry Banana Zappers.

The moment he heard her voice, he was glad he'd made it back to work, still sober.

"Thanks, Ida. Not for the warning. I knew I'd be a target when I heard of Hall's death this morning. Thanks for your concern."

Trying to hold back tears, Ida was quiet for a minute. "Hey, we're pals aren't we? That's what best friends do. They take care of each other." Sensing she might have overly dramatized his possible danger, Ida tried downplaying the warning a little. "I really called you about something much more important."

O'Shea pressed the phone closer to his ear. "Sounds serious."

Ida tried to reduce the concern in his reply with a quick explanation. "My beef stew is always serious, it's practically Irish. You're cordially invited for my famous stew, huge salad, six pounds of sourdough bread, garlic butter and five gallons of one hundred percent Colombian. Tonight, my place, 8:00 p.m. What do you say to that?"

O'Shea had quietly relaxed his grip on the phone and the knot in his stomach. "How could I possibly refuse you and my favorite meal? You couldn't keep me away, kid."

Ida smiled into the phone. "See you at eight, my dear friend. Just—well—you know, be careful."

📖 📖 📖

Sitting on a bench in the hall outside the vice principal's office, Brad Kruger seemed absorbed in his little book when Ellis approached. "Must be really interesting. Hi, Brad, thanks for waiting."

Kruger looked up with a big grin while offering Ellis a full view of the book's title, *Improving Your Social Skills.*

"Hi, Sergeant Ellis. My sister loaned me this. It's a new book by Dr. Sbazo. He's a psychiatrist who writes a lot of books for teenagers. She got it out of the San Francisco State library."

Ellis accepted the book from Kruger's out-stretched hand. After perusing the table of contents, he smiled down at him. "Maybe my kids could benefit from reading this."

Kruger shrugged with flushing cheeks. "If they're kind of shy, it might be good."

Handing the book back, Ellis gave Kruger a fatherly smile. "There's nothing wrong with being a little shy. It sure beats being a little arrogant. People really don't mind shy, but they can't stand arrogant."

Kruger quietly stared up at Ellis.

"Well, anyway, Brad, we need your help. Jill says you've got a great memory. So maybe if we go over that whole evening, you just might remember something else that could help us sort out the good guys from the bad ones. Jill and I trust you."

That's all Kruger needed. More than anything, he wanted to help catch the ones who put Jill in a tree. "I'm ready, Sergeant."

Grinning, Ellis dropped a hand on Kruger's shoulder. "Not here. Let's find a private spot where we can talk."

After locating a small side room off the vice principle's office, Brad needed no coaxing from Ellis. Seated opposite each other, Brad plunged into a steady monolog before Ellis could open his notebook. He began with their dinner at home with his sister, then their ride to the party, and where they parked in the crowded lot. His thoroughness amazed Ellis, who was frantically trying to keep up with all the details. After a half hour, Ellis was beginning to suffer from information overload. That's until Brad's comments about Erick's dialogue with Hasselburg re-ignited his attention.

"When Erick found out she was a police officer," explained Brad, "he asked her about shooting practice during training at the Academy, the kinds of weapons used and her qualifying scores. I guess he was setting her up to blow his own horn, because when she told him she was an average marksman in her class, he told her he had qualified for the state high school shooting team, and that he was top scorer in all San Francisco high school and ROTC shooting teams."

Ellis interrupted with a knee jerk question. "Did he mention the caliber of the bullets his high school team uses?"

"They use .22 caliber bullets, like the ROTC."

Ellis listened carefully to the rest of Kruger's comments without interrupting. Kruger's details offered no further indications that Karl or Erick knew Hasselburg had been drugged or waylaid. As suspects, however, they were becoming tempting possibilities. Brad recalled that Hasselburg was wandering around on her own for about forty-five minutes before her disappearance. Ellis recognized the implications of those forty-five minutes. *Erick or Karl could have noticed her leaving. Some of their friends might have mentioned her departure to them. Or, any of them could have been involved in her drugging and mysterious journey up a tree.* It was equally obvious to Ellis that next on the agenda was a review of the original interview notes and more aggressive interrogations of Erick and Karl. *Then there's the caliber of the bullets,* he thought. *Almost too good to be true!*

📖 📖 📖

Toward the close of the interview, Ellis received a call from Hasselburg. In carefully pouring over all the police reports at crime scenes related to the eight, she flagged one from an Officer Marv Cruz. He had interviewed Joe Maineri, the Poly gardener, shortly after Officer Eng was skewered by a javelin. The gardener's comments about "a couple of guys running behind the track shed right after the screams" seemed suspicious enough to warrant another interview with him. Ellis agreed and quickly changed his priorities.

After again thanking Kruger for his help, Ellis wasted no time locating Joe Maineri at the Poly track and field area. In his late fifties, Maineri was easy to spot. Every bit of him looked gardener. His craggy, tanned, leathery face was withered like a prune from years of hatless work outdoors. His thick scraggly, grayish black hair was sprinkled with blades of grass and flecks of fertilizer. He even wore the old traditional, baggy, Big Ben overalls with an assortment of tools dangling from a web belt. Ellis couldn't help smile.

Wielding a huge rake, Maineri was busily grooming the track that surrounded the field when Ellis approached. "Hi. I'm Sergeant Ellis of the San Francisco Police Department. Would you mind if I asked you a few more questions about what you noticed the day Officer Eng was injured?"

Ellis was pleasantly surprised when Maineri's face ballooned from shriveled, sour prune to a rounded, smiling plum. Ellis was more surprised when a *Farmer Brown* drawl didn't come out of Maineri's mouth.

To top off the surprises, Maineri was both thorough and articulate. "Sure. See that small wooden building beyond the scoreboard at the end of the track? Well, that's where I saw the two males. Let's take a walk over there and I'll show you." Leaning his rake against a bleacher, Maineri led Ellis to the shed, where he described the two as white, with shoulder length hair, moderately tall, about 5'10", with light colored windbreakers.

He apologized for being unable to recognize them and figured they were probably teenagers. What aroused his attention was their hasty movements away from the screams and shouts coming from the track. "Everybody else was running toward the commotion. So I watched them for a few seconds before joining all those headed for the track."

Maineri explained that, even though he didn't recognize the teenagers, he did notice they were carrying some long object with ropes. "Kinda like a crucifix. After seeing them for a few seconds at about thirty-five-feet, I really don't know what it was, if anything other than pieces of wood, rope and metal rods or something."

"Anything else at all?" Ellis asked.

Maineri looked over at a stack of hurdles, old markers, starting blocks, paint cans, miscellaneous piles of wood and other things related to track meets. "You know, I've been meaning to sort through some of the track and field paraphernalia stored over there. Especially around that tarp."

Ellis followed Maineri's pointing finger to a big blue tarp covering a pile of items behind the stacks of hurdles. "Why? Do you think they might have left some evidence?"

"I don't know. I haven't had a chance to look. But the day after the incident, I noticed that the tarp seemed to have shifted. Could have been the wind, but there wasn't any to speak of. And there've been plenty of strong winds before that never moved the tarp or anything else in the storage area. There's one more thing. I think I saw the two guys in the crowd of people on the track about a half hour later, and they were empty-handed."

Ellis was impressed with Maineri's suspicions that would have been overlooked by most people. "So you figure they might have stashed whatever they were carrying."

Maineri was still staring at the storage area. "Well, I'm not positive it was the same two, but if they were, I'd say yes."

Ellis nodded. "It's sure worth a look."

The look only took a few minutes. Beneath the tarp were rolls of tarpaper stacked tightly together in upright rows. Behind the last row were some of the objects described by Maineri. Ellis was staring at a long object with metal rods, and other stuff. "Are those the objects you saw those kids carrying?"

"Sure are." Maineri nodded with a grin.

Examining the objects more closely, Ellis discovered he was actually looking at a ten-foot two by four, with a six-foot piece of channel iron, two inches wide by two inches deep. The channel iron was bolted along the front length of one of the two-inch sides of the two by four. A five-foot length of spring steel was attached to a metal swivel just behind the channel iron. The swivel could be snapped from a parallel to a perpendicular position on a notched section of the two by four. The rope Maineri had seen was a nineteen-strand wire with looped ends that could be attached taut or loose to the grooved ends of the spring steel.

Ellis stood quietly for a moment, fiddling with the components. Then he looked at Maineri. "There's no giant here either. That's a homemade crossbow."

📖 📖 📖

What irony, O'Shea thought. *Judge Hall commits suicide and I'm more content than I've been in months.* He was again free to be himself, a detective with a complex case that finally offered viable leads. Clues were beginning to make investigative sense, and he had an attractive woman friend who cooked beef stew. As important, he didn't have to suck up to people he didn't like. He remembered Wunden's frequent clinical advice: "Play the game if you want, John, but don't take it too seriously. It's only a game." He really didn't want to play the political game. He never did. *Why the hell did I ever want to be Chief of Police? Christ, I hate politics.*

O'Shea parked in front of the Skater's Warehouse on Third Street, off Mariposa, his second stop since he left his partners an hour ago. His first stop at Surfer's Corner in Burlingame, verified that Banana Zappers are still used by a few teenagers. The owner, however, hadn't sold one in months, and had no names or addresses of prior purchasers.

Oddly, O'Shea felt he now had plenty to live for, but if situations soured, he was ready for the grim reaper. Leads were coming together; he had Ida, good loyal partners and fine friends. On the other hand he was divorced, his kids were grown, and he had done just about everything he'd ever wanted to do. Or, for that matter, things he hadn't wanted to do but did anyway. Looking across at the Skaters Warehouse, O'Shea detected that slight tingling sensation that precedes goose bumps. He had done it all, and now he was free to live or die. Either way, he was content, and as long as there were things he still wanted to do, he'd stick around. Grinning to himself, O'Shea opened his car door and headed for the store. Then he had another reassuring thought, *solving this damn case would sure keep me going for a while.*

📖 📖 📖

Inside the warehouse, O'Shea gritted his teeth against the blaring "Techno" music coming from wall speakers as big as doors. He was in another dimension. A world sacred only to pink haired, baggy pants, tattooed teenagers with rings through tongues, noses, nipples, belly buttons, and the more conventional ears. *They probably have rings through their joints,* he thought.

He knew better, however, than to offer any sarcastic comments once inside. This was their world not his, and wanting information, he had better be cool. There were kids swarming over everything the store sold. He also noticed they were all more or less keeping time to the ear shattering beat, with a variety of strange gyrations. *Why are there so damned many of them,* he thought. *This is a weekday.*

A man in his 30's approached with an answer. "Can I help you? You look a little out of place. Sorry for all the kids. Usually it's deserted this time of day, but a lot of the high schools are closed this afternoon for a teachers conference."

This tall, well-groomed man with sport shirt, slacks and wingtip shoes doesn't seem to fit either, O'Shea thought.

"Thanks for the rescue. Are you the manager?"

"I'm the owner, manager, clerk and anything else needed to keep this place going. Ted Torrentine at your service."

O'Shea figured the owner was an ex-surfer or skier who woke up one day too old and decided to become a businessman, probably on a shoestring. His stock was stacked no frills, warehouse style, including snow skis, a few surfboards, all sorts of skateboards, helmets, poles and plenty of ear-wrenching, window-rattling, floor-shaking Techno sounds. O'Shea needed to make it quick. "I'm Jack O'Shea, with the San Francisco Police."

"Juvenile Division?" Torrentine interrupted. "Since I'm 39, it must have something to do with my customers."

O'Shea let Torrentine's weak stab at levity pass. "Do you still carry the old Banana Zappers?" Once O'Shea briefly explained his official reason for being there, Torrentine was exceptionally cooperative.

First he showed O'Shea one of the five Banana Zappers in stock with the ironic remark, "It looks like a big shoe, doesn't it?"

O'Shea wanted to hug the owner. Instead, he patted him on the shoulder. "You can sure say that again."

To O'Shea's surprise, Torrentine kept good records. Back in his office he managed to find the names and addresses of four out of seven purchasers of the Banana Zapper. "They were all bought during the past two years. That's when I started this business," he explained.

O'Shea was delighted with four out of seven, especially since he hadn't really expected any names or addresses. Again, grateful for the owner's help and anxious to leave the noise, he shook Torrentine's hand with a deep felt thanks as he bolted for the front door.

It was nearing noon, and O'Shea was anxious to get back to his partners before lunch. Then they could grab a bite together while discussing their morning findings.

Driving down Third Street, he reviewed the wild, kaleidoscopic events of his morning. *What a roller coaster*, he thought. Starting with a pleasant high, followed by an agonizing low that erupted into a meteoric soar beyond any high he had known in years. Pulling into the police parking lot, O'Shea heaved a happy sigh before gleefully muttering out loud, "It really ain't over 'til it's over."

📖 📖 📖

Approaching the rear entrance to the police offices from the parking lot, he was greeted by uniformed Officer Ray Monterrazzo, a giant of a man that O'Shea didn't know well. He knew Monterrazzo worked in Lieutenant Castañeda's downtown patrol unit, which was enough information for him to avoid any friendly chitchat.

To O'Shea, Castañeda was one of those politically wired, know-nothing minority cops who had received token undeserved promotions. O'Shea realized that many minorities needed a leg up in the department. In fact, he had helped many promising minority cops. Castañeda wasn't one of them. He had never forgotten how Castañeda's poor judgment almost got two of his partners killed, on separate occasions, when he was a patrolman. Chicano political connections spared him the slightest reprimands. He was to be the shining example of a successful minority in the police department. By the time he was promoted to lieutenant at 27, Castañeda had identified himself with the white Aryan toughies who could do no wrong on his watch. He was an incompetent, bigoted, vicarious toughie, and O'Shea had once told him so, using those exact words.

Officer Monterrazzo's smile was noticeably strained. "Good morning, Lieutenant O'Shea. You probably don't remember me. I spent a day in your homicide unit after the Academy, three years ago. Now I'm working for Lieutenant Castañeda. He told me to wait here for you. He would like to see you in Room 235B, ASAP."

O'Shea sensed this wasn't good news. He smiled anyway. "Thanks, Ray. I'll drop by now."

A few minutes later, O'Shea opened the door to 235B, a small office on the second floor used by the brass to meet reporters or special clients. When not occupied, the room was available to sergeants and lieutenants by official request.

He had barely taken a step inside when he heard, "Hello, Lieutenant O'Shea. Close the door." The steely, uptight voice unmistakably belonged to Lieutenant Castañeda. Seated behind a table facing the door were five scowling, frowning faces of O'Shea's principal enemies.

Jutting his jaw, O'Shea slammed the door with the back of his foot. Like an old gunfighter ready to slap leather, he stared unblinkingly at each foe with focused, narrow-eyed contempt.

He knew this was some sort of showdown, and was equally aware that negotiations or compromise was impossible. O'Shea wasn't surprised to see Sergeant Mahoney, jaw still wired, and his lackey, Officer Logan, arm in a cast, seated to the left of Lieutenant Castañeda. Then there was Officer Tulio DaSilva, slouched to the right of Castañeda. DaSilva was a sadistic bully who O'Shea had recommended be suspended for a month without pay following an Excessive Force Charge. Internal Affairs later dismissed it. At the other end of the table sat Sergeant Ben Drake, eagerly returning O'Shea's dog-eye.

O'Shea grabbed the rickety wooden chair, obviously intended for him. It was the hot seat centered on the other side of the table facing his opponents. Sliding the chair to one side, he leaned well forward across the table, as he scanned the five. No one backed down as the slashing, laser stares pierced the deadening silence. O'Shea's impatience finally got the best of him.

"So. What the hell do you want?"

As senior ranking cop on the other side of the table, Castañeda, an inveterate weight lifter, flexed his biceps as he leaned forward with a pinched-nose sneer. "Your easy ride's over, O'Shea. You lost your punk-ass man; which means, you're out of business. You'll never be Chief of Police in this city."

Still staring at Castañeda, O'Shea pushed away from the table until looming over the five, stretching his arms over his head as if he'd just awakened from a pleasant sleep. He flashed them all a devilish grin. "Is that it? Are you some kind of pussies? I already knew that and so what. By the way, why are you gringos letting this spic speak for you?"

"You mother fucker," blurted Drake. "You're pushing your luck."

"Yeah," muttered Mahoney through his wired jaw. "You fuchen ash hoe."

DaSilva and Logan sat silently, with mean looks and slow nods of agreement as they tried to stare down O'Shea.

Castañeda waved a copy of O'Shea's service record in front of his face. "You've got your thirty years in. We've decided it's time for you to retire, one way or another…"

"Tell me about the another," O'Shea interrupted.

Drake slammed his huge fist on the table. "I'll tell you. You prick. If you don't throw it in, if you don't retire, we'll make it impossible for you to survive as a cop. You know the drill—broken bones in alleys, tripped going down the stairs. Your nigger partner busted up in accidents. You get the picture."

O'Shea knew that in front of him sat well over a thousand pounds of brawn, and that there were at least another twenty cops, all weight lifters, who would help muscle him into retirement. Despite the odds, he couldn't help chuckle to himself when it occurred to him that all five probably had about two pounds of brain.

After a minute of heavy, menacing silence, Castañeda slowly began to rise from his chair. "Get out, old man, while you can."

But O'Shea wasn't finished; in fact he hadn't started. "Sit down Mike," O'Shea roared. Then slower and more staid, "You puds have really ruined my good mood and that pisses me off. Now listen carefully and keep your candy-ass mouths shut."

Then the earthshaking unexpected happened. O'Shea's face actually softened a bit as he eased his 9mm Glock automatic from his shoulder holster. On the other side of the table they were all stunned into wide-eyed, heavy breathing. O'Shea continued. "You see, what none of you jerks understand is my personal philosophy of life. At my age, quality of life, not length of life, is vital. Right now I like my job and my partners, and as long as all that's OK, I'm in a good mood. Otherwise life isn't worth living anymore. I've had a good life and I'm ready to die if quality of life takes a dive. That's my edge on all of you fucks. You still cling to life and your shitty little jobs. You're not ready to die yet. I am."

Pointing his gun at each of the five, O'Shea added. "Look at me, you sucks. I'm perfectly calm and prepared to die. Let's have a shoot-out right here, right now. You'll kill me, but I'll kill a few of you. Are you ready to die? I am. Just remember. Fuck with me or my partners, and my quality of life takes a dive." O'Shea slowly stared at each of them. "Then, I'll kill as many of you as I can before I'm thankfully wasted. You want to do it now, you slimy pieces of shit? I've got a ten round clip, enough to kill each of you twice."

All their jaws were practically resting on the table, as O'Shea removed the safety from his automatic, mimicked an aimed shot at each of them, and stepped back one pace. Then, in a smiling whisper, he offered another calm invitation as he holstered his gun. "Come on. I'm ready. Draw, you fucks, or don't piss me off. If you do, you're dead and I'm dead, and I wouldn't give a shit. Any comments?"

The only movements were ten arms raised over five wide-eyed heads. They knew O'Shea wasn't bluffing. He casually opened the door, looked back at his enemies and patted his holstered weapon. "You want a piece of me? Come on, right now, I'm ready. Otherwise, get fucked."

Then he left.

◫ ◫ ◫

Abandoning any pretense of indifference, Ellis sprang from his desk chair as O'Shea entered their office cubicle. Hasselburg was right behind him. "Is everything OK, Lieutenant?" they practically asked in unison.

O'Shea's devilish grin had lingered all the way back to their office. "Couldn't be much better."

Ellis glanced back at Hasselburg with a teeth-clenching expression of dread. "Got an anonymous call with more of a threat than request, that you go to room 235B, ASAP. Then a hang-up. John, it sounded like Lieutenant Castañeda. Are the jackals out to get you already? Anyway, whatever you need for back-up, I'm with you the whole way."

"Me too," nodded Hasselburg eagerly.

Staring at both of his partners with a much warmer grin, O'Shea sat on the edge of his desk. "It's been taken care of, and I'm still in a good mood. Thanks anyway."

O'Shea kept looking at his partners fondly, as Ellis and Hasselburg just stood quietly and a little awkwardly. Finally, emerging from deep thought, O'Shea added, "You know, if I could choose two perfect partners from any department in the world, I'd choose you two. Now go home, have some fun, and we'll swap leads on Monday."

Both partners heaved a huge sigh of genuine relief. They trusted in their boss, whatever he had done.

CHAPTER 43

Ida watched in adoring silence as O'Shea unabashedly devoured every morsel in sight. He polished off the gigantic salad in a few minutes. Then three huge portions of stew and a half-pound of sourdough bread slathered with garlic butter.

Munching away, he smiled gratefully at Ida through his bulging cheeks. He hadn't noticed that she was rather absently toying with her small plate of food. "This has got to be the best beef stew I've ever eaten. I hate to admit it, but you're the better cook. It ain't all Irish, but it beats mine."

Ida replied with a subdued smile. She just couldn't shake her concern about some of the comments she had overheard since Judge Hall's suicide.

O'Shea's only concern seemed to be how much more food he could stuff in his mouth. "Maybe I'll have another hunk of that sourdough to sop up this gravy. Another cup of your fine coffee would also be great. I'm really piggin' out, huh."

Ida actually loved to see O'Shea happily gorging himself on her cooking. She even had to smile as she decided nothing should interfere with his gluttony. *I'll wait*, she thought.

It was another ten minutes before O'Shea slowed down to an occasional swipe of garlic-buttered bread across the few remaining specks of gravy on his empty plate. Finally, leaning back in his chair with a muffled belch, "Pardon me." O'Shea was full, content and ready to shift his attention from dinner to Ida. "You're unusually quiet, little lady." Idly awaiting some sort of answer, he waved at the furry little blurs disappearing under the refrigerator.

Clearing the table, Ida wasn't quite ready for that serious talk. "A little more coffee with your dessert?"

Rocking forward in his chair, he grinned up at Ida. "Christ, I didn't save any room. Maybe later, but I can always use more coffee. What is the dessert by the way?"

Ida feigned a curtsy, and slowly waved hot apple pie under his nose.

O'Shea took a deep sniff. "On second thought, maybe sooner."

After sharing another cup of coffee and a few minutes of whimsically smiling at each other, Ida was reluctantly ready. She knew that O'Shea was as relaxed, easy going and content as he could ever be without melting into putty.

"I truly care for you, and I don't want anything bad to happen to you."

O'Shea responded with a silly smile.

Ida continued. "This morning I heard some things I didn't need to hear. I guess these cops said them loud enough so that I couldn't miss them."

O'Shea was still displaying a relaxed smile of indifference about what she was saying.

"I'm serious, John. They said you were no longer a threat, and that you were going to retire, one way or another."

O'Shea sipped his coffee with a more attentive smile.

"But this evening when I was leaving work, the comments were strange. Some were saying, 'Stay away from O'Shea, he's dangerous.' Others said you were bonkers. What's really going on? Do you know? Is it all about Judge Hall's suicide? I just want to defend you, to fight for you. I just need to know what's happening."

O'Shea slowly got up and walked to the sink where Ida was standing with a look of bewilderment. Gently, he reached out to her with both arms. "You're a tough, loyal little shit, aren't you?"

Ida glanced up tearfully, before nodding her way against his chest.

📖 📖 📖

After a whole weekend with Ida, his good mood had soared beyond the brightest of expectations. He had convinced her that he was aware of his opponents and in full control. "No threats I can't handle," he told her. As important, he reassured Ida that he deeply appreciated her support as well as the readiness of his partners to help if ever necessary. He reminded her, he had some other loyal friends still in the department. "I'm not alone, especially with you on my side."

With that comment, Ida practically purred.

What had followed was a weekend of more good food, good sex, and long peaceful walks while holding hands, laughing and enjoying things they had rarely noticed before.

When O'Shea arrived in the office cubicle on Monday morning at eight sharp, both partners were already sitting at their desks, with somewhat furtive glances of apprehension. As he approached them, they relaxed. He seemed just fine.

O'Shea chuckled. "Yeah, I feel great. Guess it shows."

After an exchange of a few pleasantries about their weekend activities, O'Shea was on his way to his routine Jimmy Brit, with the Chronicle tucked under his arm and empty coffee cup dangling from his fingers.

"Did you check the front page?" Ellis asked.

"You mean the services for Judge Hall, when friends and relatives can offer prayers and console each other? Yeah, I'm actually going to drop by, sporting my old dark blue suit and black tie. As much as I resent most of his snobbish friends, I'll pay my condolences. It'll be my last hurrah, and his. I suppose I need the—ah—closure. Back in a while."

O'Shea returned to their cubicle in ten minutes, with a crumpled Chronicle, full cup of coffee and a look of contentment. "Anybody want the paper before it's dumped?"

Shaking their heads, both partners kept working.

"Well," O'Shea continued, "are you ready for a little catch up? You know, 'I'll show you mine if you show me yours'."

It was obvious to his partners that O'Shea was still in a good mood. Ellis grabbed some notes, as Hasselburg quickly scrolled the computer. Ellis glanced at her smiling nod. "We're ready," he chortled. He was also in a good mood.

"OK," began O'Shea, "I think we agree that we're finally on the right track."

More nods from his partners.

"Seems like new findings are leading us away from the mystical or supernatural to a bunch of high school kids.

This time his partners' nods were barely perceptible. They already knew that.

"Well anyway," O'Shea mumbled, "who wants to start?"

Hasselburg raised her hand.

O'Shea looked around with a head shaking laugh. "Just call me professor. Remember, you're being graded."

Hasselburg blushed. "Sorry Lieutenant—ah—Jack. We may have another piece to the Sutherland puzzle. I called Officer Blake, of the Park Police, who had noticed the two SCUBA divers at Aquatic Park. Paul taught me that follow-up interviews by a different detective sometimes tease out a little additional information. It did. Blake isn't a diver, and when I asked him if they were wearing tanks he said, 'Oh, yeah. They had a cylinder on each of their backs'." Referring to her computer notes, Hasselburg added, "When I asked him if he could describe them, he said, 'It just dawned on me. They were yellow, a canary yellow with a green blotch of some kind on the upper part.' Tanks come in many colors, including yellow. But the green blotch should really narrow down the possibilities."

Grabbing an unused napkin, O'Shea scribbled a few of his own notes. "What the hell's a green blotch?" he thought aloud. Then he gave Hasselburg a nod. "That's great, Jill, an A+. You know what's next, huh?"

Hasselburg glanced at Ellis. "Paul taught me that next step before he showed me the coffee machine. 'Tedious grunt work,' he said, and that's my plan. To check every SCUBA store, marine sports outlet and high school SCUBA club until I find yellow tanks with green blotches."

"Anything else?" asked O'Shea.

"Well, until I find out how I got up that tree, how Jerran was elevated over eight feet off the ground, and how a two hundred twelve-pound concrete slab was dropped on Officer Nelson's head, I can't dismiss the eerie aspects of these cases."

"Damn it. I have to agree. There are a few loose ends. How about you, Paul?"

Ellis laid down his notes, took a swallow of his super sweet, creamy coffee, and gave Hasselburg a wink. "I've been doing my own grunt work, and although we are on the right track, I'm sure not ready to toss the strange and mysterious. That last message in Beth's locker at school is a good example. Really strange and eerily prophetic. Connie, her best girlfriend, drinks a barbiturate of some kind, intended for my daughter. Her normal, high blood pressure probably saved her life. Beth has normal low blood pressure. She has no idea why she decided she didn't want orange juice and went for a glass of water instead. Same day a missile-velocity javelin narrowly misses her and pierces Officer Eng. A coincidence? Probably. But what are the odds of all these things happening the way they did?"

O'Shea shrugged in silent agreement.

"On the brighter side, I think we have one less *giant* suspect."

O'Shea leaned forward. "More good news?"

Ellis scanned his notes. "Keep smiling. The operative word is *crossbow.*"

"The javelin, of course!" O'Shea bellowed. "I was hoping there was some kind of propellant behind that velocity. You found it?"

"Yep." Ellis beamed. "The track and field gardener, a Mr. Maineri, just about took my hand and led me to it." Referring to his notes, Ellis described the hayseed looking gardener's excellent observations. "He gave me a clear picture of the javelin throw and suspects carrying an object that they later hid under a tarp behind the track and field shed. Homemade and pretty ingenious," Ellis added. "The crime lab people are running all kinds of tests for prints, special materials, even some trial shots."

"What about the suspects?" Hasselburg asked as she raised and dropped her hand almost simultaneously.

Ellis shook his head. "The gardener didn't recognize them, and I'll bet he knows most of the students. But he was fairly certain that they were teenagers."

"Well," smirked O'Shea, "that eliminates two out of, how many? Ah, four possible giants? Seems like our suspects are shrinking in size and age."

Ellis shook his head, referring to his notes. "The other two supernatural possibles may be tougher to disprove. Jill's resting place high in a tree is even more bizarre when you factor in the absence of any tire tracks around the trees, and no scratches, torn clothes, scared branches or other evidence that Jill was physically pulled up that huge tree. The two hundred twelve-pound weapon in the Nelson murder is another puzzler. Then there's the other riddle. Jerran's hanging. Maybe our two out of four is actually two out of five.

O'Shea threw up his hands. "You're trying to stomp on my good day? I'll bet they're solvable with more grunt work."

Hasselburg was carefully studying a photo in the computer. Resisting an urge to raise her hand, she caught O'Shea's roving eyes.

"What's up, Jill?"

A bit startled, she wrinkled her nose with a puzzled smile. "How did you know?"

O'Shea laughed. "Your twitching right hand is a dead give away."

Hasselburg blushed again, from light pink to a dark red.

O'Shea raised his hand apologetically. "Come to think of it, your way beats the hell out of butting in."

Ellis nodded. "You can say that again. It's hard to finish a thought with John's interruptions."

O'Shea shot Ellis a sarcastic grin. "OK. You got me. I can't argue that either. Now, what do have for us, Jill?"

"Well, I was looking over the photos taken of Officer Nelson's body at the crime scene. His head would have been about twenty inches from this big slab of concrete."

Ellis and O'Shea got up and peered over her shoulder at the computer photo.

"Go on," urged Ellis.

"Well, look at the position of the slab that crushed Officer Nelson's head. It might have been resting on the other slab, which suggests it could have been somehow pushed over instead of lifted and dropped."

Ellis patted Hasselburg on the shoulder. "God, you're right. Probably levered on top of Nelson's head."

O'Shea patted Hasselburg on the other shoulder. "Remember that pole with the disk? What do you think, Paul?"

"I think Jill and I are off to the Embarcadero."

O'Shea nodded approvingly. "Jill! You're one hell of a fine partner. While you two are checking out the Embarcadero, I have a few Banana Zappers to pursue." Frowning at Ellis, he added, "How the hell did we overlook that leverage possibility?"

CHAPTER 44

Four out of seven ... hmm, not bad, he thought. The first call was a disappointment, but not enough to jar his good mood. The phone number Ted Torrentine had given O'Shea, was out of order. It had been his first choice because the address on Parnassus was on the same block as the Likert's house. Accessing police privileges, he did, however, manage to trace the address to the actual owner of the house.

"The tenants moved back east six months ago," she said.

Scratch the first one, he thought.

The second address turned out to be on Bay Street off Van Ness.

Kevin McDougal's mother picked up the phone on the first ring. "He's in school," she impatiently replied.

"What school?" asked O'Shea.

"Galileo."

O'Shea hung up with a hasty "thanks," realizing she never asked why he needed to know about her son, suggesting that the urgent call she was probably waiting for wasn't him. O'Shea decided McDougal wasn't much of a suspect anyway. He figured no kid's likely to skateboard clear across the city to whack some guy working on a car in his garage. *Random, yes,* he thought, *but not that random.*

The last two addresses turned out to be the most promising. Fred Stanton lived on Stanyan, just a few blocks from the Likert home; and Craig Craven lived on Cole Street, a few blocks further but easily within skateboard distance to Likert's house on Parnassus. O'Shea learned from their parents, that they were both attending classes at

Polytechnic.

Robin Hungerford, Dean of Boys, had both students waiting for O'Shea when he arrived at the school, along with their school transcripts. Agreeing with O'Shea's suggestion, Mr. Hungerford had explained that the police were doing a study of skateboard safety in San Francisco.

When he introduced himself, O'Shea immediately noticed the marked contrast in their appearance and mannerisms. Both boys were seniors. Fred Stanton was tall, lanky and boyish-looking, with over-sized jeans hanging an inch or so below his navel. He slouched all over his chair, and when he got up, he still slouched. O'Shea wondered how he could use his skateboard and hold up his pants at the same time. Stanton's roving blue eyes, frizzled, flaming red hair, peach fuzzed, smooth, rosy cheeks, protruding ears and perpetual self-conscious grin, suggested he was about twelve.

Craig Craven, on the other hand, was neatly dressed and well groomed. His thick, trimmed black hair falling casually across his forehead, along with deep set, brown eyes, chiseled features and cleft chin gave him a dashing appearance of the romantic lead in a school play. Despite his moderately short height, he looked like a self-assured twenty-year-old that should be driving a convertible, not a Banana Zapper.

Stanton was first to be interviewed. Entering the small room, adjacent to the dean's office, he slogged along with his rolled up cuffs dragging on the floor. Like a loose sack of potatoes, he awkwardly slumped into a chair, head dangling above his spread legs. O'Shea sat next to him with a view of the top of his head.

In an effort to avoid any rapidly spreading rumors that the police were somehow linking Banana Zappers to Likert's death, O'Shea tried a pretty straightforward script of innocuous questions. Skateboard Clubs? Positive and negative safety features of Banana Zappers vs. the larger, new skateboard models? Number of months street skateboarding experience? Number and type of injuries? Main skateboarding areas, last three months?

With this approach, O'Shea could take notes less threateningly and hopefully learn about other users of Banana Zappers. This might lead to discovering what Banana Zapper skateboarders were in the Parnassus/Stanyan Street area, that early evening of April 8th, when Likert was murdered.

Once the interview started, Stanton was surprisingly spontaneous and talkative. He obviously enjoyed skateboarding as a sport as well as transportation, and O'Shea learned much more than expected from this sluggish, shy looking kid.

As far as he knew there weren't any official skateboard clubs. Friends just got together after school or weekends to practice maneuvers. There were a couple of places in San Francisco with "ramps and stuff" for fun and practice. He only knew a couple of guys who had Banana Zappers, including Craven, but none of them were pals. He further explained that the bigger boards were more stable, faster and much less maneuverable. That, he reasoned, made them more dangerous on city streets. He liked ten percent grades. Any steeper and it was too hairy for his skill level. Parnassus Street was nearby and one of his favorite streets to practice on. No, he hadn't had any serious injuries. Just bruises and torn clothes. He did go off a Stanyan Street curb once, right into the side of a car. Neither was injured and the driver was a nice guy. "He didn't scold me or nothing."

Stanton also said he hoped the city would build more skateboard parks because, "they're safer than the streets," and "people get mad when you chip their stairs and stuff with practice jumps."

By the end of the interview, Stanton was so comfortable he was trying to show O'Shea how to flip an imaginary skateboard 360 degree during a jump.

That's when O'Shea slipped in the casual question. "Hey, Mr. Likert, the teacher who died, lived on Parnassus. Did he ever complain about skateboarders?"

"Naw," he answered without the slightest hesitation. "He was too busy working on his race car. He was OK, I guess."

"Anything else?" O'Shea asked.

"Do you think we'll have to wear helmets and stuff like that?"

"Not in the near future," O'Shea said with a reassuring smile.

Cop instinct told him it wasn't Stanton's Banana Zapper in Likert's garage. Unless, of course, Stanton had loaned it to someone. He forgot to ask. *Maybe later*, he thought.

When O'Shea greeted Craven, it didn't take long to realize that this interview would be as different as their teenage appearances. Craven stiffly postured his way into the interview room with a rigid strut that seemed to signal his thinly veiled disdain for authority. Where Stanton was sloppily open and spontaneous, Craven was neatly tucked in, inaccessible and cautious. Where Stanton was harmlessly dull, Craven seemed cunningly sharp. O'Shea also sensed it was something more than just teenage arrogance.

Christ, this kid's worse than Taggart and Schwartz put together, he thought.

Craven sat erectly with legs crossed, arms folded over his chest, and head slightly cocked to one side. Throughout the interview he maintained a grin that said nothing friendly, and his steely blue eyes stared coldly at O'Shea through narrow, unblinking lids.

Craven seemed much too clever to openly resist. Superficially compliant, he answered all the questions on O'Shea's "Safety" list without really saying anything.

"All skateboards have unsafe features, Lieutenant.... No serious mishaps, Lieutenant.... Just transportation, Lieutenant, I travel all over.... Don't think I know any other person who rides a Banana Zapper...."

Then Craven carelessly gave his first major slip up, prompting O'Shea to inwardly shout for joy. *Gotcha, you sack a shit.*

When asked his specific street travel around his neighborhood during the past three months, Craven's evasive ploy out-slicked him. "I hit all the streets: Stanyan, Cole, Seventeenth, Grattan." He named practically every street in San Francisco except one.

"How about Parnassus?" O'Shea asked.

"No. It's too steep, Lieutenant."

O'Shea knew that the only steep part of Parnassus was on Likert's block and that Seventeenth was much steeper. Such a clearly defensive reply invited O'Shea's next question. "Didn't Mr. Likert live on Parnassus?"

"Maybe. I don't know."

"Did you know Mr. Likert well?"

"No. The whole school knows he got killed working on his race car."

O'Shea knew from his quick perusal of the school transcripts that Craven had taken drama courses from Likert for the past two years. He also knew Craven was beginning to qualify as a possible suspect, yet O'Shea decided to back off slightly until he gathered some hard evidence.

"Thanks, Mr. Craven. That's all for now."

For the first time since the interview began, Craven momentarily dropped his eye contact along with his grin. Quickly recovering, he shot O'Shea a searing stare. "You're not really here about skateboard safety, are you? You could of sent any patrolman for that."

O'Shea offered a coy smile and a little nudge. "Well, do you know something I should know?"

"You'd be amazed at all I know," Craven said smugly.

O'Shea got up and opened the door. "That's it for today, but I'll be seeing you soon."

That was the last time he saw Craven alive.

📖 📖 📖

This time it was more difficult to find the Nelson crime site. Parking on the edge of the Embarcadero rubble, O'Shea's partners gave each other a concerned glance, as they heard the rumble of bulldozers. Climbing in and around the remaining piles of debris, Ellis looked back at Hasselburg. "Last time I was here, it was the wind blowing dust and dirt all over the place. Now it's trucks."

Working her way between two huge slabs, Hasselburg shouted back. "Well, you guys found the disk anyway, so maybe we'll get lucky again."

Stopping for a moment, Ellis looked around in disgust. Bulldozers, trucks, and backhoes seemed to be everywhere, dragging, lifting, carrying and dumping tons of cement rubble. "It's no use. I can't even find the crime scene, because it's probably in one of those trucks."

Hasselburg was carefully examining a police photograph and what was left of the embarcadero area. "Wait, come here and take a look. Here's our photo of the crime scene. Now look beyond, toward the top of the picture. That's almost due west. See? That part of a big cylinder in the background is toward the bottom of the Bay Bridge anchor cable, and just beyond that, a little up and to the right is the corner of the old Ghirardelli building."

As Ellis looked the photograph over, he scanned all directions until he saw the Ghirardelli building in the distance. "I was really all turned around. I've been leading you south."

Hasselburg blushed. "And you see, we're in luck. All the heavy equipment isn't in the western part of the embarcadero yet."

Ellis stared westward before turning directly to Hasselburg. "You are incredible." Then, half in jest, he added, "You were probably an Eagle Scout, huh?"

"No, I earned the Gold Award, which, in the Girl Scouts, is the same thing."

They both laughed.

Approaching the general area where Officer Nelson was killed, it became apparent to them that the location of the crime scene was no longer clearly defined. Blown around by the winds, there were shredded pieces of yellow crime scene tape everywhere in the vicinity of the April 8th stakeout.

Ellis again realized the importance of the original crime scene photos Hasselburg had brought along. "Here's the area," he shouted. "Nothing's been moved. All the concrete lying around here is identical to the picture." Re-examining the photo as he looked around, Ellis neared the exact spot where Nelson's body had lain. There it is, Jill."

Hasselburg was way ahead of him, having memorized every square inch of the photo. "I know," she said. "Look over here. This is where his head was crushed by the concrete slab. It took one of those portable engine hoists to lift it off his head."

Deferring to her more exact discovery, Ellis asked. "Where's the murder weapon now?"

Giving Ellis an *I thought you'd never ask* grin, she pointed to a pile of concrete several feet to the left of where it had been removed. "There it is. See? There's still some blood on the side of the slab."

While Ellis examined the bloodied slab, Hasselburg practically ran back to where Nelson's body was found. Trying to keep a step ahead of her mentor, she was enjoying her brief leadership role. "Look, Paul." Pointing to the slab in front of Nelson's crushed head location, she ran her fingers along the top outer edge of the slab. "See these deep scratch marks? I bet that's where the other block was pried off onto Officer Nelson's head."

After checking the marks carefully, Ellis examined the visible sides of the other block. "I think you're right, Jill. There're similar scratches on this side of the murder weapon. You should have been an archeologist."

Hasselburg was frantically searching for the remaining piece of the puzzle. "I studied it for awhile."

Ellis shook his head with a wry smile. "You don't have to do it all. If you're looking for the pole that had the disk, O'Shea stashed it over here, under this ledge of rocks, just in case it was needed."

Ellis noticed Hasselburg's lips form a slight pout with his last comment. "Hey, partner, I couldn't have found any of this without you."

She replaced her pout with a grin. "Thanks, Sergeant."

Once they retrieved the pole, it took less than a half hour to agree that the scratches on both slabs could have been made by the pole. "Shall we take the pole to forensics?"

Pausing for a few seconds, Ellis offered a slow, thoughtful nod. "I suppose we should have taken it last time. There're probably fifty prints on it, including ours. But, what the heck."

Hasselburg picked it up with an old rag. "I haven't touched it," she declared.

📖 📖 📖

O'Shea arrived at the Judge Hall services early. He had hoped to beat the crowd, pay his respects to relatives and politely exit. So did everyone else. Entering the reception hall was like being auditioned for one of those old MGM extravaganzas. Dressed, perfumed and coiffured to the root canalled teeth, it was—lights, cameras, action— and O'Shea wanted no part of it.

The hall was overflowing with politicians, their ingratiating entourages, entertainment celebrities and the usual assortment of the high society rich who wanted to be famous.

Wandering around the outer perimeter of the mob, O'Shea felt safely invisible. Cloned pretension was everywhere. Plenty of per- formances with about as much depth as a puddle. Busily trying to impress each other with name-dropping rumors and empty chitchat, no one even noticed O'Shea. Looking down at his old blue polyester suit, he heaved a deep sigh. Watching more heads bobbing like preening peacocks, with plastic smiles, cued laughter and roving eyes, he shook his head in disgust. *Christ! And I thought I was willing to suck into this group for the Chief's job.* Loosening his old black tie, he waved to the self-absorbed crowd who still hadn't seen him. As expected, no one noticed.

Walking toward the front door, he turned and shouted into the buzzing crowd. "Goodbye."

Still no one noticed, and he left.

CHAPTER 45

Yawning his way down the third floor corridor, O'Shea couldn't help but notice the droning silence. *What the hell's that humming sound*, he wondered, *and why is it so quiet on a Tuesday morning.* Passing the coffee area, with a few dregs of cold coffee still in yesterday's pot, he figured out the noise. *Aha, it's the air vents. You can't hear them when this place is buzzing. But why's it so dead in here? What the hell, it feels good. This is the way Hall's service should have been. Quiet. Peaceful.*

Entering his dark office, O'Shea snapped on his desk lamp with the built-in digital clock that read 6:30 a.m. This time he thought, *Aw shit.* After falling asleep earlier than usual, he had an undisturbed eight hours of sleep for the first time in years. He had awakened refreshed an hour early, and never bothered to check the time. Seated at his desk, he closed his eyes and smiled to himself. *Christ, I didn't realize how much I dreaded that politicking with Hall, or all those cops gunning for my ass, or my lonely life. All that's really over. It's 6:30 and I'm in a great mood.* Still smiling in the dim quiet, O'Shea got up and headed for the coffee machine.

📖 📖 📖

On his way to their office cubicle, Ellis met Hasselburg coming out of the third floor restroom. Typical for a quarter to eight, there still wasn't much activity in the corridors. In fact, any movements or talking at this time in the morning seemed soft and sluggish, as if the whole building were tranquilized until the Pavlovian hour of eight. Following whispered good mornings, the partners heard O'Shea's voice, unusually loud and strident for the sleepy early morning. Listening on the phone, O'Shea glanced up with a quick nod, as his partners entered the office cubicle. "Thanks Mr. Hungerford, I appreciate the call. The Juvenile Division will be officially looking into it."

As he hung up the phone, O'Shea stared at his partners with a deep sigh and a thin good morning smile. "Sit down folks. The good news is that yesterday I think I found Likert's Banana Zapper intruder. A seventeen-year-old Poly senior named Craig Craven. The bad news is today he's dead as a goddamned door nail." O'Shea paused for a moment with a searching glance to his partners. "There's more good news. His killer is probably the same person, gang, club or whatever that put you in a tree, Jill." Waiting for an effusive reaction, O'Shea instantaneously got it.

"What?" shouted both partners.

Cocking his head with a perplexed frown that faded into a grin, Ellis softly asked, "OK, John, we give up. How did you arrive at that conclusion?"

O'Shea grinned back at Ellis, while Hasselburg stared in silence. "Sorry folks, no more games. Here's a copy of my interview notes with Craven. It was pretty obvious he knew more than he was ready to admit. I knew I'd eventually have the little shit. Then I got calls this morning from Tashima in juvenile and Hungerford, Dean of Boys at Poly. Craven was found dead about 2:00 a.m. up in a tree in Golden Gate Park."

Before interrupting, Hasselburg blew a puff of air through her mouth as if kicked in the stomach. "Are you going to tell us it was my tree?"

O'Shea slowly nodded. "But you're alive and he's dead. You were just a message, so are the disks. But, Craven was more than a message. I'll bet he was a co-conspirator. I suppose he knew more than they— whoever the hell they are—wanted us to know. He became a threat. He was probably going to interfere with their game plan, whatever it is. I still don't know what's really going on, but we're finally out of that maze full of dead ends. We're on the right path and getting closer." Ending his monologue with a "That's it," he jokingly bowed to his little audience, who applauded, mainly for his persistent good mood.

"Thanks, fans. I'm going to grab some more coffee, and take a hit and a miss. And when I return, let's critique what we've got."

As O'Shea hurried out of the cubicle, Hasselburg, bending over the computer, looked up and gave Ellis a squinty-eyed glance. "What's a hit and a miss?"

Ellis smirked. "My grandmother called it *number one*, some say *whiz* or *leak* or, pardon the expression, *piss*. My kids still say *pee*. I guess I don't make any announcement, I just go. Get the idea? O'Shea has his own special slang and *hit and a miss* is one of many."

Hasselburg's mouth and eyes popped open with an idea. "Hey, maybe we should publish a dictionary of O'Shea-to-English translations."

Ellis slowly shook his head with a broad smile. "You know, I've been thinking about something like that for a long time."

📖 📖 📖

Leaning over the old, stained urinal, the grayish white porcelain reminded O'Shea of the colorless look of death, when blood stops its fiery flow and all bodies resemble dull porcelain. *Ice cold and rock hard,* he thought, *without a conscience or soul. Just dead meat.* Looking beyond the old urinal, O'Shea was transfixed by the eerie images of the countless dead he had experienced in his six years as a homicide inspector. *And now there're more. Christ, how many? With Arnold Hall's suicide and this Craven kid, it must be twenty, or twenty-one? All somehow linked to the Wednesday deaths in a strange way. Some of the dead I liked or would have liked. Why don't I retire? God, I'm afraid to quit. What the hell would I do? What the hell's the use of hanging around?*

Slowly, grimly trudging to the coffee machine, O'Shea felt his mood free falling into dark, dreary gloom. He was again just a fragile moment away from the first drink that leads to the oblivion of a thousand more.

Then, unexpectedly, something of a divine, spiritual nature happened to him. As an Irish Catholic, O'Shea was the typical perfunctory Christian. He did, however, believe in God and *angels*. Not the winged, naked cherubic kind. He had searched for those as a kid with no luck. Gradually he learned that it's what they do, not what they look like that matters. So, approaching the coffee machine, with empty cup dangling limply from his index finger, he noticed Ben

Drake talking with Ida. As a squirt of adrenaline readied O'Shea to protect Ida with his life, their conversation stopped him in his tracks.

". . . If you ever hurt Jack in any way, I'll kill you myself."

"Hey! Don't get upset, Ida. O'Shea and I had a talk of our own and I agreed to stay away from you and never threaten him, and I'll honor that . . ."

O'Shea stood dumbfounded as loyalty, friendship, deliverance and angels all flashed across his mind. Seemingly invisible, he walked by them unnoticed, with coffee cup firmly clutched in his hand. He winked upward at his guardian angel who had permitted him to eavesdrop on a conversation he needed to hear. *Maybe Ida's the angel,* he thought. *Either way, the message is clear enough. Ginella, Boyd, Bender, Wunden, would deeply mourn the loss of a dear friend, me. So would Ellis and Hasselburg. Goddammit, I'm not ready to throw it in,* he grinned to himself.

📖 📖 📖

O'Shea bounced into the cubicle with a glowing smile, empty coffee cup, and in an exceptionally good mood.

Scrolling through the computer, Hasselburg was already prepared for their critique. So was Ellis, pouring over a pile of notes. Both partners smiled back, relieved that O'Shea seemed almost cheerful.

Ellis also noticed O'Shea's empty coffee cup. "We're ready, John. Did you forget your coffee?" Ellis gave Hasselburg a wink. "Or did you drink it during your *hit and a miss*? Whatever, you sure seem happy about something."

Turning to Ellis, O'Shea placed his empty cup on his desk. "It's a long, complicated story. I suppose, in a way, it has something to do with a hit and a miss, at least the urinal. Anyway, I'm fine and I'll tell you all about it someday."

Hasselburg looked at O'Shea quizzically. "Can I get you a cup of coffee before our critique? I could use another cup myself."

"Thanks, Jill. I could sure use some."

By the time Hasselburg slipped a full cup of coffee under O'Shea's nose, Ellis was starting to wade through notes and lengthy explanations, while O'Shea paid close attention. "...With the ballistic report and .22 shell casing, we jumped to the conclusion the bullet that killed Winston came from the Armory heist, and since Trickers were involved, we had a club full of suspects. More recently, arranging the disks' letters confirmed our suspicions. Solid evidence, we thought. Now, Staff Sergeant Bryant Murphy tells me that every high school rifle team in San Francisco uses .22 bullets from the same Armory. That certainly doesn't rule out the Trickers. It simply rules in high school kids, with Erick Taggart a good start. Staff Sergeant Murphy verified Taggart's expert marksmanship with a .22 caliber rifle."

For a moment, O'Shea stared vacantly at the ceiling with a pensive sigh, before giving his partners a grinning shrug. "Yeah, the timing really sucked on that one. A few days before the Winston murder, .22 caliber bullets, like the one in his head, were stolen in a wild heist at the local Armory. You see, Jill, how easily detectives can be conned, by coincidence, into thinking they're on the right track."

Bent over her computer, Hasselburg gave O'Shea one of her hesitant, *yes but* nods. "Aren't the Trickers still a suspect, especially since the disks spell its name?"

"Absolutely," replied Ellis. "And we were compelled to pursue the Trickers' lead, but not at the exclusion of other possibilities."

"Right," O'Shea added. "We're not finished with the Trickers by a long shot. Christ, Jill, you were at a Trickers' meeting the evening you were treed, and Taggart and Schwartz may not be members, but they were sure as hell there that evening and some of the last people to see you. Are we all clear on this issue?"

After each nodded their yes, Hasselburg resumed scrolling the computer and Ellis grabbed another page of notes. "I've talked with Lieutenant Tashima and Sergeant Wagner about juvenile gangs and clubs. Apparently there aren't any. At least no real organized ones capable of pulling off the eight crimes in one day. Juvenile's been monitoring all known gang and club activity in San Francisco since the Trickers' Armory heist. Nothing, except the occasional gang turf fights or drive-bys. Juvenile is also investigating all members of the Trickers as to their activities on April 8th as well as their knowledge of Jill's tree episode last Wednesday evening. High on our priority list is to reinterview Taggart and Schwartz, including their April 8th hour-by-hour activities."

Before O'Shea or Ellis could inhale for their next comment, Hasselburg flashed photos of Taggart and Schwartz printed off the computer. "I'd like to show these photos to people who live and work near Winston's crime scene; especially the woman who saw the two kids near the body."

O'Shea glanced at the photos before grinning at Hasselburg. "I'll be damned. No raised hand."

Hasselburg pursed her lips into a slight pout. "Sorry, Lieutenant."

Waving both hands in the air, O'Shea rapidly shook his head. "I was kidding, honest."

Ellis was absently studying the photo of Schwartz, whom he hadn't seen during the first interview with O'Shea. "Hey, you guys. I've seen this kid somewhere. Where? I can't place it."

O'Shea looked at the photo over Ellis' shoulder. "Yeah, that's him alright. You probably saw him at Poly."

Still looking at the photo, Ellis slowly stroked his chin, which he only did in times of deep thought. "No, John. It was out of Poly. It may come to me when I interview him."

"By the way," Hasselburg chimed in. "You two did know Schwartz lives on McLaren Avenue, didn't you?"

Ellis and O'Shea looked at each other in search of the correct answer. "Well," replied Ellis, "I guess so."

O'Shea gave a hesitant head nod.

Hasselburg added, "It's a small street, two blocks long, and a half block from the Hansen house."

Ellis and O'Shea glanced at each other with furtive shrugs.

CHAPTER 46

Stroking his chin, Ellis looked around the small side room near the dean's office that contained three chairs, a graffitied, standard three by five oak school table and three pictures of presidents over walnut stained plywood walls. *It's pretty Spartan,* he concluded. *Washington and Lincoln I can understand, but what's Eisenhower doing here?*

Actually, Ellis was trying to distract himself from the unusually long wait. Fifteen minutes earlier, the dean's secretary sent a student runner to retrieve Schwartz from his trigonometry class. The wait contributed to Ellis' mild anxiety, which he realized was common for all cops before an interview. More so for this one.

After racking his brain during his drive to Poly, Ellis still couldn't remember where he had seen Schwartz. *In any event,* he thought, *I've got to somehow cut through this kid's resistance, that's if he ever gets here.*

Just then the door flew open and in an instant, Ellis remembered the bouncing ball, the chiseled Aryan features, the acrid glare from those icy blue eyes and the acerbic scowl. Ellis also clearly remembered Schwartz's contemptuous dismissal of him and his questions, and his own sense of intimidation by a kid.

"Have a seat, Mr. Schwartz. I'm Sergeant Ellis of the San Francisco Police Department."

When Schwartz, with crossed arms and piercing stare, slowly placed his chair within a foot of Ellis, it was obvious nothing would soften this kid. *A no-win,* Ellis inwardly winced. *What the heck, cut to the chase.*

"When I caught your tennis ball out on Sea Cliff about a month ago, you said you didn't know the Hansen family. How long have you lived a half block from them?"

Without the slightest change in his smirk, Schwartz looked Ellis over as if sizing him up for a job. "I remember you. You're the guy who grabbed my ball. So, now what do you want?"

"Don't play with me, kid. I just told you. How long have you lived a half block from the Hansen's?"

Schwartz's smirk didn't budge. "I would appreciate not being called kid. Treat me with some semblance of respect, and I'll try to do the same. Incidentally, how can I answer a question that implies I know where the Hansen's live? I don't."

Ellis flushed, realizing he had impatiently skipped some questions with his leading question. "Let's start over. Do you live in the Sea Cliff district of San Francisco, on McLaren Avenue?"

Schwartz slowly nodded with a fixed stare into Ellis' eyes.

"What's your address?"

"136 McLaren Avenue."

"Now, how long have you lived at that address?"

After another uncooperative pause, Schwartz again mechanically replied with an unwavering stare. "Eight years."

Ellis stared back with an irritated sigh. "You're telling me that you lived a half a block away from the Hansen family and you never met them?"

"Now how would I know? You may know the names of your neighbors, while assuming I should know my neighbors' names as well. That's presumptuous, don't you agree?"

Ellis could feel the first adrenal signs of inner frustration. *My God, he's mocking me.* Ellis took a deep breath and offered a token smile to mask his grimace. "Did you hear of a woman's death off the cliff near your house?"

"I heard."

"You seem like a well-read young man. Didn't you see her picture in the paper?"

"Probably not. I don't read about crimes. I have more important issues to explore."

Barely hanging on to his smile, Ellis was nearing his exasperation threshold. "OK then, here's a photograph of Helen Hansen. You can clearly see her pretty face and slender figure. In your eight years living a half block from her house, did you ever see her?"

Maintaining his blinkless smirk, Schwartz gave a casual glance at the photo with no hint of recognition. "The probability of seeing residents who lived a half block from me in an eight year period is extremely likely. So? She seems familiar. So what?"

"Did you ever talk to her, Mr. Schwartz?"

For the first time in the interview, Schwartz revealed a near imperceptible defensive flaw. His smirk slipped for a fraction of a second into a glare. "No!"

Ellis offered his own smirk. "Thank you, Mr. Schwartz. I'll be talking to you again, and soon!"

☐ ☐ ☐

When her partners left the cubicle, Hasselburg felt energized by their hunches. Within a few phone calls and some deft computer searching, she was collating some revealing data.

She began with the assumption that Jerran Ramsey, Craig Craven, Erick Taggart and Karl Schwartz were somehow involved in the eight crimes. If so, what did they have in common? She easily learned that they were all seniors at Polytechnic High School, all honor students and all were members of the Thespians, the Honor Society, the Alchemists and the Omega Club. Most were physics, math or chemistry majors. Interestingly, Jerran, a math and science major, had minored in auto mechanics. As expected, Taggart was a member of the Expert Marksman's Club, an affiliate of the ROTC, and Schwartz was student president of the Honor Society.

Hasselburg was also thrilled with the information she got from the Diver Down Club's advisor. Pursuing the Poly High male senior connection, Hasselburg obtained a list of six male seniors in the Diver Down Club, fourteen in the Honor Society and three in the Expert Marksman Club. Most other clubs, such as the Omega, Alchemist and Thespians had no computerized membership record.

Another bit of data Hasselburg figured might be of value, was the names of all forty-nine male seniors. Most would probably have drivers' licenses with fingerprints to be matched to those unknown ones on the Nelson leverage pole. Scanning the male senior names, Hasselburg thought of their possible club memberships and how they might provide a new set of leads.

The top of her priority list was the Diver Down Club. She realized that the investigation of the other Poly clubs, however, would require more patient contacts and analysis, especially those with no computer listing of members. Reviewing the names of Diver Down members, Hasselburg had one burning question she couldn't wait to ask. What seniors were in possession of the Poly Parrot SCUBA tanks on the Wednesday of April 8th?

Hasselburg was just about to search the computer for the faculty member in charge of the Diver Down group, when O'Shea popped into the office. Grabbing a case file from his desk, he was almost out in the hall when he noticed his partner. "How you doin', Jill? Any progress?"

Sitting back massaging her fingers, she grinned up at him. "You're right, things are coming together. How about you?"

"You know, I've probably met more juvenile division cops today than I have in the last twenty years. They all agree no street gang caused the eight crimes. They say gangs are too turf and macho oriented to pull off such diverse crimes on a single day. Besides, those street gangs are too damned busy thumping other gangs. Tashima also told me all Trickers and guests at the get-together have been interviewed, and there're no good suspects or leads. But in your case, Jill, none of the people at the party can be ruled out. It's also becoming more apparent that Poly students keep cropping up around our eight cases."

Staring at her computer monitor, Hasselburg nodded. "Boy, ain't that the truth."

Heading for the hall again, O'Shea gave Hasselburg a thumbs up. "On my way to St. Mary's Hospital. It's my turn to give nurse Hanna and staff another shot at our dead end."

Scanning the list of Poly male seniors, Hasselburg saw the name. "There's a Jeff Hanna in the list of Poly seniors. Any relationship?"

O'Shea shouted back as he left the cubicle. "I don't know, but I'll sure find out."

◫ ◫ ◫

Pudgy faced and bright eyed, with rosy cheeks, nurse Hanna was pouring over charts when O'Shea arrived at the nurses' station.

Having never met O'Shea, nurse Hanna stood up to greet this husky, graying red-haired man with the well-worn suit and tie. "Good morning. How can I help you?" She leaned forward across the counter with a dazzling smile that matched the glow of her pure white uniform.

O'Shea broke into a sincere smile, thinking, *Ellis was right; there's something sweet about this woman.*

"Good morning to you. I'm Lieutenant O'Shea, Sergeant Ellis' partner. Is it OK if I ask a few follow-up questions about the day of Mrs. Digness' death?"

Mrs. Hanna's sparkling eyes filled with deep concern. "Oh yes, please. I'll ask Mrs. Crafton to monitor the station. I got to know Mr. Digness well. He was with Grace almost every minute. He couldn't have ended her remaining days so viciously."

O'Shea thought back to his conversation at the Java House. "I agree that Mr. Digness wasn't capable of such a thing. You do understand, don't you?"

"Yes." She nodded, dropping her eyes as if in prayer. "A violent murder followed by a grief stricken suicide. How could it happen here? How could I not have known?"

O'Shea leaned over the counter, gently squeezing her hands. "Maybe together we can find out. OK?"

With a faint smile, she looked up into O'Shea's soft gaze. "Let's try."

When nurse Crafton arrived, Mrs. Hanna led O'Shea to an unoccupied doctor's office. "Where do we start?"

"Why don't we start with that Wednesday on April 8th when you arrived at work. All the usual and unusual comings and goings of visitors, patients and staff. Try not to determine the relevance of your observations. Just tell me everything you can remember, and I'll do my best to figure out if any of it may be related to the crime."

Organizing her thoughts, Mrs. Hanna closed her eyes for a few minutes. Once she opened her eyes, she offered a detailed narration of virtually every event until she discovered Mrs. Digness' brutalized body at 4:35 p.m. She began with observations of Mrs. Washington, the night cleaning woman, who was the first person she greeted in the morning. No noticeable change in Mrs. Washington's routine. She also recalled nothing unusual about the night nurses she relieved, and no reports of any problems during the night shift.

Mrs. Hanna further explained that during her first rounds, all seven ICU patients were resting quietly, with station monitors functioning properly. Entering Mrs. Digness' room at 8:46 a.m., she found, as expected, Mr. Digness seated in a chair with arms and upper body slumped across the bed in restless sleep. The two nurses and two nurses' aides exhibited their characteristic, friendly, calm behavior in carrying out their daily assignments; and throughout the day, until Mrs. Digness' death, there were no emergencies. Rechecking her April 8th log, Mrs. Hanna noted the three groups of visitors. She said that Mr. and Mrs. Headsen, visited Mrs. Headsen's mother in room 131, while six sons visited with their mother, Mrs. Nave, in 140. She also remembered that both families stayed for an hour and left before noon.

Mrs. Hanna added that the remaining visitor was Mr. Sutton, who visited his father in room 119 daily from 2:00 to 3:00 p.m., and that after his departure at 3:15, there were no other visitors.

She looked at O'Shea, then slowly bowed her head in silent thought. "It was a very quiet day, Lieutenant. No other visitors, and in addition to Dr. Harrison in 105, the only other staff present that day was Dr. Olson who left before 2 p.m., after briefly examining Mr. Sutton and Mrs. Nave. There's just nothing else."

O'Shea nodded with an understanding smile. "That's fine, Mrs. Hanna. Now could you tell me how you discovered Mrs. Digness' body?"

Again dropping her eyes, she sighed deeply before answering. "I was returning from a conference with Dr. Harrison in room 105. When I reached the nurses' station, I waved at Candice Crafton who had looked up from her paperwork. She waved back with her nice smile. We talked for a few minutes about Mr. Sutton's failing condition. He died last week.

"There was still nothing that seemed unusual, until I viewed the monitors. That's when I discovered that Mrs. Digness' monitor was blank. Mrs. Crafton saw my startled look, followed my eyes to the monitor and shouted 'Oh my God. It was fine ten minutes ago.' I told her to stay at the station, and I ran to Mrs. Digness' room. Dr. Harrison responded to our call and confirmed that Mrs. Digness was dead."

"Officially, we nurses view the monitors every fifteen minutes. But, when at our station, we automatically look at them much more often. As you know by the police reports, Mrs. Crafton said she viewed all monitors about twelve minutes before I returned to the station, and that Mr. Digness ran down the corridor past the nurses' station a few minutes later. Nurse Crafton thinks she may have automatically looked up at the monitors, and seeing nothing unusual, she returned to her paper work. Unfortunately, she just wasn't sure."

Listening carefully, O'Shea was also following his police interview notes for possible discrepancies. "I know, Mrs. Hanna. If Mrs. Crafton had been certain the monitors were all working when Mr.

Digness left, he would have immediately been cleared. Maybe even alive today, but I doubt it." O'Shea looked uneasily at nurse Hanna. "Is there anything else you can add? Was there anyone else you remember being in ICU that Wednesday?"

Again, Mrs. Hanna closed her eyes as she viewed in her mind. Slowly opening her eyes, she replied. "No. I've reviewed that day so many times. No one else."

O'Shea believed her, yet he had to ask. "Thank you, Mrs. Hanna. I have just one more question. Do you have a son named Jeff Hanna who goes to Polytechnic High?"

Mrs. Hanna sat in stunned silence for several minutes before bursting into tears. "Oh my dear God. Why?"

CHAPTER 47

When Karl Schwartz left the interview at Poly, Ellis knew he hadn't obtained anything substantial but a headache and one momentary slip in Schwartz' cool demeanor. He also realized that turning this slip into a solid suspect hinged on the answer to a single question by a man who resented questions and cops. Gritting his teeth, as he made the call he didn't want to make, Ellis heaved a deep sigh of relief when Diger both answered the phone and agreed to meet him at the front gate.

Approaching those black metal gates, with the probing eyes, screeching sounds and austere message, Ellis could feel the earlier pangs of uneasiness. Fortunately, McGuire was away on business.

Diger surprisingly smiled with a wave when Ellis drove up. "Do you want to come in for a bite to eat?"

Remembering the time he and O'Shea last ate there, Ellis grinned a decline. "No thanks. But hop in and we'll have something on me at one of the restaurants on Geary. Is that all right?"

Diger laughed. "Sure, that's fine. This place unnerves you a little, huh?"

Ellis nodded sheepishly. "Well, where's the nearest restaurant around here?"

Other than some small talk about the weather and good San Francisco restaurants, nothing of any substance was said until they were seated in a booth at Louie's, near the Cliff House.

Perched near a cliff overlooking the Pacific Ocean, the view at

Louie's was spectacular. Ordering a Vegiburger with onion rings and coffee, Ellis scanned the clear horizon, wondering why he had never been to Ocean Beach. "Boy, what a view. I've never been here or to the Pacific Ocean for that matter."

Diger, who only ordered coffee, listened with restrained impatience while softly strumming his fingers on the table. "That's amazing, Sergeant. Where the hell have you been all these years? Did you know this area has some of the purest air in the United States? You're looking at over three thousand miles of open ocean and a westerly flow of clean air."

Ellis watched a huge container ship make its starboard turn toward the entrance to the Golden Gate. "I guess that never really occurred to me."

With the arrival of their orders, Diger decided he had politely waited long enough. "Alright, Sergeant, what's up? But before you answer, remember, the Derrick Hansen episode is over."

Turning to Diger, Ellis threw both hands in the air with a grinning shrug. "Didn't even enter my mind. I assumed you were still interested in Helen's killer, and that's the only question I have."

Diger stopped strumming and leaned forward. "You got that right. What's the question?"

Ellis spread out six photographs of teenagers, including Schwartz, taken by crime lab police after the Trickers party. "Is the kid you told me about, who kept flirting with Helen Hansen, in one of these photos?"

In a few seconds, Diger was glaring at the third photo. "That's him. He looks like one of those Nazis in the old World War II movies."

Ellis softly chuckled until Diger looked up.

"What's so funny?"

Ellis turned toward the window with a thoughtful gaze in the direction of the container ship. "A lot of things, Mr. Diger. Not really funny. I guess satisfying is a better word. Beautiful view, clean air, great Vegiburger and photo number three of Karl Schwartz."

📖 📖 📖

Pounding down the corridor toward his cubicle, O'Shea saw Ida bent over the cooler, drinking water and unwittingly displaying her firm, round posterior. That sight triggered a quick flashback about one of his old anxieties. Then his grin blossomed into the happiest of full smiles.

Ida looked up as O'Shea stopped behind her. Matching his happy smile, she furtively scanned the corridor before grasping both of his hands. "How's my man and the eight cases?"

O'Shea squeezed her hands while thoughtfully studying her face. "Call me John. Everything is coming together, and thanks little lady. You're the best."

Unaware that O'Shea had overheard her conversation with Ben, Ida stared at him searchingly. "Golly, you make me so happy. I know that only Ellis and your special friends call you John. I don't know what I did, but I must be doing something right."

O'Shea wiped a tear sliding down her cheek. "You do everything right. It's all about people caring for each other." Hearing approaching footsteps, O'Shea gently patted her face, then, glanced back as he walked away. "Thanks, little lady."

📖 📖 📖

The three partners were all in a good mood when they finally sat together that afternoon. Each was eager to learn how the new pieces they were rapidly uncovering would bring them closer to solving the mystery of the *eight*.

Clutching notes scribbled on the back of his cable bill, O'Shea sat on the edge of his desk, grinning at his two partners. "Who's first?"

All three raised their hands simultaneously, but Hasselburg added a few extras. She raised and waved both hands, shouting, "Me, me, me."

Ellis dropped his hand. "You must have been teacher's pet or a pain in school."

Hasselburg smiled back at Ellis. "Both."

Glancing at his raised hand, O'Shea dropped his notes. "You win, Jill. I gotta hunch we're on the edge of overdoing this hand bit."

Both partners nodded. "Sorry, Lieutenant. Between the computer and phone, I'm in information overload. I've got a lot to share with you guys."

Ellis grabbed pen and note pad. "Go to it, Jill."

"I think it supports the direction our new theories are taking us. Remember State Park Officer Blake and those two SCUBA divers that had green blotches on the back of their yellow tanks? Well, I had a good chat with Gary Singleton, one of Poly's P.E. teachers and Diver

Down Club advisor. He told me that all the high school tanks are yellow. And, are you ready for this, some high schools, like Poly, put their school logo on the tanks."

Ellis had attended many school functions and knew the Poly mascot well. "A green, fat parrot that could look like a splash of green at a distance?"

"That's right, Paul. A green fluffy parrot, and I checked. No other school or dive shops in the Bay Area have a green logo."

Slipping Ellis a grinning wink, O'Shea gave Hasselburg one of his inscrutable stares. "I'll bet you have a lot more to share."

Scrolling the computer, Hasselburg gave a rapid nod. "Boy, do I. Five SCUBA tanks were loaned out by the Poly Diver Down Club on April 7th and returned April 10th. Consequently, Ed Lagler, Arnie Hanes, Frank Mathews, Jesse Jones, and Cynthia Lester were added to our suspect list of Poly students. And I have a friend at San Francisco State who is great with computers and demographics. Janice Tompkins teaches advanced computer use as a research tool. So I gave her the names and basic data we have on all of the Poly students even remotely associated with the eight crimes. I also included those five students who were in possession of Poly SCUBA tanks on April 8th. My question was what do they all have in common other than being Poly students. She collated all the available data on each student and e-mailed me her findings."

Ellis and O'Shea carefully looked over the printouts Hasselburg gave them.

"This is really useful data," Ellis said, as O'Shea gave Hasselburg a quick nod before underlining bits of information.

"Christ, it sure is. It's amazing. Look at this. Jerran Ramsey, Erick Taggart, and Karl Schwartz, three of our original four, have birthdays in April. Craven is close with a March 31st birthday, and both Ed Lagler and Frank Mathews, of the SCUBA group were born in April. What a hell of a coincidence, huh?"

"You got that right," added Ellis. "They're also all seniors, all 3.9 to 4.0 students, all males and all members of the Honor Society."

Busily scrolling other computer data, Hasselburg stopped abruptly with a glance at her partners.

Ellis noticed. "What else you got, Jill?"

"Well, three of the five SCUBA divers didn't seem to fit our suspect profile. One was a 2.0, C average senior, and the other two were juniors, one a female. Eliminating them even further as possible suspects was surprisingly easy. Each of their parents reported that the three had permission to attend a two-day ocean dive field trip up north in Vernalis, California on April 8th and 9th. Lagler and Mathews were already ocean qualified, and when I called, their parents assumed the boys were in school on the 8th of April." Hasselburg flicked another quick glance at her partners. "There's more. Poly records indicate Lagler and Mathews missed all their morning classes on April 8th."

O'Shea's concentration was riveted to the printout. Using a red pencil he grabbed from his desk, he connected bits and pieces of information that formed a tangle of circles, lines and arrows. He had the determination of a general mapping an invasion. O'Shea knew that, at last, they were nearing the final assault. No bogus suspects this time. They were approaching the mysterious murderers that had teased and frustrated them for weeks. Although he still had more questions than answers, this time he was confident each of their answers were leading them in the right direction. All they needed was some hard evidence. "Have we come up with any fingerprints, eye witnesses or anything to nail all this down?"

Hasselburg turned to Ellis, who had anticipated O'Shea's question. "It's kinda weird, John. Last night's lab report indicates a clear Craven fingerprint on the pole that levered the rock onto Nelson. There're also a couple of partials they haven't identified yet, and none of the prints taken from the Trickers party match. But since we don't have all the prints on Poly seniors, we might still find a match.

"It gets even more promising and puzzling at the same time. Among others, there's a smudged partial on Likert's jack handle that's a tenable match with Craven's index finger, and that's not all. His prints are all over the pieces of crossbow we found in the Poly track storage area."

O'Shea stared up toward the ceiling as if searching for answers. "Aw shit. All that hard evidence and he's dead. What the hell was he? The organizer of all the murders? A one-man crime wave? Or just a loose cannon whacko? And you know, his goddamned death creates even more of a mystery. Not just Jill's tree, but his cause of death. Tell Paul what we found, Jill."

Glancing at Ellis, Hasselburg scrolled her way to the coroner's report. "According to this report, Craig Craven died of cardiac arrest or heart failure. Etiology unknown...."

"His heart didn't really fail," O'Shea interrupted. "I talked with Dr. Stein, the M.E., and Craven's parents. The kid was healthy as a horse. He had a physical three months ago. No arrhythmias, occlusions or any other heart irregularities. No diseases. The little shit should have lived forever. There was no failure of the heart. It just stopped beating. Dr. Stein hasn't the slightest idea why the hell it stopped. It just did. Yeah, we're getting there, but there's plenty of mystery left."

Hasselburg turned from the computer, rested her left elbow on the desk, and laid her left cheek on the palm of her hand. Staring sideways at her partners, she heaved a deep sigh. "How did I get up that tree? How did Craven end up dead in the same tree? What is the Trickers part in all of this? Yes guys, it's still very spooky, at least to me."

Ellis could feel a slight leak in their well-inflated good moods. "We are getting there, Jill. We're on the right road, but in this business we gotta crawl before we can walk. Your methodical bulldogging has been a great help. Each new clue gets us closer."

O'Shea tilted his head sideways, looked at her, and matched her solemn stare with a broad smile. "Hey. Listen up. I'm still in a great mood. And thanks to you and Paul, we're on the final stretch, when it'll all make sense. What Paul is trying to say is that patience is an important part of police work. So hang in there, it'll all come together."

Hasselburg nodded with an anemic smile.

Then, sensing a bit of levity might help, Ellis raised his hand with a corny, "Me, me, me."

Both O'Shea and Hasselburg rolled their eyes with a frown.

Ellis didn't notice. "I've got another one of those bits and pieces for you. For both of you. Karl Schwartz went from an arrogant, irritating possible suspect, to an irritating, arrogant primary suspect. Remember, John? The kid's a master at evading critical questions, while making us feel like we've lost our interviewing skills. He even criticized me a couple times for asking leading questions. Well, I was ready to pack it in when I decided to ask him directly if he had ever talked to Helen Hansen. He blew it with a big fat denial. That's when I knew he lied, provided I could prove otherwise."

Ellis paused for a moment to increase the suspense. Glancing at O'Shea, he continued. "John will find this hard to believe, but I actually reinterviewed Matt Diger during lunch."

O'Shea squinted back at Ellis. "Come on. You really returned to McGuire's fortress alone?"

"Not really. McGuire was out of town, and we ate at Louie's by the Cliff House. Anyway, Diger positively identified Schwartz as the kid who frequently flirted with Mrs. Hansen." Ellis handed Hasselburg his notes. "Here's some more evidence to download. You see, Jill, we're getting there."

O'Shea tapped his empty cup with his pen for effect. "You ain't gonna upstage me, Paul. Because of Jill's casual comment to me earlier today, we now have a primary in our dead end Grace Digness murder. Jeff Hanna, Nurse Hanna's son, was the missing link. He apparently hung around the nurses so often no one paid much attention to him. You know, just a kid and son of one of the day shift nurses. I guess he was almost invisible, like a permanent fixture on the ward. And when I mentioned his name, his poor mom instantly flashed on his unnoticed presence that April 8th. He's also a Poly senior, honor student, physical science major and I'll bet a member of most of the clubs our other suspects are or were in."

With a healthy grin, Hasselburg tapped her half filled glass of Sprite with her stapler. "Jeff was also born in April. My God, we *are* getting there."

CHAPTER 48

The next few days were filled with tedious, painstaking police work. Hasselburg doggedly searched computer websites, school files and juvenile archives for any information even vaguely relevant to the Poly seniors. Her only break was a disturbing, but necessary, visit to the tree in Golden Gate Park where she had slept and Craven had died.

Among other duties, Ellis recanvassed Seacliff and the Post Street/Leavenworth area, this time with specific questions and pictures of possible suspects. He also returned to Poly to interview students, including the two SCUBA seniors.

O'Shea was also all over the city, starting with an interview with Jeff Hanna, followed by interviews with several Trickers. Then more crime lab, juvenile department and FBI consultations to further pursue the eight disks and local gang or club activities.

It was a hectic schedule for all three partners that provided encouraging leads, gratifying answers and additional frustrating riddles.

📖 📖 📖

Driving along Seacliff Avenue off El Camino del Mar at 7:30 a.m., Ellis couldn't help replaying his backward tumble down the marble stairs, and the nervous security guards with huge guns pointed at his head. *Think I'll pass on the classical chimes and just slowly cruise*, he thought. *Let's see who's out here when Helen used to take her walk.*

He didn't have long to wait. Strolling down Seacliff toward Twenty-Fifth Avenue were two teenage girls, weighted down by backpacks loaded with books. Slightly nervous and overly cautious, Ellis needed to avoid more screaming females. Pulling along side the girls, Ellis called to them in his most official voice as he flashed his badge. "I'm Sergeant Ellis of the San Francisco Police Department. May I ask you young ladies a couple of questions?"

To his surprise, both girls quickly giggled their way to his open window. "Where's your gun and handcuffs and all that stuff?" wisecracked the chubbier girl with a round face full of braces.

"Can we have a ride?" preened the petite, rosy-cheeked one who looked about nine.

"It's OK," added the chubby girl. "Her dad's a judge and mine's a city supervisor."

Pulling away from the two heads peering into his car, Ellis knew better than to encourage their flirtatious comments with even a smile. "I need some information," he said officiously. "Do you girls go to school this way during the week, and what school do you go to?"

Trying the locked door, the chubby girl looked at her friend with another giggle. "Karen goes to Poly and I go to Lincoln"

"And what's your name?" Ellis asked as he finally managed to pull his badge away from Karen.

"He wants to know my name," she giggled. "I'm Samantha. Are you going to torture us?"

No, but you're torturing me, Ellis thought.

Barely tolerating their snickers, tee-hees and little hands reaching through the window, Ellis managed to tease a few comments out of them that made it all worthwhile.

Both girls told Ellis they had been taking the bus on Twenty-Fifth Avenue every weekday morning since they enrolled in high school as freshmen last September. On their first Seacliff walk to the bus stop, they met a tall, handsome Poly senior named Karl, who walked with them daily. Their flirtatious exchanges were fun, even when Karl got a little physical by rubbing their breasts or inner thighs. He even suggested they get naked behind the rocks near China Beach. But that was going too far. The flirtatious bus stop walks continued until about the second week in April when Karl abruptly stopped coming. The last time they saw him was about a week ago in the neighborhood. Despite their greetings, he ignored them.

Escaping from the two girls with a terse, "Thank you," Ellis cruised the area for another hour, questioning dog walkers, delivery people, more school kids and other early risers with no further success. His trip to Poly was minimally successful.

Ed Lagler and Frank Mathews brimmed with everything but uneasiness. They were polite, attentive and seemingly cooperative, with not a trace of hesitation in responding to Ellis' questions. There were no contradictions because virtually all of their answers were cleverly accurate.

Sure they were at Aquatic Park the morning of April 8th. They frequently dove there and around nearby Pier 39. Yes, all their equipment was borrowed from the Diver Down Club as usual, and after their dive, they hurried back to Mathews' car, hoping to make it to their morning Physics class, which they missed when snarled in traffic. Certainly, each had quickly nodded, they noticed Porpoise swimmers all the time.

The only two *no's* were when asked if they had seen anything suspicious or brushed against any Aquatic Park swimmers that morning. Ellis left Poly with a few more stops in mind. He had no doubt Lagler and Mathews drowned Sutherland and that, like the other student suspects, they would never admit it. Progress was on the mark but agonizingly slow, even for him. Ellis was acutely aware that the bits of neoprene under Sutherland's fingernails weren't, as legal evidence, a *smoking gun*.

📖 📖 📖

Jeff Hanna was a paragon of sincerity when interviewed at the hospital by O'Shea. He tearfully told O'Shea his heart was broken when he learned of Mrs. Digness's brutal death. Easily acknowledging he was at the nurses' station that day, he just as easily insisted he left about a half hour before she must have died. Staring at O'Shea with pleading, reddened eyes, Hanna added on his own, "If only I hadn't left, I might have been able to stop whoever did this."

He also apologetically contradicted nurse Crafton's reluctant statement, in his presence that he was on the floor near the nurses' station after Mr. Digness left and shortly before she and Mrs. Hanna discovered the blank Digness monitor. "I'm around so often they probably didn't notice that I was gone. I had to go home earlier than usual to pick up my chemistry notebook before class."

O'Shea had checked with Hanna's chemistry teacher, Mr. Frankel, who verified Hanna's presence at the 5:00 to 6:00 p.m. chemistry class. When asked, however, if there was anything unusual about Hanna's behavior that day, Mr. Frankel's reply eliminated any lingering doubts O'Shea might have had. "Mr. Hanna is a brilliant student. He'll make a fine scientist. He's always an active participant and early for the five o'clock class. Except on the 8th, he was a little late and noticeably quiet."

Similar to Ellis, O'Shea knew this Poly senior was guilty. He also felt stymied without solid, compelling evidence while knowing Hanna was not about to confess.

Recontacting juvenile authorities and other local criminal justice agencies was no major help, just a few more useful tidbits. Driving back to the office, his head was still throbbing with questions. *How did this happen to such young, bright kids? How could these kids lie so convincingly? Who the hell organized these kids...and the disks...and the Trickers...and the goddamn tree?*

📖 📖 📖

After dozens of calls, interagency computer scrolling, and exhaustive file reviews, Hasselburg thought she was getting somewhere. Adding Hanna, Lagler, and Mathews to the list of possible suspects, she was thrilled to find no change in the trend. They were all senior honor students with birthdays in April. *This has got to be more than a coincidence*, she reasoned. Embracing her hunch with a burst of excitement, Hasselburg spent half a day probing into secret student societies or meetings. Her search led her nowhere.

How about parents? She wondered. What she found was no indication of parental interest in more than any two of the seniors, nor were there any indications of groups of seniors hanging out together at some parent's home.

Trickers? Reviewing every interview, stakeout report and recorded Trickers activities since the Armory heist yielded no evidence of any connection with the Poly seniors or victims.

Disappointed, she began agonizing over what she might have missed. Hasselburg had learned from her partners that police work is method not genius. There're few brilliant insights, fewer uncanny revelations—just patient examining of every possibility. In desperation, she decided to begin again with Poly and its school organizations. That's when Hasselburg finally hit the jackpot.

📖 📖 📖

During their frenzied follow-ups over the next few days, the three partners kept bumping into each other with grinning nods of progress and tight-lipped frowns of frustration.

O'Shea had managed to hug Ida once and wave at her twice, while Ellis marveled at how his kids had grown. His wife wasn't amused. Nor was Hasselburg's roommate laughing when she forgot about their lunch and dinner dates. Even on sacred Sunday, the partners kept at it with an early morning special meeting at their cubicle.

O'Shea was a tad tired and grumpy, especially when he couldn't find any coffee on their floor. Yesterday's dregs were gone, except for Ellis' stale cup of cold, creamy, sugar with its usual dash of coffee. That sight made O'Shea even grumpier as they waited for Hasselburg.

"Jesus, this must be the first time since she started that she hasn't been the first one here. Did she get the message?"

Ellis rechecked his watch, and grabbed the phone. "I talked to her yesterday."

On the fourth ring, Hasselburg walked in with Burger King coffees, donuts and a relaxed, near saintly smile. "Didn't mean to keep you two waiting. Guess I slept too well last night."

Expecting a more characteristic breathless apology, both detectives were a bit stunned. "Everything OK?" asked O'Shea.

"Just fine," she said, passing out the coffees and donuts. "I got you four extra sugars and five little creams. Is that enough, Paul?"

Ellis nodded with a quizzical grin. "That's just fine."

Gulping down half a cup of coffee, O'Shea grasped the other cup with his left hand. "Thanks for the second cup. Christ, do I need it. Now we can get rolling and see if we can ever wrap up these goddamned eight." Slamming his fist on the desk, O'Shea half expected Hasselburg to eagerly squirm out of her seat or at least raise her hand.

Ellis was as surprised as O'Shea when Hasselburg still sat quietly with her peaceful smile. "Are you OK, kid?"

Hasselburg gave a rapid, impatient nod. "I'm great. Really. I just want to hear from you two first."

A bit puzzled, O'Shea and Ellis gave each other an, *Oh well, what the hell* crooked grin before organizing their own notes.

Ellis was ready and willing, with a detailed account of how the two giggling girls confirmed his suspicions about Karl Schwartz's murder of Helen Hansen. Equally convinced the two Poly SCUBA divers drowned Sutherland, he acknowledged that all the evidence on those seniors was circumstantial.

As Ellis began further explaining that the crime lab had a possible match on a partial print found on the Nelson leverage pole, Hasselburg calmly interrupted. "Was it Gene Richter by any chance?"

Ellis grinned at Hasselburg. "You beat me to the Lab report. Did you download it already?"

"No, Paul. I didn't know. Just a good guess."

Looking at her with restrained curiosity, Ellis continued, while O'Shea scratched his head with a frown. "On the positive side, we've got a print match from a live suspect. On the negative side, the print is so smudged it probably wouldn't hold up in court. It could be Richter but not enough points. It could be someone else."

Munching casually on a glazed donut, Hasselburg slowly shook her head as she looked up at Ellis. "Bet you a dozen donuts it's his print."

Ellis shrugged, O'Shea heaved an impatient sigh, and they both tried ignoring her, wondering if it were a monthly female thing.

After conceding all his other police work yielded nothing substantial, Ellis grabbed a chocolate donut and slumped in his chair.

Swallowing the last drop of his second cup of coffee, O'Shea took over. "My turn. You had your chance, Jill," he grumbled with a twisted smile.

"Age before beauty." She snickered.

First, O'Shea ran down his disappointing interview with Jeff Hanna. Staring down at his empty cup for a moment, he glanced plaintively at his partners. "What is it about this little shit? I knew he pulled the plug on Mrs. Digness the minute he offered those cool, plausible explanations and dramatized regrets for everything. And you know, it's like some force holding these kids together. I don't think they'll break. Craven might have run his mouth but he's very dead. His goddamned young healthy heart just decided to stop. By the way, for what it's worth, he's the only one with a juvenile record. He used to torture neighborhood animals."

Ellis was shuffling through his stack of papers. "Listen to this new addition to the Craven enigma. Remember the two kids bending over Winston's body. With pictures of our Poly senior suspects passed around, who do you think was positively identified as one of the two?"

O'Shea winced. "Jesus H. Christ. That little jerk was everywhere. What's the word?"

"Ubiquitous," Hasselburg replied without looking up from the computer she had turned on.

Ellis shot O'Shea a raised eyebrow glance. "Now that was quick, she belongs on one of those quiz shows."

O'Shea gave an idol grin. "Yeah, that was the word all right. You know, it's really ironic too. If he was alive, we could probably wrap all this up."

Ellis nodded. "I know."

"You also know that Taggart's our primary shooter suspect and, of course, no one IDed him. Right?"

Ellis stared at Hasselburg who seemed to be ignoring her partners. "Right, of course not."

"Well, we're not going to let Craven rest in peace. His death was too damned convenient to be another coincidence. I don't care what the coroner says. He was somehow whacked. None of this is random or coincidence."

Both detectives noticed Hasselburg's vigorous nods. "Hey, are you listening?" Ellis shouted.

"Back with us again?" asked O'Shea.

Hasselburg glanced up from the computer. "I've never left you guys, honest."

With new number three power reading glasses pinched low on his nose, O'Shea scanned his last few scribbles. "Here's a brand new fat piece for our puzzle. Yesterday I went to Aaron's Creamery on Irving Street. I had another chat with the owner, Aaron Vargas. None of our Poly suspect seniors, including the *ubiquitous* Craven, hung out there in the morning. But, when I showed him a year book senior class photo, he immediately pointed to a scrawny kid in the top row as a regular, every week day morning."

Hasselburg glanced over at O'Shea. "Leslie Stewart?"

Ellis tried to stifle a grin, as O'Shea threw his hands up in exasperation. "Holy shit, Jill! What do you have over there, a goddamned crystal ball? For someone who ain't saying much, you've got one hell of a lot to say."

Hasselburg cringed, wrinkling up her face. "I'm sorry, you guys. Really. Thanks to your training, I think the information I've gathered solves much of our mystery. Just in case you came up with similar evidence, I wanted to hear it from one of you first."

Both detectives shrugged at each other before slowly shaking their heads at Hasselburg. O'Shea even broke into a smile. "Thanks for your consideration." Then, glancing at Ellis, he added. "That's about all we've got. Now maybe it's your turn to teach us. We're ready."

Reddening with embarrassment, Hasselburg uneasily faced her partners with lowered head and wide eyes. "Gosh, I shouldn't have waited. Like I was mocking you. I'm so sorry."

"Hey," O'Shea replied, "age before beauty."

"Besides," Ellis joined in, "this isn't a contest. What one of us solves, we all solve. So, what have you got? "

O'Shea flashed a big grin. "Me too, but it better be good."

Hasselburg took a deep breath, smiled faintly and began from memory. "We've all been racking our brains about what these Poly seniors have in common. Well, I've had the advantage of easy computer access. Except for Craven, all the old and new suspects were born sometime in April, and like Craven they're all seniors, male, and honor students. So, excluding all but April born, high I.Q. male Poly seniors, I came up with a list of nine."

O'Shea politely raised his hand. "Including Leslie Stewart and Gene Richter I'll bet."

Hasselburg nodded. "Absolutely right, Lieutenant. I was hoping there'd be some evidence of their involvement."

"How'd you know John was going to say it was Richter's partial?" asked Ellis.

"I didn't. Wishful thinking. I guessed that it was one of the two new possibles. Since Stewart is a chemistry major, I was hoping he was involved in the Anderson drug murder. And, well, Richter's dad is a Taravel Station watch commander."

O'Shea gazed vacantly at the ceiling for a moment. "Yeah, I remember him now. We used to rattle doors out in the foggy Richmond District. Kind of a *by the book* guy. He knew all police procedures inside and out. I think he memorized the Penal Code. We got along, but for him there were no exceptions to any rule. Kind of strict. He wanted to stay a uniform, and now he's a precinct captain. I wouldn't be surprised if his kid is sick of cops."

O'Shea looked kindly at Hasselburg. "So far, Jill, there's nothing about your reasoning I can fault. You're shaping into one hell of a sleuth." Looking at Ellis taking notes, O'Shea went on. "Jill has convincingly expanded our group of primaries. One for each murder plus Craven roaming all over like some kind of facilitator."

Ellis glanced up with a nod. "Right. I'll bet we'll still end up with eight random victims but with a single motive, possibly orchestrated by Craven."

O'Shea shook his head so hard his number three's went flying off his nose. "That's not the impression I got from Craven. Maybe more of a troublemaker that the other eight could have wasted. They sure have the brainpower to off the guy. And what about the Trickers?"

Hasselburg was also shaking her head while back to rapidly waving both raised hands. "Hey, hey, you guys. I haven't finished."

Both partners stopped cold, as if a bit surprised. Ellis stood up and bowed. "Boy, we've been alone here too long. Guess our old habits are hard to break."

"Paul's right," blurted O'Shea. "I apologize, but I really thought you were finished. You have more? Great. Lay it on us."

"Thank you. Now, where the heck was I?" Turning to the computer, she did a fast scroll. "Oh, yeah. I've agreed with you two all along that there's got to be some club, gang, society or organizer behind these murders. So extending the nine primary suspect theory further, I figured there just had to be someone or some place they all met together. As you know, only a couple had anything to do with the Trickers, and Craven wasn't exactly an inspirational leader type. So I focused on Poly activities the nine might have in common.

"Although science seemed to be their primary interest, their special majors varied from chemistry, biology, and physics, to math and engineering. Except for Taggart, they also seem to have a uniform disinterest in sports, but all nine were involved in some school organization, including the Honor Society, the Omegas, the Alchemists, the Thespians, and the Astronomers. They were all honor students who were automatically accepted in the Honor Society after four consecutive honor semesters, but so were seventy-five others. And even though Karl Schwartz is now president, the Honor Society advisor, Mrs. Bramkurst, said only four or five of our nine ever attend the meetings.

"As for the other clubs, it took a bit of probing, since much of the information we needed wasn't computerized. Anyway, the Omegas are an interesting group of history buffs, exploring the demise of the Greek culture. According to Mr. Onassis, the faculty leader, of the fifteen students, mainly females, five of the nine are regulars. The Thespians' faculty head, Mr. Trisken, praised the three or four regulars of our nine. There are about thirty-five in the club and they do

Shakespearian plays.

"I had an adrenalin rush when I learned from Ms. Ho, Astronomy Club faculty leader, that seven of the nine, including Jerran Ramsey, had been members."

"Who hadn't attended?" asked O'Shea.

Hasselburg gave O'Shea one of her sideways glances. "I thought you might be curious about that. Schwartz and Craven never attended, but pursuing it a little further, I learned that these two aren't particularly fond of Orientals."

Continuing to write, Ellis heaved a deep sigh. "Craven wasn't particularly fond of anything except maybe violence."

O'Shea glanced at his empty coffee cup. "If I'm going to concentrate on Jill's stuff and finish our donuts, can we have a quick break?"

In a flash, all three were down the corridor, headed for Burger King across the street. O'Shea was in the lead with the empty corridor coffee pot.

Less than ten minutes later, they were back at their desks, loaded with more donuts, beverages and a full pot of coffee. Filling his cup, O'Shea reached for a donut. "You ready, Jill?"

"Ready," she said, accepting a Diet Sprite from Ellis. "I've saved the best for last."

O'Shea nodded with a full mouth.

"It's all about the last Poly club on my list of possibles. I never did manage to directly contact the Alchemist faculty advisor. I must have left five messages. But I did get a message from him. An e-mail on my home computer of all places. Strange, huh? He knew it was a police request with our website. Yet he sends the message to me, personally."

Hasselburg gazed thoughtfully into her partners' eyes as she presented each with a copy of the message.

All three partners were stunned by the e-mail message. It seemed like a simple encouragement that they were approaching the end of a long, mysterious journey.

O'Shea and Ellis slowly read the copy several times before turning to Hasselburg and expressing their deep felt gratitude.

O'Shea lifted his coffee cup high. "Here's to a fine detective. If I'm still breathing when you run for Chief, you got my vote."

Lifting his cup, Ellis stood facing Hasselburg. "I'll second that. Thank you, Jill."

Dear Officer Hasselburg: Well done. The list below represents all Alchemist members since its inception a year ago. Good Luck.
   Al Stricker

> *Craig Craven*
> *Jeff Hanna*
> *Ed Lagler*
> *Frank Mathews*
> *Jerran Ramsey*
> *Gene Richert*
> *Karl Schwartz*
> *Leslie Stewart*
> *Erick Taggart.*

CHAPTER 49

Monday morning the three partners barely contained their uneasy exuberance. They were on the brink of actually touching the mystery of the eight cases, yet they sensed it might cost them mangled hands. After such a long, frustrating struggle, the pieces were suddenly fitting together, perhaps a little too easily, as if being escorted to the answer or led to the slaughter. Either way, they also knew there was simply no option. They had to methodically and carefully keep going.

O'Shea was first to arrive. By 7:15 he had finished his routine and two cups of coffee when Ellis came in. Hasselburg was a few minutes behind. As she entered their cubicle with more donuts, she saw Ellis leaning over O'Shea's shoulder. Following their eyes to O'Shea's desk, there were the eight little disks in a neat row.

Glancing up at Hasselburg, Ellis nodded a quick greeting. "Come here, Jill. Look at this. The surprises keep coming. You probably figured this out already."

Peering over her partners' shoulders, she read the new word several times. "Golly. No, I didn't know. It may not be the Trickers after all. You just moved the 'S' from the last to the first letter and it spells 'Stricker'."

Removing his reading glasses O'Shea rubbed his eyes. "Morning, Jill. I'd better up the power on these babies. So, you're not a big Scrabble fan either. Last night I looked at the Trickers name for about the tenth time when the 'S' seemed to take off and fly in front of the 'T'. Got any apple fritters?"

Hasselburg laid the bag on O'Shea's desk. "There're two on the bottom, and yes I do like Scrabble. Guess I just didn't picture his name in letters."

"Me neither," said Ellis, "and I play the game with my family a lot."

Digging through the bag of donuts, O'Shea frowned at both of them. "I don't play."

Ellis grabbed the bag of donuts as O'Shea managed to remove an apple fritter. "So? Come on over some night and play with us. It's fun."

"I'd rather eat apple fritters," O'Shea mumbled with a full mouth.

$$\square \quad \square \quad \square$$

All levity faded with the last of the donuts. They agreed that, as the probable ringmaster of at least eight crimes, Al Stricker was a puzzling combination of the mysterious and the dangerous. They still didn't know what he was really up to. They did know clearly that he had to be approached with the utmost caution or arrested with irrevocable evidence.

First, they needed to learn as much as possible about Al Sticker's background, his relationship with other faculty and students and his possible connection to the Trickers. Ellis' daughter, Beth, also needed to be questioned. If Stricker were responsible for the notes on Beth's locker, why? And were the Trickers/Stricker disk letters coincidence, deception or—what?

By 9:00 a.m. the three partners were on their way to Polytechnic High School, the most obvious source for answers. Once again they were to learn that each answered question served to deepen the mystery.

While Ellis talked with Beth, Hasselburg chatted with her girlfriend's sophomore brother, Brad Kruger, and his pals Al Hoffner and Pete Baker, all Trickers. At the same time, O'Shea was astonished by the information he was getting from Robin Hungerford, Dean of Boys, and teachers at the main office.

After giving O'Shea an official printout of Stricker's background, Hungerford was delighted to discuss him. He explained that when he initially interviewed Stricker, he was so impressed with such outstanding credentials and pleasant, unpretentious demeanor that he immediately recommended him to Ms. Belotti for a top tenured appointment as head of the math and physics departments. Without prompting from O'Shea, Hungerford further stated, "Such a nice, friendly guy with degrees, publications and prior positions that would qualify him for president of most universities." Mrs. Cummings, Hungerford's receptionist and personal secretary, had a curiously different impression of Al Stricker. "His twisted smile looks like a sneer—his deep set, dark gray eyes, seem to stare menacingly with kind of a yellow glow, like a cat or panther—he walks in an ungainly lumbering way with metal clicking sounds, like a robot maybe."

Smiling a thanks to Mrs. Cummings, O'Shea started to feel those familiar pangs of confusion. *Jesus, is this the same guy? Maybe women see Stricker differently.* Searching for more opinions, O'Shea began smilingly accosting any adult who entered the main office.

Ms. Bolinger, a sociology teacher, gushingly described Stricker as "handsome, very poetic, with a charismatic manner." When asked about his gait, she nearly swooned. "Oh, gosh. He's so graceful. He seems to glide along so smoothly; I bet he's a marvelous dancer."

In glaring contrast, Miss Wagner described Stricker as, "crotchety—unresponsive—hunched over—never looked directly at me." She added that, as a physical science teacher, their offices were on the same floor, and even though she introduced herself and greeted him daily, he never replied.

O'Shea interviewed a cross section of other teachers with increasingly puzzling results. "He is tall and handsome—short and squat—openly friendly—wizened—frail—athletic—nice—sinister—strange." All faculty members did agree, however, that during his two semesters at Polytechnic, he had been unnoticed at faculty meetings and never interacted with any of them socially. No one knew Al Stricker.

Desperate for a credible opinion, O'Shea decided to contact one last faculty member, one of his most trusted old buddies, Dick Boyd.

O'Shea found Boyd about to leave his last morning history class. After a handshaking, hugging reunion, they sat at the back of the emptying classroom, complaining about why they hadn't been able to get together sooner.

When they finally got around to Al Stricker, Boyd unwittingly unnerved O'Shea with his non-opinion. "You know, pal, he's been here about a year, and I don't think I've ever seen the guy. I've heard about him. Everything from Gandhi and Batman to Gandolf and Darth

Vader. Everybody seems to see this guy differently." Patting O'Shea's arm, Boyd shook his head with a chuckle. "I guess to me he's invisible."

📖 📖 📖

Hasselburg wasn't doing much better. Expecting helpful answers to their puzzle, all she was getting was muddied puzzling answers. Rounding up Brad Kruger and his two sophomore friends was easy. All three were in the same Geometry class. But, making sense out of their comments was another matter.

As usual, Kruger was openly friendly, eager to help and very much an awkward adolescent with his over-sized, droopy pants, teenage jargon and boyish chuckles when joking with his friends.

According to him, *Professor* Stricker was the best science teacher he ever had. "He is so patient and explains everything real clear, like I knew the stuff all along." Kruger further said he occasionally received private tutoring sessions, during which times Stricker never mentioned or asked about the Trickers. Hasselburg also learned from Kruger that the *Professor* was "kind and gentle." Kruger even remembered clearly what Stricker said when asked about joining the Alchemists.

"Perhaps, when you're a senior with straight A's."

The replies from Hoffner and Baker were so different from Kruger's comments, Hasselburg thought it was like talking about a different person. Both were in agreement, during separate interviews, that Stricker was too strict, impatiently giving hasty explanations to complex issues, while scolding any student who dared ask questions. Yet, they did have strikingly different opinions of his appearance. Hoffner alluded to Stricker as "big and mean looking," whereas Baker sarcastically called him "a skinny wimp." Neither ever heard him mention the Trickers or the Alchemists.

📖 📖 📖

Sitting together in the Poly bleachers, Ellis was surprised when his daughter told him she had never spoken to Stricker. Intending to take trigonometry from him in the fall, she had, however, paid attention to friends who had taken courses from him.

"Opinions," she said, "varied from harsh and austere to easy going and friendly. They were no help." She smiled.

Asking about club activities, Ellis was disappointed when Beth shrugged, explaining she hadn't heard any of her friends mention the Alchemists or Trickers. Beth also thought it a bit curious that, even though Stricker never approached her, he always smiled and nodded when they passed in the halls.

When Ellis asked what Stricker looked like to her, she paused, as if in deep thought, "Gee, I really don't know, Dad. He just looks like a teacher."

As puzzled as his partners were about Stricker's identity, Ellis decided to see him for himself. So, after walking Beth to her next class, he headed for Stricker's office. His strategy was to introduce himself as a father interested in his daughter's science curriculum. For some strange reason, he wasn't at all surprised to learn that Stricker was away on business for a few days.

Before leaving the school, he did manage to talk briefly with four of the eight suspects on their way to classes. Taggart and Richert, as usual, were the least compliant, while Mathews and Lagler were only superficially cooperative. *At least*, Ellis thought, t*hey're all willing to describe Stricker as some kind of genius Guru who's enhanced their lives forever.*

Returning to their cubicle Monday afternoon, the partners had lost some of their optimism. There were still too many unanswered questions. *Is Al Stricker going to be as elusive as his identity is amorphous? What does he really look like? What's his involvement in all those deaths? Who is this guy? What does Beth Ellis have to do with all this? And the tree?*

Just as Ellis was about to share his morning interviews, Hasselburg, staring at the computer screen, started frantically waving her hands. Both partners glanced at her with a deep sigh of impatience.

"It's not me. We're getting an e-mail from Stricker this minute. Thought you'd want to know."

Within a nanosecond, Ellis and O'Shea were practically perched on Hasselburg's sagging shoulders.

"Oh, shit," O'Shea shouted, "I don't have my readers."

Hasselburg winced. "I think you're dislocating my shoulders. Why don't you both sit down and I'll read it to you."

Ellis and O'Shea were back at their desks in an instant.

> *To Officer Hasselburg, Sergeant Ellis and Lieutenant O'Shea:*
> *You have worked so very hard, and now it is time for your*
> *reward. Please come to our Wednesday, 5:00 p.m. Alchemist*
> *meeting at Polytechnic High School Quonset Hut 48. It will be*
> *informal. Guns and warrants unnecessary. You will learn all*
> *you need to know for some understanding and closure.*
> *Dr. Al Stricker.*

Momentarily speechless, all three partners turned toward each other with slacked jaws.

"Christ! Who is this guy?" O'Shea wondered aloud. "Big brother?"

Thumbing through his notes, Ellis shook his head. "I learned so much about him today that, you know, I actually know nothing about him."

Hasselburg joined in. "Me too. All those many descriptions I gathered today of Al Stricker say he has no specific identity."

Shuffling through his own notes, O'Shea stopped at the background information Hungerford had given him from the Superintendent of Schools. "He knows a hell of a lot more about us than we know of him. Why is he so damn polite and grateful or is this some kind of sarcastic threat. And what in hell does he intend to give us Wednesday? Damn it, what's he really up to?"

Ellis noticed the official-looking paper, idly clutched in O'Shea's hand. "What's that in your hand, John? Some school background stuff on Stricker?"

O'Shea looked at the paper, then at his partners. "I'm ashamed to tell you, I got this from Hungerford and I haven't even read it. Here I am bitching about not knowing Stricker."

"That's OK," Hasselburg grinned, "you probably couldn't see it without your glasses."

O'Shea frowned back. "Here. Why don't you look it over and run it by us?"

Hasselburg read the document carefully before staring up at her partners. "Wow."

"Wow what?" countered Ellis.

"Well, first of all, he's some kind of genius. He has more professional letters after his name than I have *in* my name. He's published well over a hundred journal articles on physics, quantum mechanics and chemistry. He even has a parapsychology degree and respected publications in India on psychic phenomena. He was an honored Harvard professor, but he resigned after a year. Gosh, he's only in his forties."

O'Shea was still frowning. "What the hell is this guy doing in a high school? Did he rape the Harvard chancellor's wife?"

Hasselburg grinned with a shrug. "I wouldn't be surprised. His whole non-academic background does seem cloudy. No explanations for leaving prestigious positions after fairly brief stays. What do you think, Paul?"

Ellis dropped his notepad, leaned back, and stretched. "You got me. The more we know, the stranger he gets. Who knows? He sure has a broad range of interests. Like a constant pursuit of knowledge. Maybe he gets bored and just likes to travel when the challenge is gone."

O'Shea broke into a smile. "Maybe he's a hit man for hire with an academic cover-up."

"Hey, you guys, there's more. This will give you plenty to speculate about." Her partners listened quietly as Hasselburg highlighted aspects of his youth and family background. "He was born in Germany on the 8th of April—his Polio at age thirteen should have prevented him from ever walking—his father, Elvin was born on an April 15th and his mom, Elizabeth, was born on April 30th"

Ellis almost fell off his chair reaching for the printout in Hasselburg's hand. "Let me see that!"

It also jolted O'Shea. "Jesus Christ. It's beginning to make sense."

Unaware of Ellis' daughter's birthday, Hasselburg looked at her partners a bit perplexed. "Golly, I didn't know I read so well."

Ellis slowly turned toward her with a thoughtful stare. "Beth is short for Elizabeth, and John knows my kid's birthday is April 30th, this Wednesday. Any wonder why Stricker has such affection for Beth, with the same name and birthday as his mother?"

Hasselburg appeared genuinely stunned. "Wow. His whole life seems engulfed in Aprils."

O'Shea gently leaned over Ellis with a soft smile. "You OK, pal?"

Rereading the printout, Ellis nodded.

"Yeah, Paul. That info's probably the tip of the iceberg. I'll bet he's one bitter guy, packing a bunch of grief. But your daughter is no doubt the safest kid on the block."

Looking up at both partners, Ellis gave a crooked, tentative smile. "I know you're probably right, just hope he's not like the old King Kong movie, where the big terrifying brute kidnaps the damsel. You two know whatever Stricker is or isn't, he's still a mysterious, formidable opponent."

O'Shea sat quietly for a few moments, pondering their contradictory information. "I can't argue a word you said. He not only has the advantage of genius, he's driven by the power of rage and love and grief. The son of a bitch could just as easily kill us as kiss us."

Turning off the computer, Hasselburg glanced soulfully at the ceiling. "In a showdown with him, I guess I would feel powerless. He didn't kill me and I wasn't born in April." Hasselburg closed her eyes with a deep sigh. "He has another power over us. I think he's evil."

Slamming his fist on the desk, O'Shea offered a wide grin. "Evil, ambivalent, brilliant or just another asshole, we'll find out a lot more Wednesday."

"You got that right," Ellis added. "So let's decide how we want to do this. Just the three of us, or the SWAT team?"

CHAPTER 50

Waiting together outside Quonset Hut 48, O'Shea and his partners looked at each other with reassuring nods that everything was under control. They had decided police back-up was unnecessary. There weren't going to be arrests, they were simply invited to a meeting. After all, it was *both* Elizabeths' birthdays, certainly not a day of violence, they hoped.

It was 4:55 p.m. and lots of other thoughts were swirling through their minds. *Five more minutes and the mysteries will be revealed or we'll be mocked—maybe even dead.*

Hasselburg was the first to speak since they parked their car. "Oh, my God."

Sliding their hands towards their weapons, O'Shea and Ellis stiffened in readiness. "What, where?" they whispered.

"Don't you hear it? I think it's Frederick Chopin."

"Is he in there too?" Ellis replied with a strained grin of relief.

O'Shea wasn't amused. "This isn't the time for your corn."

Pressing a finger over her lips, Hasselburg turned slightly toward her partners. "Shhhh. Can't you hear the music? It's Chopin's *Funeral March*. Not exactly a welcoming tune."

O'Shea glanced at his watch. "Hell, he's European. Maybe he has funeral services for his mother every year."

Ellis gave Hasselburg a wink. "Oh sure, John. Now who's joking?"

O'Shea responded with one of his eye-rolling sighs. "It's just about five. Let's do it."

Approaching the Quonset hut door, the music became clearer, more foreboding. Ellis imagined shadowy zombies mourning their deaths.

O'Shea figured the sounds were warnings, to scare them off, while Hasselburg found Chopin's music beautiful, sad and eerie.

Within reach of the Quonset hut door, O'Shea rechecked his watch. It was exactly 5:00 p.m. Concerned they might disrupt whatever was happening inside, O'Shea gave a loud, friendly announcement as he slowly opened the door. "Hello! It's Jack O'Shea and his partners. Can we come in?"

Other than Chopin's *Funeral March*, there was no answer.

Virtually tiptoeing through the door with fixed smiles and arms waving, all three partners were stunned. What they saw sagged their arms, smiles and jaws.

With no outside light through the drawn shades, the large room was aglow with brilliant flickering lights from hundreds of multicolored candles casting dancing, swaying, gargoyled shadows on the curved ceiling.

In the center of the floor was a perfectly symmetrical white star ringed by a red circle, about twelve feet in diameter, with each of the star's five points touching the edge of the circle. Bordering the red circle were ten equidistant chairs facing inward toward the center of the star. Directly behind the ten chairs, was an outer green circle. One additional chair was situated just behind the outer green circle, to the right of a leather wing-backed chair. It was obvious to the partners that the wing-backed chair, directly opposite the first point of the star, was special. All the others were metal folding chairs placed clockwise, like the numbers on a ten point clock, except the wing-backed chair at the top represented number one rather than ten.

All but the first, second and eleventh chair were occupied by students. The eeriness amplified when the partners realized none of the eight seated students were looking at them, or showing any signs of movement. Repeating his friendly greeting, O'Shea and his partners scanned the students carefully for some response. There was nothing, not even an eye blink.

Moving cautiously toward the outer green circle for a closer look deepened their confusion. Ellis stopped behind the third chair from the top. It was Karl Schwartz, as arrogant as ever, with a smug, chiseled smile, jutting jaw and a piercing stare that could cut through steel.

Creeping up on the sixth chair, Hasselburg recognized Richert from his photo. Despite his ramrod posture, she thought he looked peaceful. Eyes closed, rosy cheeks and a pleasant smile.

O'Shea was studying Hanna, seated stiffly in chair number eight. He noticed the half closed, droopy eyes focused on the center of the star, and the protruding lower lip that suggested sadness.

While the music continued its dreary procession, the three partners slowly walked the outer circle looking for some sign of consciousness. All three were pondering the same questions. *Are they drugged, under some spell or performing for us? And where's Al Stricker?*

Hasselburg finally looked up at her partners. They were standing uneasily on either side of the special chair. "I had a course in cults and witchcraft," she whispered. "Can I tell you what some of this means?"

O'Shea and Ellis nodded as they continued to scan the room.

"That interlaced star in the center is called a Pentagram. Each point represents one of the five elements or senses. Earth, air, fire, water and Akasha, the spirit. Akasha is a symbol of power or protection in witchcraft."

O'Shea's eyes stopped at the wing-backed chair. "I guess we know whoever sits here is the fifth element, the power."

"That's correct, Inspector O'Shea."

Startled, all three partners spun around searching for the voice that seemed to be coming from everywhere and nowhere. "I apologize for my absence, but you will understand why."

"Will we meet later?" asked O'Shea, frantically searching the room.

"During our, or rather my, self-disclosures, I would deeply appreciate no interruptions. The format is simple. I will talk, to provide you with sufficient information to close the eight cases. You will listen, take notes, but record nothing. You may speak to my voice or each other only when I give you permission, such as now. Is that satisfactory?"

O'Shea looked at his nodding partners who were standing within inches of him. "We agree, Dr Stricker."

"Fine. Despite the ritualistic appearances here, I'm no devotee of mysticism; my mother was. Being a scientist, however, I have dabbled in parapsychology and conducted comprehensive research into psychic phenomena. Officer Hasselburg may be able to explain the differences later. If you are wondering why the Wicca symbols, well, we are all influenced by our parents, especially mother. I cherished my mother.

My bio, the one you received from Mr. Hungerford, should expand your understanding of me and my parents.

"Starting with the two empty seats to my left, the one outside the green circle was occupied by Craig Craven. You must know from my bio that the month of April in my life has extraordinary significance. It is no coincidence that my parents and I were born in April. It is a special, prophetic month for special persons. Mr. Craven was the only Alchemist not born in April. Betrayal of my ancestral instincts was an unconscionable mistake.

"I met his father, Craig Craven, Sr. several years ago at an International Hypnotic Society Convention in Frankfort, Germany. Professor Craven presented a brilliant paper on Functional Genomics and Hypnosis. He is a world-renowned neuroscientist and an incredible hypnotist who studied with the great Milton Erickson. He was head of the Neurophysiology Department at Stanford University. I learned a great deal from him about how hypnosis can alter gene expression. I also knew he had a son in elementary school. I didn't know his son was flawed until it was too late.

"Craven Jr. was born with the intellectual genius of his father and the violence potential of the Boston Strangler. He tainted the purity of our experiments with his ecstatic preoccupation with the witnessing of dying and death."

Then the voice stopped as the funeral march droned on. The three partners stood quietly awed, completing notes and awaiting more disclosures; which came after an agonizing five minutes of nothing.

"Understand, detectives, that the human body is life in motion. When those incalculable coordinated body movements stop, the body must die. During my studies of psychokinesis and the power to move inanimate objects, I learned how to reverse the neuro-psycho-physiological process. Hence, Mr. Craven Jr.'s heart stopped, and his death ended his thrill in the death of others. Questions?"

Hasselburg quickly raised her hand before realizing Stricker probably couldn't see her. When she glanced sheepishly at her partners, they both nodded their approval to ask the voice. "Was the chair to your left for Jerran Torres or Ramsey?"

"Yes, it still is. Mr. Jerran Ramsey honored the number two chair. He was a loyal, highly moral boy who discovered he killed his mother and sister. He was blessed as well with my birthday, April 8th. Craven Jr. encouraged him to commit suicide, and for obvious sadistic reasons, he offered to help. Since Jerran was willing, the death was easily executed. Craven borrowed a four-step ladder from the janitor's supply room, he and Jerran entered the Gymnasium carrying their shoes, Jerran climbed the ladder, and secured the belt to the pipe and his neck. Craven pushed the ladder over, watched Jerran strangle, replaced Jerran's shoes and returned the ladder to the supply room. You detectives created a ridiculously complicated, excessively mysterious scenario. Questions?"

Ellis blanched and O'Shea frowned.

"What is the condition of the eight students sitting here?" asked O'Shea.

"That would have been my first question. Alchemy is a Greek term meaning the art of transmutation practiced by the Egyptians. Consequently, part of our Alchemist agenda was to study mind over matter through Eastern meditation, Yoga, and hypnosis. They are all in self-induced trances relevant to their individual personalities. At the conclusion of our discussion, a prearranged phrase from me will bring them out of their trance state. Questions?"

Sighing deeply, Ellis focused his narrowed eyes on the winged chair. "I have a lot of questions about your apparent interest in my daughter, Beth."

"Though your daughter was in danger because of her close relationship with Jerran, she was also the safest student at Polytechnic once I learned of her peril. All of my knowledge and psychic power was mobilized to protect both of them. I failed Jerran because he wanted to die. I couldn't, I wouldn't fail your daughter. My God, how could I not protect Beth? She has my mother's name, mother's birthday and her courage to defend a friend, a boy like a son to me. Questions?"

"Who tried to kill her?" Ellis asked with a slight quiver in his voice.

"Craven, of course. He was a compelling speaker with an uncanny persuasiveness. He easily talked Mr. Stewart into injecting a toxic chemical into Beth's orange juice and persuaded Mr. Richert to shoot his cross bow at Beth. Providence spared her the poison and psycho-kinesis deflected the javelin that hit Officer Eng. Craven's death also eliminated his plan to kill the three of you. Questions?"

Still carefully scanning the room in frustration, Hasselburg waved to her partners who nodded back their permission. "I can't locate the source of your voice. Are you somewhere in the Quonset hut, or maybe nearby using psychic powers like telepathy?"

Both detectives shot a glaring glance at Hasselburg.

Stricker's reply was higher pitched, and softer, as if amused. "Officer Hasselburg, not everything here is supernatural or unfathomable. It's simply a conference call with multiple speakers, receivers and a cell phone, not telepathy—just the latest telecommunication technology. Questions?"

Hasselburg instantly turned a scarlet red, while O'Shea patted her on the back.

Staring at her partners, Hasselburg's red face slowly paled into a lower lip pout. "That was stupid. Can I ask some good questions?"

O'Shea and Ellis smiled a yes.

"Dr. Stricker, were the Trickers involved in any of the eight cases?"

"This may surprise you. I know nothing of such organization, club or gang. The disks were planted by my Alchemists to discourage you from badgering innocent suspects and to offer a single clue, my American name. Now you can appreciate the irony of the letters. The connection between the Trickers and the Alchemists was pure chance."

"But what about the Trickers' party?" O'Shea interrupted.

"Patience is not one of your endearing qualities. Remember the rules for my self-disclosures."

Glancing at his partners, O'Shea flinched an apology. "I'm sorry, Doctor. I guess I'm too eager to clear things up."

"You will, Lieutenant, and what I don't tell, you and your partners can sort out. Suffice it to say, the Trickers were not part of Officer Hasselburg's abduction. You see, I love trees, she loves trees, and Craven liked to hurt them. You have three more questions. Choose them well."

Huddling for a minute, Hasselburg agreed Ellis and O'Shea had the most critical questions.

Clearing his throat, Ellis spoke slowly, as if in a courtroom. "To your knowledge Doctor, were any of the other deaths during the past several weeks caused by the Alchemists?"

"No. However, in addition to fate and chance, I imagine you're familiar with the domino effect. Two more questions."

O'Shea knew this was just about it. Stricker would probably vanish after the two. "Does the experiment you mention have anything to do with our eight cases?"

Chopin was the only sound for the next three minutes. The partners uneasily scanned the room, afraid to say anything that might break an interview rule or cause Striker to disappear.

At last, they thought, when Stricker finally replied.

"Indeed. And now for your last question."

O'Shea didn't hesitate. "Will you please tell us about your experiment?"

As another *Chopinesque* silence loomed, O'Shea's aching knee, from an old injury, gave out. "Been standing too long in one spot," he whispered. "Gotta sit down." Just outside the green circle, they all squatted cross-legged on the floor of the old Quonset hut, anxiously awaiting the finale. After ten minutes, the floor was painfully hard while Stricker's silence was nearly unbearable.

For Hasselburg, Chopin and bladder tolerance were also reaching their limits. "Think he's gone for good?"

Massaging his knee, O'Shea was about to answer, when Stricker's voice broke the silence. This time the tone was decidedly reflective, hesitant, almost wistful. With a show of curious deference, the partners struggled to their feet.

"Answering your last question is difficult for me. I succumbed to the demon that lurks in all of us. I had the power and insight to stop the process; and I, alone, choose not to."

For a moment, Stricker's voice again faded beneath the sounds of Chopin. Then it returned stronger, yet more casual and composed. *More like a lecture than a confession,* Ellis thought.

"In the fields of neuroscience and hypnosis, I can think of no person I have professionally respected more than Dr. Craig Craven. I have read every research paper and book he wrote. Dr. Craven was killed several years ago in a commercial airline crash while traveling to a symposium in Chicago. When I later discovered in San Francisco that his son was an honors student at Polytechnic, I applied for a teaching position here. Craven was my reason for teaching at a high school. I, of course, was hoping the son was not only as brilliant as his father, but had access to unpublished papers and manuscripts I could read.

"The Alchemists was an outgrowth of my pursuit of Dr. Craven's son, plus my passionate interest in the power of the mind over matter, and my appreciation of brilliance. Prerequisites for membership included Honor Society status, senior year, science majors and interest in the study of psychic phenomena. Dates of birth and other personal data I learned during interviews with each interested student. Of course, I courted Craven Jr. with an invitation to be the first qualified member of my Alchemist group. I wanted a maximum of ten, all with birthdays in April. Craven was the single exception.

"You have obviously noted the absence of females. Perhaps it's partially because of my father's Aryan, patriarchal influence and the dearth of April born female seniors with science majors. Our group began with basic hypnotic trance inductions and an enthusiastic exchange of information, ideas and theories. It was enriching for all of us.

"Then Craven challenged a statement of mine that had been supported by his father's earlier publications. I maintained that post-hypnotic suggestions, regardless of trance depth, could *not* be followed if contrary to a subject's values of morality, of right and wrong."

Busily taking notes, the partners were jolted into heart-pounding vigilance by the sound of a metal chair scrapping along the floor.

"Did you hear that?" murmured Ellis.

O'Shea slowly scanned the circle. "We'd have to be deaf not to hear it."

Nudging her partners, Hasselburg had zoomed in on the empty chairs. "Doesn't Craven's chair look further behind the wingback chair than it was?"

Stricker's voice again seemed pleasant, almost cheerful. "I apologize for alarming you with a brief demonstration of psycho-kinetic motion. Officer Hasselburg is correct. The eleventh chair moved two feet to the rear. Now, back to the experiment.

"Craven insisted his father was doubting the power of personal, moral belief systems to resist post-hypnotic suggestions. According to Craven, his father died before he could prove his doubts with new experiments.

"When I disagreed, he argued that, in respect for his father, I should conduct an experiment to test his father's doubts. I maintained, of course, that there were no studies supporting such doubts. Craven agreed, and proposed an experiment that would settle his father's doubts. An experiment with a post-hypnotic suggestion to randomly kill someone—anyone. Despite his persistence, I refused until he pointed to the flaw in my refusal, which clearly proved my own doubts. If I truly had no doubts, there was no reason to fear such an experiment. As they say in movies, the rest is history.

"All of my Alchemist students were well within the range of deep trance potential on Dr. Craven's famous Hypnotizability Scale, and after months of hypnotic inductions in preparation for the experiment, all my students were easily hypnotized and uniformly responsive to a wide variety of post hypnotic suggestions. They were ready."

All three partners were back on the floor diligently taking notes, more like grad students on a field trip than police on an investigation. Ellis, leaning against the wingback chair, frequently paused to shake his head in awe, while Hasselburg sat cross-legged and erect, thoroughly engrossed in recording each word in shorthand. As usual, O'Shea was frantically scribbling on every scrap of paper he could find in his pockets, while sprawled on the floor trying to rest on an elbow.

Suddenly, Stricker's voice hardened, with a terse edge of thinly veiled rage, as if thinking aloud. "Perhaps I naively believed Craven's loyalty to his father and my absolute certainty the students would never violate their moral principles. Or maybe the untimely death of my parents, and the negligible punishment of their killer have generated an underlying bitterness toward the lives of others. Probably a bit of both, and don't ever forget how my tortured body has screamed for mercy."

Simultaneously feeling Stricker's inner torment, the partners cautiously stood up, not knowing what to expect. Another tense five minutes elapsed before Stricker's voice returned—softer and more subdued.

📖 📖 📖

"On Monday, April 6th, each boy was guided into a deep trance and given the identical post-hypnotic suggestion to randomly kill someone on Wednesday, April 8th, before twelve midnight. But the experiment was flawed the minute it started. Discovering that most seniors intended to resist hurting anyone, Craven added altered hypnotic instructions, which he gave on April 7th to each senior without my knowledge or permission. These instructions were focused on the morality of sending struggling humans to a spiritual life beyond, so that death, not life, was the victim's salvation. They were told I had changed the hypnotic instructions and, as their *Akasha*, they worshiped me without question. Such worship is certainly not the role of clinical or experimental hypnotists.

"Jerran was the most resistant, yet so obedient to me, he tried diluting his compliance by cutting the brake lines, hoping the crash at the bottom of the short descent would not seriously injure the driver.

"Craven eagerly participated in at least three of the deaths while intending to kill anyone who got in his way."

This time Stricker's silence was accompanied by a shower of sparkling embers from the more vigorously flickering candles and a louder, more sinister Chopin. Hasselburg cringed, expecting some wicked spirit to materialize. Ellis uneasily scanned the room for Stricker's dramatic appearance, while O'Shea was thinking, *It's show time folks.*

In less than a minute, the voice returned with a quivering, breathy, rasp of an extremely old man. "When I learned from Craven Jr. of the death of the woman crossing the street with her child, I knew there was something far more sinister than a botched experiment. We were tampering with fate and destiny. I didn't try to stop the others; perhaps it was out of control. Or maybe this was my vengeance to a world indifferent to my life of pain and loss.

"I am responsible for all the deaths associated with the experiment, yet I only grieve for Jerran. The other seniors will remember nothing about the experiment or the deaths. So I have completed my self-disclosures with one final declaration. Only I permitted random killings of nameless others by young boys. That, I consider *the ultimate evil.*"

The instant the last two words spewed from his mouth with a loud choking gasp, the candles died along with Chopin. The darkness and silence were momentarily deadening. Then the overhead Quonset hut lights went on, and like the end of a long sinister movie, the seniors stood up and quietly filed out of the room—as the partners stood frozen in a stunned silence of their own.

TWO MONTHS LATER

EPILOGUE

A full two months had passed since the Quonset hut meeting with Dr. Stricker's voice. Breaking the eight cases was a colossal news event; even for street savvy San Franciscans. It was a great political speech opportunity, with politicians emerging from everywhere, shyly boasting their long support and congratulations to the best police department in the nation. Ironically, for the three partners, it was a time of sheer drudgery with plenty of frustrating paperwork. Thanks to Hasselburg, they survived the ordeal.

There were also endless debriefings by the mayor and police commissioner on down the sloping hierarchy to Captain McInerney. Invariably they ended in photo ops, that were marginally tolerated by O'Shea and Ellis, while Hasselburg, the rookie, couldn't restrain gushing smiles to the flashing cameras.

The district attorney's office was trying to tiptoe through the minefield of public and official opinions. Starting with the governor's office, everyone wanted immediate arrests, indictments, punishment, vengeance, even voodoo. Unfortunately, for vote hungry politicians, Stricker had vanished without a trace, and Craven Junior was dead. No undisputed bad guys to beat up in superior court, no justice, no retribution. The evidence on the remaining nine seniors was too vague; and the last thing Ronald Holm, the DA, wanted was flimsy cases and a bunch of under-age defendants who pitifully zombied themselves into murder under the spell of a Svengale. Jerran's suicide also wouldn't help the prosecution.

Holm's decision was politically wise and a sound compromise. He declined prosecution of any of the young suspects. Instead, following parental agreement, which wasn't too difficult to arrange, they were all adjudicated wards of the juvenile court. This meant they were primarily answerable to the courts, rather than their parents. They were then ordered to undergo bi-weekly psychotherapy with a California licensed therapist, board qualified as well in clinical hypnosis. That decision seemed to satisfy the general public, except for the *rednecks* who wanted them tried as adults and executed.

Still under post-hypnotic, retrograde amnesia, the nine juveniles were more than a tad confused about their court status. They weren't quite sure why they were suspects in multiple murders, because they couldn't remember anything associated with the actual killings.

📖 📖 📖

Nine weeks after the Stricker disclosures, the political, self-righteous dust had just about settled and the city's journalists were getting bored with *old news*. The partners had finally filed their final reports and it was time for O'Shea to kick back with his old friends for a more personal debriefing.

The Java House was the perfect place for their get-together. O'Shea scheduled the event for 3:00 p.m., Sunday, the deadest time of the week for the little restaurant.

Driving by the front door on his way to park at Pier 42, O'Shea couldn't miss Phil Papadopoulos standing at the entrance with arms folded and the gigantic handle-bar mustache dangling from an otherwise average looking, pony-tailed guy. *What a combination*, he thought, *an old Greek pony-tailed hippie.* "Hey Phil," O'Shea shouted.

"Park in my place. No car today, and hurry up," Phil ordered.

Knowing how tight parking was near Pier 42, he complied with no argument ▪

After parking his car, O'Shea was gratefully surprised to find all his most loyal friends already there. Ellis was sitting with Ida, Ginella, and Bender. Wunden and Boyd were seated nearby at a separate table.

All were dressed casually, except Ellis. He awkwardly wore the only suit and tie.

O'Shea smiled and nodded his way to his partner where he gave Ellis a firm arm on the shoulder as he whispered in his ear. "Thanks, pal. Now why don't you take off the tie and coat before they think you're with the FBI."

Loosening his tie, Ellis grinned up at his boss.

The next stop was Ida. O'Shea squeezed her hand before grabbing a nearby chair.

Following an exchange of introductions, handshakes and hugs, they all settled down to cheerful conversations, coffee, Sprites, beers, and Papadopoulos' hors d'oeuvres of deep-fried sausages and bigger, greasier plates of French fries.

The usual slurping, munching, laughing and joking were briefly interrupted when Hasselburg came limping in wearing full make-up, professional hairdo, expensive dress, matching purse, pearl earrings and necklace—and old worn sneakers. Moving unsteadily toward O'Shea, her glistening eyes, and slightly smeared makeup said the rest.

Ida and O'Shea leaped out of their chairs with open arms. Ellis, seeing Hasselburg's entrance a second later, knocked over his chair on his way up.

As they gently embraced her, she heaved a deep, jerky sigh. "I'm so sorry I'm late," she sniffled. "I wanted to look nice for your friends. I tripped over a curb in my high heels and had to go home to bandage my knees and stuff."

O'Shea cupped a hand under her chin and smiled into her teary eyes. "Christ Jill! You and Ellis don't need to dress up for anyone. You're great as you are."

Shouldering his way past O'Shea, Papadopoulos grabbed Hasselburg by the hand and led her to an empty table. "I'm Phil and you are a beautiful lady. I'm going to fix you a special Greek dish. No sausage and fries for you. Now you sit here and let the others come to you."

It didn't take long before Hasselburg's table was filled with old and new friends, and the whole room was teeming with more laughing, joking and teasing. Phil, always the lady's man, fought off all those who wanted some of Hasselburg's Greek dish, except, of course, Ida.

By 4:30 the group had mellowed, and conversation finally got around to the *eight.*

"You guys think they'll ever find Stricker?" Boyd asked.

Hasselburg and Ellis looked at O'Shea.

"Hey. Don't look at me. I don't have a clue either. He could be dead. Remember those gasps before he shut down? But like Elvis, there've already been sightings all over the world."

Pausing for a moment, O'Shea realized all his friends, including

Phil, were quietly focused on him. "You know, folks, I wouldn't care if they never catch him. But, for me personally, I'd like to see him in the flesh just once. Everybody saw him differently and I keep wondering how he'd look to me."

"Yeah, me too," added Ellis.

Dramatically slamming a fist on the table, Papadopoulos stood up clutching his beer bottle. "In my country, we find and hang him by his balls."

"Phil! We're running out of fries," quipped Ginella.

As Papadopoulos picked up one of the plates, Bender grabbed its last two French fries. "It's probably just as well we don't find Stricker. There's no clear, eye witness evidence against him, and his admissions to you are somewhat vague posturing with a dash of metaphor."

"What about wasting Craven?" Boyd asked.

"DA investigators have checked into that with the best of cardiologists. They all agree there's no scientific evidence a heart can be stopped by mind power."

"That doesn't mean it couldn't happen," protested Hasselburg. "What do cardiologists know about the mind?"

Downing a piece of sausage, Bender nodded. "Oh, I agree. But that's irrelevant in court. No jury is going to convict someone of doing something medical science says hasn't been done. Anyway, a trial of such a brilliant, incredibly slippery guy would no doubt go on for months and cost millions."

Hasselburg slowly shook her head. "Doesn't matter. He's gone for good."

"How do you know?" Bender asked.

"I don't know how I know. I just know."

Wrapping some new hot fries around a piece of cold sausage, O'Shea stuffed the whole thing in his mouth with a smiling, nodding agreement.

Building his own sandwich of fries and sausage, Ginella glanced at Ellis. "How about you, Paul?"

"Yes, I think he's gone for good, and just between all of us, I hope so. I believe he did protect my daughter, no matter why."

During the brief silence, O'Shea threw a napkin ball at Wunden. "Hey, Doc, you haven't given us your professional wisdom about Stricker."

Shaking his fist at O'Shea, Wunden threw the balled napkin back with a smirk. "I really don't have any. I never met the guy and from what I've learned from all of you and the papers, he's a one-in-a-billion special genius, whom I couldn't possibly understand. I'm not in his league."

"Come on, Jerry," countered O'Shea. "Your guesses are a hell of a lot better than ours."

Wunden frowned into his empty cup as Papadopoulos stopped at his table. "See, Doctor, I pour you more coffee. Now talk."

"You assholes. I'm as awed by Stricker as you are. I already gave you a profile. He's a goddamned world-class genius, and if anyone could reverse psychokinetic movement or protect Paul's kid, he could."

"Doctor," Hasselburg said softly with a raised hand. "What do you think he meant by his comment about me liking trees and Craven hating nature?"

"Do you care about nature?" Wunden asked.

"I love nature," she answered solemnly.

"Then seems like Stricker, using his clairvoyance, was right. My best guess is that for you, Jill, the tree represented loving protection and for Craven, exile and punishment."

"And the funeral march?"

"Come on, Jill." Wunden grinned. "We all have our own opinion of that one. I think the constant Chopin loop was a combination theatre, his way of mourning the twenty who died because of the experiment, and he probably likes Chopin's music, realizing that everyone views Chopin, a Pole, as differently as they view him."

"Twenty-one," announced Hasselburg.

O'Shea gave a surprised look at Hasselburg. "What? It's twenty, isn't it?

"Sorry, I forgot to tell you. The hospital left a message this morning. Mrs. Hanna died last night in her sleep of an apparent overdose of sleeping pills."

Looking at Ellis' bowed head, O'Shea bit his tightening lips. "Shit. Damn it all. She was a fine lady."

"Am I through?" Wunden asked, trying to change the subject.

Stroking Hasselburg's shoulders, Ida stared at Bender. "Does anyone have any hunch who drugged Jill?"

Bender gave Wunden a wink. "Guess it's my turn. The DA's office received Craven Jr.'s appointment book with all kinds of notations. It arrived a week after Stricker vanished, and of course, there's no return address. Just a San Francisco postmark."

"How come we didn't know?" O'Shea fretted.

"I'm glad you asked, John. I'm beginning to think our investigators are dyslexics. They still haven't finished analyzing the little book or sending us a report with a copy to you. Anyway, you guys were so busy writing your own reports, I figured it could wait."

"We're all ears," O'Shea grumbled with a slight grin.

"Well, at least you heard this before the press and the rest of San Francisco. According to a scribbled entry the day of your abduction, Jill, Craven was sneaking around at the Trickers party. That's where he talked Taggart into lacing your drink with some kind of upper to make you act exuberant and foolish. Of course, he didn't level with Taggart that the pill would make you feel nauseous, woozy and eventually unconscious. There's also a lot about how he sabotaged Stricker's experiment, and his participation in several of the killings. But there's nothing about the tree or what actually happened to you when you left."

Searching her memory as she listened, Hasselburg gave Bender a slow, nodding sigh. "Thank you, Richard. Every little bit helps."

At a quarter to six, the group had just about run out of drinks, the fourth order of Phil's hors d oeuvres, and any purposeful conversation. They were all satisfied that Craven was really the evil catalyst, that Stricker was indeed a brilliant wizard who, wherever, was retarded when it came to street savvy. He still had plenty to learn about people, they agreed, but it didn't matter. He was probably gone for good. They also concluded that, since there were no friends or relatives of victims to fan the smoldering demands for justice and vengeance, the flame would soon flicker out along with a search for Stricker.

After the usual hearty handshakes, hugs and waves, they all headed their separate ways. Silently walking Ida and Jill to their cars, O'Shea and Ellis were feeling pretty good about putting their eight cases to a much-deserved rest.

Stopping at the curb for an approaching P.G. & E. truck, they noticed the hydraulic lift on the back. They all stared curiously at the lift basket, then each other.

Hasselburg spoke first. "I wonder how I got up that damned tree? What do you think?"

Simultaneously they shrugged as the P.G. & E. truck bounced down the street with the basket swaying behind. Slowly they turned to Hasselburg with big grins. "Yeah. It's possible."

THE END

ABOUT THE AUTHOR

Athletic scholarships eventually led Larry Wonderling to college, a doctoral degree in clinical psychology, athletic Hall of Fame honors and careers as clinical psychologist and international cross cultural consultant.

Retiring into a writing career, his critically acclaimed nonfiction books express his lifelong observations and experiences, while his present mystery novel reflects his twenty year background in forensic psychology with the criminal justice system.